Three

# THREE

# Mark Sennen

# Cast of Police Characters

### London UK
Detective Inspector Jessica Chase
Detective Inspector Nick Green
Detective Sergeant John Stafford
Detective Chief Superintendent Jeff Boyle
Detective Constable Sam Hasting
Detective Constable Nikki Ghosh
Detective Constable Kyle Willem
Dr Pat Kendle - pathologist

### Montana US
Detective Frank Locke
Detective Leo Sullivan
Jim Swanson - FBI
Dr Adam Hem - Medical Examiner
Kerri Dunstan - CSI

### Darwin Australia
Detective Senior Sergeant Takeo Sasaki
Detective Sergeant Linda Malroony
Assistant Commissioner Fred Cooper
Sergeant Kevin Anderson
Officer Ken Royston
Officer Bryce Mitchell
Dr Arthur Benson - pathologist
Kieran Lamb - CSI

# *Prologue*

The Architect has three horrific stories to tell. For now. Later, there will be more. Many more. But three is enough for now.

He kicks out, leans into the high-backed chair, and swings his feet onto the desk. He is in his home office, a spare room in the attic of the house. A round window provides a good view through the tall pines surrounding the small development where he lives. Snow-capped mountains are visible in the distance. The shimmering blue of a lake is closer. There was a time when the office was neat and tidy, but now there is a sense of disarray. Scraps of paper lie scattered across the desk and the floor, scribbles of pencil spidering on each piece. Books pile in teetering stacks or sit haphazardly on surfaces. A chest of drawers has one drawer missing, another half open to reveal a jumble of pens and pencils and protractors and dividers. A pencil sharpener is mounted at one end of the chest of drawers, but the little tray used to catch the shavings is absent, and slivers of pencil have fallen on the floor in a heap. Once fastidious, the Architect now appears to be sloppy and slapdash. However, appearances are deceptive, and his thinking is as sharp as ever, his focus pinpoint and unerring, his purpose resolute and unwavering.

Single-minded...

Since the accident, focusing on anything but his mission is difficult, if not impossible, and in other areas of his life, he's not doing much more than getting by. Coasting. Freewheeling. Or, as his mother used to say, just rolling.

He can hear her voice in his head as clear as if she was right next to him:

'Keep rolling, son, and then you'll be OK. Keep rolling along and heading for the horizon because the stars are too far away for mere mortals to reach. It's down-to-earth advice, son, and that's where we're at. On the earth. God's earth. He wants us to roll, roll, roll. Roll with the punches. Roll with the waves. Roll along those grassy slopes. Don't let life get you down, and just keep rolling. Do that and you'll be fine. More than fine. Understand?'

'Sure, Ma, sure.'

Not that rolling got his mother very far in life. No further than a bar job she supplemented with blowjobs given around the back of the car lot. Truckers and salesmen and local cops that, as a small kid, he peeked at from behind a stack of empty beer kegs. His mother, on her knees, head bobbing, the soiled greenbacks already stashed in the pocket of her cut-off jeans. To think she got given a second chance, and this was what she did with it. Threw it away. Flushed her life down the pan.

The Architect remembers when she disappeared. She was gone one evening and didn't turn up until a month later, her decaying body contorted into a drainage gully a couple of clicks beyond the town limits, the consequences of the side hustle catching up with her eventually. They never caught the trucker who did it. Or was he a salesman? Perhaps a cop.

Whoever he was, she brought it on herself, and the Architect was the one left alone to suffer. Kids' homes, foster homes, and, at one point, a runaway. He grew up unloved. Neglected. Beaten. Abused. But at some point, the tears wouldn't come any longer, and he began to fight back. He forgot about rolling, forgot about his mother, forgot about the reason why the pair of them ended up in the one-street town where she worked in a bar for minimum wage and did the other things for not much more.

2

*He forced himself not to think about the place where she died for the grubby twenty-buck note found on her rotting body. He put the memories behind him, worked hard at school and college, and, against the odds, he excelled. He found a decent job and earned more than decent money. He aimed for the horizon, aimed for the stars, and many would say, looking at his career and his rise to the top, that he got there.*

*Which begs the question, where did it all go so wrong?*

*For a moment, he thinks back. First to the accident, and then to decades ago, to when it all started. Thirty-three years... hard to believe it has been so long. He begins to ponder a dozen 'what ifs' before snapping back to the present, cross with himself for pointless reminiscing. History is unchangeable; creating the future is what matters.*

*He pulls his feet from the desk, disturbing a pile of notes. Sheets of paper glide to the floor, adding to the detritus. He swings the chair forward and taps the red leather desktop. Grasps for a tiny notebook and flicks it open. The pages contain all the pertinent details: times, places, people. He glances at the wall, where a vast map provides a visualisation of his plan. He follows the threads that go from drawing pin to drawing pin, and his gaze alights on the yellow Post-It notes stuck at each location. He traces the lines of latitude and longitude. This is geography as memory, the future turning to history. Two dimensions of ink and paper telling the sordid tale of each place, each girl, each bloodied, frenzied, utterly sickening, killing.*

*Three stories to tell...*

# *Chapter 1*

She wakes in the near dark. Indistinct shadows. Water drip, dropping close at hand. Cold air wafting across her face, carrying an odour of damp earth. She shifts, uncomfortable on the hard surface on which she is lying, but her hands are bound with rope, and her legs clamped by some form of shackle. She shivers as the chill breeze slips over her skin and realises she is naked. Last night is a blur, as if she has a monumental hangover, but one thing she knows for sure is that she wasn't drinking. Never when she is working. Never.

She turns her head to one side and spies a rectangle of dim light that marks an open door. Where this is and how she got here, she has no idea, but there are flickers of memory: A car journey through streets slick with rain; The rhythmic flash of lights passing at speed on the motorway; Being thrown side to side as the vehicle drives miles along a twisting country lane.

And before that?

She can't say.

She moves her gaze to the other side. Close by, there is a wooden workbench. An array of tools glinting in the faint glow from the doorway.

Not tools... instruments: forceps, scalpels, a suture needle and thread, a bone saw.

She struggles, pulling hard against the rope and chain, wanting to cry out but at the same time fearing to do so because her screams might just bring him here.

Him?

4

Another slice of memory. No name, no face, just a voice that was soft, low and precise. Intelligent. Knowledgeable. Trustworthy. Persuasive. Perhaps, in the end, threatening.

And, without knowing quite why, she had complied with his requests. Leading to... she glances at the surgical instruments again. Feels her heart racing. Palpitations. A clammy sweat on her forehead despite the cold.

She takes a breath to calm herself. And another. Looks over to the workbench once more. Next to the instruments, a rectangle of glass reflects the room. She squints, resolving the piece of glass into a mobile phone. Her hands are bound by her sides, but she reckons if she wiggles a little, she might be able to stretch a finger out to the bench and reach the phone.

A stomp of boots on the hard floor causes her to swing her head back to the doorway. A silhouette surrounded by radiance. Some sort of floodlight. There's just enough illumination to make out his features, and now she remembers everything.

'Please,' she pleads as he strides into the room. 'There's no need to hurt me.'

He pauses and turns to her. No smile, no anger. If there's any emotion she senses it is one of reluctance or even fear.

'PLEASE!' She fights now, flinging herself back and forth, trying to break her bonds.

'Don't worry,' he says as he moves over to the workbench. 'You won't feel a thing.'

# *Chapter 2*

*London, United Kingdom.*

The alarm warbles and Detective Inspector Jessica Chase opens her eyes.

Groggy.

Too much wine the night before.

A splitting headache thumping as if a pound of lead is smacking her on the left temple.

Nausea.

Yesterday, Chase turned thirty-four. Celebrated with a few friends and plenty of booze. Memo to self, she thinks: Stick with the friends, lay off the alcohol and stop acting like you're eighteen.

The alarm plays again. Louder and more insistent. Not. Going. Away.

'Fucking hell.'

She reaches for her phone to silence the racket and realises the trill is a call, not an alarm. She blinks and focuses on the screen. The caller is DI Nick Green. Doesn't he know it's her day off?

Yeah, she thinks, he probably does. His idea of a joke. Ha, ha. Very funny. Go to hell.

She lets the phone chirp away, and Green hangs up, but as she leans back on the pillow in relief, the rings come again. When she holds the phone up, his name floats on the screen like a recurring bad dream.

'Christ all-fucking-mighty.' Chase thumbs to answer. Spits into the phone. 'The restaurant ran out of cheap red because we drank so much, and you're ringing at...' She pulls the phone from her ear and looks at the time. 'Seven twenty-five?'

'What is it, Goldilocks, ended up in the wrong bed?'

'I'm in *my* bed, at home, alone.'

'That's good because I'm on my way there now to pick you up.'

'You're fucking not.'

'I recommend some Alka-Seltzer, a can of Red Bull and plain white toast with no butter. If you haven't got Red Bull, then Coke, but not Diet or Zero. Failing that, then a black coffee with three sugars. You've just got time because I'll be outside in exactly ten minutes.'

Chase reckons if this is a joke, it's gone on long enough. 'Cut the crap, Nick, I need to go back to sleep.'

'Not possible, Jess. Got a body. It's been there a couple of days and it's all cut up. There's weird stuff, too. *Really* weird.' The tone in Green's voice suggests the joke, if there ever was one, is long over. 'This isn't your standard gun and run, not a domestic, not a drug deal gone wrong. This is bad, understand?'

Chase doesn't need a hangover cure to sober her now; Green's words have done that. She pushes herself up, the room spinning, the light seeping from behind the curtains and needling at her eyeballs like pins rammed into a pincushion.

'You're at the scene?'

'No, but I've had a call describing everything in glorious Technicolor detail and asking if we might be interested in this one. Always good to get in at the start, right?'

'Sure.' Chase can't argue with that, but the timing's shit.

'Satnav says my ETA is now seven minutes. See you soon.'

Green is gone, and Chase resists the urge to lie back on the bed. Instead, she gets up, heads for the bathroom, and sits on the toilet. Then she flicks the shower on, strips out of her T-shirt and steps under the rush of water.

*We might be interested in this one...*

*We* being the SCU. The Serial Crimes Unit. Newly formed, barely out of nappies, but thrown in at the deep end to sink or swim.

Chase soaps up and washes off. Thinks: we need to do this by the numbers. Rules and regulations. Procedure. Tickbox paperwork. In its brief existence, the SCU has only had one case. One *unsuccessful* case. They went out on a limb to get results, and the branch snapped off, the SCU in freefall, the landing painful and undignified. This time, if the SCU is to have a future, that won't do.

Three minutes gone.

She half dries herself, returns to the bedroom, and grabs some clothes. Puts them on.

Two minutes more.

Goes to the kitchen, pulls a can of Red Bull from the fridge (DI Green knows her all too well), gropes in a cupboard for a cereal bar, and finds a couple of paracetamol in a drawer.

Another minute gone.

She dry swallows the painkillers and sits for a moment on a stool at the breakfast bar, promising herself the drinking has to stop.

One minute.

The door buzzer vibrates, Green on time to the second as always. Chase slips into a pair of shoes, opens the door to her flat, and heads down to greet him.

When she emerges onto the pavement, he's sitting in his old Land Rover Defender, the engine idling. The vehicle, dating from fuck-knows-when, is all pimped out as if Green is about to enter the Paris-Dakar rally. Wire mesh on the windows, wheel rubber like the tyres have been stolen from some humungous earth-moving digger, and a bloody big snorkel snaking up the side of the windscreen in case Green ever needs to go sub aqua, which, in central London, seems unlikely. Green slides the window open and smiles at her before offering a greeting.

'You look like shit,' he says. Green is tall, dark and handsome when viewed through a fancy filter but stocky and prematurely greying in plain, honest daylight. Good for a wisecrack twenty-four-seven. 'That is if a shit was one sixty-five in a pair of Guccis.'

Chase stops at the curb and looks down at her feet. She's wearing the shoes she had on last night — not Guccis, not on a police officer's salary — and sensible footwear they aren't. Too late to go back and get a different pair now.

'Thanks for the confidence booster,' she says as she climbs into the Defender. 'How come you're so perky?'

'Half a pint of water for every unit of alcohol before I went to bed. A big fry-up with plenty of tomatoes when I woke up. The water stops you from dehydrating, and the fry-up lines the stomach, right?'

Chase feels her insides heave at the thought of an oily fried breakfast. She pops the can of Red Bull and opens the cereal bar. Takes a gulp and a tentative nibble.

'Where?' she says, hoping it's miles away so she can nap on the way. Hoping, too, that Green will do the talking when they get there.

'Brentford Ait.' Green clanks the Defender into gear and pulls off. 'In case you're unfamiliar with the name, that's an island in the river just upstream from Kew Bridge.'

'Who found the body?'

'A canoeist on an evening paddle went ashore to take a piss. He saw something suspicious in the undergrowth and called it in.' Green takes his hands off the wheel for a split second and shrugs. 'The on-duty slackers didn't check it out until this morning. Go figure.'

9

'You ever been on nights? Do you know how much shit they have to deal with?'

'A body, Jess. Doesn't that get kicked to the top of the pile?'

Should do, Chase thinks, but then again, getting out to the island in the dark would have been tricky, and she can imagine a watch leader deciding their team could do without the hassle. Why bother with all the health and safety crap if the job could be bumped to the morning crew?

There's no time for sleep; it's only a few minutes from Chase's place in Hounslow to Kew, and now they're stuck in traffic as they inch across the bridge. She looks to her right, where the Thames ebbs in great boils of grey and brown. Unlike many Londoners, Chase hates the Thames. Detests it. The river is no more than a festering line of pus meandering through the city. It divides north from south, significantly contributing to the appalling traffic jams since the bridges are choke points, and if Chase never had to go within half a mile of it again, she wouldn't be sorry.

A cluster of trees lines a finger of island just upstream from the bridge. The main section of the river lies to the left, while a smaller channel weaves to the right, houseboats hugging the bank, mud sucking at their hulls. The island, known as Brentford Ait, is only a few metres wide but hundreds long, and it follows the curve of the river as it bends south.

Green turns right at the end of the bridge and powers across two lanes of traffic to the accompaniment of a chorus of car horns. Then he swings into a road that doubles back towards the Thames and pulls up at a set of bollards. Beyond, a wide path borders the river, and a police RIB is nudging into the shallows on the far side of a concrete wall.

'Our taxi,' Green says, getting out. 'Come on.'

They cross the path, climb over the low wall, and clamber down shelving cobbles that lead to the water. Green hops over the bow of the RIB and nods a greeting to the police officer at the helm. Chase follows and sits down, hoping the crossing to the other side won't be too rocky. The officer puts the outboard into reverse and pulls back before gunning forward and sweeping across the river.

In a minute, they're approaching the island, the helmsman guiding the RIB parallel to the bank for a hundred metres before nosing onto an expanse of mud, unable to get closer because the tide is half out. Green jumps off the boat into ankle-deep water, and Chase notices he's wearing Wellington boots. She reckons he must have been a Boy Scout because he's the kind of person who's always prepared. He probably has all the badges: first aid, knots, astronomy, remembering your fucking wellies when you attend a gruesome murder by the Thames.

She looks down at her own footwear as she clambers up to the bow. Brand new and worn for the first time last night. She swears as she drops into the water and squelches through the thick mud.

'Hey, Cinderella?' Green says. 'Careful you don't lose a slipper.'

Chase steps out of the water and onto the bankside. Something is clinging to her right shoe — a translucent rubber balloon a few inches long.

'For fuck's sake.' She swings her foot and the condom flies back into the river. 'Dirty fucking wanker.'

'You're just jealous.' Green is alongside her now, patting her on the back. 'Not getting much these days, are you, poor thing.'

'Your sympathy is noted, but your interest unwelcome.'

'Touchy, touchy.'

Chase has recently split up with her long-term boy-friend. At least she thought it was long-term. He had other ideas. Green's been ribbing her about the breakup every chance he can. It's banter, nothing more, but these days, the top brass frown on anything that might affect someone's mental health. Chase thinks the top brass should get off their arses and out in the real world more often. What has the most detrimental effect on an officer's mental health is what's waiting for them up ahead.

Another body.

Chase has seen two this week: a shooting in Wandsworth and a bloater fished from the river near Hampton Court. Neither sight was conducive to her well-being. She wonders if she should ask for a spot of counselling followed by an extended period of leave. Take a nice break somewhere hot. Somewhere with a beach and lots of ripped men. On the other hand, when she got back, the extended joshing she'd get from Green would be intolerable.

'Let's go, lover girl.' Green is forging up the river bank and following a path into a dense thicket. The island is just a few paces wide in some places, a finger of land following the course of the river for several hundred metres. A handful of riverboat moorings line the main bank, but on the island, the water's edge is fringed only with the dead remains of last year's bullrushes, their leaves whispering in the stiff breeze.

Chase squelches through the mud, her shoes already beyond hope and ruined. The path slips beneath a weeping willow, the tips of the branches touching the water, early spring growth bright green. Beyond, half hidden by the thicket of shrub, three white apparitions talk in low voices: the pathologist and two CSIs dressed in PPE suits. There's a flash from a camera as one takes a picture. You could post the snap on TripAdvisor. Three and a half stars.

A lovely spot for a picnic beside the river, but the ambience ruined by a rotting corpse and the unexpected arrival of half a dozen police officers.

'Christ.' Green steps into the little clearing, blocking Chase's view. 'The shit did this?'

One of the CSIs points to a line of blue and white tape. 'Keep that side,' he says. Chase can see the CSIs are on plastic stepping plates, and little flags poke up from the undergrowth everywhere she looks. She moves to Green's side. Wants to swear but doesn't. Wants, in truth, to spew up the cereal bar she's just eaten.

'Female?' she says. Although the corpse is naked, it's hard to tell as a mass of tangled hair shields the face, and mud and river debris cover the torso.

'Yes.' The woman pathologist nods across at her.

Behind the mask, Chase recognises Doctor Pat Kendle's round features. Kendle is short and wide, her hair cropped to a fuzzy length, all spiked up and tinged with purple. A 'blue rinse', Chase wants to call it, except she wouldn't dare. Kendle rides a big Moto Guzzi, dresses in full leathers and has a soft spot for hard metal music with a jackhammer beat. She also has a soft spot for pretty women; men, she says, have never been able to handle her. That Chase can believe: according to Green, who was there when she did it, Kendle can sink a pint of bitter in under three seconds. Not many male egos (or stomachs) can deal with that.

'Jessica and Nick.' Kendle pulls the mask down and smiles. 'Your names have a ring of daytime TV about them even if your faces don't.'

'Ha, ha. You should be on stage.' Green sticks out a hand and gives Kendle a raised thumb. 'Sweeping up after the performance.'

13

Green and Kendle go way back, both hailing from the West Country. 'She reckons she's the only PhD in Cornwall,' Green once joked. 'And doesn't she let you know it.' But, for all her ego and bossiness, Chase likes Kendle. Sure, she's a little big-headed, but the pathologist is a take-no-prisoners, suffer-no-fools type of woman and all the better for it.

'Did she die here?' Chase asks.

'Unlikely.' Kendle points at the body. 'The wounds on the chest happened pre-death. Plus, there's the removal of the arm to consider.'

Chase leans forward to see better. She runs her gaze down the body. No right arm. Three deep slashes across the breasts. Blood between the legs. She swallows. A man did this, she thinks, and not for the first time in her life, Chase wonders if half the human race is an entirely different species.

'Butchered?' Green asks. 'Literally?'

Chase knows what he's thinking. A couple of years ago, there was an infamous case where several arms and legs were found in the Thames. Eventually, the limbs were matched to three torsos discovered in a burned-out car. It transpired the murders were gang-orchestrated, and one of the members had learned his trade in an abattoir. Chop, chop, chop. Nice work if you can get it.

'More like surgical,' Kendle says. 'Fine cuts made with a razor blade or a scalpel to start with and then a bone saw on the arm. Some skill involved.'

'Fuck.' Now Chase does swear. 'You're kidding me?'

'No.' Kendle bends over the body and pushes a finger down against the skin. 'And then there are these.'

Chase spies a line of brown dashes across a cut above the belly button. 'Stitches?'

14

'Yes, she's been sutured.' Kendle glances up. Smiles. 'Although it looks like a bit of a rushed job. Still, whoever did it used proper surgical thread.'

'So what's gone on in there?'

'I can't begin to think, can you?'

Yes, Chase can, and that's because, one, she's got a sick fucking mind, and two, she's dealt with some right nutters in the past. She's seen the results of the worst depths of human depravity. Crimes where the details had to be withheld from the public because they were so disturbing. So, it's all too easy to imagine the horrors perpetrated on this woman.

'You were right to call us,' Green says. 'I don't think this is going to be a one-off. It's the first of a series. You don't do something like this and then pack it in and go back to masturbating over your iPad in your bedroom, do you?'

No, you probably don't, Chase thinks.

Ten years on the Met as a detective means she's seen a lot, and experience tells her there are two types of killers. In the first category are those who want to make some grand statement, almost as if the killing is a piece of art. Without an audience, the act is nothing. They want to see headlines in the newspapers and coverage on TV. They want to see the flashing blue lights, the forensic teams, and the senior officers at press conferences trying in vain to reassure the public. They love the stories of grieving relatives, the creation of a nickname for the killer, and the emergence of a whole industry following the case. On the other hand, the killers in the second category like to work in the shadows. They couldn't care less about the notoriety. The *process* is the whole thing for them. They plan and execute, and after the killing, they re-enact. The involvement of the police can only hasten the end game, and that's the last thing they want. The killers in the first group get all the glory, but the ones in the second group are the most dangerous.

'You could be right,' Chase says, belatedly answering Green's question. She throws a hand at the surroundings. 'But this isn't public and it's not easy to find. So I'd say he — and I'm saying "he" for the moment because these types of killers inevitably are — didn't want the body discovered.'

'There are certainly more straightforward places for a dump site. He'd have had a hell of a time getting across here undetected.'

'We found a rowing boat,' one of the CSIs says. 'It was grounded on the shore under the bridge. Looks like it was stolen from one of the houseboats or the marina upstream.'

'Right,' Chase says. She glances round at the tangle of trees and briars. 'Perhaps this place has some significance. Perhaps he's got a thing for islands.'

'Is there a term for that, Doc?' Green turns to Kendle. 'For getting your rocks off surrounded by water?'

'Rocks. Excellent,' Chase says, but Kendle's not listening. She's got better things to do. Better things like gently turning the body and inserting a rectal thermometer. Chase thinks that's just adding insult to injury. First, you get attacked and murdered and butchered, and then when it should all be done and dusted, some medical type shoves a thermometer up your arse without a by-your-leave.

But then it goes with the territory.

As she thinks that, she regrets the words but knows why she used them. She's already wondering who this woman is and why she ended up here. Perhaps she was on drugs or had mental issues. Maybe she'd been in trouble since she was a kid. Serially abused. People tried to help, but she slipped through the net. Pretty soon, she's stealing and fighting. Running drugs for some dealer. Bad company. Running drugs, using drugs, hooked on drugs. And the next thing is the dealer's moonlighting as a pimp, and the woman can't say no because if she does, she won't get her next fix. The demands get worse, the men more depraved, until finally, she doesn't return one night. But what's the pimp going to do? Call the cops? The fuck he is.

Well, we're here, Chase thinks. Phone call or no phone call. Better late than never. Then again, perhaps she's in danger of overanalysing this one.

'Jessie?'

'Sorry, somewhere else.' Chase shakes her head, sad she's already written the girl's life story before they've even got an ID. But that's how it goes in police work. History repeating itself, just a different name each time. The name becomes a number, and the number goes on a chart. The chart goes to a government department where a minister looks at it, and perhaps a few pounds get added to one budget and taken away from another. The victim's name is long forgotten. 'She could be a sex worker.'

'Could be,' Kendle says. 'But I wouldn't want to jump to conclusions at this early stage.'

'Have we got any idea on the cause of death?' Green says. 'Only I wouldn't want to jump to conclusions either.'

Kendle smiles again, and Chase wonders if she's flirting with Green. Doubts it. Kendle doesn't do cocky, self-assured men. Doesn't do men at all.

'Exsanguination,' Kendle says. 'Hardly surprising.'

Exsanguination is the medical term for bleeding to death, and no, it's hardly surprising that if you have your arm cut off and your stomach cut open, you'll bleed out.

17

'You said they might be a pro.' Chase indicates the suture marks. 'That they might be in the business. Care to expand on that?'

'Not really. Leastwise, not here. Best to wait until we get her on the table. Be a lot easier to work out what the hell's going on back at the mortuary, right?'

'Right.' Chase nods at Kendle and then asks Green if he's got any more questions. When he says he's done, Chase turns and tramps back towards the river. She thinks about her ruined shoes and how bad the traffic will be on the way to HQ and what she might do later after work and whether there's something worth watching on Netflix tonight and any other subject aside from the girl with the missing arm and the slashes across her breasts and the strange suture marks on her stomach.

# *Chapter 3*

The Serial Crimes Unit has a suite of offices on the fifth floor at New Scotland Yard. At least *suite* was how an officer described it to Chase before she joined. In reality, the SCU occupies a series of cubbyholes clustered in one corner of a vast open-plan area. Reception, complete with the obligatory plastic rubber plant, has space for all the staff members to sit. That is if they wheel their chairs out from the cubbyholes and ride them, Dalek style, to the meeting area. Typically, if someone wants to give a briefing or ask a colleague a question, they stand up and shout over the top of the low room dividers.

The SCU's permanent roster is just three strong, which, Chase reckons, shows the genuine sentiment towards the unit. Making up the trio of herself and Green is Detective Sergeant John Stafford. He's the office manager and does data analysis on the side. He's known as Johnny, Johnboy, JJ, Rubberman (hence the plant), Condo, or anything as long as it's not John. Stafford is a Cambridge dropout. Mathematics. Was halfway through a doctorate when he decided Euclidean geometry no longer did much for him. He turned his career around, as he likes to say, one hundred and eighty degrees. He's good-looking in an upperclass way and is the only person Chase has ever met who can wear a tweed jacket, cords and brown shoes and make them look halfway stylish.

Aside from Chase, Stafford and Green, the SCU is also a temporary home-from-home to three detective constables who are rotated in and out as needed. Currently, the lucky three are Sam Hastings, Nikki Ghosh, and Kyle Willem. The DCs are given the shit jobs and do the legwork, while Chase, Green and Stafford get the fun stuff.

As a legal entity within the National Crime Agency, the SCU should be able to draw on officers from across the country, but inevitably, recruits come from the Met. Green is the exception, as he's from way out west in the sticks. Cornwall. Same place as Doctor Pat Kendle. There's usually a shake of the head at the idea of a country boy bumbling along in the big city. Jokes about sheep rustling and speeding tractors. Lame attempts at a West Country accent. That is until Green mentions he worked in Truro. Then the heads stop shaking and start nodding. Truro, right. The Cornish Ripper. And all of a sudden, Green's appointment to the SCU makes a whole lot of sense.

Two years ago, the Cornish Ripper was front-page news. In the space of a few months, he raped or sexually assaulted fifteen women, and the effect the crimes had on the region was devastating. Female applications to Falmouth University were down by a third, tourists began to shun the area, and several newly-formed hi-tech businesses expressed their intentions to relocate up country. That's when questions were asked in parliament, as if it only mattered when people were getting screwed *financially*.

Under pressure from the Home Secretary, Devon and Cornwall's Chief Constable makes a left-field play and replaces the entire investigative team, appointing the ageing but experienced DI Nick Green as the SIO in charge of a revitalised task force.

Green, untroubled by the pressure, identifies a new suspect, a second-homer from London whose occasional visits coincide with the crimes. However, after extensive surveillance and a fruitless honey trap, there's still no evidence.

Undeterred, Green uses a pseudonym and books a stay in the suspect's holiday home. While there, he discovers a rape kit hidden in a locked cupboard. He rigs a transmitter to the cupboard, moves into a nearby property rented at personal cost, and waits for months. Then, alerted late one night by the transmitter, Green stumbles out into the darkness and trails the suspect, intervening as he is about to attack a young female student.

Guy goes down for twenty-five years minimum, and Green receives a commendation and an invitation to move to London to join the newly set up SCU.

Which is when the fun starts.

On day one of the fledgling unit, Chase, Green and Stafford are briefed by their new boss, Detective Chief Superintendent Jeff Boyle. The SCU, even though it's an NCA subagency, comes under the jurisdiction of the Met. And why wouldn't it? Boyle argues. Met resources, Met staff, Met fucking pencils and paperclips. Never mind fledgling, Chase thinks, we're getting our wings clipped before we even leave the nest. She wonders if the SCU isn't some PR exercise, something to make the Home Secretary, the Commissioner and the Mayor look good.

Chase and Green will head up the unit under Boyle's ever-watchful gaze. He jokes that he likes the name *Chase,* but *Green* doesn't cut it. Laughs all round until Boyle leaves them to it, and Green says 'wanker' under his breath. That's when Chase knows she'll get along fine with the country hick from way out west.

Green has well over a dozen years more experience than Chase, although that's not to say that she's inexperienced; prior to the SCU, she spent five years working on major investigation teams where she saw her share of murder and mayhem. Still, Green has never looked down on her, never pulled the wise old copper routine. She respects him for that because his attitude is unusual in an organisation built on rank and long service and a good dollop of misogyny, racism and the odd dodgy handshake.

The SCU idles for the first six months with no real sense of direction. Chase, Green and Stafford set out the policy and parameters of the unit and write a dozen briefing documents, but in terms of actual policing, they do sweet FA. Zilch. Nada. Nowt. They find time to help out on other investigations into a couple of murders, several rapes and a nasty celebrity abuse case, but there's nothing *serial* about any of the crimes, and that's where their expertise supposedly lies. Playing the long game. Seeing the bigger picture. DPP.

DPP: Data. Patterns. Persistence. That's a catchphrase Stafford came up with for the PR department to flash around on the fancy brochures and social media posts, but when the SCU finally gets a legitimate *serial* case, DPP pays dividends.

The papers tag him the Soho Sleeper for his liberal use of flunitrazepam, better known by its trade name of Rohypnol. The drug is a benzodiazepine that induces drowsiness, and that's precisely how the Soho Sleeper uses it. He targets young men, specifically straight young men he knows won't be keen on going to the police after he's raped them. Chase and Green start tracking reports and eventually, after a public appeal, discover dozens of incidents. The MO is the same in each case: the victims remember talking to a friendly guy in a bar. They share a drink or three, the guy making a point of ogling any women and commenting on them, clever small talk to reassure the victims that he's one hundred per cent heterosexual. Later, he persuades the victims to come home and watch some porn flicks. They take a taxi and then walk across a park. The victims describe a maisonette in a posh cul-de-sac. Multi-million-pound houses. Expensive cars. Other details are sketchy, including the location. West? South of the river? Suburban? Out of London? The victims have no idea because the Rohypnol fuzzes their memories. They can't remember much more than going inside with the man and, at some point, falling asleep. The following day, they awake as they are bundled out of a large 4x4 in a random London street.

To Green, if it looks like a mess and sounds like a mess, then it's a mess.

'No way we can untangle this crap,' he says. 'We're fucked.'

'We're not fucked and it's not a mess,' says Stafford. 'It's DPP.'

Data. Patterns. Persistence.

Stafford plugs in various datasets to his analysis software: pickup points, drop-off points, and any landmarks the victims can remember. Chase and Green concentrate on the flunitrazepam. The drug isn't licensed in the UK, so it has to have come in illegally, probably from Europe. They make contact with dealers. They know none of them will spill the beans on their customers, so they merely ask whether they've ever sold the drug. More data.

Next, taxis and minicabs. The team hand out little report pads, and every time a driver picks up two men, they make a note of the journey. More data.

The attacks continue and correlations begin to appear. Chase sticks an enormous map of London on one wall. Soon, it's filled with circles and arcs, and Stafford says that an old Greek philosopher called Euclid might be helpful after all.

A few months in, Stafford fires up a little machine-learning algorithm he's written. The algorithm traces routes, linking drug deals with taxi rides with landmarks with the vehicle licensing information of expensive 4x4s — a hundred other data points.

'A mess,' Green reiterates. 'A pretty mess, I'll give you that, but still a mess.'

Chase agrees but thinks watching Stafford work is like watching Cumberbatch in *The Imitation Game*. Only Stafford is better looking than Cumberbatch and cleverer than Turing.

'Really?' says Green.

'Drinks more,' answers Chase. 'And can still come up with the goods, so overall, yeah.'

'Point taken,' says Green.

Stafford's algorithm narrows the search down to a street in Richmond. Big, fuck-off houses, several converted into multi-million-pound flats. There's one particular guy in a maisonette who's been acquitted on a charge of possessing cocaine. It's years back, and he was found not guilty, sure, but there you have a possible connection to the drug dealers. He's also a consultant at a private London hospital, which explains how he can administer the correct quantity of Rohypnol. Then there's a recent trip to the US to consider. The consultant goes on a two-month exchange visit to the States, and during that time, the attacks cease. And — guess what? — a week after he returns, there's another attack. Finally, they discover he's active on the fetish scene, into leather and whips and cuffs.

'Who isn't these days?' Chase says. 'Vanilla is so passé.'

But still...

The team do a 'Green' and moves into a vacant apartment opposite. The weekly rent is eyewatering, and Boyle gives them just two weeks. They work double shifts, doing their regular job during the day and carrying out surveillance at night. Nothing. The two weeks are up, and the

Dodgy Doc is in the clear. Chase doesn't buy it, and neither does Green. Boyle doesn't care. 'You're done,' he says. 'Fuck him,' Green says, and they use a car instead of the flat, working the surveillance while off duty and each doing one night on, one night off. Fifth night — Friday — Chase gets delayed and doesn't get to the street until late. She watches into the small hours and, at three o'clock, hits the jackpot. The doc comes out half carrying, half dragging an unconscious young man. Packs him into the back seat of his Merc 4x4. As he drives off, Chase rams the vehicle with her own and then calmly calls for backup. The Soho Sleeper — real name Doctor Alan Grainger — is arrested, and months later, the case goes to trial. The jury doesn't believe a word Grainger says, and he gets a lengthy sentence.

The Commissioner takes the credit. And Boyle. And the Mayor. And the Home Secretary. Chase, Green, and Stafford give a collective shrug because they're not in this game for the glory. They gather the rest of the team, pop open a bottle of bubbly, drink a toast from plastic cups, and return to work.

And then, three months after the verdict, Grainger's case goes to appeal. The judge orders a retrial, and this time, it's Grainger opening the champagne as the jury, weighing the new evidence, finds him *not guilty*.

Not. Fucking. Guilty.

Chase, Green, and Stafford go down to the local pub and get well and truly hammered.

~ ~ ~

Chase is back at New Scotland Yard by mid-morning, leaving Green at Kew to coordinate with the locals. She senses a buzz as she gets to the fifth floor and cuts across the open-plan office towards the corner belonging to the SCU.

A few people are clustered around a TV screen, others staring at monitors.

'Huh?' she says, tapping a colleague on the back and peering over his shoulder. 'What's going on?'

'Where have you been this morning, Jessie?' her colleague says, momentarily turning his head. 'You've not heard the news?'

'No.'

The officer gestures at the TV, and Chase reads the scrolling ticker at the bottom. On the screen, shaky video from a phone shows three masked men surrounding a car. One of the men holds a shotgun, the other two pistols. The windscreen crazes and caves in as the guy with the shotgun fires. The other two men discharge several rounds, and then all three run to a waiting black BMW and drive away.

'Gangland execution,' the officer says. 'Two shot dead in broad daylight on Croydon high street. Not going down well with the powers that be.'

Chase shakes her head. Fuck knows what the world's coming to. She walks away but is spotted by DCS Jeff Boyle before she can get to the safety of the half-a-dozen little cubbyholes that make up the SCU. He waves, but she keeps her head down and pretends she hasn't seen him. The anonymous girl by the river who's all cut up has probably got him all cut up. Word gets around fast, she thinks. As she strolls over to her desk, Boyle makes his move and arrives as she plonks herself down in her chair.

'Morning, Jessie,' he says. 'Just want a quick word.'

*If only*, she thinks. Boyle doesn't use one word when he can squeeze three or four in instead. Doesn't make do with a paragraph when he can concoct ten. Busy-busy Boyle. Like a bee on a good day, flitting from desk to desk, a smile and a chat, and he's off again. On a bad day, Boyle is more like a boil on an arse cheek: irritating as fuck, and the more you scratch, the redder and more painful it gets. The best thing on a bad day is to try to forget that he exists.

'Just a word, Jessie,' Boyle says. 'Or two. About the, um, *situation*.'

Boyle is tall and thin and looms over her like one of the towering cranes that constantly push their way above the London skyline. He swivels as if he's about to dump a bucket-load of cement right in her lap. Which, she figures, he probably is.

'You're talking about the woman at Kew?' Chase says. 'She was in a bad way. Sliced open. One arm missing. Other things.'

'Other things? I'm not too fond of *other things*, Jessie, you know that. It's easier when it's a simple knifing or a couple of people taking potshots at each other.'

What the DCS means is that he likes it when a murder is criminal on criminal, like this morning's incident in Croydon. No innocent victims, no bystanders caught in the crossfire. Definitely no room for a pesky woman to be so foolish as to allow herself to be sliced open.

Boyle is off on one now. He wants this sorted before it gets out of hand. With the horrific events earlier, the last thing they need is another shocking news story.

'We don't want panic,' he says. 'And the best way of avoiding panic is to keep the gory details under wraps and feed the media as little as possible.'

Chase thinks the best way to avoid panic is to catch the killer, but she keeps quiet.

'We need to reassure the public they are quite safe and remind them that killings like this are incredibly rare.' A pause as Boyle lets his words sink in. Then, repetition and emphasis just in case she hasn't got the message: '*Incredibly* rare, right?'

Chase nods and hopes Boyle is correct.

'So?' Boyle has finished wittering. He cocks his head towards Chase's monitor. 'Where are we at?'

'Nowhere yet, sir.' Chase doesn't want to give Boyle any sense they'll wrap this soon. 'Anonymous woman dumped a couple of days ago. Possibly homeless and or trafficked since we don't have any pressing missing person reports. She was found on a small island in the river at Kew. No useful forensic evidence so far. PM scheduled for tomorrow.'

'How did she die?'

Chase wants to say *painfully,* but instead, she shrugs. 'Not sure. It looks like her attacker inflicted multiple knife wounds. He amputated her right arm.'

'Did you say *amputated*?'

'Yes.'

'At the scene?'

'Probably not, no.'

'So where?'

'It would have to be somewhere secluded or soundproof. She'd have made a lot of noise.' Chase thought about the cuts and the agony endured. Can't help but flinch. 'She'd have been screaming unless she was drugged or unconscious.'

'Christ.' Boyle shakes his head. 'Fucking Christ.'

'Fucking Christ? Yeah, that's about the state of it, sir.'

Chase can see Boyle doesn't want to deal with this. He wants to get back to his gangs and the underworld killings. Black on black. White on white. Black on white on black on white. What happened earlier this morning in Croydon was disturbing, but it's Boyle's area of expertise. Yes, the killings were nasty and brutal, but not this, not *depraved*. Boyle doesn't do *depraved*. This is a problem because, notionally, one of Boyle's duties is supervising the SCU and seeing the team get everything they need. It's also a problem because right now, Chase needs to tell him stuff he won't want to know.

'I think,' she says cautiously, 'this could be part of a series.'

'Fuck off, Jessie. I don't want to hear that.'

Even though, Chase thinks, the entire raison d'être of the SCU is to solve *serial* crime. But that's Jeff Boyle. Give him a couple of heavies gunning down a security guard, and he's in heaven. Show him a picture of a woman all sliced open, breasts cut up, arm cut off, and he doesn't want to know anything about it.

'Sorry, sir, but that's the way it is.'

'DI Green with you this morning?'

'Yes.'

'And he agrees?'

'His notion, so pretty much, yeah.'

'I see.' Boyle is thinking. Cogs in his head whir around until a lightbulb flashes, and a chime rings out. He waves across at a nearby island of desks where several detectives hunker down over keyboards. 'You've got Hastings, Ghosh and Willem. I'll see if I can spare another couple from the Croydon job. For a week or two at least.'

'OK, sir, that'll be good.'

'It's not good, Jessie, not good at all, but it's doable.' Boyle smacks his lips together in a grimace and looks over at the trio of young DCs. 'So get it done, right?'

'Yes, sir.'

# Chapter 4

The post-mortem takes place the next day, and considering the lack of progress so far, Chase hopes it will give the team something to work with. With Pat Kendle at the helm, that's almost a given. Kendle does autopsies like she enjoys them. No, not enjoys, *savours*. No cut-and-shut for PK. No wham, bam, thank you, ma'am. Her PMs are always drawn-out affairs. Early morning stretching to well past lunch and afternoon creeping into the evening. Once, Chase had arrived at half-three, leaving a bright sunlit day behind; she'd come out a little before nine and stumbled into a murky night, the darkness engulfing the last vestiges of hope the daylight had offered.

'You eaten?' Green says to Chase as they park up and head into the mortuary.

'No.' Chase says.

'Here.' Green flips his jacket open and shows an inner pocket. The tops of a couple of Mars Bars poke out. 'Let me know if you get peckish while we're in there.'

'You do know how to treat a girl, Nick. I can't understand why you're still single.'

'Me neither. Must be the stories I tell them about me and PK.'

'That'll do it every time.'

Kendle is waiting in the little atrium. White walls, floors, and ceiling. Plastic flowers in a vase on a desk. A painting of waves rolling onto a sandy beach hanging above a stark metal bench. Chase isn't sure if the conflict of metaphors is intentional: the everlasting plastic flowers as opposed to the inevitable rise and fall of the tide. Eternity versus the passage of time. Stasis or erosion and decay.

Fuck knows.

'Still no ID?' Kendle turns to Chase.

'Nothing yet,' Chase says. 'She doesn't match any mispers. My initial hunch is she's an illegal immigrant, probably trafficked here and forced to earn her keep.'

'You might think I'm a bit of a liberal,' Kendle says. 'Lesbian, lefty, enviro-freak. Not for the people who do this kind of thing, though.' She waves through to the next room, where a slab of stainless steel awaits. 'Bring the perp in and I'll harvest his organs. Genitals first, no anaesthetic. Does that sound good to you?'

'Sounds great.' Green claps his hands together. 'Now we just have to catch him.'

Kendle gestures at a row of gowns hanging on the far wall. Time to get suited and booted. Time to get down to business. 'Any leads?'

'Not so far.' Chase moves to the gowns and selects one. 'Hoping you're going to help us out with that.'

Appropriately dressed, they move to the next room, where a blue sheet lies over the body. Kendle nods to the mortuary assistant, and he removes the sheet and reveals the cadaver.

'Bloody hell.' Green sucks in air and half turns his head away. Chase doesn't think he'll be scoffing his chocolate bar any time soon.

The victim isn't looking great this morning. In the shadows on the river bank, the true nature of the injuries hadn't been apparent, but under the bright lights, everything is revealed in full colour. Or rather in a set of muted colours: the brown riverbank mud smeared on the body; the black of multiple bruises; the blueish purple of livor mortis across the skin; the dull grey eyes wide open but seeing nothing; the dark red splatter marks on the stomach; the pale white stick of bone jutting from the shoulder.

31

Right now, Kendle's offer of a spot of retributive justice sounds pretty good.

The pathologist reaches for an overhead boom and pulls a microphone down. She makes some preliminary observations on the woman's height, weight and approximate age. She details some of the injuries, the state of the corpse, and the presence of day-old instars. She picks up a couple of the tiny maggots — dead now because they've been in the cool morgue drawer — and pops them in a Petri dish.'

'There's a tattoo,' she says. 'On the right shoulder. Or rather half a tattoo, the rest of it is on the missing arm.'

The missing arm.

Extensive searching of the riverbank and the river itself has drawn a blank as regards the arm, and Chase reckons either the tide swept the limb away or the killer kept it for some nefarious purpose.

She moves closer. The tattoo is a dolphin leaping through a wave, a curl of blue and grey, although the lower half of the dolphin is missing.

'As I said at the scene,' Kendle says, 'neat, tidy cuts.' She leans in closer. 'And removed with a fine-toothed saw. And those three slashes on the chest are very precise, not part of a random attack. It's almost like they are part of a sigil or something.'

'A gang marker,' Green says, turning to Chase. 'As if the girl was a hanger-on and got targeted by an opposing gang. The marks are a message.'

'Could be,' Chase says. 'But if the killing was intended as a message, then why secrete her away on the island?'

Green shrugs and goes back to studying the body as Kendle moves around the autopsy table, making a second circuit. Always fastidious, PK. Never slapdash. Sometimes, Chase would prefer a quick bodge-it and scarper.

The details, the time and cause of death, the weapon. Out of the mortuary and down the pub and sinking a pint. And another. And another. Shit-faced because anything else and the memories return. Coils of grey intestines. The chest cut open and the skin peeled back. The brain removed and plonked on a tray for weighing. My round again, is it? And another. And another.

'She bled out.' Kendle's made her mind up on the cause of death, but then she's only confirming what she proposed at the scene. 'Either from the removal of the arm or from that.'

A finger points at the scar across the stomach where a line of sutures zigzags above the belly button.

Green coughs and shifts uncomfortably from foot to foot. There's an obvious question, but it looks as though Chase will have to follow through.

'Was she conscious when she was cut open?'

'There are marks on the wrists and ankles consistent with restraint.' Kendle indicates the friction burns. 'On the other hand, that wouldn't stop her from thrashing about as she was opened up.'

Too right. Chase blinks. Doesn't even want to imagine the pain. She remembers a story about a patient coming round during an operation but unable to speak. The agony. The feeling of helplessness. In their victim's case, she *would* have been able to speak and shout and scream, to strain with every sinew to escape. But her words would have fallen on deaf ears.

'... too neat for her to have been struggling.'

'Sorry?' Chase missed the start of the sentence. 'Are you saying she *wasn't* conscious?'

'She was almost certainly unconscious. And if not unconscious, then so drugged up that she was beyond caring.

We'll know after we send some blood and stomach samples for toxicology tests.'

'So she didn't wake up before death?'

'I very much doubt it.'

'Small mercies.' Green shakes his head. He holds up one hand, finger and thumb a hair's breadth apart. 'Very, very small, mind you.'

Kendle straightens. 'Now, let's see what went on behind those stitches.' She nods to her assistant, and he comes across with a wrap of scalpels on a kidney dish. 'OK?'

'Can't wait.' Chase steals a glance at Green. He half smiles and points to his breast where the Mars Bars are concealed in a pocket. Gives her a wink and mouths, *saving them for later.*

Then, someone's mobile rings, muffled by a layer of scrubs. Kendle frowns, annoyed. She glares at Chase and Green. Jokes she likes, interruptions not so much, and she's known for imposing a ten-pound fine if anyone's phone disturbs proceedings. Green pats himself on the bum. Shakes his head.

'Not me,' he says confidently.

'Nor me.' Chase touches her jacket pocket through the gown. Her phone is silent.

'Mine is in my office,' Kendle says as her assistant steps back, hands raised. Not him, either. 'So...?'

There's another chirp, chirp. Kendle leans forward and peers down at the floor as if looking for a phone that might have been dropped and kicked out of sight beneath the mortuary table. She straightens, her gaze moving to the body. Cocks her head to one side.

'What the fuck?' Green steps closer and lowers his head. 'It's...'

'Scalpel!' Kendle snaps, and the assistant moves across to offer her a kidney dish with an array of instruments.

She selects a thin blade and moves in close to the body. There's a flash of silver as she slices in below the line of stitches. The skin slips apart, yellow puss oozing forth from the gash.

'Jesus.' Chase tries not to breathe in as a waft of foulness escapes the suction of the ventilation system. The stench is awful. Rotten eggs, putrid meat, an open sewer. Tendrils of death fill the air and grab her throat.

There's another pair of chirps, louder now. No doubt about where the sound is coming from. Kendle slices again and peels back a layer of skin. She eases a hand into the gash, yellow slime rising on the blue latex of her glove, an overflow of liquid frothing up from the opening. Half her forearm is gone now as she delves inside the cadaver.

'Got it!' she says, slowly removing her hand. There's a layer of clear plastic wrapped around a slab of black, the whole package glistening with bodily fluids. Kendle moves to the side of the room to a sink with a set of taps with extended levers. She nudges one with an elbow and runs water over the package, clearing the muck away as the chirp chirp from the phone continues. 'Right, let's see.'

Chase moves over as Kendle holds up the phone.

And then the ringing stops.

'Fuck,' Kendle says.

Chase peers at the phone through the plastic. Sees something flash at the top of the screen.

'One new voicemail message,' she says.

~ ~ ~

Tempted as she is to play the message immediately, Chase holds fire. She needs tech support in the form of John Stafford. Green hovers beside her, impatient.

'You don't think we should bite?' he says, pointing at the phone.

35

'The message could be garbled or in a foreign language, or it could disappear after one playback,' Chase says. 'Yes, we could record it, but we also need to contact the carrier and ensure they preserve everything, track down the number and grab all the records relating to the phone. Better wait, right?'

'I guess.' Green glances back at the body. There's not much more to look forward to than another couple of hours of PK stripping away skin and sawing through bone. Trepanning the skull and slipping the organs onto trays. He pats his breast pocket. 'Fancy a break?'

~ ~ ~

They grab a coffee and eat the Mars Bars. Chase alerts Stafford that they're coming in hot and that he should be prepared. Then it's back to the PM. Kendle wields the bone saw, opens the chest cavity, extracts the internal organs, cuts through the skull, her blue-gloved fingers curling around the pale purple tissue as she carries the poor girl's thoughts and dreams from the lifeless body and places the brain on a stainless steel dish. Chase stares at the organ and wonders if chemical and electrical signals are all there is to life because, if so, the young woman got the shitty end of a crap deal.

When it's over, Chase and Green return to base with the mobile phone and find Stafford waiting by his mini-tech lab. He's rigged cables and power supplies and installed a program that can emulate the phone's operating system on his computer. He pulls the phone apart and connects up his gear. In a few minutes, he's made a backup of everything. While he's doing that, Green tries to contact the phone company and track down the origins of the phone. They'll need a warrant to get the records, but for now, he wants to make sure the account is locked and nothing will be deleted.

There's a problem, though.

'Pay as you go SIM,' Green says. 'And the phone is a grey import, likely purchased at a dodgy car boot sale.'

'So it's untraceable?' Chase says.

'Yeah, looks that way. Plus, credit was put on with a top-up card, which doesn't help. We'd need to throw considerable resources at it to get anywhere.'

'Well, there's nothing stored on the phone.' Stafford shrugs. He's completed his job and sounds frustrated that Green can't hold up his end. 'There are no calls or texts out, only the missed call in.'

'If it's a burner, then that could be all there is,' Chase says. She nods across to the three junior detectives. 'Kick the paperwork over to our loyal Musketeers and let them deal with it.'

'So, we're good to go?' Stafford says.

'Yes.' Green says.

Stafford waits for Chase.

'Do it,' Chase says.

Triple four accesses the voicemail, and Stafford taps the numbers on the keyboard of his computer.

'Are you recording?' Chase says.

'Duh.' Stafford points to the computer monitor, where a red line peaks with spikes of noise. 'Of course I am.'

*You have one new message. Press one to play. Two to save. Three to delete.*

Stafford clicks one.

# Chapter 5

*The Architect is in his home office, thinking about the events he has set in motion. The three stories aren't a random set of killings, and he's not some nutter; quite the opposite. The killings are a calculated response to circumstances he didn't initiate, didn't want and certainly didn't expect.*

Didn't expect? More fool you, son.

*He has been hearing his mother's voice ever since the accident nine months ago. Scolding and berating and nagging and bleating. It's as if the way things turned out was entirely his fault.*

Well, they were, son. And now you've made your bed, right?

*Nine months ago, in the course of his work, he falls and hits his head. The ER doctor says he's suffered a mild concussion, and the effects should pass in a few days. Only they don't. He finds himself getting frustrated at the most minor of things and angry at events outside his control.*

*Somebody on the sidewalk goes to step into the road as he drives by, and he leans on the horn.*

*BLOODY IDIOT!*

*He's loading his shopping trolley with groceries in the store, and a woman moves the trolley to get by.*

*LEAVE IT ALONE, BITCH!*

*During a stroll in the park, a homeless man approaches with an empty coffee cup held out for loose change.*

*GET THE HELL AWAY FROM ME OR I'LL BEAT YOUR FUCKING BRAINS OUT!*

*Even as he says the words, he's appalled. It's like someone else is talking for him. Someone very different from the calm and ordered person he knows.*

*At work, he can no longer concentrate. Tasks pile up and colleagues, aware of his failing health, step in to help lighten the load. HR, in consultation with his physician, suggest some time off. He takes it.*

*But back home, with nothing to distract him, the nightmares start.*

*At first, they're the usual kind: Falling. Being buried alive. Running from an unseen beast. But then the usual kind becomes the utterly bizarre kind.*

*Gone are the dreams about falling, internment and monsters. Now, he is haunted by a hag who comes to him in the small hours. She creeps up one night, crawls into his bed, and cuddles up. Her clothes are torn and dirty, and she's half-naked, with black bruising on the side of her face.*

*Which is when the Architect realises this is no random ghoul, no ordinary demon or night terror.*

I'm back, son, back from the dead. Back to remind you that this is a situation all of your own making.

*It's his mother.*

Of course it is, son! I'm here to look after you since nobody else can.

*The ghoul leans in close, peeling skin on her neck revealing dried sinew beneath.*

Give Mommy a kiss!

*NO!*

*He wakes in a tangle of bed sheets, dripping with sweat, the minutes ticking by until he realises it was only a nightmare. But a week later, she's back again, creeping under the sheets sometime before dawn.*

That's alright, baby. Mommy will help you sleep. You've been a bad boy and caused all kinds of problems, but I forgive you. Come closer. There, there. Give Mommy a big hug, and all will be forgotten.

*GET OFF ME!*

*He tries going to bed with the lights on, the radio play-ing, and an alarm to wake him every half hour so he doesn't ever doze off long enough for her to slip into his dreams. But eventually, worn out, the radio and the alarm aren't sufficient, and he falls unconscious.*

Sweet baby, cuddle time!

*NO!*

*The Architect returns to his doctor, and the doctor ex-plains the concussion might be worse than first thought. He prescribes sleeping pills, and the Architect takes dou-ble the dose, knocking himself out, a wall of black enveloping him. But the black fades, and his mother ma-terialises in a mist of grey.*

We're rolling, baby, rolling. Riding and writhing to-gether. Mommy's here for you. Closer than ever. After all, you're so alone now.

*Yes, he's alone. The truth is the Architect's wife left a while ago, and even before she did, his marriage had been a wreck for years: No children, an unhealthy work-life balance, an unfulfilling physical relationship.*

Let her go, and it'll be you and me against the world, baby. Rolling towards the horizon. Riding. Because, yes, I can give you a fulfilling physical relationship. And remem-ber, you owe me. You ruined my life back then. Ruined all our lives.

*I WAS TWELVE!*

Yes, you were, honey, but you were a clever little boy. You knew what you were doing.

*I WAS DOING THE RIGHT THING!*

I don't think so, but Mommy loves you whatever, right? Come on, cuddle up close. Slip inside me. We can solve this problem together if we put our minds to it.

*Solve this problem...*

The Architect shakes his head; there is no problem other than the witch and her nightly visits.

He gives up on the doctor and visits a therapist. He tells her about his life from start to finish, including the stuff from way back, but he doesn't mention the dreams. He does one month with her, twice weekly sessions. He tells her he has fantasies but leaves out the lurid details. He doesn't tell her about his mom's nocturnal visits. Doesn't tell her the other fantasies that involve taking retribution for the mess he's in. The ones where he's out cleaning the streets and washing the filth away, a lone vigilante ridding the world of profanity one fallen woman at a time.

'Fantasies are quite normal,' the therapist says. 'We all have them. They're harmless as long as they remain just fantasies.'

Harmless? Right... and as for everyone having them? No, they fucking don't. Not like his. Nobody has fantasies like his.

Still, the therapy works for a time, and the succubus vanishes for several weeks. But then a bout of severe flu lays the Architect low, and she returns, sliding into his dreams and underneath the bedclothes. Sliding him inside her body.

You didn't think you'd banish Mommy that easily, did you?

Her voice wakes him, and he leaps from the bed and runs downstairs. Turns all the lights on. Flicks the TV to a twenty-four-hour news channel and paces the room, glancing at the stairs, half expecting the demon to come gliding down.

The nightmares start over, and this time, the dreams come more frequently, barely a night when she doesn't visit him.

He takes speed to keep himself awake in the small hours and sleeps in his car during the day. But the neighbours, concerned for his mental health, call the cops, and he has to make up some story about an infestation of bed bugs.

And the next night, when he's back inside the house, she's there again, not long after he falls asleep.

You know what you must do to be free of me, right?

Her voice screeches inside his head even as he wakes from the torment. He pops some more uppers and stalks round the house, close to breaking point. This has been going on for too long. Week after week, month after month. Much more and he'll lose his sanity for good. He slumps on the sofa, puts his head in his hands, and thinks back. Not to the accident, but to long, long before, back to the route of all his problems.

Thirty-three years...

He leans back and closes his eyes and dreams, transported to another place, another time, hoping that when he wakes, he will have the answer to his problems.

# *Chapter 6*

*Story Two*

It's late in the city as she walks down the street past deserted warehouses. Every few minutes, cars cruise by, windows down. Wolf whistles. Lewd comments. The occasional beep of a horn. These aren't the players; they are tourists or rubberneckers. Guys with a couple of beers sloshing around in their guts, just driving down here for a laugh. Jocks on a bachelor party night out. Couples getting some sort of kick from seeing streetwalkers in the flesh. The players don't make a sound, and the window doesn't come down until they're alongside. Then there is a whispered, 'How much?' She gives them the long and the short of it. The price for a handjob, a blowjob, full sex, anal, bareback. She tells them she has her own place five minutes drive away. That isn't true. The walk-up belongs to her pimp; she hasn't had anywhere to call home since she ran out on her mother age fourteen. She tells the clients she is clean. That's a lie, too, since the pimp is also her dealer. Keeping her hooked ensures she's meek and pliable. If she runs, she doesn't score, and if he finds her, she'll get a hiding. Better to do as he says and secrete a few dollars away each day under the rotting floorboard behind the panel in the bathroom. Save a little here and there, and perhaps she can make a break. A hundred more blowjobs, a hundred more handjobs.

She's returning to the walk-up now to catch a few hours sleep. She ignores the rubberneckers and a potential client in a white Tesla who asks her how much for a quickie.

'I'm done for the night,' she says when he persists. 'Try down the street.'

Carolina's down there. And Tracey. Friends, of sorts. Same pimp. Same crazy idea to save a little here and there and get the fuck out while they still can. Same hopeless dreams.

The Tesla drives on to be replaced by a large truck with out-of-area plates. The letters and numbers on the plate are superimposed over the image of a mountain. Below the characters are the words *Evergreen State*. She doesn't register any other details because the window is down, and the driver is leaning across.

'Hello, sweetheart.'

'I'm not working.'

'You're a doll. Just what I'm looking for.'

'What part of...'

The driver is waving a bundle of notes in her direction. Five hundred.

That's a lot of cash, she thinks. Put that with what she's got saved, and she could get out tomorrow. Only...

'Are you crazy?' She points at the money.

'My wife was blonde, like you. Exact same figure, same mouth, same eyes.'

'Get lost, weirdo.' She starts to walk off. She doesn't want some dude beating her up because she looks like the woman who walked out on him.

'She died, see... cancer... and I... I just wanted to...'

She turns back. The man lowers his head, sad, wistful. He could be acting, chancing his luck, but her gaze is drawn to the five hundred bucks. The golden ticket.

'No funny stuff,' she says. 'Straight only, OK?'

'Sure,' the man says as he clicks open the passenger door. 'Get in.'

She gets in.

# *Chapter 7*

'Isn't this just about the most fucked up thing you've seen?'

Detective Frank Locke considers the question and then looks at the man who asked it. Name of Robert Kell, a freelance photographer living at Seeley Lake. At least those are the details the man has given, but Locke is beginning to wonder whether he's telling the truth.

Locke has driven up here through the trees, the blacktop running out before a five-mile switchback along a rough fire truck road to where he found Kell hanging around, nonchalant as could be. Since Locke has come on a call from a forest ranger about a man behaving suspiciously, possibly linked to remote crack houses, that's odd. But, odder and more disturbing still is what Kell has just shown him.

Locke takes a deep breath and looks around. They're about seventy miles northeast of Missoula in the Lewis and Clarke National Forest amid a landscape of sharp ridges, deep ravines, grassy valleys, and ice-blue lakes. There's a backdrop of mountain peaks, plenty still white with snow despite the spring warmth. Getting here from Missoula, Locke's base, has taken a couple of hours, but he's philosophical about that. Getting anywhere in western Montana usually involves a dog leg at least twice the straight-line distance.

'Well?' Kell wants an answer, some sort of validation. 'The most fucked up thing, right?'

'Pretty damn close.' Locke has seen a lot of fucked up things in his time. Doesn't want to go back to dwell on any

45

of them just so he can answer. Dwelling is something you try not to do when you're a homicide detective, especially when you've worked the cases Locke has. Madness that way lies. Mind you, Locke's done his fair share of dwelling in the past. Difficult not to. Considering. 'Tell me how you found her?'

Her. No doubt about it because the corpse is naked. Even if it hadn't been obvious, Locke would have had a hunch based on all those years he's done, all the dead bodies he's seen, all the crime scenes he's had the dubious pleasure of visiting. Not here in Montana, of course. But then Locke's not from Montana.

In Locke's experience, when the victim is a woman, it's most often down to so-called domestic troubles, and the husband's usually holds his hands up as the cops arrive. Shows them where the body is. Tears and apologies and crap.

*I just meant to hit her the once, officer, but then she went for a knife. The next thing I knew, she was lying on the floor, and I don't remember how she got there.*

The self-defence angle. Locke's heard it before, even from a three-hundred-pound beefcake with a petite wife.

But this sure isn't a domestic, and the reason Locke would have guessed it was a woman even if he hadn't seen the body is that only a sexual predator brings a victim deep into a forest and leaves the body above ground.

He remembers a statement from a tutor during his time on a course at the FBI Behavioural Analysis Unit in Quantico:

*So, you might think that's because the perpetrator wants animals to scatter the remains, right?*

A roomful of green detectives nod in agreement until the instructor tells them the truth.

46

*Wrong. The perp leaves the body exposed so he can come back to it. So he can jack off over it. So he can penetrate the mouth or the anus, or the vagina. So he can lie with the rotting body, caress it, and relive what he's done. Does it turn your stomach even to contemplate something like that? Get the fuck over it! You need to slip inside his mind, understand his desires, and think the way he thinks. You'll end up a half-mad loner driven to drink, but here's the thing: you'll catch your prey more often than not, certainly more often than the clock-in, clock-out, leave-it-at-the-precinct type of cop. In the end, it's your decision. Is this just a job to you, or is it a vocation? Are you just playing at this, or is this your life's work? It's make your mind up time, fellas, make your mind up time...*

'Tell me how you found her?' Locke repeats the question because Kell hasn't heard the first time; he's too focused on the cadaver, fingers caressing his fancy Nikon camera, his gaze sweeping up and down the torso. It's as if he's studying the dead girl and noting every detail on the expanse of naked flesh. Perhaps he's even getting a thrill from viewing the body. Locke takes the man's arm and guides him away until the corpse is lost in the maze of trunks behind them. 'How did you come across the body since it's not on a path?

The chance of stumbling across the scene by accident is minuscule, and Locke isn't entirely convinced by Kell's attitude. Too calm and collected.

'I was looking for my drone,' Kell says. 'Came down somewhere near here, and I was following a GPS line to retrieve it.'

'GPS line?'

'Following a bearing on the control unit.' Kell fishes something from his jacket pocket. Several buttons and a small screen. 'The drone's another four hundred yards down the hill, but once I stumbled across the body, I didn't bother retrieving it.'

'How were you able to guide me here without using the GPS?'

'We came off the track, right?' Kell nods back uphill. 'There was a treefall on the stream where I crossed over on my way down. So I looked for the treefall and followed an animal trail. I'm used to being out in the wild, and signs like that stick in my mind.'

'Right.' Locke hadn't noticed the treefall, but then he'd been concentrating on not smacking flat on his fanny or tripping forward and catapulting himself headlong. 'When did you last come down this way?'

'This way?' Kell cocks his head to one side like Locke is the crazy one. 'Never. I don't usually go wandering around off-trail for the fun of it. Why would I need to come down here except to retrieve my drone?'

Why indeed? Locke glances down and studies the soft loam. Plenty of footprints. His own and Kell's and possibly some others too. He needs to get the CSIs out here.

'That drone controller,' Locke says, pointing at the unit in the ranger's hand. 'Can it give me the coordinates for this exact spot?'

'Sure thing.' Kell raises the unit. Messes with a couple of buttons and reads out a stream of figures. Doesn't make much sense to Locke, but he pulls out a notepad and writes them down verbatim. Reads them back.

'Any chance of making a cell call?' he says. 'I need to get some people out here to deal with this.'

'Forget it.' Kell turns his head to one side. 'You'll need to get back to the road before the signal cuts in.'

There's something there, Locke thinks. A spark of anger, a tiny hint of disappointment, like Kell hadn't figured on

48

a bunch of police stomping around in *his* forest. Or perhaps it's something else. Locke flips his notepad closed and puts it in his jacket pocket. His hand brushes his shoulder holster, and there's the reassuring presence of a Glock 22. He's not exactly worried, but Kell looks fit and muscled, like a lean bear. Entirely appropriate, considering the location up here in the woods. Still, if you put a bullet in a man's chest, it doesn't matter how strong he is; he'll hit the ground like a proverbial ton of bricks.

'Let's go then,' Locke says. 'I need to make that call.'

Kell glances through the trees towards the body, and Locke's sort of hoping the man just cracks open and goes crazy, draws the knife he's got secured on his belt. Locke would step to the right, draw, aim, shoot. There'd be some paperwork to run through, but the case would be done and dusted. He can't see how it's going to work out otherwise. The body's been here for a couple of days at least, tending to suggest this is an unknown, someone not reported missing, someone unloved. Witnesses will be non-existent. Forensics a nightmare. After cursory enquiries, the killing will be chalked up to some random predatory male, and the mystery woman will never get justice.

Be a lot easier if Kell just went for the knife...

'Sure thing.' Kell nods and heads away uphill towards the track.

Locke stands for a moment, noticing how light-footed the man is. He takes his own glance through the trees at the body. Getting an early break on this one would've been nice. Of course, he could always whip out his gun and pop Kell in the back anyway. Say the man attacked him and then made a run for it.

'Would I do that?' Locke says out loud to the surrounding forest. 'Would I fuck.'

He turns and follows Kell up the hill.

~ ~ ~

Three hours later, Locke's got company. The CSIs with their truck and the medical examiner in his car. There's a stiff wagon, too, and a couple of orderlies lean against the vehicle, bored. One strikes up a cigarette until he's balled at by the CSIs. Locke stands by the corpse with the medical examiner, Doctor Adam Hem.

'What do you reckon?' Locke says. 'Do you think the arm was cut off here or somewhere else?'

The missing limb is the *most fucked up thing you've seen* that Robert Kell was talking about, and Locke's been pondering how and why the arm was removed ever since he first saw the body. So far, he hasn't come up with a decent explanation.

'I don't know,' Hem says. He peers at the ground. 'But then there's no blood, so I guess somewhere else, right?'

Well, I could have fucking told you that, Locke thinks, and he wonders what he's done to deserve Adam Hem. The ME looks like someone who's spent way too long in the education system. Locke hasn't met Hem before. He's new to the area and likely got a zillion qualifications and a Ph fucking D shoved up his ass, but Locke doubts he's seen anything like this before. Welcome to the real world, sonny.

'What about the striations on the right side of the sternum?' Locke had a good look before the crowds got here. Noticed the marks on the exposed rib bone. Three, to be precise. 'Couldn't that be an indication of stabbing or slashing wounds?'

'A knife? Yes, it could be.'

Diploma Boy is struggling, partly because the early spring bugs have come out for an evening buzz around. Hem seems to be attracting swarms of them. Locke isn't a country boy born and bred, but he always carries a repellent spray in his car. Hem waves his arms in a series of futile gestures at the growing cloud of insects.

'But the slashes are evenly spaced, precise. And something odd down in the genital area. Mutilation.' Locke grimaces. Odd is a polite way of putting it. There's enough flesh left so that not much imagination is needed to conclude that the killer didn't just dump the body. 'To be honest, Mr Hem, this is something out of the ordinary.'

'It's not mister, I'm a doctor,' Hem says.

Well, you could've fucking fooled me. Locke says nothing. Doesn't even nod to acknowledge his mistake. Hem peers at the remains for a minute, then rises and steps back.

'She's been mutilated in the chest area. I can't say if it occurred post-mortem or not. We'll find out at the autopsy.'

'Great.'

Locke nods across at the CSIs. They're up next. They clump down to the body like they don't care about making a mess of the scene because they figure this is a lost cause.

'Frank.' The lead CSI, Kerri Dunstan, nods a greeting as she stands and studies the scene. Dunstan's small and dumpy and wears her hair in a bun, the hair grey, she claims, ever since she attended her first slice and dice. She looks like she should be sitting on a rocker at home churning out knits for her grandchildren, not inspecting corpses for a living. 'This is a helluva fucking thing.'

Dunstan says *helluva thing* a lot. Doesn't matter how bad or how *not* bad things are, it's always a helluva fucking thing to Kerri Dunstan.

'The prints, Kerri.' Locke points at the soft loam, which bears several footprints, including Kell's, Doc Hem's,

Dunstan's, Locke's own and — possibly — the looney tunes who did this. 'What do you think?'

Dunstan kneels and examines an impression. Pushes her fingers into the soil. The marks she makes spring back.

'Indistinct,' she says. 'We might be able to get the size of the shoe, possibly something about the weight of the man. A couple of these suggest somebody your size or bigger. Tread patterns will be a stretch, though.'

'Right.' It's pretty much as Locke expected. 'Other traces?'

Dunstan stands and considers for a moment, then reaches out with a finger and thumb and snares something invisible from a nearby branch.

'A hair,' she says. 'Caught by the tree. Could be more. We'll check around.'

'Colour?' The victim has blonde hair, so anything but that would be a result.

'Ginger,' Dunstan says with a grin. With a flourish, she pulls an evidence bag from her coat and slips the hair inside. 'Howabouts that?'

'Nice,' Locke says, and he means it. The discovery of the hair is a minor breakthrough, and the fact it's ginger is a big help. There aren't many redtops around, and fewer still with hair long enough to get caught in a tree. 'So we're looking for a long-haired, overweight, ginger, hippy incel with a woman problem then.'

'That's about the size of it, Frank.'

Dunstan waves the two other CSIs down to their position and instructs them to begin a fingertip search radiating out from the body. Then she stares down at the corpse and shakes her head. Opens her mouth.

Here we go, Locke thinks. A *helluva thing* followed by a long rant about the state of the world, the state of law enforcement, and how the whole bloody mess is going down the tubes in a handcart overloaded with shit.

But Dunstan just stands there, focuses her gaze on the ground, and says nothing.

~ ~ ~

Later, the body's gone, Hem's gone, and Kerri Dunstan and her team are gone. It's just Locke and the forest. The light's going too, a gradual seep from day to night, as the colour drains from everything except the sky. The clouds are crimson red as if all the dead woman's blood has been sucked to the heavens, swirling round, angry, disturbed. There's a final display of radiance for a few minutes until even that fades, and the only remnant is whatever spirit the poor woman left behind. Only Locke doesn't believe in spirits, ghosts, ghouls, or anything supernatural. And there certainly isn't a god or a supreme being watching over all this crap.

He reckons his lack of faith is part of what makes him a good detective. The only people looking out for the poor victim are cops like him. No priest will save her soul, no prayer will bring her back, and no words of comfort will provide the relatives with anything approaching justice. Only Locke can do that.

He walks from tree to tree, circling the spot where the body had been lying. It's almost pitch black in the forest now, and he can't see anything but the outlines of the branches against the sky. He closes his eyes, listens, senses. Off to his right, there's a rustle in the dead leaves on the forest floor. Some creature emerging from its daytime hidey-hole. A bird calls out a sharp warning from a roost high above. There's a whisper in the breeze as the air caresses the treetops. He stands in the dark with his eyes shut. He imagines the killer with the woman, kneeling over the lifeless body and revelling in some perverse pleasure only the demented can experience.

*He'll come back*, he thinks. Even though the body's gone and the scene has been disturbed, even though there's a risk of capture, the killer will be drawn to this spot again and again. Perhaps not tonight, though.

And then a twig snaps off to Locke's right.

He opens his eyes. No animal made that sound. He stays still, his body pressed tight against a large tree trunk. He looks towards the forestry track as a shadowy figure passes between two trees and moves down the steep slope and into darkness. Earlier, to give space to all the arriving vehicles, Locke had moved his car round a corner and out of the way; it's possible whoever this is hasn't seen his car and doesn't know he's still here.

He slips his hand up to his gun. Releases the strap on the holster and eases the weapon out. Checks the clip.

Silence now. No animal sounds, no wind noise, nothing. Locke can almost *feel* the killer's presence beneath the trees, drawing closer and seeking out this sacred place. He turns his head, scanning the darkness for anything. Then, just a few steps away, a tiny light floats in the darkness before fading.

Someone is right where the body had been. Getting his sick-as-fuck rocks off.

And then there's a blinding flash that illuminates everything for a split second, freezing the scene, a man standing there staring at the tape that Kerri Dunstan had pegged to the ground.

The light snuffs out and leaves nothing but black, and as Locke blinks, he sees the image of the man burnt onto the back of his retina. He blinks again, trying to regain his night vision. He wraps both hands around his weapon and steadies his grip.

'Don't. Move. An inch,' he says.

# Chapter 8

'The fuck you doing up there?'

Robert Kell sits on a crappy plastic chair in the crappiest room in the precinct. Doesn't answer Locke's question. Just tries to stare him out. Gives up after a minute and blinks.

'What d'ya think, Frank?'

That's fellow detective Leo Sullivan playing the tag team shuffle. Standard procedure to move things along. Sullivan's got a couple of years on Locke. A couple of pounds, too. What he doesn't have, unlike Locke, is much patience. When Locke turned up with a prisoner in tow, Sullivan was about to head home. Instead, Locke grabbed him for a quick chat with the pseudo-photographer Mr Robert Kell.

Locke and Sullivan work for the Montana Department of Justice Division of Criminal Investigation. The DCI is based in the state capitol, Helena, but Locke and a handful of other detectives work out of Missoula, sharing space with the local PD. Locke gets to cover the state's mountainous northwest, and that's how he likes it.

Kell was pissed that he'd been clamped in cuffs and taken into the station. He claimed to have returned to the scene to try to retrieve his drone.

'Well?' Sullivan shifts in his seat. 'We could just charge him and get it over with?'

'Not yet, Leo,' Locke says. 'I'll keep asking Mr Kell the same questions until he tells me the truth.'

Sullivan rolls his eyes in the direction of the clock on the wall. Eleven thirty-one. Patience running thin.

'So, again,' Locke says. 'What were you doing there?'

'I told you. I was looking for my drone.'

'If there'd been a drone, our CSIs would have found it. Also, it doesn't explain why you were taking pictures.'

'I dunno.'

'There are a dozen pictures of the body and a dozen more of the surrounding location stored on the camera, and they were all taken before I first arrived. You took the pictures so you could relive the murder, didn't you? You wanted to jack off to the snaps later.'

'What I want is a lawyer,' Kell says.

He does the staring thing again, this time with Sullivan.

'We're trying.' Locke spreads his hands in apology. 'But it's late. Far simpler for us to have this friendly talk and get everything cleared up.'

'You think I killed the girl?' Kell breaks eye contact with Sullivan and tries it on with Locke again. 'Well, I didn't. You're more wrong than you could ever guess.'

Locke meets the stare and holds it until Kell blinks and looks away. Locke doesn't read too much into the pained expression on Kell's face. He doesn't believe anyone who says they can detect a lie, nor does he reckon there's such a thing as a universal tell, a narrowing or dilation of the pupils, some kind of physical response. Distinguishing truth from fiction can only be done by correlating a statement with known facts. Kell says he didn't kill the girl, but in Locke's experience, if you're the type of guy who likes to photograph dead bodies for fun, your name gets bumped right to the top of the list of suspects. At least until there's some overwhelming evidence to the contrary.

'We'll keep him in overnight,' Locke says to Sullivan. 'Get a lawyer here for a proper interview in the morning.'

'But I'll be missed,' Kell says. 'Karen will be worried.'

'Don't worry,' Locke says, thinking this Karen must be the pervert's poor wife. 'We'll let her know where you are

57

and everything you've been up to. And I mean everything, you sick fuck.'

Kell is taken to the cells, and Locke thanks Sullivan for his help.

'Overtime, Frank,' Sullivan says. 'Double rates and payback from you for the favour, right?'

'Sure thing, Leo.' Locke pats Sullivan on the back. 'The next time we're at Fat Tam's, I'll get your order.'

'Night, Frank.'

Sullivan heads off. Back to a dark apartment, with a cold meal and an empty bed waiting. His wife left a good few years ago. Locke's wife, Elsie, is still hanging on in there even though their relationship has gone frigid in the same way Sullivan's apartment has lost its soul. Leave a place long enough, and the fire goes out. His fault, he knows. So much crap in his life day to day that he feels like he's covered in shit. Doesn't want to touch anybody he loves because he's scared it might rub off. And he had loved his wife.

*Had* or *did*?

Still did in that odd way you love a place you've once visited even though you know you're never going back there. After their children — a boy and a girl — had grown and left the nest, Locke had assumed he'd spend more time with his wife. It hadn't worked out that way. Having more time meant more hours hunched over a desk reviewing old case files or out on the street chasing down leads. Every new year, he made a resolution to cut back, but resolutions were made to be broken and he always obliged.

With Sullivan gone, Locke is the last one left in the office. He should head off, too, but his wife usually goes to bed early while he's a night owl. After the day he's had, he's still buzzing and unable to relax, so he weaves across to his desk and logs onto his computer. Taps out a report, ticks boxes, arranges files. There's a stack of paperwork and a backlog of cases to deal with. Never enough time, never enough time.

When he's made a small dent in the paperwork, he returns to the current case and their suspect, Mr Robert Kell. Kell said something about only having arrived in Montana in the last couple of days. His previous address was Otero County, New Mexico, and before that, DC. Said he travelled around a lot. Didn't like staying put in any one place for too long.

With a couple of clicks, Locke pulls up a map on his screen. Otero is on the border with Mexico, yet here is Kell in Montana, bang up against Canada. You could hardly get farther away unless you switched countries. So what makes someone up sticks and head thousands of miles across the US? Well, Locke thinks, either you're chasing a dream or you're running away. Kell, bland and unassuming, doesn't look like he'd have the energy to get up and follow a dream, so it's far more likely he's running.

Sure, there are legitimate reasons to run away. Locke should know; he and his wife moved cross-country too, only west to east, and just four hundred miles from Seattle. Were they running away or chasing a dream? His wife likes to tell people it's the latter. Elsie's folks, on her mother's side, came from just outside Missoula, their ancestors settling there at the end of the nineteenth century. So here they are, simply following the trail home again. Only that's not the whole truth, not by a long and crooked Montana mile.

Locke kicks back. He brings up another map, this one of Seattle and the surrounding area — specifically the national parks: Olympic, Mount Rainier, North Cascades, and Glacier Peak. There are several little icons dotted across the various wilderness areas. This is Locke's personal project. Perhaps more like an obsession than a project. A habit he can't kick. An addiction. Click an icon, and a little card with all the details comes up. Name, if known; age; biography; date of discovery; probable date of death. He's spent too many late nights staring at this map instead of making eyes at his wife across the dinner table. He knows she thinks he's crazy and would prefer he was the clock-in, clock-out, leave-it-at-the-precinct type of cop. He also knows she understands the reasons he isn't, and that's why she doesn't complain.

Locke clicks a couple of icons, but the action is futile because the dates are all wrong and out by years. Kell wasn't up north when these women were killed. He may well be responsible for the Lewis and Clarke National Forest murder, but Locke *knows* who killed the women in the adjoining state of Washington, and it wasn't Robert Kell.

Running away or chasing a dream? Robert Kell's motivation for heading north isn't known, but for Locke, moving east was a little bit of both.

~ ~ ~

The following morning, Locke is back in early. He talks to the custody officer, who says Kell had a quiet one.

'Sobbed a bit at first,' the officer says as he winks at Locke. 'But then I made him a cocoa and told him a bedtime story, and he curled up with a teddy bear as sweet as you like.'

'You spat in his tea, rapped on the bars, and put a big hairy biker in with him?'

'About it, Frank. Can't be going too soft on them, can I?'

Half nine and a lawyer shows up to see Kell. Gets the same cosy interview room as last night. Locke gives them thirty minutes to talk sweet and then heads in. Sullivan's back and wants to sit in, too.

'Just for curiosity's sake. See whether my money's safe.'

'Your money?'

'Got a Benny on you being right on this one. Charlie, Doug and Ethan are on the other side. Odds of three to one. That's three hundred for me.'

'But they're risking one hundred to get thirty-three? Nice to know how little faith they have in me.'

'Well, they don't know your record from back in the Seattle smoke, do they? Hoovered 'em up like a street sweeper from what I heard.'

Like it was easy, Locke thinks. Like it didn't take much more than to steer in the general direction, and those killers would lie down and surrender to ace Detective Frank Locke. Like there was no effort or cost involved, no emotional price to pay.

If only.

'You got anything else?' Sullivan asks before they go into the interview room. 'Something to knock him for six?'

Locke tells Sullivan about how Kell travelled from New Mexico and turned up in Montana for no apparent reason. Sullivan whistles and grins.

'Highly suspicious. I reckon that money is as good as in my billfold.' He heads for the door, bullish. 'Let's do this.'

Locke follows Sullivan in, and they sit at the table. Kell sits opposite, his attorney alongside. The attorney is a walk-in, publicly appointed. Name of Gavin Bead. Long in the tooth. Jaded. Grey hair and gold-rimmed specs, the specs kind of fuzzy in the lenses like Bead has polished them with the wrong type of cleaning fluid. He's only here for the fee and half asleep by the look of it. Not a good start for Mr Kell, and Locke sees Sullivan pat his back pocket and try to conceal a smile.

Sullivan switches on the recording equipment, reads Kell his rights again, and explains the interview format. The preamble over, Locke jumps right in.

'Why did you take pictures of the dead woman, Robert? Is it because you're a necrophiliac?'

Bead nearly has a seizure there and then, and if he's been half dozing, now he's wide awake.

Locke passes several printouts across the table to Bead.

Bead skips through the pictures, face crumpling in distaste. Kell obviously hasn't told Bead about the photographs, but all credit to the old legal eagle because he tries his best to rustle up a defence.

'The explanation,' he says, 'is that my client was worried he might not be able to find the location again or it might be disturbed. So he wanted to ensure a photographic record of the body and the scene.'

'Most people usually leave evidence gathering to the police. It's kinda our job, you know?'

'Sure, but he committed no offence; thus, his actions are irrelevant.'

'Of course they're fucking relevant.' Sullivan rocks forward and slams the table with the flat of his hand. Locke thinks the behaviour is a bit overdramatic, but then the man does have three hundred bucks on the line. 'And Mr Kell *returned* to the crime scene later with the intention of taking *further* piccies. How do you explain that?'

'Mr Kell?' Locke wants to hear Kell's side of the story rather than his lawyer's. 'You got anything to add?'

'What he said.' Kell gestures at his lawyer.

'And the second time?' Sullivan isn't giving up. 'If you returned for your drone, then why take more pictures?'

'Well... you know.' Kell dips his shoulders. 'I thought I could sell them. The ones with the body, probably not, but images of the crime scene would be marketable. Especially if there was another killing.'

'What?' Sullivan says. 'You Robert-fucking-Capa now, are you?'

Even if Sullivan isn't buying it, Kell makes a fair point, Locke concedes. Some less reputable publications would pay a few dollars for the pictures, but just because Kell says that's why he returned doesn't make it so.

'Why did you up sticks and move a squillion miles north?' Locke says. 'Trading all year sunshine for three months of warmth and a whole heap of snow?'

'You've got the wrong end of the stick.' A shrug from Kell. 'I haven't moved to Montana. I'm just here to take pictures. A sort of working holiday. No law against that, is there?'

No, there isn't, but Locke wonders if he needs to get in touch with the locals down Otero way and find out if they've any unexplained murders, any women turning up in shallow graves way out in the desert.

'And how's the photography working out?' Locke doesn't think the images on the camera are up to much. They're not even up to local newspaper standards and no better than anyone could take with a phone. 'You making a living?'

'Not yet, but I've only just started. I'm just wandering around, taking pictures of what I see. When I've enough, I'll try to sell them.'

'Wandering around... must be nice, all that freedom.' Sullivan nods. Reaches out and taps Locke on the shoulder. 'That's what we like, isn't it, Frank? Single crewed on the open road. Put a country station on the radio, crank up the volume and cruise the blacktop. No one looking over our shoulders. Nobody checking up on what we're doing. No sneaky peeky little eyes watching us if we want

63

to pick up a piece of cheap skirt and get super friendly even though she might not want to.'

'Where are you going with this, detective?' Bead folds his arms. Defensive. He's trying to act like he knows what he's doing and deserves his paycheck, but while he might be competent at serving divorce papers, he hasn't got a clue how to defend a scum sexual predator like Kell.

'Motive and opportunity, Mr Bead.' Sullivan jabs a figure at Kell. 'We've established a motive, and I'm pretty sure Mr Kell had the opportunity.'

'I didn't kill the girl.' Kell says. 'It was just like I said; I came across the body by accident.'

Bead puts an arm out. 'Before we go any further, I have a proposition. Perhaps we can step outside and discuss it?'

Locke focuses on Kell. He's looking down at the table, embarrassed. 'Why don't we stay *inside* and discuss it?'

Bead hums for a moment, then turns to Kell and flips his palms up as if apologising. 'OK with you?'

A twitch of the head, a nod, barely.

'So, propose away,' Locke says, pretty sure he knows what's coming next.

'Right.' Bead leans forward, his voice grave, something approaching his best courtroom tone. 'My client is willing to admit to visiting the crime scene after dark to take pictures for his sexual gratification. You can charge him with a minor offence or let him off with a warning. We can wrap all this up in the next hour and be on our way.'

Blindsided, Locke thinks. He'd been expecting Bead to come up with some excuse for Kell returning to the scene — perhaps from morbid curiosity, possibly working up the *pictures to sell* angle — he hadn't reckoned on this. He taps Sullivan on the shoulder. Nods to the door.

Out in the corridor, Sullivan is buzzing.

'We got him, Frank, we got him.' Sullivan pulls a smile that says he thinks he's three hundred dollars richer.

Locke isn't so sure. At first sight, Kell admitting he returned for some nefarious purpose puts the man firmly in the weirdo category, so his confession isn't a good look. But this begs the question, why did Bead go along with the plea deal?

'Let's work this through,' Locke says. 'Say Kell did kill the girl. Admitting the lesser offence draws a line. He goes deep because he knows that otherwise we'll keep probing.'

'Exactly.' Sullivan's bobbing as if he's going to pinball off the walls back and forth down the corridor, hit the ten thousand score at the end and set the bells ringing and lights flashing. 'It's like when you pick up some druggie. They empty their pockets and show you a tiny bag of weed, hoping you won't do a full search and find the foil wrap of crack they've got in their shoe.'

'Right. On the other hand, by telling us, he tags himself as a sexual deviant, thereby putting himself in the frame. Why risk that?'

'Rock and a hard place, Frank.' Sullivan balls his right fist and rams it into the palm of his left hand. 'Bam! Know what I mean?'

'But plenty of sickos can get off on the sight of a corpse without ever being the type of nutter who goes in for brutal murder. Kell knows that. And if it *was* Kell, why on earth would he lead me to the body?'

'Ego. Self-importance.'

'Could be,' Locke says, but he's beginning to have doubts.

'So what's your hunch?' Sullivan scratches his head. Chews his lip. He's a Montana guy, born and bred. Doesn't have Locke's experience of fifty murders a year in Seattle, not all of them simple shootings. 'Did he kill the girl or not?'

'If he did, he's just walked into a trap of his own making.' Locke turns back to the door of the interview room. 'Which doesn't make a lot of sense to me.'

# *Chapter 9*

Early afternoon, Kerri Dunstan comes to see Locke. She flips open a folder and pulls out a few sheets of paper.

'Let's start with the boot prints,' she says. 'Round the body, there was nothing worth looking at. The ground was soft loam, and only general outlines were visible. However, a little up the hill, there was an area with a spring bubbling over shale and mud. Got a couple of good impressions. According to the shoe print database, they're Timberland Rustics, size eleven.'

Dunstan hands over the first sheet of paper. Locke shakes his head. Robert Kell was wearing Timberlands, so that proves absolutely nothing.

'I've eliminated everyone else's, and they're the only useable prints.' Dunstan holds up her hands. 'Of course, the body had been there a few days, so earlier evidence might have gone. That loam springs back like a sponge. After a while, you wouldn't know anyone had walked on it.'

'What about the hair you found?'

'I was coming to that.' Dunstan glares at Locke like her whole day has just been ruined. 'But first the vehicle tracks.'

'What vehicle tracks?'

'So you, Kell, Doc Hem, me, and the CSIs went up and down the fire access road. There's a barrier at the bottom, but it's not locked in position. Anyone can drive up there if they can be bothered to get out and lift the barrier. Plus, the road is mostly hard gravel, and vehicles don't leave any meaningful tracks.'

'I'm sensing a "but" here.'

'There was a place to turn round where we all parked, and I checked to see if there were any tyre markings at the edge of the road.' Dunstan shook her head. 'No such luck.'

'Good work, Kerri, now what about—'

Dunstan repeats her acid stare. Carries on. 'So I took a hike up the road. I went about half a mile until there was a junction with another road, this one just dirt and no gravel. When I examined the verge, I found several tyre marks. The rain had softened the impressions, but they were large, something like a heavy truck turning round.'

'Not Kell's Jeep Renegade?'

'No, bigger and heavier. Something like a Ford Ranger or a GMC Canyon.' Dunstan spreads her hands expressively. 'And with big, chunky tyres. Oversized, I guess. They don't match those on Kell's Jeep.'

'Could it have been a forestry vehicle or something?'

'Could have been. It could have been someone cruising the track looking for a spot to dump the body. Or worse, perhaps the victim was still alive at that point.'

Locke tries visualising it: The perpetrator picks up a hitcher or a hooker. Drives her somewhere quiet. Takes it from there. Perhaps there'd been nothing sinister to start with, but then something happened. The guy reads the hitcher wrong or doesn't want to pay the hooker. Things get violent. Maybe the guy keeps a big wrench under the driver's seat. Possibly, he's carrying a knife or a gun. Out in the wilds, the woman doesn't stand a chance.

'Can you get anything from the impressions?'

'Sure. Probably the size and make of the tyre, but it won't help much unless we can find the truck.'

Locke nods. It isn't Dunstan's fault, but the information about the truck isn't what he wanted to hear. It means Kell could be getting a pass to walk.

'And the hair?'

'Saving that for last,' Dunstan says with a grin. 'Because I know you love dealing with the odd curve ball, right?'

Wrong. Straight up is how Locke likes it. 'Go on.'

'I'm pretty sure the red hair came from a woman.' Dunstan smiles as Locke does the opposite. 'Under the microscope, I can see heat damage. The curl isn't natural and probably made with a pair of tongs. Luckily, the sample is a whole hair, root and all, so DNA analysis should confirm my hunch.'

Never mind a curve ball, Dunstan has launched a pitch from a bazooka. The ball whistles past Locke's ear, and he just stares. 'You're fucking with me, Kerri?'

'Nope. Can't say how the hair got in the tree, but it likely belongs to the female of the species.'

'Could it have blown there?'

'And somehow find its way through the canopy and land in a tree next to the body?'

Locke shrugs. He has to admit it sounds implausible. 'An accomplice then?'

'That's certainly possible. She comes along for the ride, so to speak. Hair gets snagged in the tree while she's watching.'

'Shit.'

'Yeah, I can see that.' Dunstan is silent for a moment. 'Has Kell got a girlfriend?'

'A wife, I think, and no, I don't have any idea what colour hair she has.'

'You'd better find out, right?' Dunstan reaches out and pats Locke on the back. Consolation. Like the whole case is slipping away.

When Dunstan has gone, Locke finds the contact details for Karen Kell, the woman Robert Kell put down as next of kin. He gives her a call. She wants to know when Kell is getting out. 'Not until I've spoken to you,' Locke says.

~ ~ ~

An hour later, he's pulling off the eighty-three just north
of the little town of Seeley Lake. He drives down a hard-
packed dirt road towards the expanse of water that gives
the place its name. Several log cabins sit beneath tall
pines. Summer lodges and vacation rentals, mostly, but
one or two full-timers live here year-round. The road
turns right and runs along the foreshore, ending at a small
cabin, two beds at the most. A separate garage and a big
wood store stand to the right, and down by the water,
there's a dock with a small boat tied up.

Sweet, Locke thinks as he gets out. Quiet, too.

A knock and Kell's wife opens the door. Locke tries not
to show his excitement.

'Karen,' she says, flicking a curl of her red hair. 'Karen
Kell. Yeah, I know how it sounds.' She laughs. Big smile.
Brown Eyes. Nice teeth. Full lips. 'Stupid, right?'

'Frank Locke.' Locke sticks out his hand. Karen might be
married to the prime suspect, but she's so friendly he's
disarmed. 'Frank Locke 'em up. More than stupid, right?'

'I guess it suits you.' Another laugh as she shakes his
hand. 'You want to come in, or I could bring some coffee
out?'

There's a picnic table down by the dock. A gentle breeze
blows off the water, and ripples dance like liquid silver in
the warm afternoon sunlight.

'Out is great,' he says.

Never mind the excitement about the hair colour, Karen
is a looker. Out of Kell's league. Out of Locke's league. And
it's not simply the looks. There's something about her
manner, the way she moves, the sexiness of the slight
southern lilt that comes with her soft voice. And the way
she doesn't seem phased that Robert is banged up on suspicion of murder. Could be bravado or overconfidence,

but Locke doesn't think so; it's more like she's convinced he's innocent. Or even more worryingly, she *knows* he's innocent.

He ambles down to the dock, leaving Karen to bring the coffee. He sits at the table and stares out at the lake. When he was Kell's age, he was in Seattle struggling to pay the mortgage on a grimy apartment in a dodgy neighbourhood. He wonders about the pressures for a young couple like the Kells: seemingly itinerant, no place to call home, no permanent job. But then that's a thing with youngsters these days, isn't it? Digital nomads or something. Like roots don't matter anymore. Still, difficulties or not, sharing that sort of lifestyle with Karen Kell would make it pretty near damn perfect.

*Steady*, he says to himself. Karen being attractive doesn't discount her being party to a brutal murder. Often, appearances *do* matter, but it's dangerous to be swayed when somebody doesn't fit the standard cut-out. Evidence is what counts, and the hair snagged in the tree places Karen at the murder scene.

'Here you go.' Karen has brought a tray down. Coffee in a pot, cream and sugar. Cookies, home baked by the look of them.

Locke declines the cream and sugar but gives in and takes a cookie. 'Do you work, Karen?'

'I'm a landscape artist. Just dabbling, really, but I sell a few.'

'So you were in New Mexico with Robert and came here to paint?'

'Yes. Me to paint and Robert to take pictures. It was my idea, and he decided to tag along.'

*Tag along* — that sounds an odd way of putting it to Locke, but he lets it go. 'You move around a lot?'

71

'Uh huh.' Karen nods. 'It's good to see new places. I get bored if things get too routine.'

'And before New Mexico, where were you then?'

'DC.'

'That's some contrast.'

'As I said, I get bored. Variety is the spice of life, right?'

'Bereavement, divorce and moving house are supposed to be the most emotionally charged events in your life. It's tough on a relationship, shifting around all the time, right? My wife would never stand for it. You must have a strong marriage. Good luck to you.'

'*Marriage*?' Karen laughed. 'I think you've got mixed up, Mr Locke. Robert is my *brother*.'

~ ~ ~

Locke chuckles to himself as he drives away from Seeley Lake. Makes sense, he thinks, that Karen is Robert Kell's brother. It certainly makes a lot more sense than the two of them being married. However, it complicates Locke's theory about Kell moving north in search of easier prey or running from trouble in Otero County.

After the revelation, Karen Kell chatted on. Locke got the impression she cared very deeply about her brother and that they were close. But close enough to cover for him? Locke doesn't think so. Karen seems the honest type, and if Robert Kell is the killer, then she doesn't know, and the strand of hair must have been carried to the scene accidentally by him. Locke hadn't told her about the hair, though, deciding to hold the nugget of information back. Instead, he'd steered the conversation around and asked about Robert's love life so he could get some kind of angle on Kell's sexual proclivities. However, Karen said Robert was single and hadn't had a relationship recently. So did that make Robert an incel, desperate to get what he'd been denied? A woman-hater? A sexual deviant? A serial killer?

It's a stretch, and Locke has to admit he's back to square one, the only positive being he'd got to meet Karen Kell.

'You're married, you dick,' he says aloud as he tucks in behind a slow semi on the road back to Missoula. 'She's twenty years younger and even ignoring that you wouldn't have a chance.'

Still, nice to daydream once in a while. Nice to remember what the world felt like when it came at you fast, dishing you surprises. These days, life's a bit similar to his progress home: pretty much the same as being stuck behind an eighteen-wheeler on a twisting road with nowhere to overtake. There is nothing to do but admire the view and count off the miles until the destination.

Locke edges the car out as a sweeping curve becomes a short straight but dives back in as a horn blares from an oncoming vehicle. He settles back behind the wheel, content to follow the semi for the next dozen miles.

Robert Kell moved north with his sister because it was the simplest. Just turn up and unpack his bags. Locke imagined Karen would be cooking, cleaning, and washing and all Kell had to do was bung her a few notes once a month for food. If she was paying the rent, there'd be no worries about finding an understanding landlord who'd overlook that Kell didn't have a job. No hassle from nosey neighbours wondering what a single man was doing out in the sticks on his own. Kell wanted an easy life, and his sister provided it.

And so what?

Locke raps the steering wheel and shakes his head. The evidence, sadly, is beginning to point to Kell being in the clear.

But when he's back at the precinct and settled at his desk, Locke finds an email from a detective in Otero

County responding to his query about unsolved murders, specifically of women.

*You don't keep up with the news, then...* the email began. Then, a link to a web page. A contact number for the detective should Locke want to talk it over.

Locke clicks. Reads. Thinks. Changes his mind once more.

Fuck.

He remembers the story now. The X-Mex Slayer. Five women immigrants were murdered over the past two years near the White Sands missile testing range. Perhaps that's why Kell followed his sister. Locke imagines the heat building, local law enforcement closing in, and possibly the FBI on the case as well. The easy option is for Kell to get out, and where better to go than a sleepy little town a thousand miles north of trouble? Locke wonders whether he'll be taking some bad news about her brother back to Karen Kell. Shame because he liked her. It's not her fault she ended up with a psycho for a sibling.

'Plughole.' Sullivan pops up and slaps Locke on the back.

'Hey?'

'As in, you've gone down a Wikipedia plughole. Don't worry, I've been there, Frank. One minute, you're looking for pictures of some celeb you fancy; the next, you're reading about perpetual motion machines or the chemistry of Jupiter's upper atmosphere or the Yom Kippur War.' Sullivan leans over. 'Only this looks like work. What-da-ya have there?'

'The X-Mex Slayer.'

'Is that the X-Files or something?' Sullivan shakes his head. 'Area fifty-fucking-one? I dunno, Frank, you must be getting old. When I'm browsing the web, I'm checking up on Jessica Chastain's chest size or something, not getting my kicks from some true-crime bullshit. Hell, we do that for a living, right?'

'Might be linked to Robert Kell.'

'You got him pegged for this, too?' Sullivan scrapes up a chair and plonks himself down. Pops a stick of gum in his mouth. 'Really?'

'Could be.'

'He's turning into a regular little Ted Bundy, our Mr Kell.'

Locke wants to click the webpage closed and log off from the computer. He can't think with Sullivan chewing his menthol gum close by. It might clear Sullivan's airways, but the odour clogs Locke's brain. Nothing Locke can do, though, unless he wants to be rude, which he is rarely inclined to be.

'Five women killed in the past two years,' Locke says. 'Kell moved north just a few days ago, and a girl turns up in the Lewis and Clarke forest. Coincidence, I doubt.'

'No shit.' Sullivan shakes his head. 'I should've had a sweepstake on you, Frank. Could've just about retired on the winnings.'

Locke reads the webpage. 'Two of the victims were between the ages of twenty and twenty-five, the third in her late thirties. A nineteen-year-old. A woman in her fifties. Remains not found for several weeks.'

'Single, attached, married?'

'Doesn't say, but they were all illegal immigrants.'

'Working girls?'

'No idea. We're going to need to get more information from the Feds.'

'Serial crimes? Are they in on this?'

'You'd think so, on account of the numbers.' Locke reads down. He wants to know the MO and compare it to the killing in Montana. There's something about possible strangulation but not much more — nothing about a missing arm. Wikipedia can only get you so far, it seems. 'Might need to take a trip.'

'Now I get it.' Sullivan gives Locke a pat on the back. 'Looking for a few days away. You'll be wanting to bring a partner with you, right?'

'If I do, you're first in line, Leo.'

'And Robert Kell? We can't hold him any longer without some sort of charge, but right now, despite all you've just told me, we've got jackshit that isn't circumstantial.' Sullivan dips his shoulders. 'Much as I want my money, he's got to walk, right?'

'Yes. Release him, but tell him to remain in the area.' Locke closes the browser and logs off. Stands. Sullivan looks disappointed. He'd be happy to chinwag for the rest of the shift, but Locke has better things to do than chat with Sullivan. 'Sorry, gotta go.'

Better things like heading home so he can get an early start the next day. First thing tomorrow, he's got an appointment with Adam Hem and the dubious pleasure of watching the ME chop the insides out of the forest girl.

~ ~ ~

He sleeps badly and rises at dawn. Heads into Missoula for a date with Doctor Hem and Jane Doe. Hem, Locke thinks as he stifles a yawn, is a morning person. Bright-eyed and bushy-tailed. Ready to go. And in the mortuary, he no longer seems like a fish out of water. Up in the woods, he'd been tentative, unsure. Striding round the autopsy table, he's confident. He's the master of all he surveys; this is his domain, and he wants Locke to know that.

'Not Mister,' he reminds Locke. 'Doctor.'

Prove it, you dickhead, Locke thinks. Prove all those hours hunched over textbooks at med school translate into real-world knowledge. Prove those wealthy parents of yours invested their money wisely.

An hour later, it turns out Mom and Pop backed a winner. Hem has explained about the severing of the arm, arguing it's a neat job carried out by someone with sharp tools and the knowledge to know where to cut. He's pointed out a puncture wound in the woman's back as likely being the cause of death, the weapon — a sharp spike or similar — penetrating the heart and killing her within seconds. And now he's found something else of interest.

Locke conceals a modicum of disappointment at the young ME's competence and leans over the corpse as Hem wields a pair of long forceps and prods at a lump in the upper reaches of the chest cavity.

'What is it?' Locke asks as he tries to make sense of the mess.

'Something lodged in the gastrointestinal tract.' Hem moves the forceps, pushing at a bulge in a pale tubular organ. 'Something hard and solid.'

'That caused death? Suffocation or choking?'

'I told you the puncture wound killed her.' Hem turns to Locke. Sneers. 'And this is the oesophagus, not the trachea.'

'How did it get there?'

Hem shakes his head. He moves up the body and tilts the head, opening the mouth. He takes a penlight from the trolley. 'Extensive damage to the pharynx,' he says. 'Either they swallowed it or...'

'Or it was forced down.' Locke imagines how you'd go about doing that. First, the victim would need to be well restrained, unconscious or dead. Then, you'd tilt the head, just as Hem had done, and push the object with a stick. Locke swallows a lump in his throat, nothing but air. Stifles a retch. He points back at the chest. 'What is it?'

Hem replaces the penlight on the trolley and shakes his head again. The young man is having trouble processing what's before him. Hem's bread and butter are myocardial infarctions, a car crash or two, prescription overdoses, and occasionally gunshot wounds — self-inflicted or otherwise. Not something like this.

'I need a break,' Hem says, his earlier confidence ebbing. 'We'll take five minutes, OK?'

'Sure.' Locke nods.

Looks like Hem's a fucking lightweight after all, Locke thinks as the ME heads out of the room. He might know the textbooks back to front, but his experience of the brutal reality of murder investigations is sorely lacking. Locke moves to a stool and takes the weight off his tired feet for a moment. Laughs at the irony. Youth equals inexperience and vitality; age brings knowledge and a host of aches and pains, not all of them physical.

Who's the fucking lightweight now?

Locke shakes his head. Even as Hem is away in his office, hastily Googling *types of objects swallowed*, Locke is reflecting on the stuff he's seen in his long career and how it has messed with his mind. There are things he can't unsee, but then unseeing is part of the problem with the world. Cross the street, look the other way, turn the channel over, and move to the next story.

He glances across at the corpse — correction, young woman — and wonders how long he can keep her story going. There's only so much effort he can expend before the law of diminishing returns kicks in, and the narrative has to come to a premature conclusion. Locke doesn't want that to happen because it means a triple dose of failure. He'll have failed his victim, failed the community and, last of all, failed himself. He can rationalise the first and live with the second, but the third will inevitably induce another bout of decay. Bit by bit, he can feel his soul rotting away, leaving only a paper-thin exterior that a light breeze could carry off into the void.

His morbid introspection is interrupted as a ringtone trills out from somewhere. Locke turns to the anteroom, expecting to see Hem bending to his phone, but there's no sign of the young man. Locke slips off the stool. He left his own phone in the car — force of habit.

The trilling continues.

'Doctor Hem?' Locke says, moving across to the anteroom and cocking his head. The ringing isn't coming from there, and Hem has disappeared. He turns, aware the sound is echoing off the bare walls, coming from close at hand. He steps towards the autopsy table and looks at the trolley where a spread of Hem's instruments sits on a green cloth: forceps, scalpels, bone saws, scissors. No phone.

His attention moves to the girl. The abdomen is open, and the ribs are cut through. At the neck, there is that tube of greying pink with a hard, oblong object inside.

'Christ.' Locke steps forward. 'Doctor Hem!'

Hem still doesn't answer. For a second, Locke stands frozen. Then, he reaches for a scalpel and turns to the body. He realises he isn't wearing gloves, but there's no time to find a pair and put them on. His left hand slips in and grasps the oesophagus. It's slimy and semi-hard, like a damp cardboard tube. As his hand closes on the pale organ, he feels a lump in his own throat, like he's choking himself. He shakes off the sensation and slices in with the scalpel. The blade is razor-sharp, and the tissue parts, a chunk of black easing from the opening like an alien birthing from some reptilian beast.

Except the amniotic sac is composed of clingfilm and, wrapped within, the alien child is a cell phone.

He discards the scalpel and picks up the phone. It's an older retro type with a small LCD screen and a keypad. The plastic film is slick, and Locke's fingers can't get enough grip to remove it. Instead, he prods at a key with a green icon and raises the phone, pressing the gunge-covered object to his ear.

'Hello?' he says.

# *Chapter 10*

*The Architect dreams of long ago, of when he was just a young boy:*

Black flies alight on her pale skin as the sun rises over the dusty field. She's naked. Unmoving. And quite dead, he's sure about that. After what happened last night, there's no way she couldn't be. The violence. The rage. The inevitable consequences of actions taken without thought.

The sight is shocking even though he knew this is what he would find. He walked for hours to get here, praying that what he witnessed in the dark wasn't true. That the screams and the blood were somehow a figment of a perverted imagination or a nightmare dreamed but not seen. But now the truth lies before him in appalling candour, the dawn revealing everything to everyone, the story told by the bruises on the face, the cuts across the breasts, the torn clothing scattered across the sun-baked soil.

He gulps dry air and feels the tears come at the same time as giddy nausea causes his knees to buckle. He falls to the ground and lies sobbing with his face in the dirt. He cries and moans and begs, and his hands scrabble in the soil, clenching fistfuls of tiny stones so tightly that the pain causes him to gasp.

When he is done crying, he rolls over onto his side, his face mere inches from the girl's breasts. The deep lacerations have stopped weeping blood just as he has stopped weeping tears. The girl is dead, her soul no more, her spirit gone. There is nothing he can do to her body now to make her situation any worse. That's good because there is work to do if he is to prevent more mayhem.

He picks up the small package he's brought with him, a towel wrapped around something long and thin. The carving knife drops out and bounces once on the earth — God's earth — the blade flashing sunlight in his eyes.

It's a sign that someone is watching and judging. Someone is waiting. The truth will out, and there's nothing to be done about that.

He takes the knife and moves to the body. His left hand pushes down hard on the girl's right shoulder while the other hand brings the knife to bear on the upper arm. He slices once, twice and then hacks over and over again. The blade hits bone, and he grits his teeth and forces the serrations back and forth, little splinters of white spraying out. The sun beats relentlessly as he saws away, and his hand cramps and his body sweats with the effort. And then the bone gives up its resistance, and the knife slips through the remaining flesh. The arm is free.

For a moment, he simply stares. Then, he carefully wraps the knife in the towel, bends, and picks up the arm. It's heavier than he expected, but the sensation of the girl's flesh between his fingers is, worryingly, not unpleasant.

He faces in the direction he has come, his mind calculating, working the numbers, doing the sums. Then he starts to walk...

~ ~ ~

*When the Architect wakes from the dream, everything is clear. He realises he made a mistake back then. He owes someone an apology. He needs to fix his error.*

You're going to do that for Mommy? What a good boy!

*But he isn't listening. This isn't for her. He needs to pay homage to the past by revisiting history and bringing it to the present. Two wrongs CAN make a right.*

*But it won't be that simple. To pay a meaningful tribute, he must prove himself by doing something bigger than before. Bigger and cleverer and totally unsolvable. Yes, there's still everything to play for. As long as he ensures things are properly connected precisely like they were all those years ago.*

Connected? Oh yes, you thought you were so clever, but you never saw the consequences coming down the tracks, did you? Still, what goes around comes around, right?

*He ignores the voice and heads up to his home office, taking the stairs two at a time. He finds a pencil and grabs a pad. Begins to plan, knowing the preparation will take months.*

*There are things to buy, people to speak to, places to research and victims to select. Much of the time, he sits at his desk, tap, tap, tapping away at the keyboard or scribbling notes on pieces of paper. He searches through names, checking all the details, looking for the slightest hint of an anomaly he can use in his mission. He measures distances and seeks out connections and revels in the complexity of the task. Since he went on sick leave, he has been bored out of his mind, and this gives his life purpose. It is like everything has been leading to this time and place.*

*After a month of hard work, he sticks a large map on the wall to give himself something physical to work with. It enables him to see the bigger picture, and at some point, he begins to feel as if he is an ancient God peering down on his subjects from the heavens. The participants in his drama are like ants moving on the chequerboard of life, his invisible hand pushing them this way and that, deciding their fates on a whim.*

*That's when he begins to call himself the Architect, reasoning that as he draws and plots and measures, he is taking control of his life, building the future with lines and angles and distances.*

*All the while, his mother continues to visit him at night, and it is only through the use of copious amounts of drugs that he can function during the day. Luckily, the extended period of sick leave allows him plenty of time to work on his project, and his extensive contacts mean he can get all the narcotics he needs.*

*One morning, the Architect stands in front of the bathroom mirror and notices his face has an unhealthy pallor. His eyes are sunken, the skin on his jawline loose. He realises that he has lost weight and his muscles are wasting away. Still, whether the cause is the drugs, the stress or the lack of sleep, there is nothing to be done but plough on.*

*The work becomes all-consuming, and from here on in, he barely has time to cook. Luckily, Grubhub, Uber Eats, and DoorDash are but an app away and soon, the weight he's lost begins to return. The living room becomes a mess of discarded cartons and wrappers, and since he dismissed his cleaner a few months back, the clutter accumulates until it is ankle-deep. Still, the sooner the project is done, the sooner the nightmare will be over, and he can return to a normal life.*

You're not getting rid of me that easily!

*The Architect turns from the desk to see the whore standing in the doorway. Recently, she has been blinking into existence during his waking hours. He puts the delusions down to the cumulative effects of the drugs and tries to ignore her as she saunters over. Even so, he swears he feels her caress as she wraps an arm around his shoulder. And the smell: spilt beer from the bar she used to work in, the scent of someone who's spent a month lying in a drainage pipe, and the unmistakable tang of decaying flesh.*

Slow down, son. Relax. Let's just get back to rolling along the way we were before.

*No way. The Architect is done with fucking rolling. Now it's time for action. Trying not to gag, he focuses on his work. The final pieces of the jigsaw are clicking into place, and the first set of stories is almost complete.*

# Chapter 11

*Story Three*

He's handcuffed her hands behind her back, so when he pushes her towards the car, she stumbles, falling face down in the dirt.

'You fucking pig,' she says, spitting out a wad of dry soil.

'Get up and get in.' He's holding the rear door open like a gentleman would, but this guy's no gentleman. 'Your choice,' he says. 'Get up and get in or else I'll beat the shit out of you and shove you in once you're unconscious. I don't care either way.'

She pushes herself up onto her knees. She looks around, hoping to see someone. There's not much they'd be able to do, but at least having a witness might make things go a little easier down the line.

There's no one. The place where she dossed last night is an old abandoned shack round the back of a long-since-closed store. Time was people living round here would have used the shop, but now the supermarkets in town are bigger and cheaper. You don't know what you've got 'til it's gone, she thinks.

Except nobody is going to notice when she's gone.

She gets up and moves to the car, ducks in and slides onto the seat. He reaches in, pulls the seatbelt across and secures it.

'Health and safety,' he says. 'Regulations.'

The door clunks shut, and he gets in and starts up. Pulls away from the front of the store and hits the highway.

Fuck. She should have made a run for it. As soon as she'd seen the car, she should have edged out the back of the shack and headed across the fields. Sure, he had a gun, but would he have shot her in the back in cold blood? And she doubts he'd have bothered chasing her, not in this heat.

But then she doesn't understand why he's bothering at all. Why come all the way out here just for her?

'What am I supposed to have done?' she says.

'Shut up,' he says. 'Don't make this more difficult than it is.'

She slumps back in the seat, uncomfortable with her hands behind her. The landscape slips past. Irrigated fields here and there, drab dry brownness between. She blinks and swivels her head as a bus passes on the opposite side of the road, its destination written in fluorescent letters above the windscreen.

'Hey,' she says. 'We're going the wrong way.'

He looks forward, one hand on the wheel, the other on his gun. He waves the gun into the rear.

'I told you to shut up,' he says. 'Shut up, keep quiet and act like the obedient little whore you are. Do that, and everything will work out fine.'

'I want you to call it in,' she says. 'Call your dispatcher and let them know you're bringing me in.'

'No can do,' he says.

She stares out the side window. Only the occasional farmstead now, nothing much else to see but a vista of seemingly endless outback.

Up ahead, there's a turning to a squat house surrounded by dilapidated outbuildings. He swings right and pulls the car to a stop in front of the dwelling.

'You want to fuck me, you can,' she says. 'I won't say anything. Just fuck me and let me go, and we're quits, right?'

He gets out of the car and goes into the house.

She moves to the door, wriggles sideways and tries the handle, but the door is child-locked. There's a grill between the front and rear, so there's no way out there. She

87

looks around, panicking now.

And then he's back.

He opens the rear door.

'I said you can have sex with me,' she says.

She glances down to where his right hand hangs low, the fingers clenched around the handle of a large bush knife.

'I don't want to have sex with you,' he says.

# *Chapter 12*

'Alright, mate?'

'Yes, fine.'

'Good. We don't want you getting the blues, do we? Don't want you leaving your job and heading home. Where would Darwin's finest be then? Up shit creek with no paddle and plenty of crocs, that's where.'

The door clicks shut, and Assistant Commissioner Fred Cooper walks away, a darkened figure through the smoked glass panel of the tiny office. Detective Senior Sergeant Takeo Sasaki watches Cooper moving from desk to desk, jaw working fast, filling everyone in on the day's big news. He stops next to Sergeant Kevin Anderson, a uniformed officer, and bends to say something. Sasaki can't lipread, but he can guess Cooper's words.

*The Jap's wife has left him, poor bugger.*

Both men laugh, and Anderson half turns towards Sasaki's office, a sneer on his face. At least Cooper will have omitted the *chink* between the *poor* and the *bugger*. Back in the day, when Sasaki's father was on the force, *chink* was in casual use. His father was known as Detective Butterhead. At school, Sasaki was called Chinky, and in the street, it was worse. 'Don't worry,' his father said. 'These people are so ignorant they can't even get their racial slurs correct.'

Sasaki knows Anderson, especially, had been right up there with the worst of them. Thankfully, the sergeant is on the way out. He'll be fifty-five in a few months, and his retirement party is looming. A clock and a certificate of long service to take home. A photo on an inside page of the *Northern Territory News*. A grateful sigh from most of those serving in the Darwin police force that the dinosaurs are moving on and dying out. Soon, they'll be no more than fossils studied by future generations, who will find it hard to believe that such creatures ever existed.

Sasaki bends to some paperwork, but after a few minutes, he gives up and leans back in his chair. He's finding it difficult to concentrate. Anyone peering in through the glass door would have assumed it was down to his marriage difficulties, but what has recently become public knowledge has been private between Sasaki and his wife for months. It's only his move to an apartment in Palmerston that has set eyebrows raising and tongues wagging. Someone had seen him carrying boxes into his new place over the weekend. Figured he was on duty and wanted to know what was going on. Was it a crime scene?

The irony isn't lost on Sasaki. His marriage *had* been a crime scene. A standoff, a warzone, a disaster area. It happens, he tells himself. Marriages break up all the time, Two in five. Those are not good odds if you are a gambler, which Sasaki isn't.

They'd had eight years together, good years, mostly. No kids, though. *Barren*, Sasaki knew the gossip was. He wasn't sure if it was him or Anna. They'd never bothered to find out, something unsaid between them as if they both knew the relationship would always be finite. In the end, they drifted apart. Anna had been elected to parliament and spent long periods away in Canberra, and increasingly, the distance between them was political, too. Sasaki did his job and cleared up the mess on the streets, but everything for Anna became ideological. There'd recently been a spree of violence and disorder in Darwin, undoubtedly caused by poverty and deprivation, which

90

the police had dealt with as best they could. For Anna, it was as if he was somehow responsible.

He turns his head. A picture of his father hangs on the wall to his right. 'To make you feel at home,' AC Cooper said when Sasaki received a promotion and moved into his own office. Sasaki senior is in a dress uniform, buttons sparkling, shoes gleaming, not a thread out of place.

'It's a lot to live up to.' The chief's words again. 'Your father was quite a policeman. Earned a great deal of respect for what he did for this town. We owe him big time.'

If he's heard those words once, he's heard them a thousand times.

His father stares out of the frame with dark, piercing eyes. While in the office, Sasaki can't escape the gaze or the implied censure. He'd like to take the picture down and shove it in a drawer, but that wouldn't be respectful.

*... quite a policeman.*

Sure, but perhaps not all there as a father.

Sasaki wonders if that's what it takes to be a good cop, perhaps what it takes to be good at anything. He remembers an HR seminar from a couple of years back on the importance of recognising that you can do *anything* you want but not *everything* you want. His father had chosen to be a great cop and a below-average father.

*It's a lot to live up to.*

If that's what you aspire to.

He thinks of Anna again. Sasaki would have taken being a good father over an above-average cop, but perhaps the infertility was a symptom of their incompatibility as a couple. Biology provided the answer to the question they'd never fully asked each other.

'Sir?' Sasaki missed a tap at the door, and now, the face of DS Linda Malroony peers round. Malroony is half Aboriginal, half white. Dark hair above a face that always seems to be smiling. Unlike Sasaki, she's hard as nails and never allows herself to be run over. He wonders if that's because this is her land. She has an attachment to the country he, even as a second-generation Japanese immigrant born and bred here, can never have. It's literally part of her makeup, her body formed of atoms from the ground she walks on, her soul connected by bloodlines to the continent's prehistory. Sasaki feels like he's forever an alien, struggling for breath as he sucks in the unfamiliar foreign air.

'I'm fine, Linda. This is a personal matter, and I just—'

'No, there's a call out.' Malroony jerks her thumb over her shoulder into the main office area. 'Tortilla Flats.'

'Over near Batchelor, isn't it? Ken Royston?'

'That's him. Friend of your dad, wasn't he?'

'Yes.' Sasaki tries not to speak through gritted teeth because there it is again. Every day, there's something to remind him of his father.

*Knew your dad, good man.*

Or *he's a legend around these parts.*

Or *like father like son.*

Or *Darwin's got a lot to thank your old man for. He'll never be forgotten.*

Sometimes, Sasaki wishes his father *would* be forgotten. No one would care if old man Sasaki had been a taxi driver, plumber, or real estate agent. But he was a police officer.

*Like father like son...*

Perhaps the fault is Sasaki's. Perhaps *he* should have become a taxi driver or a real estate agent — anything but a policeman.

'So what sort of problem is it that Ken can't deal with?' he says.

'Someone's found a body out near the Adelaide River. A woman.'

'Another domestic?' Sasaki doesn't mean his question to sound dismissive, but domestic homicides make up over half of all murders in the Northern Territory. Alcohol is usually involved, and solving the crime is simply a matter of tracking down the husband. You don't need to be much of a detective, and you certainly don't need to have a name like Sasaki.

*He's a legend around these parts...*

'Doesn't look like it. There's some stuff Ken's not happy with.' Malroony glances down at a pad where she's scribbled some notes. 'Weird stuff.'

'Weird stuff? He doesn't say what?'

Malroony shakes her head. 'No. Says we best come and see.'

'Right.' There's nothing out at Tortilla Flats except a couple of homesteads and an old army base used in the Second World War. Batchelor, the nearest town, is ten miles to the west, but the flats are a sixty-mile drive from Darwin down the Stuart Highway. It's a good road for most of the way, but the journey will still take well over an hour. Sasaki would usually send someone else, but today, he could do with the air. 'You want to come?'

'Does a girl want to dance?'

Malroony smiles and Sasaki, for a guilty moment, is glad somebody's dead out at Tortilla Flats.

~ ~ ~

The road south is flat and wide, and the countryside is sparse but surprisingly green. Visitors to the Northern Territory are often surprised by the subtropical climate. There's plenty of rain for half the year, and temperatures rarely exceed the low thirties. Still, today, it's hot enough to have the windows shut and the air-con on.

Malroony drives, and as they head south, she chats over the hum of road noise. She's been seeing someone new and is keen to tell Sasaki all about the ups and downs. The ups are all to do with the guy's prowess in bed. Pushes her buttons, she says with a giggle and a smile. The downer is she's just discovered the prick is married. What to do?

The question is rhetorical. Malroony would no more ask Sasaki for relationship advice than she'd ask him to cut her hair. The way it goes is that she asks the questions, he listens, and then she provides her own answers. It's been like that since day one: Malroony always a buzz of words, Sasaki providing a calming silence. Like a therapist, but he's not on two hundred an hour. Somehow, the friendship works in a way it never did with his wife.

Malroony's talking again, but now she's moved on to some drug intelligence received via an anonymous tip. The problem is the intelligence points to a family who've already had a complaint about police intimidation upheld. Back on safer ground, Sasaki chips in and offers guidance on how to best deal with the issue.

Ken Royston meets them at the turn-off for Tortilla Flats. He's standing by his ute, a Toyota Landcruiser with four doors and a white GRP truck body on the back. Malroony brings the car alongside, and Sasaki lowers the window, the cool chill of the air-conditioned interior drifting away to be replaced with a waft of heat.

Royston strolls across, casual as you like. He's a big, lumbering man suited to the wide-open spaces he patrols. Stick him on a city street, and he'd collide with every second person.

'Takeo,' Royston says, leaning down to the window. 'Been a while.'

Royston's a lower rank than Sasaki, so by rights, he shouldn't be so familiar. But, then again, Sasaki once sat on 'Uncle' Royston's knee at a party, played hide and seek in the park with him, and had his hair ruffled by him on numerous occasions. All that back when he was a kid, of course, but Sasaki reckons Royston still sees him as waist high and in short trousers, never growing to achieve the height nor stature of his father.

'It was at Jimmy Follet's funeral.'

'Right.' Royston nods and keeps nodding. Like Sasaki has set a train of thought in motion. Nothing will stop it until the train hits the buffers with a bang.

Jimmy Follet, Sasaki remembers, had pulled over to intervene in a brawl between two groups of bikers and got a knife in his ribs for the trouble. He received a posthumous award, the medal given to his wife, but Sasaki didn't think a bit of shiny metal on a silk ribbon was much compensation for the loss of somebody you loved.

'Should we go?' Sasaki asks, seeing the train still hasn't arrived. After a moment, Royston nods again, walks back to the Toyota, and climbs in. It's like something is bothering him, something more than poor Jimmy Follet, something to do with Sasaki.

'Great start,' Malroony says, easing their car forwards. 'Let's hope it gets better.'

Royston is pushing his ute along at a fair pace, but the road is metalled, and Malroony has no trouble keeping up. They drive through scrub and low trees for the first few miles, and then the landscape opens up to sparse fields. Tortilla Flats was once a government research station where experimental agricultural trials took place. There was some hope rice could be grown on the land surrounding the Adelaide River, but nothing ever came of it. There was an airstrip here in the Second World War, too, and once the Japanese bombed it. Sasaki wonders if that's what's bugging Royston. As if Sasaki is personally responsible for the actions of his distant kin sometime before the middle of the last century. He mentions it to Malroony.

'If you're different, you're to blame,' she says. 'That's how it is with men like Royston, Cooper and Anderson.'

'And my father? How did he get away with being different?'

'The distinction is he earned it, boss.' Malroony turns her head and winks. 'You not heard that before?'

Sasaki laughs.

They're nearing the Adelaide River, a strip of lush greenery in the distance marking its twisting route. Farm buildings loom ahead on the left, but Royston swings right onto a dirt track. Malroony follows but now the going isn't so easy. She slows a little, and Sasaki worries Royston will disappear over the horizon, but then he pulls off the track and stops at an open gate next to another police ute. Malroony parks behind the ute as Royston gets out. Close by, tangled wire fencing lies in coils, remnants of the experimental rice plots. Beyond the gate, the land rises gently to a mirage of shimmering heat, something up there on the horizon, white against the blue sky.

'Bryce,' Royston says as Sasaki and Malroony leave the cool of their vehicle. 'Been up there all morning looking after the scene. Good kid. Hell of a job.'

Bryce. Sasaki searches for a surname, but it doesn't come. His father had a thing for names and faces and knew everyone on the force, everyone in Darwin. Perhaps it was part of being an immigrant. Make the unfamiliar familiar. Make the locals feel like you belong.

'Mitchell?' Malroony says.

'Yes.' Royston appears surprised. 'You know him?'

'Training college,' Malroony says, and there's a smile there as if Bryce Mitchell is more than just a remembered surname.

Royston misses the smile. He nods and then gestures to the gate. The three of them walk through, climbing the low rise. The mirage blurs ahead, the mysterious white blob no closer. Distorted perspective, Sasaki thinks, his mind for a moment back on his marriage. What you see isn't always what you get. Travelling forwards but getting nowhere fast.

'The body's female?' Malroony is asking the questions Sasaki should ask. 'Local?'

'Yes to the first, not local to Batchelor to the second,' Royston says.

'Domestic?'

'Don't think so.'

Sasaki is glad. A domestic is the pinnacle of a relationship gone wrong, and he doesn't want to go there. Not today.

'You said weird?' Sasaki says. 'How so?'

'Weird as in peculiar. Unexplained. Fucked up.' Royston stops walking and puts his hands on his hips. Takes a momentary breather. 'Forgot to say, we found this close to the body.'

He pulls a little GripLoc bag from a back pocket and hands it to Sasaki. A silver chain curls to a swirl of letters spelling the name *Kirsty*. Sasaki shows it to Malroony.

'Shit,' Malroony says. 'I recognise this. It belongs to Kirsty Downland. I must have pulled her in a dozen times for various things. She's a user, gets her fixes however she can. Begging, stealing, selling anything she can get her hands on, including her own body.'

'Has she been reported missing?' Sasaki says.

'She's always missing, but nobody ever misses her. I guess that's been her problem all along.'

'These girls,' Royston says. 'The thing is, they never learn.'

After dispensing his nugget of dubious wisdom, Royston sets off again, puffing. He looks older now, and Sasaki realises Royston, like Anderson and Cooper, must be heading for retirement soon. He'd been a young detective when Sasaki's father was in his prime, with a bright future ahead of him. Unexpectedly, he resigned from CID and went back to regular policing. Married a woman from Batchelor and moved out there. Everybody said Royston had chosen the quiet life, but Sasaki wonders if that was the whole story. His father once told Sasaki their adopted country was a great place to hide secrets, and Sasaki has, during his detective career, learned the truth of that. In the outback, no one can hear you scream.

The mirage is dissolving now, the white blob revealed as a popup police forensic tent, the sides billowing in the breeze. As they approach, a stocky man appears from the shady side. Bryce Mitchell is like a ranch hand in uniform. Cropped hair under a giant hat. Big arms. Bow legs. The size of Royston and then some, but his smile is large and generous, not tight and cynical.

'You OK, Bryce?' Royston says.

'Sure.' Mitchell stares at Sasaki for a moment and then turns to Malroony. '*Linda*?'

'Yeah, buddy.' Malroony walks forward and fist-bumps Mitchell. 'Good to see you.'

The two officers exchange words as Sasaki and Royston look on. Royston gobs out some phlegm and taps Sasaki on the arm.

'Let's get on with it, mate.' He lifts a flap on the side of the tent. 'In this heat, she's cooking like a pig on a spit at a Christmas barbie.'

Sasaki follows Royston into the tent. Immediately wishes he hadn't. A rush of rancid air invades his nostrils. Putrefaction. Meat gone bad.

For a second, Sasaki's confused. This is supposed to be a homicide, but there isn't a body, just a mound of something blotched and black in the centre of the tent. Then Royston waves an arm, and a cloud of flies buzzes up, leaving a red shape on the dry earth.

Sasaki can make out a head and a torso. A string of sinew spiralling out from where the right arm should be. The face is gaunt, the skin as dry as parchment and stretched tight over jutting bones. The hair might have been blonde once but is now earthy and discoloured. A fake eyelash has slipped from a shrivelled eyelid and lies over an empty socket. The other eye is covered with dirt. On the torso, three gashes run diagonally across the breast area.

'This heat we've been having,' Royston says. 'Dried her out in a day or two, I'd say. Plus, I reckon some critter has been at the body. Explains the state she's in.'

'Who found her?'

'A local from Coomalie Creek was looking for his dog with a couple of pals. They came out here and got the shock of their lives.' Royston stares ruefully at the corpse. 'They never found the dog, though.'

There's a sad irony, Sasaki thinks, that a missing dog gets more attention than poor Kirsty Downland.

'Forensics?' Sasaki is gagging at the smell, so he keeps his sentences short and tries to open his mouth as little as possible. 'You didn't think to call in the CSIs?'

'Bryce took a couple of pictures.' Royston shrugs. 'I wanted you to get here first.'

'Ken, you should have been on top of this.' Sasaki steps back. Takes a breath. 'What about Benson?'

Doctor Arthur Benson. The pathologist.

'As I said, I wanted you to see this first. I thought it was important.'

'To see what exactly?' Sasaki peers at the corpse. The flies have returned with a vengeance. The body is under sustained attack, and every minute is crucial. Benson should be here, the CSIs should be here, and the whole place should be a hive of investigative activity. This isn't a routine Darwin killing. Not a domestic or a bar room brawl got out of hand. Not an argument over money or drugs. This is going to be front-page news and lead to sensationalist headlines. There'll be TV crews and reporters and all kinds of lurid speculation. Locals will buy an extra dog or gun or both. Tourists might consider changing holiday plans. Careers are made or broken on this type of crime. Royston has either messed up badly, or there's something else. 'What am I missing? Why haven't you followed procedure?'

Royston flinches as if Sasaki has landed a heavy blow. He moves back to the entrance and pushes past to the outside. Sasaki follows.

It's ten degrees cooler out here. A gentle breeze wafts across Sasaki's face, and even though the air is hot and dusty, the difference is welcome. Royston is stalking off, heading away from the tent at an angle, moving farther into the vast field. Sasaki chases after him, but Royston's got his second wind and forges ahead, eating up the ground. After several hundred metres, he stops, and Sasaki catches up.

'First thing I did when I got here was follow bloody fucking procedure, mate.' He points to a square piece of plastic on the ground a couple of strides away. A small rock at each corner stops it from blowing away. 'Did a perimeter search and found this. Take a look and tell me I fucked up. Tell me your dad would have done anything differently.'

Sasaki steps over to the plastic and lifts one of the rocks off. The wind catches the edge of the plastic, and the other corners slip from beneath the stone weights. The plastic flies away and he jumps back. A disembodied arm lies stretching out, shredded tissue and sinew where it's been severed above the elbow. The hand is clenched in a half fist, the forefinger extended as if pointing somewhere to the northeast.

'I don't...' Sasaki's having difficulty taking it all in. Perhaps his father might have made a better stab at it. Perhaps, after all, Sasaki is merely a shadow cast from a brilliant point of light. When the light fades, the shadow vanishes, and nothing of substance remains. Sasaki is an afterthought, and when he dies childless, he won't have even had the satisfaction of passing on his father's genes.

'History, Takeo.' Royston's agitated. He's moving from side to side as if to keep still would be to atrophy. 'It's thirty-three years this year, isn't it?'

'Since what?' For a moment, Sasaki thinks he really is stupid, but then something clicks, almost as if his dad has kicked him up his backside. His mind clutches, grasps and reaches for an alternative answer, but it's a forlorn hope. 'You're talking about—'

'Yes.' Royston nods. 'Thirty-three years. I was there with your dad back then, and I can tell you it's not something you forget. Ever. That's why I wanted you to see it first.'

Royston says nothing more, turns away and walks back towards the forensic tent.

Sasaki looks down at the hand and follows the line of the finger to where it points to the horizon. Thinks about how space and time are the same things. Go far enough, fast enough, for long enough in one direction, and maybe you can end up back where you started. Maybe you can even go back to *before* where you started. He blinks, unsure if the blurring is from the tears in his eyes or another mirage in the distance. He feels a shiver even as the sun beats down.

'Shit,' he says.

# Chapter 13

Assistant Commissioner Fred Cooper doesn't like surprises, so the news the dead girl at Tortilla Flats is in some way connected to three murders that happened over thirty years ago isn't welcome. And, by the look of his pained facial expression and the way he's just popped a couple of Rennies, it's giving him indigestion.

'You what?' he says to Sasaki when the details are laid out for him. 'Do you mean the Black Ute Killer?'

'Yes.' Sasaki waits for the retort, the anger, the venom. It doesn't come.

'It's a copycat?' Cooper looks reflective, perhaps even worried. 'Or are you telling me...?'

He leaves the question hanging. Derek Pearce, AKA the Black Ute Killer, is being held in maximum security at the Alice Springs Correctional Centre. He's got a release date somewhere well north of 2040. Given he's in his late fifties, the only way he's leaving prison will be feet first in a six-foot box.

'I don't know, sir.' And Sasaki doesn't know. His father may have been the detective who caught Pearce, but Sasaki was just a kid at the time. However, after Pearce was put away, rumours circulated about an accomplice. Two decades later, with the advances in DNA technology, the sequencing of some skin samples did suggest there may have been a second person at the crime scenes, but the results were far from conclusive and led nowhere.

'Not good enough. If your old man was here, he'd know, right?' Cooper huffs and then chews his lip. 'Talking of Endo, how is he these days?'

'Fine,' Sasaki says, lying.

Endo Sasaki isn't fine. He's spending his days in a care home on the outskirts of Darwin. There is a nice view over a lake and park, good food, and compassionate care. But Endo's eyes are cloudy, he doesn't see so well, and he's also lost his appetite. Plus, he is a proud man and doesn't cope so well with the indignities of hands-on nursing. His days are spent staring blankly at the TV, watching meaningless cartoons, an old biscuit tin stuffed full of photographs clutched in his lap, like the pictures within are a substitute for his memories. Sasaki tried to look inside once, but his father wouldn't let him, as if for anyone else to see would corrupt the contents.

'Be sure to send my regards the next time you see him.' Cooper leaves a few seconds of respectful silence and then presses Sasaki for action. 'We need this cleared up pronto, OK? And I don't want a whiff of the connection to the Black Ute Killer getting out to the public. Whether it's a copycat, an old accomplice, or something completely different, stories of a bogeyman are a no-no. Puts off tourists, scares the locals and brings the bloody national media swooping in like flies round shit. That's trouble we don't need.'

Sasaki nods. Remembers the clouds of flies rising from the torso of the dead woman. The putrid, gagging odour. The way the body fell apart as the forensic team tried to remove the woman. The severed arm limp and half rotten. He wants to tell Cooper that dealing with a few journalists pales in comparison.

He returns to his office and watches as the clock on the wall at the far end of the room ticks past three. Officers stir, heading out to get their mid-afternoon coffees. He opens his office door, beckons over Malroony and several other junior detectives, and tells them to come in and settle down because it's time for some background context on the case in the form of a little story about the Black Ute Killer.

~ ~ ~

Middle of March, thirty-three years ago. Sasaki is seven years old, and he's sat in a booth in a milk bar. Giant chocolate milkshake in front of him. A couple of straws through which he slurps the drink. His father sits opposite, staring ruefully at an empty cup of coffee. As Sasaki slurps again, Endo looks up and opens his mouth to say something, but then he stops. He has to contain himself and not censor his son at every opportunity. What would have seemed gross and rude to Endo's parents in Japan is normal here in Australia. And more than anything, Endo wants his son to fit in, to be accepted.

Fitting in is something Endo has struggled to do. His parents were Japanese, and his son is Australian, but he isn't sure exactly what he is. Locally, he's known as the 'The Jap cop.' In Darwin, in the whole of the Northern Territory, there is only one Japanese police officer. In fact, he's probably the only Japanese detective in Australia anyone has ever heard of. Say *Jap Cop* to people in places as far away as Sydney or Canberra, and folk know precisely who you mean. Endo Sasaki. The face of the modern police force. Several newspapers had run features, and then ABC turned up with a request for an interview, possibly a fully-fledged documentary. The newly promoted Endo had been against it, but his boss had insisted.

'Looks good to the minorities,' he'd said. 'The Abbos. And you've got a thing for them, right? Plus, they also think the world of you, from what I hear.'

Endo knows the reason for that is because speaking to a white cop is about as helpful as talking to a brick wall.

'Father?' Sasaki has finished slurping. 'Can I have another one?'

'No. We need to get home.'

His son doesn't protest, and they leave the milk bar and head to the street where Endo's car is parked. As they get in, a squad car pulls up alongside, a young cop, Kevin Anderson, at the wheel. He leans out the window. Anderson is a rookie, cocksure and unpleasant.

'Chinaman,' he says. 'We found the girl.'

The girl.

Even at age seven, Takeo Sasaki knows Anderson is talking about Tina Davidson. Tina, twenty-four, went missing two weeks ago. She vanished from the streets of Darwin as if the pavement had opened and swallowed her whole. Sasaki saw the headlines in the evening paper and heard a smatter of words on the radio news. And the missing girl is the talk of the town. Hushed whispers from teachers in the corner of the playground. People gossiping in the supermarket. Friends at school — girls mostly — complaining that their parents are keeping them home rather than letting them out to play.

Then, there are the off glances at Sasaki because his father has something to do with all this.

Endo climbs back out of the car and closes the door. The young Sasaki cracks the window a little so he can hear the conversation.

'Melacca Swamp?'

'Yeah,' Anderson says.

'Is she dead?' Endo says.

'Of course, she's dead.' Anderson grins. 'You think a chick like her could survive out there alone all this time?'

'Anything else?

'Well...' Anderson pauses, a reluctant tone in the following words. 'The arm... she... it was... it was pointing precisely like you said it would be. The boss says you need to take a gander before they bring her in.'

106

Endo glances back to his car for a moment and then turns to Anderson.

'Give my son a ride home, please. I'll head out there.'

The grin vanishes, Anderson not best pleased at having to play nanny to a seven-year-old kid. Sasaki gets out and slips into the back of the squad car, and the little boy is the one who's grinning now.

Late March, thirty-three years ago. A ride in a Darwin black and white the highlight of the day but not the abiding memory.

Sasaki is in bed when his father finally comes home late that evening.

But he's not asleep.

*We found the girl...*

Sasaki wants to know what's happened. Is she really dead? Or is she back with her mummy and daddy?

He creeps from his room and crawls along the corridor, where he nestles on the floor close to the door to the living room.

His father is sitting in his usual chair, bent over with his head in his hands.

Crying.

Sasaki's never seen him cry before; Endo rarely shows any emotion except when he occasionally loses his temper. Never tears.

Words are tumbling out from behind the wall of fingers that hide his father's embarrassment, but they're Japanese words, and Sasaki, who was taught only English to make him fit in, struggles to understand.

*Forced... cut... horror... dead...*

The girl isn't going home tonight; that much is clear. And Sasaki senior doesn't seem to be able to make much sense of the situation.

*She's number three...*

Everyone knows she's the third victim because the newspapers have been plastered with pictures of the girl and the previous two women. But his father seems to be obsessed with the number.

*Three... It never should have come to this.*

Over the next few days and weeks, young Takeo Sasaki, even then a nascent detective, puts together the pieces of the story. There's a black ute cruising the streets, someone picking up young women, taking them into the wilderness, assaulting and killing them. The full details won't become clear to Sasaki until he's much older and a police officer himself: the fact the three women were all sex workers; the right arm of the second victim cut off and laid out pointing to the location of the first, the third victim's arm to the second victim. The cause of death a large round stone rammed down the throat of each victim, the word *whore* scratched on the surface of the rock. The arrest of Derek Pearce for the murders, his motive revealed as a twisted logic that made little sense to anyone but himself. The case solved by Endo, preventing Pearce from killing God knows how many more women. Pearce gets a life sentence, and Endo Sasaki becomes a local and national celebrity, feted everywhere he goes, nominated for awards, and forever known as the *Jap Cop*, a real Australian hero.

And Takeo Sasaki, aged seven, doesn't understand the irony of the label and decides he wants to be a policeman too.

~ ~ ~

'So this killing is related?' Malroony says. 'But how? Pearce is in prison.'

'There were rumours he may have had an accomplice,' Sasaki says.

'And he's waited thirty-three years to commit another murder?' Malroony makes a characteristic tutting sound she usually reserves for AC Cooper's more outlandish claims. 'I don't buy it.'

'Well, if not an accomplice, we must be looking at a copycat. Someone who wants to emulate the crime for some reason. You've got to admit the severed arm is a pretty distinctive feature.'

'That's true, but if the details came out in the trial, the copycat could be anyone, right?'

'Anyone who's read up on the case, yes.'

'But why would they go back and troll over the details of an ancient crime?'

'Because they were somehow involved back then.'

'That doesn't make sense.' Malroony bites her lip. Thinks for a moment. 'They'd risk exposing themselves.'

'Unless it's some sort of bluff or double bluff.'

'Even if it is, why now?'

Sasaki shakes his head and can't help glancing across to the portrait of his father. Endo stares out with clear, piercing eyes, the certainty of belief written on his face.

*He's a legend around these parts...*

'That I don't know,' Sasaki says.

~ ~ ~

The post-mortem takes place late the next day, with Doctor Arthur Benson presiding. Benson is a drunk, widely rumoured to have been shunted into forensic pathology because he couldn't uphold the Hippocratic Oath. He's of an age where he remembers Sasaki's father, and like Cooper, Anderson and Royston, Benson is heading for retirement. It's a generational shift, a changing of the guard, the passing of the baton to Sasaki, Malroony and others.

Can't come a moment too soon, Sasaki thinks, when he and Malroony traipse into the autopsy room. Benson is standing over the cadaver, swaying slightly. He looks up, little red veins in his eyes spidering across the sclera, a web woven, thread by thread, by each bottle of Timboon single malt he's consumed. Benson's a slight man with oversized hands and would, at first sight, seem to lack the dexterity required for his job, but the whisky steadies his nerve, if not his manners.

'You ready?' he says. There's no greeting, no enquiring about their health, no chit-chat. Par for the course with Benson if you're not one of his drinking pals.

Sasaki and Malroony don the necessary PPE and move closer. The odour from the Timboon is only partially masked by the smell of disinfectant and decay, but Sasaki doubts Benson cares. And, as long as the pathologist does his job, Sasaki doesn't care either.

Benson waves his forceps over the woman's remains. Slurs out the basic details and fills them in on the state of the body.

'With this amount of exposure, we're not going to find much,' he says. 'The larvae have had their way with the soft tissue, and various wild animals have played with what's left. Plus, she's had a few days to bake in the sun.'

Sasaki nods. Great start.

Benson gets to work, dissecting where he can, pulling flesh from bone where there's nothing to cut. Using tweezers to pick up the white maggots and deposit them in a jar.

'I'll use these for my weekend fishing trip,' he says, and Sasaki knows Benson's not kidding. Then he tells them about the cuts below the right shoulder and the indentations made by the saw that rasped through the bone to sever the arm. 'The amputation occurred after death and was carried out using a razor-sharp knife and something like a rough wood saw.'

'Did they know what they were doing?' Sasaki says.

'No.' Benson gives Sasaki a stare. 'The arm was hacked off.'

Sasaki glances across to where the limb lies on a nearby trolley. Jagged tears of skin and lumps of muscle lend substance to Benson's statement.

'The perpetrator was nervous,' Malroony says. 'Or in a hurry or both. There was no pleasure for him in removing the arm, so he must have had other reasons.'

'To place it four hundred metres away,' Sasaki says. 'And arrange it to point off into the distance.'

'Like the BUK?'

'Exactly.'

Benson sways slightly, a hand reaching for the stainless steel gurney.

'Are you OK, Doctor Benson?' Sasaki says.

'This isn't the Black Ute Killer.' Benson swings around, angry. 'The BUK is in prison, and he's going to die in there if there's any justice in this fucking world.'

The outburst is uncharacteristic for a medical professional but perhaps reflects that Benson is less a medic and more a drunk.

'Do you remember Derek Pearce?' Sasaki says.

A pause as Benson lets out a long sigh and composes himself. 'I was training back then, didn't pay much attention to the details, but I do know Pearce should've been hanged for what he did to this town.'

And there, Sasaki thinks, in a nutshell, is a perfect summation of the attitude of the authorities and the general public to the three historical killings: Pearce is hated not for what he did to his victims but for dragging Darwin into the mire. The three murdered women were seen as lowlifes and, as such, got what they deserved. If Pearce had kept under the radar and done his brutal business without attracting attention, there'd have been more than a few people agreeing with the sentiment of his actions, if not the results.

'Any other wounds?'

'Marks on her wrist consistent with being handcuffed or otherwise restrained.'

'Handcuffed?'

'Or some form of manacle, perhaps a chain or a rope.'

'Anything else?'

'Difficult to tell because something's been at her.' Benson points at the throat and upper chest area, where there's a gaping hole. 'A wild dog, probably, so we'll never know what happened here.'

It seems that's not the only thing they'll never know, as an hour and a half in Sasaki is no wiser as to how the girl died. He asks Benson.

'What was the cause of death?' he says. 'Because unless I missed it, you haven't specified, right?'

'No, I haven't specified.' Benson looks up from the cadaver. 'The three slashes across the breasts were likely made post-mortem, so they didn't kill her. Likewise, the arm. Whatever animal ripped away the throat area means there's no way of knowing if she was strangled or asphyxiated.'

'And no stone,' Sasaki says, thinking of the MO of the original BUK.

'No stone.'

The rest of the PM is a waste of time, and Benson sums up the lost hours with one word: *inconclusive.*

'The value of Arthur Benson to the police force,' Malroony says once they're out in the fresh air. 'Inconclusive.'

As they walk back to their car, Sasaki wonders how many people in Darwin think the same of him because, for all his hard work, he's been unable to emerge from his father's shadow and prove his value. And the severed arm with the pointing finger suggests this is Endo Sasaki's case to solve.

'You going to visit him?' Malroony says, reading his mind. 'See what he can recall?'

Sasaki thinks of the wizened man sitting in the chair at the care home. The biscuit tin of old photos clutched in his lap. Staring at the TV. Smiling at whatever is on the screen, a thin rivulet of drool on his chin. Scowling at the appearance of Sasaki and waving him away when the nurses introduce him as 'your son.'

'I'm sure I'd remember if I had a son,' Endo Sasaki had said the last time Sasaki visited. 'I remember my wife, and I remember my daughter. I remember a dog I used to have.' A glance at Sasaki. 'But not a son.'

'Sir?' Malroony stands at the car and blips the locks. 'I said do you think it's worth going to see your dad?'

'No,' Sasaki says.

# Chapter 14

Sunday morning and Sasaki's in his flat. A week after the move, the place is still a mess. There are boxes in a stack on either side of the TV. A crate of cooking pans in the kitchen. A couple of bin liners full of clothes shoved inside a wardrobe in the bedroom. He tells himself he hasn't had the time, that he's been working too hard. That's partly true — the Tortilla girl has been taking up most of his hours — but there's another reason. Anna's been in touch. She wants to meet up for a coffee, perhaps dinner. Sasaki knows he's kidding himself, but he wonders if there might be a chance of getting back together. He thinks about his father. The patter of tiny feet. Passing on the precious DNA.

Is that all he's looking for from Anna? What about love? Sasaki isn't sure. Perhaps it's just that he's feeling lonely. Malroony says he should get out more. Use a dating app. Perhaps try a smile or two in the supermarket.

But there isn't much to smile about at the moment, certainly not at work. They've spent several days on the Tortilla case, and it isn't going anywhere. AC Cooper wants it to be put on the back burner, and Sasaki can see his point of view. He and Malroony have been working the case full-time with nothing to show for their efforts. Four other detectives, too. Still, Cooper has so far humoured him, but that's only because the chief remembers what happened thirty-three years ago.

Yes. Sasaki Senior. Still influencing poor Sasaki Junior's life. Reaching out from the past, a shadow following him even out at Tortilla Flats in the midday sun.

He's heading there later. First time since they found the girl. He wants to go back alone and see if he can find an answer written in the dusty soil. He knows that's unlikely to happen, but there's something he's missing. The autopsy report, the forensics, the offender profile compiled by a so-called expert in Sydney — none of it adds up to much. Plenty of detail, yes, but detail leading nowhere. Can't see the wood for the trees, Sasaki thinks. Except out at Tortilla Flats, there aren't any trees.

He arrives in the early afternoon, and this time, the sun isn't beating down. Cloud hangs in the sky, holding in an oppressive, humid heat. Rain is imminent. He parks next to the coils of barbed wire and trudges to the scene. There's not much left now, just a wooden stake where the body was, another way in the distance marking the location of the severed arm.

Sasaki stares down at the wooden stake. It isn't much of a marker for a life. He drops to the ground and kneels. The soil is dry and dusty, with dark stains blotching the earth. Sasaki puts a hand in his pocket. He considered bringing a wreath or bouquet, but flowers won't last long out here. His fingers close around a small, hard object. It's a piece of polished soapstone carved in the shape of a lotus blossom. The ornament belonged to his grandmother, given to him when she was still alive.

He places the stone on the ground and rises as the first raindrops begin to spatter down. Little explosions in the dusty soil around him, like the ground is alive. The lotus flower. Birth, death, rebirth.

He walks away from the first stake and towards the second, feeling the damp shirt on his back, the sleeves clinging to his arms. He should leave before he gets too wet, but he wants to visit the other stake. The severed arm is the link back to his father. The Black Ute Killer murdered three girls and laid each out with their severed right arms pointing to the location of the previous victim. Endo

115

Sasaki caught the killer, and he was locked away for life. His son hasn't achieved the same heights, but — as his grandmother used to say — perhaps there are as many lessons to be learned from the successes that evade us as from those that fall lightly into our laps.

The rain is heavier now, slatting down and soaking him to the skin. He's a quarter of the way to the second stake when he stops and wonders what he's doing. For a moment, he stands there as the tears come, mingling with the rain. Crying has never been easy for him. There was too much expectation as a child and not much room for emotion. Now, the expectation has gone. There's nothing left but raw feelings. Everything's flown from his reach: his father, Anna, his unconceived child, a successful police career. He wonders what can lie ahead that can fill the void.

He blinks, already embarrassed at his gross self-indulgence, and turns away. He wipes his face, prisms of light forming from the rain and tears. Lines streak across his vision. Parallel lines. He blinks again, the tears gone, the lines now on the ground a few strides away. He walks towards them and stares down. Two indentations, four metres long, a couple apart, perhaps a hand wide. The rain soaks into the low depressions, darkening the soil as rivulets run down the lengths. Before the rain, they'd been all but invisible. He bends and examines the closest. It's as if a long pipe has been pressed hard into the ground and left a semi-circular mark.

Sasaki straightens and looks across at the other line. Tries to visualise what made them.

And then he has it.

~ ~ ~

Malroony's there in ninety minutes, and Kieran Lamb, Darwin's head CSI, is with her in the car. Lamb's nickname is Long-in-the-tooth Lamb because he, like Cooper and the others, is heading for retirement. At a crime scene, Lamb is slow but meticulous. Moves like he needs a walking frame. It's all that time spent bending forwards, hunched over, squinting down. Lamb's brought a load of kit with him: surveying gear, cameras, a laser scanning device that can map three-dimensional objects; Malroony turns up with a flask of hot coffee, some spare clothing and a bright smile.

'Boss.' She greets Sasaki as he gets out of the car. Takes in his dishevelled appearance. He's wet and muddy and still a little emotional. Lamb doesn't notice Sasaki's mood, but Malroony does. 'You OK?'

'Better for you being here,' Sasaki says, meaning it.

The rain has stopped, so he figures he should get changed. Malroony turns away as he drops his trousers, removes his shirt, and pulls on the sweatpants and top. She pours him a cup of coffee. His hand shakes as he takes the cup.

Lamb is already heading up towards the stakes, laden down with equipment.

'We'd better help him,' Sasaki says, pointing to the remaining bags.

'Yes.' Malroony puts out a hand and steadies Sasaki's arm. 'Are you *really* OK?'

'Right as rain now.' Sasaki glances skywards. Shakes his head. 'Heaven sent, would you believe that?'

Sasaki finishes his coffee, puts the cup on the roof of his car, and grabs a large crate. Malroony bends and picks up a couple of bags.

'Are you going to tell me then?' she says as they follow Lamb. 'Or do I have to guess?'

'You mean why I was out here or what I've found?'

'Both. Either.'

'Cooper hinted that it wouldn't be long before we're done with the case. He doesn't want to waste time on the likes of Kirsty Downland. And the sooner we let it lie, the sooner the media ghouls stop hanging around Darwin, and the less likely somebody links the killing to the BUK. I returned to pay my respects and say I was sorry.'

'To your father?'

Sasaki glances sideways at Malroony. He wonders how this woman can see inside him in a way Anna never could. 'Yes, but also to the victim. I thought we'd failed her and were failing all the other victims this guy might have killed or be going to kill. I don't ever want to get like Cooper or Anderson or Benson, where the job is just a job.'

'Honey, you needn't worry, you're a million miles from those three.'

'That's just it, they weren't always so cynical.'

'I wouldn't be so sure.'

They reach the first stake and Sasaki pauses. The stone lotus flower glistens with moisture, shiny in the lightening sky.

'You put that there?' Malroony says. Sasaki nods. 'That's nice, real nice.'

'It was my grandmother's.' Sasaki wants to say something else, but a lump has formed in his throat. For a moment, there's silence.

'Tell me about what's over there.' Malroony gestures to where Lamb has already unshouldered his bags and is examining the depressions.

'I think they're skid marks.' Sasaki sets off again, keen to get Malroony and Lamb's opinion.

'How's that possible? If a car had been up here, we'd have seen the tracks, surely?'

118

'Not a car and not that type of skid.'

'I don't get it?'

'Wait.' Sasaki's teasing now and wants to prolong the surprise. They reach Lamb and drop the rest of the equipment on the ground. 'What do you think, Kieran?'

Lamb is measuring the lines and noting the results on a tablet. He shakes his head. 'I don't know. Something heavy made these, though. A tonne or more.'

'Takeo says they're skid marks,' Malroony says. 'But I can't see how they're from a vehicle, especially now I'm looking at them.'

'No,' Lamb says. 'They're not tyre tracks. Look at the shape of them.' Lamb points at his tape measure. 'Three point five metres long, eight point five centimetres across, the two markings two point four five metres apart. No car or truck made these.'

'I agree,' Sasaki says. He looks at Malroony. Delivers the punchline. 'They were made by the skids on the bottom of a helicopter.'

~ ~ ~

The helicopter clue has blown the case wide open, and even though it's late Sunday afternoon, AC Cooper has come into the station. Sasaki can smell barbecue smoke on the chief's clothes and remembers it's the Coopers' wedding anniversary: big party, family, friends, plenty of free alcohol. Most of the station have been invited. Not Sasaki or Malroony though. Funny that.

'You're telling me somebody used a chopper to dump the body?' Cooper stinks of beer as well as smoke. There's a brown sauce stain at the bottom edge of his white shirt. It's past six and the party started at one. Cooper's well on the way. 'Because that doesn't make any fucking sense at all.'

'No, sir, it doesn't.' Sasaki needs to take this easy. When Cooper's had a few coldies, he tends to get defensive. 'But that's what happened.'

'Who the fuck flies out into the middle of nowhere with a body in a helicopter, hey?'

'I don't know,' Sasaki says. It's a good question, but you may as well ask who kills a woman and cuts off her arm. 'Somebody with money.'

'Doesn't take a genius to work that out, Sake.' Cooper gives a wink. 'Sake. Get it, right?'

Sake. Oh, that's funny. The AC drunk isn't a good look for the force, Sasaki thinks. 'Enough money to both have a pilot's licence and charter a helicopter or own one.'

'They flew themselves?'

'They'd hardly be able to charter an aircraft and pilot to take a body out here, would they?'

'Don't be flippant, mate. I'm trying to work out why I'm not at home enjoying myself rather than listening to this drivel.'

'Sir?' It's Lamb. He's stuck around for the after-show fireworks. 'We've got the measurements of the helicopter's skids. We can correlate them with dimensions from various makes and start looking for matching aircraft. We can cross-reference with state registrations, visit owners and check alibis. It won't take long by my reckoning, so Takeo might just have cracked the case.'

'Huh?' Cooper grunts. Sasaki can see he's picturing himself in front of the TV cameras. Nationwide coverage. Perhaps some kind of police chief's award. Something to talk about at the next party and every other social from now until well into his retirement. 'Right. Good work.'

Except the work isn't done yet. Not by a long stretch. Cooper heads off back to his party, leaving Sasaki and Lamb.

'Thanks,' Sasaki says. 'For backing me up.'

'No sweat, mate.' Lamb stands there looking at the space where Cooper had been. Smacks his lips. 'But it might have been nice if he'd invited us back for a jar to celebrate.'

'You want to get one?' Sasaki doesn't drink much, but he owes Lamb. 'Over the road?'

There's a bar opposite the station popular with cops. Sasaki pushes himself up from his desk and feels in his back pocket for his wallet.

'What?' Lamb looks at Sasaki like he hasn't heard and then seems to come to his senses. 'Nah, mate, you're OK. Better get back to the missus. She doesn't like me being out on a Sunday. We'll start on this helicopter stuff tomorrow, right?'

'Right.'

Sasaki stands looking at the space where Lamb has been. Shakes his head.

'Sir?' Malroony pops up from behind her monitor. 'I could do with a drink, perhaps something to eat.'

'Over the road?'

'I think we can do better than that, don't you?'

Yes, Sasaki thinks, we can.

~ ~ ~

They find the phone the next day.

He returns to the scene with Malroony, thinking about how they'd missed the helicopter skid marks. When they first visited Tortilla Flats, Ken Royston told Sasaki he'd done a perimeter search. That's how he'd discovered the arm. He'd missed the marks, though. Perhaps that wasn't surprising, considering it had taken a rainstorm to reveal them. Then again, Royston wasn't the type of officer who'd carry out a thorough search on a baking hot day when he probably had a couple of tinnies stashed in a coolbox in the ute.

'What are we looking for, sir?' Malroony says as they stick in marker flags. 'More mysterious lines in the sand? Gold nuggets? Alien footprints?'

'I don't know, Linda,' Sasaki says, 'but I want to be sure we haven't missed anything.'

His dad never missed anything except several times his son's birthday.

'It's becoming an obsession, right?' Malroony holds up her hands in apology. 'Not that there is anything wrong with being obsessive about this. Nobody else cares about the poor girl but us, do they?'

It's true. Cooper got excited on Sunday afternoon, but he'd been fuelled with more than a few beers. This morning, he'd reigned in a little, explaining to Sasaki that they had limited resources and not to go off on a wild goose chase. The helicopter skids could have been coincidental and made sometime before the girl was dumped. Cooper is clutching at straws. Sasaki knows he wants the case to fade away, not blow up in his face; the similarity with what happened thirty-three years ago is something he doesn't want to confront.

They divide the area around where the body was found into a grid 800 metres square with lines every twenty metres. The land is barren, just a few wispy pieces of scrub, and Sasaki thinks they'll spot anything if they stick to the grid lines and double-work each line. There's no guarantee they'll find any evidence, but it's worth a try.

They start at ten, Sasaki suggesting they break every half hour. It's tedious and hot, and they can't keep up a conversation since it would be too easy to be distracted. After an hour and a half, with several drinks breaks, they're still only on the sixth line of the grid. That leaves thirty-four lines. At this rate, they won't finish today.

'We're making progress,' Malroony says, ever optimistic. She takes a pull of water from her bottle and stares out across the barren landscape. 'Bit by bit.'

'You wonder how they ever thought they could grow rice out here,' Sasaki says.

'It was a research station, right?'

'Supposedly.'

'Genetic engineering?'

'No, a long time before that.'

'And the airfield at Coomalie Creek? The one Royston holds you responsible for bombing?'

'A squadron was based there in World War II. There was also an artillery range.' Sasaki turns back to Malroony. 'Do you think there could be a link between either of those and the girl?'

'I don't see how. Not after all this time. You're talking decades and decades back to the war.'

'The research station only closed in the early nineties.'

'That's still a good while. And why would a young woman be murdered because of some experimental farming research? Rice wars?'

'Never mind.'

Sasaki starts walking again, eyes flicking left and right, taking in every little stone or clod of earth. His mind wanders, trying to find an answer to the mystery involving the girl and the helicopter. He tries to link World War II to hybrid rice grains to Darwin sex workers, hoping for a clue.

'Takeo.' Malroony bends to an object on the ground. Pale pink and covered in dust. She prods the lump with her aluminium probe. 'You need to take a look at this.'

Sasaki steps over and peers down at a length of gristle half chewed by some critter and then baked hard in the sun. But there's something else too. A piece of plastic wrapping pokes from beneath the dried entrail, a bag enclosing a flat rectangle of glass.

'What is it?' Sasaki asks. He turns his head, trying to understand. Malroony jabs at the plastic again, and the bag splits open, revealing what's inside.

'A phone,' she says.

~ ~ ~

Kieran Lamb is there within an hour. He trudges up from his van and nods approvingly at the marker poles and the exclusion zone around the evidence. Makes a face when he reaches Sasaki and Malroony.

'Be nice if you could make it Darwin next time, mate,' he says. 'Save me spending half my life on the road.'

'Speak to Royston,' Malroony says. She turns to Sasaki. 'He's the one who fucked up, right, sir?'

'What do you think, Kieran?' Sasaki says. He can't bring himself to dump Royston in it, but Malroony isn't wrong.

'He shouldn't have missed it,' Lamb says nonchalantly. He drops his bag and moves over to the piece of flesh and the phone. Raises an eyebrow. 'This was *inside* the girl?'

'Seems that way. An animal tried to grab a tasty morsel and dragged it out to here.'

'Which is within Royston's perimeter search,' Malroony says. She's not letting go. 'His *so-called* perimeter search.'

'But...'

Lamb is staring at the phone, and Sasaki guesses he's thinking the same thoughts Sasaki and Malroony have run through for the past hour. Who? How? And, most pertinently, why?

'We don't know,' Sasaki says. 'But stones were placed in the throats of Pearce's victims. Each had the word *whore* on them. Perhaps the phone is in some way related to that.'

'Fuck.' Lamb bites his lip and then reaches for his carry-all and delves inside. He pulls out gloves, forceps, wipes, evidence bags, Petri dishes, and a couple of acrylic boxes. Bends. 'Well, this is part of the oesophagus. Looks like the phone was rammed down the woman's throat.'

Sasaki nods, steps back, and lets Lamb do his job, watching as the CSI takes samples and carefully removes the phone from the plastic bag. When finished, he holds up the phone, now sealed in one of the boxes.

'The screen's cracked,' he says. 'Plus, the battery has leaked, and there's condensation inside the housing. I doubt it's going to work.'

'But you can get the data, right? From the sim or the memory card?'

'Possibly.' Lamb begins to tidy up. The remainder of the girl's throat is in the other acrylic box, with soil samples and a couple of insects in the Petri dishes. He places everything in his bag. 'We'll see back at the lab.'

Sasaki isn't hopeful. Lamb's lab is a nook in the station basement. There's a cluttered workbench and a broken oscilloscope. A computer running a version of Windows that looks as if it was released in the nineteen eighties. Cutting edge, the lab isn't.

'Do we need...' Sasaki hesitates. As with Royston, he's too polite and doesn't want to offend. 'Do we need a specialist?'

'You what, mate?' Lamb puffs himself up. 'You casting aspersions?'

'No, I mean... I just... we could... perhaps...' Sasaki looks to Malroony for help, but she has a smile plastered across her face. When he turns back to Lamb, the CSI laughs. The bravado is just a joke.

'No worries.' Lamb closes his bag. 'When we get back to base, we'll take a quick shufty. Any doubts then I promise

I won't cry myself to sleep if you think we need to fly in someone who knows what the fuck they're doing.'

Back in Darwin, Lamb gets down to work.

He connects the phone to his ancient computer, finds and fits a spare battery, and the phone springs into life. Sasaki is disappointed when Lamb says there's nothing on the phone.

'The thing hasn't even been set up,' Lamb says. 'Just the basic apps and no personal data. It doesn't look like the phone has ever connected to the internet, and the location information has been turned off. There's not even a password to get in.'

'It doesn't make sense.' Sasaki stares at the phone. 'What about the number?'

'Well, we can try getting further information from the carrier, but the sim looks like a standard pay-as-you-go. It's possible it was never used. We might be drawing a blank when it comes to evidence.'

As if in response, the phone pings and a text notification appears on the screen.

*Welcome to T-Mobile. To continue setting up your phone...*

Then there's another ping and another text.

*To purchase credit call 444 or go to the TMobile.com website where you...*

And another.

'Hang on,' Lamb says. He accesses another screen which contains a record of calls and messages. 'There's a voice message.'

He plays the message.

# Chapter 15

*Let's play a game. A game with numbers. Shall we start with three? Three times three? Perhaps three times three times three? And after that? Well, I guess it depends on whether you can catch me.*

*You know, I thought it was wrong back then, thirty-three years ago. Killing those whores. For a long time, I didn't understand, but now I do. Killing back then was a rational action, and today it is rational, too. Which is why the new girls have to die. You will try to stop me, but your attempts to shield the sinful from retribution will be in vain. The debased can no longer be allowed to stain God's earth with their tainted footprints.*

*I am no monster, even though you may label me as such. Each time I kill, I reduce the potential level of misery in the world, not only satisfying my desire for revenge but bringing benefits to others as well. But this message isn't about justifying my actions; you see, the telling is part of the process. You could even say the telling is all of it. People must know of my work and the connections I am making because making the connections resurrects the past, and once something is born again, it can die again, too. And when I kill a whore I also stop a nightmare. Two birds with one stone. A win-win situation. And yes, it is like last time, only this puzzle is bigger and better because it has to be. I have to surpass what went before and prove it can be done without giving the game away.*

*I know your job is to track me down, and because I am like you in more ways than you know, I understand this is not simply a career. It's an unhealthy obsession. You worry, you fret, you don't sleep enough, you find yourself alone with your thoughts. You're often the last to leave the office, and you don't switch off even when you're at home. You overthink everything. Try to make those little connections from A to B to C. When ordinary people see a car passing on the street, you see the make and model, and you note the tag. Who's inside: a family, a couple, or a lone man? A man on his own draws your attention. Is he white, black, young or old? Where have you seen his face before? Is he a work colleague, or is the face from a mugshot? Could he be the one you're looking for?*

*Probably not, because serendipity is something only a fool would rely on. Instead, you will resort to wild theories and blind guesses, consult databases and scour crime scenes, engage in freeform thinking, construct mind maps and spider charts, and, who knows, you might even employ the services of a medium or mystic. In the end, you'll resort to kneeling by your bed and praying. But here's the thing: your efforts will prove fruitless because, this time, I'm giving nothing away gratis.*

*Perhaps it would be for the best if you simply gave up now. The victims are no loss to anyone. They shouldn't be on the streets, and I'm simply fulfilling society's unspoken wishes. I'm cleaning up the dirt. Removing the sullied. Sweeping away the tainted flesh and starting anew. You should thank me, for you call yourselves the guardians of order, yet you preside over this abomination.*

*And I guess if you'd done your job properly years ago, none of this would be necessary.*

# Chapter 16

DI Jessica Chase and DI Nick Green play the message several times. More than several times. In fact, they listen to the strange, distorted, rasping voice repeatedly until Chase reckons she could stand up on stage and recite the whole thing from memory. When she returns home that evening, the words echo in her ears.

*Let's play a game. A game with numbers...*

A game?

She cooks herself some crap food and chills in front of a mindless Netflix series. Goes to bed. Her head hits the pillow, she closes her eyes, and text floats in a grey fuzz.

*This puzzle is bigger and better...*

Bigger and better than what?

*Perhaps it would be for the best if you simply gave up now...*

And then she's asleep, and when she wakes in the morning, there's no sudden revelation, no dreams to interpret, no clarity brought by the new day. Nothing.

*In the end you'll resort to kneeling by your bed and praying...*

It could well come to that, she thinks.

Back at the SCU, Green looks like she feels.

'Bad night?' she says.

'No night,' Green answers. 'I went over the bloody thing again and again, and I still can't make sense of it.'

'Me neither, but we're listening to a deranged killer, not a rational actor. He cuts open his victim and places the phone in her abdomen, knowing we'll find it. I don't think we can take anything from the message, at least not anything at face value. The whole thing could be an act of misdirection.'

129

'Self-evidently, but this guy is too big for his boots. His boasting might well be his downfall.' Green lowers his voice. 'You do the praying thing yet?'

'Thought about it.'

'Me too.' Green stays quiet for a moment. 'He said he was like us.'

'You think he's police?'

'Why not?'

'Because that's what he wants us to think.'

'So it's a double bluff?'

'There is one thing,' Chase says.

'Go on.'

'He says something about a car: *you note the tag.* That's not how we say it here, is it? We say *index* or *plate.* And I looked up *tag,* and sometimes it refers to a registration sticker you stick on the licence plate in the US.'

'So he's American?'

'Could be, unless it's another attempt at misdirection.'

'But if the whole thing is fake, why bother to leave a message in the first place?'

Chase doesn't answer. Says: 'He mentions thirty-three years. Does that refer to a previous crime he's committed or something else?'

Green raises his shoulders, opens his hands and shakes his head. Then he turns to Stafford. 'You got anything new?'

Stafford is hunched at his computer screen, over-ear headphones rammed tight on his head as he stares at a wavey red line representing the audio feed. Yesterday, while Chase and Green were listening to the content of the message, Stafford worked on the technical side, running the clip through various filters designed to clean up the sound.

Stafford doesn't answer, so Green taps him on the shoulder. Stafford raises one side of the headphones, and Green repeats the question.

'Not yet,' Stafford says. 'But it's definitely DP.'

'Deep Penetration?' Green says with half a grin.

'No.' Stafford looks offended. 'Digital processing. He used an audio effect to disguise his voice and slur the words.'

'Jess thinks he could be American.'

'The line about the tag?'

'You knew? Why didn't you say?'

'Not conclusive, not yet. We go on evidence, not hunches, and so far, I've got nothing to tell you.'

Par for the course, Chase thinks — nothing following nothing. Yesterday, the three of them had a stand-up row about the accent, with Chase thinking the man was from somewhere across the pond, Green reckoning West Country and Stafford arguing the voice was a put-on northern accent designed to throw them off the scent. In truth, the digital processing has removed any easily identifiable traits, but Stafford worked late and was in early, not ready to give up.

'I'm off,' Green says, moving quickly away. 'An urgent appointment with the little boys' room.'

Chase doesn't get it for a moment, but then she blinks and spots something in the corner of her vision: DCS Boyle heading for the SCU like a heat-seeking missile.

'DI Chase,' he shouts, causing heads to at first turn and then duck for cover. 'An explanation.'

'Christ,' Chase mutters. Boyle doesn't look happy, and she's sure it's not simply because they've made no progress.

'Sir?' she says.

'Several of the tabloids have it.' Boyle waves a sheaf of red-top newspapers at Chase like he's brandishing a baseball bat. Chase flinches, half expecting to get hit. 'We've got a fucking leak.'

'The tabloids have what, sir?'

'They know a phone was found *inside* the girl.'

Chase hasn't told Boyle about the message, but the DCS has the report from Pat Kendle that details the reverse c-section mobile phone insertion event — as the pathologist called it.

'It's quite enough to have got them all in a tizzy.' Boyle waves the papers close to Chase's face. 'They're putting two and two together and coming up with some very unpleasant conjecture.'

'Does it matter?'

'Of course it matters. It's about the optics, Jessie. What appeared to be a killing of some unfortunate druggie or immigrant now takes on a different shade. There's talk of a psychopath on the rampage.'

'Perhaps that will persuade someone to come forward with information.'

'Well, it's persuaded a whole lot of scum journalists to ask some uncomfortable questions. They want to know if we've gained access to the call logs, if there were any messages, and if we've been able to track the phone's owner.' Boyle waits. In the neighbouring cubicle, a junior detective bobs down and stays low. 'Well?'

'We're working on it, sir.'

'Is that egghead of yours not living up to his billing?' Boyle swivels his head like an owl looking for prey, but Stafford has followed Green to the toilets and is nowhere to be seen. 'Looks like DS Stafford is turning out to be more of a Camden Market trader than a Cambridge University don.'

'There are technical issues I don't fully understand. You'll need to speak to John.'

'You speak to him, Jessie.' Boyle wags a finger. 'And get those issues solved and the investigation moving because so far there's not a hint of a decent lead, no ID for the victim, no motive, and we sure as hell don't have a suspect. Do I need to tell you that's not good enough?'

'No, sir.'

'Well, sort it.' Boyle finally relinquishes his hold on the newspapers, and they sprawl out across Chase's desk. 'Or else.'

With that, he's gone, the threat unspecified but likely somewhere between a severe reprimand and the closing down of the entire unit, the latter suiting Boyle's agenda to a T.

'Technical issues?' Green reappears, popping his head over one of the room dividers. 'That's crap. Why haven't you told him about the message?'

'I didn't think it was... um... pertinent.' Chase watches Boyle weave between the maze of desks. He may think he's spreading his good cheer and raising morale, but officers and civilian workers alike visibly flinch as he approaches. Chase turns back to Green. 'But we are in serious need of a lead, or Busy Bee is going to be wielding his sting.'

'You're right,' Green says. 'We're one nil down, and if the message is correct about the numbers, it's only going to get worse.'

Chase hears the distorted voice echo through her thoughts. Hopes Green is wrong.

~ ~ ~

A breakthrough comes the next day in the form of a missing person's report for a woman matching the description of the victim.

'Alison Madden. Twenty-five, brown hair, lives with her girlfriend in a house out at Southend on Sea,' Green says. 'Her mother has been on holiday out of the country and couldn't make contact when she returned.'

'Anything else?' Chase says.

'Yeah.' Green nods. Looks downcast. 'Big dolphin tattoo on her right shoulder.'

Chase gives an involuntary shiver as euphoria and horror mix in a mush of emotions. This is the first concrete lead, and identifying the victim could point to possible suspects.

'Pretty much confirms the ID,' Green continues. 'But there's more.'

'Go on.'

'Her partner is missing as well.'

'The girlfriend?'

'Yup. Her name is Lizzie Thomkin. So either the partner is a suspect...' Green turns his hands palm up and shrugs. 'Or...'

He doesn't say anything else. Doesn't need to.

*Shall we start with three?*

The killer is attempting to live up to his promise.

Fuck.

'Is she a sex worker?'

Green shrugs blankly.

The inaction lasts all of five seconds, and then Chase and Green head down to the car park for a journey to Southend in Green's Landy, the DI laying odds that this will be the breakthrough they need.

'Could be,' Chase says. Thinks: too good to be true.

The drive is the usual London slog through traffic, roadworks, and more red lights than is fair in one day. Lady Luck isn't smiling so far, and Chase crosses her fingers as they arrive in Southend. They need this.

Alison and Lizzie live on Hainault Avenue in a nonde-script little terrace house. There's a BMW Z3 outside that belongs to Alison. A tidy little front garden behind a low brick wall. The upstairs window frames look like they could do with some TLC, but downstairs, everything is freshly painted. It appears as if Alison and Lizzie were making a life for themselves. Just another couple strug-gling with day-to-day ups and downs. They probably had arguments, money worries, holiday plans, and long-term goals. They didn't expect one of them to get murdered.

A uniformed officer stands by the front door and in-spects their identification before letting them in. He tells them a forensic team has just left, and the place has been searched. Doesn't seem impressed by a couple of detec-tives from the SCU poking their noses into Essex Police business.

The front door clicks shut, and Chase and Green stand in the quiet of the hall, the only sound the hum of a refrig-erator from the kitchen. Chase knows Green is doing the same as she is: letting the atmosphere seep in. After a mi-nute, she breaks into the silence.

'What do you think?' she says.

'Not sure,' Green says. 'You?'

'Alison knew her killer,' Chase says. 'If Lizzie went miss-ing at the same time, then I'll double down on that.'

'Because?'

'This is nice and cosy. The two of them were inseparable. Loved each other deeply and never went anywhere alone. Most of the time, they stayed in, watched boxed sets, and held little dinner parties. They weren't the kind of young women who went out, got drunk or high, took risks, slept with strangers.'

'You're jumping to a hell of a lot of conclusions.'

'Am I?' Chase gestures to the living room and then up the stairs. 'Let's take a look around and see.'

Half an hour later, nothing she has seen goes against her intuition. Of course, the disappearance of the two women could be some kind of random forced abduction, but the more Chase gets a feel for Alison and Lizzie, the more she backs her hunch.

'Anything?' she asks Green when they reconvene in the snug little living room.

'Found these.' Green casts his hand over the coffee table, discarding half a dozen business cards. Black embossed with gold. An image of a stiletto boot to the right, *Double Trouble* on the left, a mobile number and a web address on the reverse. Green nods at the mantelpiece, where there's a picture of Alison and Lizzie. 'I checked the website and it's them.'

'They were *escorts*?' The news shakes Chase. She looks at the image on the mantelpiece. Alison and Lizzie are locked in an embrace. Smiling happy faces on a beach somewhere warm. Crystal blue water, white sand, palm trees. It's a world away from the miserable, sordid death Alison suffered, a world away from creepy punters, the ever-present threat of violence and everything else that comes with selling sex for a living. 'My hunch was wrong. Very wrong.'

'The message said, "When I kill a whore I stop a nightmare."' Green picks up one of the cards. 'Well, *Double Trouble* fit the bill even if they are high class and very expensive. The website says they do in-calls in central London and out-calls anywhere if the client is willing to pay travel expenses. There's no address for the London pad, just the phone number.'

'Did you try it?'

'Yes. It goes through to an answerphone. We'll need to get the logs for that phone and also liaise with the locals to get access to their personal phones and other devices,' Green says. 'We can pass the data to John and see what he can do. Then there's the interviews, door-to-doors, and all that.'

Chase groans. The Essex force won't want detectives from the SCU muscling in; that's clear from the reaction of the PC at the front door. And yet, every hour spent chasing them for information is an hour less to catch the killer.

'Where does Alison's mother live?' she asks.

Green pulls out his phone, and a moment later, he looks up and smiles.

'Upminster,' he says. 'Which last time I checked is not on Essex's patch, but across the border in Greater London.'

~ ~ ~

Upmarket Upminster, if there is such a thing, is where they find Helen Madden, Alison's mother. The house is a neo-Tudor new build bordered by fields and close to a church. Although only a mile from the M25 motorway and within the Greater London area, it's a world away from city living.

When the door opens to their ring of the bell, Helen Madden turns out to be *the* Helen Madden, star of stage and small screen. Chase remembers her from guest star parts in *Doctor Who*, *Endeavour*, and *Casualty,* and, more recently, she played a sultry matriarch in *Bridgerton*. It's all Chase can do to restrain herself from saying how much she admires Madden's work; Green looks as if he might ask her to autograph his notebook.

Inside, tea politely declined, the actor face Madden wore on the doorstep vanishes. This is a mother in deep distress at losing her daughter. Transpires, too, that she's only just

137

returned from identifying Alison's body. However carefully Alison's injuries had been disguised, and however tastefully the body had been posed, the experience hasn't done much for her composure.

Green, who Chase knows comes over the verbal equivalent of fingers and thumbs in these emotional situations, lets her do the talking, and that's probably for the best.

She begins by offering their profoundest condolences and heartfelt sympathies. Blah, blah, fucking, blah. Madden, being a professional actor, sees through the bullshit and waves Chase's words away like she is dismissing a butler in a period piece.

So Chase moves on and works through the usual questions before getting to the more delicate stuff.

'What did Alison do for a living?' she says.

'She's a sales rep for a pharmaceutical company,' Madden says. 'Was, I mean.'

'Well paid?'

'Absolutely. All those holidays abroad with Lizzie? Goodness knows I'd never have been able to afford to travel to the exotic destinations she's been to when I was her age.'

'And Lizzie?'

'Magazine publishing. *Cosmo* or something similar.'

Chase nods. Wonders how to broach the subject that Alison and Lizzie have been living a lie. That Helen Madden has been deceived by her daughter. Before she has a chance to say anything, Green steps in.

'Did you have a problem with Alison and Lizzie being together?' he says.

'Of course not.' Madden snaps.

'Sorry, but I had to ask. You'd be surprised. Even these days.'

'They were deeply in love, and that was enough for me.' Madden's brow creases. 'My only issue was they were so bound up with each other that they barely had time for anyone else. They were virtual recluses, but if they hadn't been so self-sufficient, perhaps this wouldn't have happened. Perhaps there'd have been someone else around to look out for them. As it is, they didn't need anyone but each other. And Max, of course.'

'Max?' Chase says. She glances at Green, and he makes the slightest shake of his head. 'Who's Max?'

'Max is their dog.' Madden follows Chase's gaze to Green and back. 'Haven't you...? In the horror of this whole thing, I'd...'

Tears then. Like Max is a symbol of the bond between Alison and Lizzie, and if he's gone too, the end of the world truly is nigh.

Chase thinks she might as well hit her when she's down, so she breaks the news about Alison and Lizzie's little business — the one which involves them hustling in latex and high heels and brandishing whips and handcuffs.

At first, Madden doesn't believe it, but after she's been shown the embossed card and told about the website, she comes round. There's a wry smile for a moment, a shake of the head, a finger wiping away a stray tear.

'Acting is prostituting yourself,' she says. 'You sign a contract and then do what a director tells you. Wear this, walk here, say that. Even sometimes, remove your clothing. Occasionally — rarely these days, but it still happens, I'm certain — an invitation to drop your knickers and lie on the casting couch. If you want to work, you go along with it. I would imagine Ali had a similarly pragmatic view to earning and perhaps being in a relationship with a woman meant she could perceive sex with men as purely transactional.' Another smile. 'I guess it explains the holidays, the house, the car. Silly me to have been taken in, but she played a role better than I ever could.'

Back outside, after Green has made tea and Chase has found a neighbour to come and stay with Madden, the actor's reaction is front and centre.

'She didn't seem much fazed,' Chase says as they walk to the Land Rover. 'Very matter of fact about the whole thing.'

'Maybe she had suspicions.' Green stops and turns back to the house. 'Or perhaps she's been on the casting couch herself.'

Whatever the truth — and Chase reckons Green is wide of the mark with his casting couch comment — Madden hadn't been able to come up with much to help them aside from the one helpful bit of information concerning Max, the dog.

'I didn't see any signs of a dog,' Green says. "No water bowl or bed or anything.'

'There were some pictures,' Chase says. 'But I thought it was a friend's pet.'

A call to the lead detective on the Essex force reveals that a bed with dog toys and food and water bowls have been taken away for analysis. Max had not been in the house, and the neighbours hadn't seen or heard him in the past week.

'So where the fuck is the little mutt?' Green says as they drive away and head back to central London.

Chase stares through the windscreen and turns her head to focus on a professional dog walker with half a dozen assorted canines on a tangle of leads coming down the lane towards them. Where the fuck, indeed? It's a good question because if they find Max, they might just find the killer.

# *Chapter 17*

As the message played, Detective Frank Locke had the sense to turn the phone's volume up and raise it to the overhead microphone Dr Hem used for dictation. He'd missed the first few words, but the rest had been recorded. When Hem finished the autopsy, Locke played the call back. Now, with the cadaver snug in a drawer in the morgue, they are drinking strong coffee in Hem's office, and the ME is having a hard time digesting what just happened.

'Beyond understanding,' Hem says. 'What sort of person kills someone and tries to justify the act by leaving a message like that? And why kill the girl and cut her arm off? Is that part of whatever game he's playing?'

'I have no idea,' Locke says, but he knows if it's possible, someone, somewhere, will do it. Torture, necrophilia, bestiality, rape, murder, incest, child abuse; the list is long, and humans are endlessly and sickeningly creative. A sensitive soul like Hem has some hard yards ahead of him. Perhaps he chose the wrong career. Perhaps he should have become a dentist dedicated to making crooked smiles straight. Or a plastic surgeon with the job of enhancing breasts, removing sagging skin and smoothing furrowed brows.

'And the message?' Hem stares down into his coffee for inspiration. 'What does it mean?'

'Not your problem, Doctor Hem,' Locke says. Thinks: fucking mine. He takes a sip of his coffee and then gets up. 'You'll be in touch when you've written your report, right?'

Hem barely nods as Locke leaves the room.

Back at the precinct, he gives the phone to Kerri Dunstan. When he explains where it was found, she mutters an *ah huh* but doesn't seem phased, as if it's every other day you find a phone rammed down someone's throat. She promises to get it to the DCI tech lab in Helena, where they'll trace the number, contact the carrier and get all the call logs.

Locke slips behind his desk and uploads the recording he made at the mortuary to his computer. Plays it a dozen times. The voice is distorted and fuzzy, as if it's been run through some sort of effect you might use for a hard rock guitar, and Locke can't make much from the accent or style of speech. He spends a few minutes transcribing the recording and then types several phrases from the message into a search engine. Nothing comes up. Zilch. Blank. He finds a website dealing in biblical quotes and searches that. Nada.

*I'm cleaning up the dirt. Removing the sullied.*

The five women killed in New Mexico were sex workers.

He kicks back and thinks for a moment. He could contact the local force, but this sort of thing would be way out of their league. Instead, he heads outside to the parking lot and calls an old colleague of his. When he'd been in Seattle, Jim Swanson had been Locke's go-to contact at the FBI. He'd first met him years back, soon after Swanson had left his tech job at Microsoft and moved to take control of data gathering with the FBI's Behavioural Analysis Unit-2 section. He was the brains behind setting up the Global Serial Crimes Database. The database recorded crimes worldwide using a standardised format, and an algorithm searched for patterns in offences that could be used on live cases to screen suspects. Swanson had left the Bureau and recently moved back to Seattle, but still did consultancy work and continued to help maintain the database. He had high-level clearance and the ability to get information that Locke couldn't. Few in law enforcement knew more about murder — specifically serial murder — than Swanson, and he'd helped Locke on previous cases.

'Jim,' he says when Swanson answers. 'Frank Locke.'

'Frank?' Swanson says. 'My old mate Frank Locke, the hero of the Emerald City force? Well I never.'

'I'm looking for some info on one Robert Kell,' Locke says. 'He's a possible for multiple homicides, at least one here in Montana, five or more in New Mexico, God knows how many elsewhere.'

'Robert Kell?' Swanson hesitates before spelling the name out. 'Doesn't ring a bell. Should he?'

'You tell me? You guys are supposed to be the experts in serial murder. I just wondered if he was on your radar for anything.'

'I'm no longer one of those guys,' Swanson says. 'I'm not up on the latest info on who's killing who and why.'

'You could find out though?'

'Sure I could, if you want.'

'It'd be appreciated.'

Swanson mutters something and says he'll call back within the hour.

Locke crosses the road to the little diner opposite the station. The Daily Grind serves the best local coffee and has patisserie to die for. Inside, there are truckers and local farmers. A couple of young mums with prams and bawling babies. Two traffic cops nod as he enters. Locke buys a skinny latte and a gooey brownie and sits on a bench outside, answering his phone when it rings.

It's Swanson. Somewhere noisy.

'Frank. Jim.'

A pause. More noise. Traffic?

'You get anything?' Locke says.

'This Robert Kell, what did he tell you he did?'

'He claims he's a photographer, but I'm not sure about that. He's just arrived in Montana, and I suspect he left New Mexico on the heat over the murders down there.'

'I'm going to talk off the record, Frank. I shouldn't be telling you this, and I'm in trouble if anyone finds out I've spoken to you, so play it sweet, right?'

'Sure thing. This conversation never happened.'

'Robert Kell was with us, with the emphasis very much on the *was*.'

There's a burst of vehicle noise, the blare of a horn. Locke isn't sure he's heard Swanson correctly. 'What did you say?'

'Kell was a federal agent but left the Bureau under inauspicious circumstances.'

'What sort of circumstances?'

'Harassment of a female agent.'

'Figures,' Locke says.

'In his defence, he claimed he had long-term mental problems exacerbated by the job, but that doesn't wash in these days of competing rights. Sure, we had a duty of care to him, but sexual harassment trumped that. So the long and the short of it was he was kicked out and lost his pension and other benefits.'

'When did this happen?'

'About nine months ago.'

'Can you send me all the details?'

'Sorry, Frank, no can do. The file is sealed and requires level-five clearance. That means permission either from the Director or Deputy Director.' There's a pause. More traffic noise. 'As it is, my search might raise a flag on the file. If anyone asks, I'll have to come clean and tell them I was just trying to help an old buddy with a routine enquiry, OK?'

'So what you told me was...?'

'Just common knowledge at the Bureau. When you first mentioned Kell's name, it threw me. I thought it might have been someone else, but it seems like your man is, or rather was, our man. Still, without going directly to the Director, you can forget about discovering anything else.'

'And what do you think my chances are if I do that?'

'Minimal. See, here's the thing. The file will likely identify the female agent, detail what went wrong with the complaints procedure and how Kell got away with the abuse. It's not information the Bureau will want out there. Sorry I couldn't do more, Frank. Look me up next time you're over this way.'

Swanson ends the call, and Locke stands up and returns to the precinct. He puts his coffee cup on his desk and finishes the brownie. He wipes his fingers on a tissue and stares at the computer monitor. Robert Kell is setting alarm bells ringing now, what with the possibility of sexual violence and intimidation and his mental health problems. He wonders how to proceed. He could confront Kell with the facts and ask him straight out what the hell is going on. But, on the other hand, maybe there's more to Kell than Swanson is letting on. The Feds may have Kell pegged for the New Mexico murders and haven't yet got enough to charge him. Locke wouldn't want to blow an op by putting his foot in it. Still, Kell is his only suspect. Feds or no Feds, if Kell killed the girl in the woods, then he's a legitimate target for Locke's investigation.

He hunches forward and logs into his computer. He brings up the phone message once again.

*Let's play a game.*

He taps the table, cursing. He'd meant to ask Swanson about the message and whether the FBI had any experience of such a thing. Also, any priors where items were left inside bodies, information on any end-of-days groups or

145

weird religious sects that might be relevant. He opens a new email and fires off a few questions. Sticks Swanson's address in and sends it.

He returns to the file on Kell and tries to get a handle on the new information. According to Swanson, Kell left the Bureau nine months ago. Tick. Trucked up in Otero County. Tick. Got a little too familiar with some local girls. Tick. Locke thinks about how that plays out. Perhaps Kell gives the girls his photographer spiel:

*Hi honey, would you like to make some money doing a few shots? Nothing lewd, just some classy glamour pics. Now, how about you loosen your top and show me a bit of cleavage? That's it. Good. A bit more. A bit more.*

It is easy to imagine Kell flashing a bit of money and his expensive camera to dupe a naive young woman into coming with him to some remote location.

Locke pulls up the details on the X-Mex murders to check exactly where the bodies were found, but before he does, he is thrown by something: the dates don't tally. The murders were committed in the months *before* Kell arrived in New Mexico, which doesn't compute. If Kell killed the women, why on earth would he move *to* the area?

Time, Locke thinks, to have another word with Mr Robert Kell. He stares across at the clock on the far side of the room. It's late now. Dark outside. Seeley Lake is an hour there and an hour back. An appointment with Kell is going to have to wait until tomorrow.

~ ~ ~

He's thinking about Kell as he stands in the queue for his first coffee of the day over at The Daily Grind and when he's back at his desk drinking the coffee and eating a triple chocolate chip cookie. He jots a few questions on a pad and calls Kell's cell.

Voicemail.

146

Locke leaves a message and then phones Kell's sister, Karen. When she answers, he asks her if Robert is there. No. Any idea where he is? No. When he'll be back? No.

'Karen, help me out here, would you?' Locke says, trying to sound conciliatory. 'I need to speak to Robert, and it'd be a lot easier if he'd simply cooperate rather than forcing me to haul him in here and do the good cop bad cop routine all over again.'

'He had business out of state.'

'*Out of state*?' Locke swears to himself. Kell had been released on the condition he wasn't to leave Montana. 'What business and where?'

'I don't know. He took the truck and said he'd be gone a day or two.' Karen pauses. 'Look, Mr Locke — Frank — Robert didn't kill that girl. He didn't kill anyone here or anywhere else. Believe me, if you're looking for a serial killer, you're after the wrong guy.'

'Well, he's doing an excellent job at making me think otherwise. If you speak to him before I do, tell him to call me.'

Locke hangs up, cross with himself for being curt with Karen Kell. He taps the desk, something bothering him.

*Believe me, if you're looking for a serial killer, you're after the wrong guy.*

'I never said anything about a serial killer, sweetheart,' he mutters. 'So why bring it up?'

He pulls up his notes for the interview on the screen in front of him and double-checks whether he mentioned anything about multiple homicide to Kell. Nope, not a word. So what's going on here? Did Robert Kell kill the women in New Mexico after all, despite not living there then? Odd that Karen would bring it up if he did; even odder that if Robert is a serial murderer, she'd stick by him.

147

'Reverse prejudice. You're just disappointed in the woman for not meeting your expectations.'

'What chick are you disappointed in?' There's a waft of menthol as Leo Sullivan slips up close, his jaws working the gum. 'And perhaps she could live up to my expectations instead.'

'Karen Kell.' Locke snaps, annoyed at being disturbed. 'Her brother's gone AWOL, yet she claims he's not the killer.'

'Well, she might just be right about that.' Sullivan waves a sheet of paper enticingly in front of Locke. 'Got an ID on the Doe. One Monica Granton, a good old-fashioned streetwalker, most recently working down in SLC. Kerri Dunstan got a partial off the remaining hand, and it matched Monica's prints. She'd been arrested two years ago on a drug rap.'

'So? Salt Lake is only, what, four hundred miles from here? Robert drives down there, picks her up, kills her, brings her back here to secrete the body in the forest for later fun and games.'

'Sounds plausible, Frank, but they've got someone they suspect of abducting and killing Monica in SLC. A boyfriend pimp who kept his charges needled up and happy until they got too lippy or too skanky. The boyfriend's in custody on multiple narcotics charges, but the detectives down there would love to hook him to a murder wrap as well. I'm going to send all the details through to them.' Sullivan pats Locke on the shoulder. 'The only bummer is it looks like I've lost my bet.'

'Fuck, this is my case, Leo. Kell's involved in the girl's death, I'm sure of it.'

'My winnings are vanishing into thin air, so I wish he was, but it's not looking that way. Sorry.'

And menthol breath is gone.

Crap. Locke smacks the desk, but Sullivan doesn't look back. No surprise; Sullivan is lazy and takes the easiest route. But the easiest route isn't always the right one, and in this case, Locke is convinced it's a blind alley. No pimp from Salt Lake would be imaginative or even sick enough to ram a phone down someone's throat. Nor would they leave a cryptic message. The whole point of a pimp bringing her up here into the wilderness would be to ensure she could never be found. But, despite the remote location of the body, the phone and the message suggest the killer wanted the opposite. Sullivan's hypothesis doesn't ring true. No pun intended.

Still, Sullivan's information is a downer, and without some new evidence, the whole case against Kell looks shaky.

Locke spends the rest of the morning in a sulk. He does some paperwork, bills for expenses, and gets lunch. A call comes in from a detective in Billings. Locke is part of an investigation into remote crack cook houses, and the team in Billings has made an arrest; by rights, Locke should drive down there and be in on the interview. But that means a day and a night away; right now, that's the last thing he wants to do. Still, he doesn't have much choice.

He grabs his things, intent on heading home to pack an overnight bag and driving to Billings. Sullivan glances at him as he passes his desk. Locke says nothing. Outside, he gets in his car and sits for a moment, calming himself. Kell is out of the picture; you're done with the Lewis and Clarke forest girl; focus on the next task.

Then his phone vibrates on the dash, buzzing like an angry hornet.

He stares at the cell, reluctant to touch it. Like all ringing phones have now been tainted. He shakes his head, picks it up and looks at the screen. Kerri Dunstan.

'Kerri?'

'Frank,' she says. 'Got something for you.'

'Shoot.'

'Those tyre marks in Lewis and Clarke are from a brand often fitted to Ford Bronco Raptors.'

'Sweet, Kerri, that's great. I'll start checking out local registrations.'

'Wait, there's more. I trawled local traffic violations and found an out-of-state Bronco pulled over just last week for a dodgy tail light somewhere near Superior.'

'We can't charge them for murder because they blew a bulb, Kerri.'

'Sure, but don't you want to know who the truck was registered to?'

'Yeah, I'd love to.' Dunstan's going the long way around like she usually does, but Locke humours her. 'Especially if you're going tell me Robert Kell has a second vehicle.'

'No, he doesn't. The truck had Washington plates and it's not Kell's.'

'OK, so who does it belong to?'

'Henrik Mattich.'

And with the mention of the name, Locke knows he won't be driving to Billings this afternoon.

~ ~ ~

Henrik Mattich. That's a name he's not heard for a while, but it doesn't mean Mattich hasn't been in his thoughts over the past few weeks, months, or years. Hell, ever since Mattich walked out of a courtroom on a sunny Seattle morning seven years ago, leaving Locke's boss, SPD Chief Lenny O'Reilly, to face the media and explain why the murders of several black women were now listed as unsolved. That was also the morning when Locke decided he was done with city policing and finally gave in to his wife's request to move east to Montana, the state of her birth.

150

There'd been seven of them. Seven dead black women between the ages of eighteen and forty-nine. The women were down-and-outs and sex workers, and this led to the general level of disinterest in the case. The media didn't care much, and neither did the police. The mayor did, for a while, but only long enough until more pressing matters took over. There weren't many votes in dead prostitutes — black or white.

After the third killing, Locke is passed the baton, picking up the case from half a dozen bored detectives who've made little progress. They have no suspects, various conflicting motives, and little interest in pursuing a dead-end investigation that won't enhance their careers one jot. Locke doesn't care about his career any more than he does about the mayor's votes or the lack of media coverage. These women are daughters snatched from their parents, and in two of the seven cases, they're mothers with young children. There is no scenario in Locke's mind where they deserve anything other than compassion and justice.

The mutilation, Locke thinks as he looks at the crime scene pictures of the first three bodies and, later, stares down at the pathetic sight of the subsequent victims lying in their entrails, is far from a random act from a crazed individual. There is a method to the madness. Butchery is a misplaced term for a butcher is a skilled artisan wielding a knife and a cleaver to make precise cuts. A butcher joints and slices and fillets. And, in this case, skins, for the bodies have been flayed and the skins taken. Disturbingly, according to the pathologist, it had happened while the victims were still conscious, drugged up on massive doses of fentanyl.

Locke compiles a profile that includes surgeons, butchers, vets, and undertakers. He consults a psychologist who posits that it is the combination of the victim's race and profession — black sex worker — which drives the killer to such extremes.

*Well, duh,* Locke thinks, but he runs with it.

A week later, he gets a lead that takes him fifty miles east to Kachess Lake where, close to Interstate 90 after it's twisted through Snoqualmie Pass, he finds an old mining shack repurposed as a vacation chalet. What's led him here is a macabre painting brought into SPD by a concerned citizen. The picture, an oil of some detail and not inconsiderable artistry, shows several human skins draped over furniture in a neat, tidy room. The room is gothic in style, but the skins look like Salvador Dali melting watches in the way they seem to slide across a chaise lounge, wrinkle over a wooden rocker, and bend over a marble washstand. And the skins are all black.

The painting comes from a thrift store, but there's a signature on the bottom right. It could have been painted anytime by anyone, but when Locke inspects the rear of the canvas, he spies a little *Michaels* sticker, complete with a website address. There are half a dozen of the art supply stores in the Seattle area and others close by. He gets a couple of juniors to do the on-the-ground legwork checking the stores while he investigates the name of the artist: Henrik Mattich.

Mattich immediately raises several red flags since he's got a conviction for assault against a black sex worker for which he served four years in Stafford Creek Corrections Center. In addition, a neighbour once reported him for a peeping tom offence, and he was at some point a member of a white power group. He is also a taxidermist.

Now, Locke doesn't have taxidermists on his list of suspect professions, but he figures they must be good at cutting up things, eviscerating, de-jointing. And at skinning.

Mattich, according to the few locals who reside in the area, uses the chalet as an artist's retreat and spends most of his time there. Despite the elevation of Snoqualmie Pass, I-90 is kept open all year, so as long as Mattich is prepared to walk to the chalet from the main road, visiting is never a problem.

It's fall when Locke turns up and finds what turns out to be little more than a hut at the end of a rough track. Rabbit pelts lie stretched on frames out front, and two dead cats are hanging from the bough of a nearby tree. Half a dozen crows have been nailed to a rickety gate, and on the porch, a full-size skin of a deer folds over an Adirondack chair.

Henrik Mattich answers the door, and never mind the red flags waving because now the whoop, whoop of sirens are going off inside Locke's head. Mattich is forty-some-thing with a scraggly beard and long, unwashed hair. He's wearing an old-fashioned preacher's suit like he's just walked off a Western movie set, and there's a silver cross on a chain swinging at his neck. When he smiles, there's gold in the teeth, and as he turns his head, Locke spies a swastika tattoo on the side of the man's neck. The inkwork looks homemade, something done during his spell in prison, perhaps.

Mattich speaks in monosyllables as he invites Locke in, but inside the shack, the main room is lined with book-shelves. Locke notes works by Nietzsche and Machiavelli. There's an old set of Encyclopaedia Britannica, dozens of atlases, and all the classics of American and English liter-ature. Unless Mattich simply likes the look of old books, there's more to him than meets the eye.

To one side, there's a workbench with instruments laid out. Scalpels and forceps, needles and catgut. Some critter that Locke can't identify, its innards slopping in a bowl, a curl of skin drawn back from the pale torso of exposed flesh. And then there are the paintings. Half a dozen are similar in style to the one from the thrift shop. Big sellers, Mattich says, and when Locke asks about the offensive content, he gets an *it's a free country or at least it used to be* answer.

When Locke leaves half an hour later, he's convinced Mattich is worth investigating further — suspect numero uno.

And yet...

After a month of work trying to tie Mattich to any of the crimes, all Locke gets is a blank sheet. He heads out to the cabin in the woods once more, and this time, he hikes in round the back, waits, and watches. Eventually, Mattich drives off in his old jalopy, and Locke enters the unlocked shack. He pokes around, looking for murder weapons, trophies or trinkets. The skins of the dead women.

Nothing.

He stands and peruses the bookshelves. Finds a leather-bound journal beside a copy of *The Lord of the Rings*. Hits the jackpot.

The journal contains a scrawl of Mattich's thoughts on women, on race, and on the downward trajectory of the human species. And descriptions of skinning techniques that might be applied to humans.

Locke puts the journal down as Mattich walks through the door.

'You killed those women,' Locke says, gesturing at the journal.

'Prove it,' Mattich taunts. He claims the journal is a fantasy. A story. That's why it's shelved next to Tolkien. 'Ha, ha, ha. Ha, bloody ha.'

The next moment, Locke is pinning Mattich to the floor, his fist pummelling the face. Punch. Punch. Punch. Punch.

'Tell. Me. The. Truth.'

Mattich slips into unconsciousness before saying a word. Locke cuffs him anyway and hefts him outside and into the back of his car. He shoves the journal on the front seat and drives Mattich back to Seattle, where he's charged with multiple counts of murder.

Then comes the bullshit from the lawyers.

A search without probable cause. Failure to properly arrest Mattich or to read him his rights. Assault by a police officer.

The case goes to trial anyway, but somehow Mattich gets top representation, paid for, Locke suspects, by some far-right-wing admirers. His lawyers try to prevent the journal from being entered into evidence, but a whizz kid on the prosecution team invokes an ancient precedent that Locke has never heard of, and the judge allows it.

*You're going down*, Locke mouths at Mattich the following day as he's led to the witness box.

Only he doesn't.

The jurors believe the crap about the journal being the jottings for a novel, they don't like Locke's attitude and appear to detest the Seattle police even more than violent men like Mattich. So the fucker walks. He returns to his shack, and the hotshot lawyers get him substantial damages. Locke hands in his badge, knowing he can't face this kind of crap any longer. Elsie persuades him they should move east, back to where she was born, back to where life is simpler and safer. But before he heads east, he pays Mattich a final visit.

There's a new vehicle out front, paid for with the wrongful arrest settlement money, but the shack is as squalid as ever. Mattich cowers as he opens the door to Locke. He starts moaning about police intimidation and his rights and being innocent, but Locke doesn't care. He pushes

155

Mattich back inside and slaps him on the face once, twice, three times, trying to provoke him. Mattich staggers back but doesn't react.

'I'll be watching,' Locke says. 'You won't know when or where, but I'll be there. You go within ten feet of any woman, and I'll fucking kill you, understand?'

Locke doesn't wait for an answer. He turns and walks out. Back in the city, Locke and his wife pack up their lives and drive east, crossing the state border into Montana. They build a house on the side of a mountain, and Locke signs on with the DCI. The Seattle streets fade to distant memories. There isn't a night, however, where Locke doesn't think of the dead women, of Mattich wielding his taxidermy tools, of the abomination he perpetrated. Not a night when he doesn't think of heading back to the shack, ramming a gun in Mattich's mouth, and blowing his brains out.

# *Chapter 18*

Word has got back to Assistant Commissioner Cooper that there's been a significant development in the Tortilla Flats' case, and the next day, he accosts Detective Senior Sergeant Sasaki, wanting to know about the phone and the message.

'Well, Takeo?' Cooper says. 'I've got a meeting with the Commissioner this afternoon, and I don't want to sit there with my trousers round my ankles and my dick hanging out.'

Sasaki shows him a transcript of the message, and after reading it, Cooper looks at him with contempt. Like it's all Sasaki's fault this unpleasantness has surfaced in the first place.

'Who is this fucker?' Cooper says. 'Some crazy God Bod? All that crap about whores. Just what does he expect us to do?'

Good question, Sasaki thinks. Sex work is legal in the Northern Territory. The police can no more remove women from the street and shut down brothels than they could arrest flower arrangers and close florists.

Cooper is off on one, and there is more than one reference to abbos and prossies in his lengthy spiel.

'Can you imagine if this gets out?' Cooper stares at Sasaki.

The rant continues until eventually Cooper waves Sasaki away. He heads back to his office and beckons Malroony in.

'They've given him a name,' she says as she dumps a newspaper on his desk. 'The Tortilla Torturer. TT for short.'

'That's all we need,' Sasaki says. He moves the paper to reveal a transcript of the message. 'I've listened to it again.'

In truth, he's listened to the message dozens of times. There's plenty to suggest the current murder is related to the BUK killings: the mention of *thirty-three years,* as well as the severed arm and the victim's profile. However, the Black Ute Killer is in prison, which is a pretty good alibi in Sasaki's mind. Back in the day, there were rumours the BUK had an accomplice, but the DNA evidence reviewed more recently was inconclusive.

'So, a copycat?' Malroony says after Sasaki has explained his thinking. 'But why?'

Sasaki doesn't know, but however unlikely, it feels personal and targeted at him, in which case there has to be some link back to the original killings.

'Kirsty Downland was a sex worker,' Sasaki says. 'As were the three women killed by the BUK. We also have the severed arm pointing and the mutilation of the genitals. The phone and the message are new, but perhaps our assailant is simply moving with the times and expanding on the stone with the word *whore* scratched on it found in the throats of the victims. The three slashes across Kirsty's chest, I guess, hint at the three killings.'

'And in the original case, the arms pointed to the location of the previous victim?'

'Yes, although my father didn't work that out until the final murder.' Sasaki recalls the night Endo broke down in tears. 'He beat himself up about that. Still does, I reckon.'

If he can remember, Sasaki thinks.

'But, sir,' Malroony says. 'That means if the new killer follows the MO of the BUK, there's already another body out there. Surely we can search for it?'

'I don't think it's so simple. First, we might know the rough direction where the body is, but it could be anywhere along the line. The arm pointed to the northeast, which means we've got two hundred and fifty kilometres of mostly wilderness before the line reaches the sea. It will take a massive search operation to cover the area. And if there is a second victim, then they've already gone missing and, likely, they're another sex worker, another woman whose disappearance won't be noticed.'

Sasaki begins to realise he's been reliving his father's case instead of concentrating on this one, hooked on the idea that he, Sasaki junior, would save lives where Endo failed. But if the next victim is already dead, then his efforts are futile.

'When was Kirsty Downland last seen alive?' he says.

Malroony glances at a calendar on the wall. 'Twelve days ago is the final confirmed sighting, but I wouldn't place too much store on that since she was always wandering off.'

Sasaki drums his fingers on the desk. He swallows and takes a moment to glance sideways at the picture of his father hanging on the wall. If he can stop the killer, he may have a chance to emulate Endo Sasaki. But if he can't...

'We need to pull this together quickly,' he says. 'If number two is already dead, then we must stop the killer before he gets to number three.'

'Action points then, right?' Malroony smiles at him. Picks up a notepad and a pen.

'Yes.'

'One?'

'Helicopters. Which models match the imprints at Tortilla Flats, registration and owners, charter and hiring if appropriate. There are a dozen or more at Darwin airport, and some down at Sandford airstrip used for wildlife

159

tours. That's just the aircraft close at hand. If we factor in the range and expand a circle from Tortilla Flats, we'll have a rough idea of how far afield to look. Officers can begin checking the helicopters and alibis at once.'

'OK. Two?'

'Missing persons, specifically sex workers, but also tourists and anyone else who might not be immediately missed.'

Sasaki goes through several other points, and Malroony comes up with a few herself. Then Sasaki gets to where he knew he was going to end up all along.

'The Black Ute Killer,' he says, resisting another glance at the picture of his father. 'In other words, Derek Pearce.'

'What about him?'

'AC Cooper isn't going to like it, but we need to visit Pearce and see if he can shed any light on the murder at Tortilla Flats.'

'Do you think he'll cooperate?'

'From what I've read, he's an egoist. He'll be happy to talk if only to relieve the boredom. The severed arm and the fact the victim was a sex worker link the case to him. Whether he can provide any useful information is another matter.'

'I wasn't talking about Pearce,' Malroony says, a grin on her face. 'I meant the AC.'

Sasaki laughs. 'Cooper is another matter altogether.'

~ ~ ~

The next day, the newspapers and broadcast media, having concluded there must be some link to the Black Ute Killer, abandon the Tortilla Torturer moniker for the more sequel-friendly BUK2 acronym. The only upside is that now it's out in the open, AC Cooper has little option other than to agree to Sasaki's suggestion that a visit to Derek Pearce, the original BUK, might be in order. Even then, in a neat about turn, he berates Sasaki for his lack of foresight.

'We should have been on this earlier,' Cooper says. 'Stayed one step ahead of those media rats by interviewing Pearce from the get-go.'

'Yes, sir,' Sasaki says through gritted teeth.

It takes a day to arrange the visit, and then it's an early start for Sasaki and Malroony so they can catch the six AM scheduled flight to Alice Springs. Malroony dozes most of the way, but Sasaki stays awake, thinking of Derek Pearce, the three girls he killed, and, inevitably, of Endo Sasaki, hero cop of Darwin, the Northern Territory, and just about the whole of bloody Oz.

Two hours later, the Qantas 737 is pushing into shadow. Bright sun one moment and then in the clouds as the pilot scrubs height and guides the plane down. The aircraft slips beneath the murk and lines up for the final approach to Alice Springs.

With no baggage, they're off the plane and through the terminal in minutes. Like the airport, Alice Springs Correctional Centre is south of the city but out to the west. They take a taxi and drive through the flat countryside on the A87. Low scrub and red soil. Not much to see. A road sign says Adelaide is 1519 kilometres away, Uluru National Park a mere 441. Their starting point early this morning, Darwin, is a fifteen-hour drive due north. It's hard to imagine a better spot for holding one of Australia's most notorious murderers in splendid isolation.

The taxi driver recognises Sasaki and wants to talk.

'Seen you on the TV, mate,' he says. 'About the girl at Tortilla Flats. That's why you're here?'

'No comment,' mutters Sasaki.

'Sure, mate, I understand.' The driver raises a hand and taps his nose with a finger. 'Hush, hush, right? Well, I've got a length of rope in the boot you can take into Mr Pearce if you want. Call it a present from Mr and Mrs Public Opinion. Tell him he can do us all a fucking favour. Save the honest taxpayer a fortune.'

The journey is mercifully short, and ten minutes after leaving the airport, they swing off the highway and take an access road to the prison. A few low buildings pass on either side, and they pull into a car park. Sasaki asks the driver to wait, and they get out and walk to the reception building. A guard behind a screen calls out their names as they push through the doors.

'Been expecting you,' he says, holding up a printout. 'Not every day we get a visit from royalty.' He gives a wink. 'And not every day we have to wheel out our most infamous prisoner and prepare him for an interview.'

'Sorry for the inconvenience,' Sasaki says. 'I'm afraid trying to do it online wasn't going to cut it.'

'No worries. It gives us a chance to get hands-on with Mr Pearce. A complete cell takedown and cleanout. Leg irons and cuffs for our guest. A full and very intimate body search. He loves it and so do we.'

Sasaki flinches. He's no softy, but the Correctional Service has come in for criticism in recent years. Malroony plainly doesn't share his concerns.

'Listen, boss,' she says as they wait for an escort. 'The stuff with juveniles and all was wrong. The service had a worrying culture and some bad apples that needed chucking out. But Pearce? Deserves all he gets, and if that means a flashlight shoved up his arse, then so much the better.'

'Pearce has been inside for nearly thirty-three years,' Sasaki says. 'When does that become long enough?'

'For him, never.' Malroony makes a face. 'He raped, killed and dismembered three women, remember? They didn't get a chance to live their lives, so neither should he.'

Sasaki nods. He understands the sentiment, yet there's a nagging sense that hiding Pearce out here doesn't do much for anyone.

A second guard takes them through a series of locked doors and across an outdoor area. They're inside the prison proper now, a huge compound surrounded by tall wire fences, and the only way in or out is the entrance block they've come through. The guard shows them to another unit. More doors and then a corridor. Two further guards stand outside a door with a large Perspex panel.

'He's in here,' their escort says. 'Don't approach the prisoner, don't pass anything to him or receive anything from him, understood?'

'Of course not,' Sasaki says.

A pass key on the door buzzes the lock open, and the escort shows them in. Turns and leaves. The door thuds shut.

Pearce sits with his back to them, his chair pushed up to a small table, legs in chains connected to the base of the chair. Grey hair in a ponytail, head bent forward as if he's dozing. He's in his fifties but scrawny and lean. It's like he works out but doesn't get enough to eat.

Sasaki and Malroony skirt the table to the two chairs on the other side. Pearce raises his head. Takes a second glance at Sasaki as he sits down.

'Knew they'd be sending someone. Didn't think it would be you.'

'Takeo Sasaki,' Sasaki says. 'And Linda Malroony.'

'Delighted to meet you.' Pearce smacks his lips together. Stares at Malroony. 'Especially you. The female guards here are a bit on the rough side, if you know what I mean.'

'Just so we don't get off on the wrong foot,' Malroony says. 'You can fuck right off.'

Sasaki gestures at Malroony to sit. Confrontation isn't what he wants.

'Mr Pearce—'

'Derek or Dezza or Dez,' Pearce says. 'All I hear from the guards is Mr Pearce do this, Mr Pearce do that. Give me a break.'

'Derek—'

'Endo's kid, right?' Pearce tuts to himself. 'Incredible. All these years and he's still coming after me. It's like a bad dream repeating itself. I guess I'll never be rid of him.'

'My father is no longer a cop. He retired a while ago.'

'Yeah, I heard that. Good luck to him. Retiring isn't something I'll ever get to do because I've got a non-parole period of fifty years. I'm going to die in this place, and I guess that suits some, but it sure as hell doesn't suit me.'

'Mr P...' Malroony. Impatient. 'Derek. We're here about—'

'The Tortilla girl.' Pearce grins. Tosses his head so his ponytail flicks up and down. 'I know why you're here.'

'I don't know what you've heard,' Malroony says. 'But there are similarities between the killing out at Tortilla Flats and what you did to your victims.'

'I only know what I saw on ABC News before a kindly prison officer changed the channel to save my blushes. So you'll have to tell me exactly what's been done to the Tortilla girl and how it relates to what I did to my victims.' Pearce smiles. 'I guess you'll need to explain the grisly details bit by bit, entrail by entrail, right?'

'Cut it out, Derek,' Sasaki says. Pearce is getting a thrill from this, and he wonders if bringing Malroony along was such a good idea because the presence of a woman can only excite him further. 'I'll explain what happened, but only enough so you can help us.'

'Why would I even bother then?'

'You don't have a conscience? A slice of remorse? A desire to do something good in your life?'

'Assuming there isn't a God or a heaven or a hell, then what difference will it make?'

Silence. Sasaki hasn't got an answer because it's unlikely Pearce is getting time off for good behaviour.

'It's a puzzle,' Malroony says. 'And we aren't clever enough to solve it. You just might be.'

'An intriguing admission.' Pearce nods. 'Then again, you're clever enough to come here, right?'

Sasaki says nothing, but it's a good line Malroony is taking. Pearce has an ego, and getting him to show off how bright he is to the stupid dumb cops might just work. Sasaki tells Malroony to show Pearce the pictures they've brought. She slides the brown envelope onto the table and extracts the photographs. Spreads them in front of Pearce.

'You placed a stone engraved with the word "whore" in your victims' throats; this woman had a phone rammed into her, a message on the phone about "killing whores". You cut the arms off the bodies and pointed them at the previous victims. The line between the body and the arm was an exact bearing. Here we have what appears to be a similar set-up.'

'I assume you read the trial transcripts?' Pearce shakes his head. 'I never cut the arms off anyone. I certainly didn't point out the bodies of the victims to help the police catch me.'

'Your defence was based on the stupidity of the act, that it was something you'd never have done, but DNA tests proved you did kill the three women. Are you still claiming you didn't arrange the arms?'

'I'm not claiming anything, it's fact.' Pearce raises his shoulders a little. 'I couldn't care less whether you believe me or not.'

Sasaki wonders about Pearce's state of mind and why he continues to play games. Perhaps it's simply the chance to have control over something.

'The pictures.' Sasaki points to the photographs.

'This stuff about the arm wasn't in the news.' Pearce is eager. Agitated. Moving on his seat, the leg irons rattling. His tongue flicks out like a snake tasting the air, and he stares down and takes in the images. 'Have you got a second body?'

'Your accomplice arranged the arms, right?' Sasaki ignores Pearce's question. 'If you say you didn't, then he must have. For some reason, he went back to the scene.'

'There was no accomplice. That theory was flogged to death by the media but never proved. If there was, why didn't I shop him for a reduced sentence?'

'I don't know, but humour me.' Sasaki points at the spread of photographs. 'Who else but your accomplice would know how to commit exactly the same crime?'

'A cop,' Pearce says, looking up and grinning. 'There's a lot of bad apples in the Darwin force, you know that.'

'True, but hardly anyone knew the full details. I still think an accomplice is the most likely explanation.'

'Let's say, hypothetically, I did have an accomplice. Why would he start killing after all these years? Doesn't make sense. I think you're pissing against the wrong tree, mate.'

But Pearce cocks his head, and Sasaki sees a tiny spark of something on the man's face. It's like the photographs have triggered some memory and raised a worry that wasn't there a moment ago.

'All I'm asking for is a name,' Sasaki says. 'Give me that, and you'll get the credit for preventing another murder.'

'What about my sentence?' Pearce smiles. 'You'd get me time off for good behaviour, would you? Or perhaps a nice big TV for my cell, a tight-bod hooker once a week, and a dozen cans of beer delivered with a Domino's on a Saturday evening? I could go for that.'

Sasaki doesn't answer. There's a zero per cent chance Pearce will ever be freed. Some home comforts might be possible, but certainly not what he's asking for.

'Thought not.' Pearce returns his attention to the map. 'Anyway, you might be too late. There could already be another body out there.'

'You think so?'

'The arm suggests so. I assume you've been looking?'

'We've…' Sasaki hesitates.

'No,' Malroony says. 'The arm points northeast, towards or across the Kakudu National Park, hitting the South Alligator River near the mouth. There's a lot of territory to cover, and we have no idea if the body is two kilometres away or two hundred.'

'We need to narrow it down,' Sasaki says. 'We need a clue.'

'You could fly along the bearing.' Pearce raises a hand and flattens his palm. Glides it over the table. 'You might spot the dump site.'

'Or we might not.' Sasaki notes the casual way Pearce talks about the crime scene with zero empathy for the victim. 'That's why we need a pointer from you.'

' A pointer? Very droll. Thirty-three years ago, your dad was the bright spark in the heap of dung that was Darwin PD. He worked it out.'

'We're talking about now, Derek. Can *you* work *this one* out?'

Pearce looks down at the photos again. Says nothing for a good minute before raising his head. 'You got a map?'

Sasaki reaches for his phone and then realises he handed it in at reception. Curses.

'I'll go.' Malroony stands and goes to the door. She raps on the Perspex and a prison officer opens up.

Five minutes later, someone has pulled a large map from the wall of one of the prisoner classrooms. Malroony brings it in and lays it on the table, the southern edge towards Pearce.

'Where exactly was the body found at Tortilla Flats?' Pearce says, bending his head over the map.

Sasaki finds the Adelaide River and points at the map. 'There.'

'And the arm was where?'

'Northeast about four hundred metres.'

'So pointing to wilderness, mostly.' Pearce moves his hand over the map and traces a line with his finger to the northeast. 'Even though you're guessing she'll be on this line, it'll be hard to find anything unless you know exactly where to look.'

'We're not even sure there's been another killing yet. That's why we're here.'

'And there's the rub.' Pearce leans back. 'You want me to speculate what this killer is up to, give you everything I've got. But for what?'

'As I said before, to do some good. And if that isn't enough, you could help us simply for the intellectual stimulation.'

'I can read a book for that.'

Pearce crosses his arms, and Sasaki senses he isn't going to cooperate. They've flown down here for nothing, and when they return empty-handed, Cooper will be livid.

'So you're not going to help us?'

'I don't see what's in it for me. Earning a few Brownie points from you guys doesn't make anything change. To be honest, I think I'm done.'

Pearce shifts in the chair and turns his head towards the door, trying to catch the eye of one of the guards through the window.

'What about a day trip?' Malroony says. 'As per your suggestion, we fly down the bearing in a small aircraft or helicopter. You come with us, and we'll see what we can spot from the air.'

Sasaki almost falls off his chair. It's not within his power or remit to grant Pearce even a minute outside the prison wire. He glares at Malroony as Pearce turns back to face them with a broad smile.

'You're on,' Pearce says.

# Chapter 19

*The first night after it's all done, the Architect sleeps like the proverbial baby. Twelve hours solid. Birds joyous with spring wake him, and he throws back the drapes to see sun and blue skies. His headache has gone too, just a dull throb, which he guesses is simply a memory of the pain he's endured these long months.*

*It's worked, he thinks. All the planning, all the effort, and all the risks have been worthwhile. His mother is no more, her evil grip around his heart loosened. He is FREE! Sure, there is much more to be done to keep her at bay, but this is the first step on the long road back to normality.*

*The Architect showers and dresses and almost skips out the front door. He takes a long walk, ending at a diner where he orders breakfast. He doesn't deny himself anything. He sits at an outside table where it's a little chilly, but the spring air is fresh and invigorating. The meal comes, and he relishes every morsel. He drinks a coffee, followed by another. Reads a newspaper and feels the sun warm his face. He spends a good hour at the diner, and when he leaves, there's a generous tip under his coffee cup.*

*YES! He is FREE! Life is GOOD!*

*In truth, the Architect is surprised it was so easy. Not the practicalities — working everything out and executing the plan took every last piece of his guile and cunning — no, he's surprised this was all it took to banish the witch. But then, that's the type of woman she was — a giver-upper. Not like him.*

*Of course, there are still threads to tie up down under, so he hurries home to finalise the details, ticking off items with a pencil on an A4 pad. Then he kicks back and thinks about the last few months. Thinks about the stress. The sleepless nights. The doctor was concerned about his blood pressure and weight fluctuation, but that's history. A corner has been turned, and things will be very different from here on in. The only sad thing is that his utter brilliance will go forever unknown. He consoles himself that perhaps someday in the future, some clever detective — cleverer than poor Frank Locke, the Jap cop, and the dozy Brits — might work it out.*

*And then, suddenly feeling quite drained, he leans back in his armchair and falls asleep...*

*... waking in his bed, the bedclothes thrown to the floor, his mother astride him, naked and putrid, him inside his mother as she is rocking and riding, riding, and laughing.*

And rolling, my son. Always rolling, right? Rolling to the horizon. You and me rolling, rolling, rolling. Together forever. Happy ever after. Just—

*NO! NO! NO!*

~ ~ ~

*Hours later, the Architect wakes from one of the most fitful nights he's ever had. He's drenched in sweat, the bed sheets a tangle, red weals on his chest where he clawed at himself to try to end the visions. He sits on the edge of the bed. Puts his head in his hands and sobs, crying tears until there's no more to give. He can't carry on like this. It's time to find a way out, head for the exit, and end it once and for all.*

*He reaches out to the bedside cabinet and slides a drawer open. Inside is a standard-issue Glock 19M. It's a 9mm, 15 rounds in the clip, but he only needs one.*

*He pulls the gun out, the heft in his hand comforting. He closes the drawer and looks at the pile of clothes on the floor. He wonders if he should make the bed or perhaps tidy the house a little. He doesn't want to be found living in a tip, the word out on the street that he was some nutter.*

*But no, let them think what they like.*

*The Architect raises the gun and places the barrel against his right temple. Slips his forefinger onto the trigger. Starts to squeeze.*

Baby, no, don't do it! Stay with mommy. I can make it better.

*He twists to the right and swings the gun towards the bedroom door, where a shadow stands motionless. He fires a shot and another. Rises from the bed and runs to the doorway. Fires blindly into the corridor. Bang, bang, bang. He turns and points the gun at the bed, now convinced the lump under the duvet must be her. He looses another shot, tufts of feathers exploding into the air. Then he lurches to the right and aims at the open door in case she's hiding behind it. Three rounds splinter into the woodwork. He wrenches the door back and fires into the space. Bang, bang, bang. And again, bang. He rushes to the built-in wardrobe and slides the door open, firing in rapid succession, the rounds shredding a row of his best suits. If she's in there, she's dead, so he steps back to the bed and sits on the mattress, and without thinking any further, he slams the gun under his chin and squeezes the trigger.*

*Click.*

*If he hadn't traded his G17 a few years ago for the lighter, more compact 19, he'd already be dead. But the G19M has two fewer rounds than the 17, so he's not.*

*He laughs, giddy on adrenalin, but as his heart slows, a strange calmness comes over him.*

'Nothing's fucking working,' the Architect says.

*The knowledge that he couldn't kill himself and that the plan to get rid of his mother didn't work — perhaps can never work — is almost liberating. He realises that he's done with clever ruses and silly games. He's done with self-pity. He might never be rid of the hauntings and the nightmares, but that doesn't mean he can't continue what he's started. There can still be a purpose to his life, a reason to go on, because while the streets are littered with filth and abomination, with women degrading themselves for money, with women like his mother, his work isn't done.*

*He grabs the pad he used for planning and rips off the top pages. Begins to scribble down random thoughts. There's so much to think about now. How many more should die? Where? In what manner? He will pay homage to what happened in spades, a fitting tribute, a lasting legacy. And, of course, there's still the Black Ute Killer to think about. Derek Pearce will soon be free, and then the Architect and the BUK will be reunited. The Architect smiles to himself. He never envisaged that he'd see Derek again, but now he realises it must have been predestined, a conjunction of cosmic importance. This will be a new beginning for both of them and once they're together, they'll go down in history as the greatest serial-killer pairing of all time.*

*The Architect recalls that movie by Tarantino. The guys with the sharp suits and bags of attitude. Reservoir Dogs, right? He smiles to himself. Grins. Laughs. Cackles. He is beyond help now. As demented as his demon mother, as twisted as Derek Pearce.*

*'Let's go to work,' he says.*

# Chapter 20

Max doesn't turn up at the local dog shelter, and there's no call from Lizzie Thomkin. It's gone dog and gone girl. But, on Tuesday afternoon, Stafford beckons Chase and Green over to his workstation.

'The message,' he says. 'Been working on it.'

Chase knows Stafford's been working on it. Hour after hour, he's been sitting there with his headphones on, playing the recording over and over.

'And you've got something?' Green says. 'About fffing time.'

'Listen,' Stafford says.

The voice is muffled, almost non-existent, and Chase can't make out the words at all now. Whatever Stafford has done, it's turned the whole thing into unintelligible gibberish.

'Huh?' Green says. 'That's bloody useless, JJ. Worse than ever.'

'Wait.' Stafford holds a hand up and then points at a window on the screen where spikes of audio slide from right to left. 'Here.'

There's a brief burst of static followed by a strange musical-tweeting-pinging-singsong sound.

'And?' Green looks puzzled.

'I think the whistling sound is a bird,' Stafford says. 'A bearded reedling, to be precise.'

'A *what*?'

'Otherwise known as a bearded tit. A reed dweller that's quite rare in the UK. A few hundred breeding pairs at most. It must have been singing in the background when the call was made. What's more, in the process of isolating the bird sounds, I discovered that the call is actually a recording played into the phone.'

'Hey?' Green says. 'Are you certain?'

'Ninety per cent. Someone dialled the number of the phone inside the girl and then played back a prerecorded message.'

'Why?' Chase asks.

'Perhaps they were nervous; by prerecording the message, they made sure to get it right when they called. Another possibility could be that whoever made the call is not the same person as the voice in the message. In any event, it serves to obfuscate the whole thing further. Still, the reedling gives us a rough geographical fix as to where the call was made.

'Enlighten us then,' Chase says.

'South Coast around Hampshire, Norfolk, Suffolk, outer Thames Estuary, Romney Marsh, the Somerset Levels. As its name suggests, places with reed beds.'

'It's a stretch,' Green says. 'But if that is all you've got, I guess we've got to go with it.'

'All I've got?' Stafford sighs. 'Do you know how many blooming bird calls I've listened to narrow it down to this one?'

'We can cross reference it,' Chase says, keen to stop the bickering. 'Use one of your geolocation grids that worked so well with Grainger.'

'You can't cross reference without something to cross reference with, and we don't have anything else yet.' Stafford pointedly stares at Green.

'Then let's focus on the *yet* and try to come up with something, shall we?'

~ ~ ~

The *try to come up with something* doesn't happen fast. In fact, it doesn't happen at all that day, and by close of play, they're no better off.

'We could investigate all bearded reedling sites,' Stafford suggests. 'Even without anything to cross-reference the locations, we might get lucky.'

'Us and whose army?' Green says. 'Boyle might give us a couple of extra bods, but you're talking about hundreds of places, right?'

Stafford nods, looking sheepish, and Chase reckons he regrets bringing up the bird in the first place. They've wasted hours going down a blind alley, and his suggestion they might get lucky shows how desperate the situation is because he doesn't usually do lucky. Boyle, she imagines, will not be happy.

And then something *does* turn up. DC Nikki Ghosh answers a phone and stands and shouts across the room to where Chase and Green are bent over a map of London. It's not Lizzie, not the missing dog, Max, nor anything to do with the stupid bearded reedling.

'We've found Alison Madden's arm,' Ghosh says.

Chase wheels round. 'Where?'

'Top of those posh flats at Kew Bridge. A lift engineer performing maintenance up on the roof spotted it.'

'Let's go,' Chase says.

It takes thirty minutes to barge through the traffic to Kew Bridge, where they pull up outside a complex of apartment buildings. There's subterranean parking, a ground-level bar, two restaurants, and various businesses, and above them, staggered balconies rise to rooftop terraces. There are views over the river and to the botanical gardens beyond. Views, too, across to Brentford Ait, the island where they found Alison.

'You're looking to move, aren't you?' Chase says to Green. 'This would be ideal.'

'Yeah,' Green says. 'Just need to find a rich girlfriend to sub me the money.'

They get out, and Green waves his ID at a uniformed officer who comes across.

'Inside?' Green says.

'Stairs to the roof in the lobby,' the officer says. 'For obvious reasons, the lift is out of order.'

Chase cranes her neck and gazes skywards, counting floors as she does.

'Seven,' she says. 'Might want to pre-empt any issues and call an ambulance for my colleague.'

'Seriously?' the officer says.

'Yes,' Green says. 'And a chiropodist too. While I might be a bit unfit, Jess has shoe problems.'

They leave the bemused officer at the curbside and head for the lobby. Inside, there's a reception desk with a concierge. The man gives them a harsh stare until Green flashes his ID again and makes for the stairs. Round and round they go, footsteps echoing in the well, Green's breathing increasingly laboured. They stop just before the top, and Chase peers over the balustrade, getting vertigo as she looks down.

'The concierge probably isn't twenty-four-seven, but still, choosing this place feels risky.' She turns back to Green. 'Building staff, other residents, CCTV. Begs the question, why take the chance of getting caught?'

'Right.' Green stands with his hands on his hips, sucking air, red in the face. 'Well, we can certainly rule out smokers over forty carrying a few extra pounds.'

'I thought you'd given up the fags?'

'I've given up giving up more like.'

Chase nods. Wonders when Green last had a medical.

It's only one more flight to the roof, and Green appears to get his second wind as he sprints up ahead of Chase. When she arrives at the top, she finds him arguing with a man wearing a fluorescent vest. A uniformed officer stands just inside the door to the roof, trying to look disinterested.

'The fuck we will,' Green says.

'I'm in charge of building maintenance, and there are health and safety regulations,' the man says, pointing at a pile of rope, carabineers, and harnesses. 'Anyone on the roof has to wear a harness and clip onto the fall arrest system.'

'What about the railings?'

'They're decorative and might not provide sufficient support in an accident.'

Green turns to the police officer. 'Where's the arm?'

'On top of the central lift tower.' The officer points to a shed-like structure in the middle of the roof. It's the height of a man with louvred panels on all four sides. A galvanised metal ladder snakes up one corner. 'You have to climb up the ladder.'

Green nods and pushes past the health and safety guy. Chase follows but turns to the man.

'He's survived a fight with the Cornish Ripper, a twenty-a-day habit and the climb up here,' she says. 'Anything else isn't worth bothering with.'

Chase catches up with Green as he reaches the lift tower.

'Why?' Green says.

'Why cut the arm off or why here?' Chase says.

'Either. Both.'

'Let's see.' Chase pulls a pair of latex gloves from a pocket and moves to the ladder. It's only a couple of metres high, but she takes it slow. Pointless giving the Health and Safety guy the satisfaction of a *told you so.*

She hauls herself over and onto the flat roof area and bobs down on her haunches. The arm lies to one side of the roof, three fingers bent, one finger outstretched. The flesh is pale and white, curling and torn on the upper section of the arm, where a grey dolphin tail is just visible.

'It's Alison's,' Chase says as Green's head appears at the top of the ladder. 'Definitely.'

'Christ.' Green says as he scrambles up and kneels beside Chase. 'What a fucking horror show.'

'She's... it's pointing.' Chase raises her head and squints out across London. 'But to where?'

'You think he did that deliberately?'

'Yes, I reckon.' Chase shuffles closer, noting a mark on the concrete next to the finger. 'There's a black line. A marker pen or something.'

'Like he drew on the ground so as to know exactly where to place the arm?'

Chase nods and stands unsteady on her feet in the buffeting wind. She's got a better view to the northeast now, but nothing jumps up shouting *here, here, here*.

'What's in that direction?' Green says.

'Close there's Shepherd's Bush, Islington, then Romford, then farther away there's the M25, Chelmsford, Colchester, Ipswich. I mean, how far do you want to go?'

'Ipswich must be fifty miles away. More maybe. And beyond that, it's the sea. Why would the killer be pointing there?'

'I'm not saying he is, just telling you what lies over there.'

'Doesn't make any sense.'

'He's a psychopath, Nick. Any attempt at making sense disappeared when he sliced poor Alison open and stuffed a mobile phone in her abdomen.'

'Point taken.' Green stands and follows Chase's gaze. 'But there must be a reason.'

'The body was just over there.' Chase turns one hundred and eighty degrees. They're high above the river, and Brentford Ait lies close by. 'What do you reckon, three or four hundred metres to where she was found?'

'Yeah.' Green swings round. 'You think there's some relationship?'

'He put a lot of effort into placing the body where he did and even more effort into putting the arm up here.'

'You just said he was a psychopath, and sense was out the window.'

'Changed my mind. It's a woman's prerogative.' Chase rotates once more, looking out to the northeast across London. 'This sort of thing is right up Rubberman's street, forgive the pun.'

'Hey?'

'If we can get John all the right data — the direction the arm is pointing, the time it was placed here, the height of the building, that sort of thing — I'm sure he'll be able to come up with some sort of hypothesis as to what exactly is going here. Whether it makes sense or not, who knows?'

'Got to be a better shot than the bloody bearded reedling.' Green pauses and then casts a glance at Chase. 'Unless...'

Chase makes the connection at the same time. She raises her arm and points, mimicking the pathetic shape of the severed limb.

'The outer Thames Estuary, Essex, and Suffolk all lie in that direction,' she says. 'Prime wetland habitat for the reedling, right?'

Green swivels, his gaze following her outstretched finger. He pats Chase on the back.

'John Stafford lucks out again,' he says, then turns to the ladder, shaking his head. 'Fucking geometry.'

# *Chapter 21*

Locke calls Jim Swanson and asks about Henrik Mattich and the possibility he's started killing again.

'Mattich has been in Montana recently,' Locke says. 'Did you know that?'

'No.' Swanson is silent for a moment. 'But it's only a couple of hundred miles from his chalet to the state line, and no law says he has to stay in Washington.'

'Tell me about it,' Locke says. 'But what if he's up to his old tricks again, only this time he's abandoned his prejudices and is targeting white girls?'

'Bullshit, Frank. Your case doesn't fit his MO.'

'Thanks for the confidence vote.'

'Look, you and I know he committed the Seattle murders, but trying to conjure up something ain't going to work. This time, it needs to be watertight.'

'But you've been keeping an eye on him, right?'

'I made a promise to you, as you did to me. I'd check up on Mattich every few months if you promised to stop thinking about him. Anything amiss I told you I'd contact you. And up until now, I haven't, right?'

'When did you last see him?'

'Just after Christmas, I drove to his place, and he was still there. Miserable life if you ask me. Surrounded by all those dead animals. I watched from a distance as he hung out a couple of rabbit pelts and then went and chopped some wood.'

'So he's still into taxidermy?'

'Looks that way, but it's the same old same old. No new incriminating evidence.'

'But say he was ranging out of his area, would you know about that?'

'If nothing flags up, then no.'

'His vehicle was pulled over in Montana last week.'

'It's a free country, Frank.'

'What about New Mexico?'

'I know where you're going with this, buddy, but you're barking up the wrong tree.'

'But has he been there?'

'No idea.'

'Couldn't you check?' Locke realises he's beginning to sound desperate. 'Credit card payments, bank withdrawals, minor traffic stops.'

'You know I'm no longer operational, and anyway, obtaining that kind of information requires more than just a wild hunch.'

Ouch.

Locke pulls the phone away from his ear for a moment. Breathes out to calm himself. Tries a different tack.

'Could you run him through the database alongside the parameters for the girl in the forest? See if he comes in with anything approaching a fifty-fifty probability?'

'I can tell you he won't come in close to that. Even with your evidence of him being near Missoula, it will only be twenty per cent.'

Locke shakes his head. Twenty per cent. One in five. If he was at his monthly poker night with Leo Sullivan sat to his left, he'd want better odds than that to make a call. But this isn't poker.

'OK,' Locke says, downbeat.

He thanks Swanson for the information and hangs up. Puts his cell back on the dash and stares at it.

Swanson's probably right. One moment, Kell is out of the picture, and the next, Mattich pops up to take his place. It's all too convenient. Then, there are the odds of twenty per cent, although he feels sure that if Swanson had run the algorithm, the numbers would have been better than that.

Call or fold?

He grabs his phone from the dash, gets out of the car and heads for The Daily Grind. Black coffee in a white cup. A toasted English muffin slathered with a slab of butter. He sits on a stool at one end of the counter and nobody comes near. A couple of patrolmen nod as they grab some food. No words. Not for Frank Locke, the outsider.

He knows that's what they think of him, despite the fact he's lived here for nearly seven years, and that's one reason they don't come across for a chat.

But the tag of the failed detective is another.

He's past the stage where he beats himself up about it. What happened with Mattich was a cooler, but Locke took a punt and it didn't pay off. Better luck next time.

Except this isn't luck, it's a calculated gamble. Twenty per cent. Not good odds on which to risk a career, but surely decent odds to try and save a life? Even better odds when it might be several lives.

Locke takes a bite from the muffin and wipes butter from his chin with a tissue. The cafe is half full. A few cops, a couple of truckers, and a posse of construction workers in from the site down the strip. Snippets of conversation drift Locke's way: the truckers lament some new legislation, while the construction workers moan about building codes. Locke thinks about how Mattich got off on a technicality and wonders about the good old days before building codes and fancy lawyers.

He takes another sip of coffee as the conversation at a nearby table turns to sport, and Locke zones out and swivels to face the window. There's a view across the street to the station, and right by the little 7-11 next door, an older man with long, lank hair and a thin beard stands staring towards the café.

Henrik Mattich.

Locke leaps from his seat and pushes past a burly worker in a lumberjack shirt and Caterpillar boots.

'Watch it, bud, you—'

He doesn't hear the rest because he's at the door, wrenching it open, scanning the street for Mattich...

... only it's not Mattich. As the man walks along the sidewalk, Locke realises that although he has the same scraggly beard, lank hair, and thin frame, his eyes are warm blue, not the cold grey steel of Mattich's. No tattoo on his neck. No mole on the bridge of his nose.

Locke goes back inside and apologises to the worker. He returns to his table, finishes his coffee and muffin, and thinks about Henrik Mattich. The *real* Henrik Mattich, not some phantasm conjured up by his over-active imagination.

According to Swanson, it's less than twenty per cent he did the girl in the forest. Long odds but a big reward. Things seem clearer now, and this time, Locke doesn't have to think about it for long.

Call or fold?

'Call,' he says to himself.

~ ~ ~

His mind made up, he drives home. Once back, he dials up Adam Hem. There was something in the autopsy report that piqued Locke's interest. With Swanson's reluctance to help out, he wants to revisit the information.

*The cuts were made by a scalpel and were possibly the work of someone used to wielding such a tool. A medical professional, perhaps.*

'Doctor Hem,' Locke says, making sure he starts on the right foot. 'I wonder if I could draw on your considerable expertise?'

He asks Hem about the statement in the report. Hem seems to withdraw from his claim a little.

'Perhaps, I said. Only perhaps.'

'But a scalpel?

'I'd say so, based on the depth and narrowness of the blade.'

'And someone used to a scalpel?'

'The precision and lack of hesitancy. No half-hearted slicing, but straight in with a high degree of accuracy. Someone who knows what they're doing.'

'And the puncture wound in the back, could that have been made by a hunting arrow or crossbow bolt?'

'I thought it probable a screwdriver or spike was used, but an arrow would fit too.'

Locke thanks Hem, hangs up, goes to a drawer, and pulls out a folder. Takes it over to the dining table and opens it. Spreads the contents. Dozens of pictures, some of stuffed animals, some of pelts hanging on a rack, some of skinned corpses, some of tiny bodies dissected. Finally, a photograph of a gaunt man staring at the camera.

Mattich.

The tattoo. The mole on the nose. A no-brainer he wasn't the man on the street, but the intervening time has taken a toll on Locke's memory, and the mistake was understandable.

*He's teasing you, Frank. Come to haunt your dreams.*

Was it possible Mattich had crossed into Montana to target Locke specifically?

He picks up his phone and swipes his fingers across the screen. In a few moments, he's plotted a route to Henrik

Mattich's place at Snoqualmie Pass. A little over four hundred miles door-to-door. About six hours of driving if he pushes it. He'll be there just before sunset if he leaves now.

~ ~ ~

He's driven through Snoqualmie Pass en route to or from Seattle a few times in the intervening years since Mattich's arrest, trial and release. Always thought about pulling off the I-90 around ten miles before the pass and taking the road towards Kachess Lake. Driving through the pine forest to where chalets dot the woodland on either side of the road. From there, taking a side track that leaves any semblance of civilisation behind and wends into thicker forest, eventually reaching the rundown cabin. And when he got there, pulling his gun and finding Mattich and firing several bullets into the man's addled brain.

*Steady.*

The journey takes the time it takes. Plenty of hours to think about what he's going to do. This time, the evidence must come first, he decides. Head must rule heart. Otherwise, Mattich will get another fat check from his lawyers, and Locke will be handing in his badge once again.

He stops at the tiny halt of Easton a few miles before the turn-off. There's a general store with a little diner inside. Gas outside. He fills the car's tank and uses the bathroom to empty his own. Takes a cup of coffee, a beef sandwich and a side of fries. Another cup of coffee.

Back outside, the light is fading, and the sun is long gone behind the high peaks. He re-joins the interstate, pushes the car to the limit, and eats up the remaining handful of miles in a few minutes. He turns off the freeway and onto a small road that leads to Kachess Lake. Tall pines on either side, snow beneath the trees and packed hard on the verges, streams full of meltwater. The sky above the trees has turned pink, the firs jagged and black against the lightness.

He drives past the chalets he remembers last time and takes a track that winds into denser woodland. He guns the car on the rough gravel, wheels spinning. Threads between the trees into a monochrome landscape where it's as if the colour and vitality have been sucked from everything living. Like Mattich, the taxidermist, is eviscerating the world one luckless animal at a time.

As the track nears the cabin, Locke pulls over to the side. The house is a dark rectangle a couple of hundred yards ahead, the sky behind now a spider's web of crimson clouds.

*Blood red*, he thinks before quickly censoring himself. Overthinking is dangerous. He needs to sift the evidence and deal with the facts, not elevate Mattich into some bogeyman.

And yet...

Out of the car and standing in the still woodland, it's not difficult to sense something wrong here. A tingling caresses the back of his hands as his hairs react to a static charge in the air. He takes a breath, and a sour taste bites at the back of his throat. To either side of the track, a low mist hugs the ground, tendrils curling round tree trunks like the miasma is a nocturnal creature awakening for the night.

'Get a grip,' Locke says to himself. He reaches into the car and opens the locker on the dash. Pulls out his gun and checks the clip. Then he grabs his jacket and puts it on, slipping the gun into his shoulder holster.

He walks down the track towards the house. The place is exactly as he remembers it. More of a shack than a house, less of a home than a hovel. A single room to the front and a low lean-to at the rear. A small round window high in one gable end where there's a sleeping area up in the roof space. Off to the right, there's a dilapidated barn, and as Locke nears the house, he can just about make out a faint glint of light slanting out from a window to the left of the front door.

*Somebody's home.*

Locke eases off to the left and picks his way into the woodland, skirting the house to approach from the side. He wouldn't put it past Mattich to be sitting at a window cradling a crossbow.

His foot splashes into a patch of icy water, electric cold biting at his ankle and freezing liquid oozing into his shoe. He moves on until he is square to the gable where only the little round window faces in his direction, the house about twenty-five paces away across a patch of yard. He stands behind a large tree and listens for signs of life, but there's nothing. He steps forward and crosses the yard, jogging to the edge of the house, where he stops in shadow. He pulls out his gun and once again checks the clip. Better safe than sorry. Better to be sure he can take Mattich down if the nutter tries to spring something.

To the front of the dwelling, there's a veranda, a step to a low deck that stretches the property's length. Locke places one foot on the deck and eases up, the wood creaking as he does so. He slides along a pace at a time until he gets to the window. A dim glow comes from behind a hessian curtain, and he tilts his head and peers in through a gap. There's a kitchen table above which an old oil lamp hangs from a twisted cord. A pool of congealed blood on the table, the essence of some creature after it has been dissected and eviscerated and then, presumably, stuffed. There is no sign of Mattich.

Locke ducks low and moves beneath the bottom of the frame until he's past the window. He pads to the front door. He stands to one side, reaches for the handle on the flyscreen and pulls the screen open. Now for the actual door. The round knob squeaks as he turns it. There's a click as the latch gives. He pushes the door and it swings inwards. He waits.

Nothing.

He edges round and peers into the gloom. There's a waft of bad air, a tinge of chemicals and something rotting. Inside is a kitchen, living room, and diner all in one. Cosy, were it not for the blood on the table. Locke steps over and kicks something soft at his feet. He stoops and uses one finger to poke at a pile of clothes: a short leather skirt, bra, panties, and a skimpy top. He straightens and looks at the dark red blotch on the table. Fragments of white bone dust the stain.

Locke recoils, feels his knees buckle, and reaches out for the table for support. He looks away momentarily, and when he turns back, he's calmer. Wonders how Adam Hem would react.

'Amateur hour,' he says, scolding himself. 'Fucking amateur hour.'

He remembers the women in Seattle, the skin flayed from their bodies in an attempt at imposing racial purity, Mattich the prime suspect, but never enough evidence for Locke to make a case. Now, it looks like Mattich has moved on to a new project. He's undoubtedly ignored Locke's warning to stay away from women.

'Going to put a bullet in you, you fucker,' Locke says, his right hand wrapped tightly round his gun. 'Just give me the opportunity.'

All he needs is for Mattich to appear. Bang, bang and who's going to question Locke's story of self-defence? Locke is ninety to ninety-five per cent certain about the Seattle murders, and never mind Swanson's twenty per cent crap, the evidence Mattich is killing again is right here in front of him. In the end, that's all that matters.

He checks the gun again and then walks across the room to a side table. Pulls open a drawer, looking for something, anything. Strikes gold: Inside, there's a roll of c-notes, Locke guesses about three K's worth, and a box a cell phone came in. He opens the box, but it's empty. He looks at the picture on the front. Retro. Miniature. The same model he extracted from the throat of Monica Granton.

~ ~ ~

Locke takes a few snaps of the phone box, the clothing and the blood on the tabletop. He'll need to call someone but doesn't want to get involved. There'll be too much paperwork and too many questions. A dozen hours stuck in a room with a couple of local dicks who know nothing about Mattich and will need to be filled in from the start.

He takes a final glance around the room and then steps out onto the deck. A pair of lights float like a will-o-the-wisp in the trees, flitting to the left and right and then coming straight at him, a sudden glare in his eyes, the sound of tyres crunching on gravel swirling into his ears.

Locke moves to one side and shields his face with his left hand while his right grips his gun and holds it low.

The car draws up in front of the house, the headlights so bright that Locke can't see who's inside.

If it's Mattich, then Locke is ready to take the role of judge, jury and executioner. No need for a trial. Not with what he's discovered in the house.

'Frank?' A voice comes a moment after the driver's door clunks open, and Jim Swanson walks round in front of the headlights, his bulky form casting a huge shadow. 'What the fuck are you doing here?'

'What you told me to do,' Locke says. 'Gathering evidence on Henrik Mattich.'

'That's why I came.' Swanson saunters up to the veranda, a big Maglite in one hand. Shrugs. 'After our conversation, I felt uneasy, guilty, even. I knew the Bureau wouldn't put anyone back on the job, so I thought I'd better get on the case myself.'

'Fuck, Jim, I drove half the day to get here. You did it from Seattle in, what, an hour?'

'With the traffic, a little over.'

'Well, F.Y.I., he's not here.'

'A wasted journey then.'

'Not exactly.' Locke waves his gun back at the house. 'He's left a little present on his dining table, and it ain't anything to do with cutesy stuffed animals.'

Swanson climbs the steps and stands beside Locke. 'No?'

'No. Proves he murdered the girl in the forest.'

Locke waits as Swanson enters the house. Torchlight bounces round, and Swanson mutters a string of obscenities. He comes out a couple of minutes later, shaking his head.

'You were right all those years ago, and this proves it.'

'Seems that way.' Locke wonders how many more there are because it's odds on that Mattich never stopped killing. Seven women in two years in Seattle is over three a year, and he's been living here out in the boondocks for ages. Locke nods into the darkness. 'Probably need to get a search team out here. Bearing in mind the terrain, a couple of cadaver dogs wouldn't go amiss, too.'

'Sorry, Frank,' Swanson says, swinging the Maglite down and turning it off. 'I shouldn't have doubted you. Hell, I should have insisted the Bureau kept up the surveillance.'

Locke reaches out and taps Swanson on the shoulder. 'Short of twenty-four-seven, three-six-five, I don't see what else you could have done. If it's anyone's fault, it's

191

mine. I should have got the evidence the first time around.'

'I'd better call it in.' Swanson steps off the veranda and makes for the car.

'Can I ask a favour?' Locke says.

'Ask away.' Swanson turns.

'I want out of here.' Locke jumps down from the deck and looks back. 'I can't be doing with all this. Plus, there'll be questions about why I'm here way out of my jurisdiction.'

'So you want me to claim I found the blood and clothing?'

'Yup. You can say we talked, and you came out here to check on Mattich. I can return once you've proposed the Lewis and Clarke girl as a possible victim.'

'Sure.' Swanson waves his torch at his car. 'You driving back home tonight?'

'No.' Locke's already decided that's impossible. 'I'll stop somewhere.'

'Right.'

Locke waits with Swanson until he confirms a search team is on the way and heads off. Once he gets back on the interstate, he drives southwest for forty minutes until Ellensburg, where he finds a Holiday Inn Express. He grabs something to eat from a nearby Taco Bell and then hits his room and sleeps for ten hours straight. Doesn't dream.

# Chapter 22

If arranging the visit to see Pearce in prison took some effort, getting approval for the BUK to go on a one-day vacation is an almost Sisyphean task, and that after Sasaki has endured the wrath of Assistant Commissioner Cooper for even asking.

'The fuck you thinking of, boy?' he says, turning a dark shade of puce before launching into a tirade that has Sasaki fearing the AC might have a coronary.

Eventually, persuaded by the fact Pearce might be able to help clear up the case, Cooper agrees. From then on, Sasaki spends every waking minute dealing with the not-inconsiderable paperwork. There's clearance from various government bodies to obtain plus the security to arrange. Risk assessments by the dozen, a telephone call with the minister responsible for prisons, transport to and from Alice Springs, a charter plane, flight plan and insurance, vetting for him and Malroony, a safety briefing, and more. Some of the work inevitably falls on Cooper's shoulders, and to say he's not thrilled is the understatement of the century.

On the day of the flight, Cooper calms a little, although only because there is a glimmer of hope that Pearce might help them find the killer. If there is any other result, Sasaki knows who will get the blame.

Pearce had been flown up the day before and spent the night in police cells in Darwin. Now he's sitting in the back row seat of a police minibus with a minder on either side, one of whom he's cuffed by the wrist to.

'Going to be a beautiful day,' Pearce says as they wend through the streets to the airport. He looks over to Sasaki. 'And I see you've packed a picnic.'

Describing the supplies Sasaki is bringing along as a picnic might be stretching it, but yes, he has food and drink for himself, Malroony, Pearce and the pilot. Pearce has insisted it's just the four of them, and the only reason he's got his way is there's no more room in the plane. Sasaki also suspects the Correctional Service are happy to pass custody over to the police since if anything goes wrong, it'll be the police who get the blame. This means that, ultimately, Sasaki is carrying the can for the whole operation.

Make or break, he thinks. A place alongside his father or the rest of his career issuing parking tickets in downtown Darwin.

The vehicle pulls into the general aviation area of the airport, and they coast across a concrete apron to where the plane awaits. Nat Walker, the pilot, stands by the plane, a tiny Cessna 172. It's a four-seater, and with the wings above the fuselage, the aircraft is ideal for spotting something on the ground.

Walker is well-known in Darwin. He's a big drinker, brawler, an all-around redneck. He's also one of the best pilots in the Northern Territory, and if they're going to be swooping low over the remote wilderness, Sasaki can think of nobody better to be at the controls. Besides, there's no choice: Walker is a mate of AC Cooper.

'Buddy.' Walker holds out a hand. 'I always respected your dad.'

Of course, Sasaki thinks, Walker must have met Endo Sasaki at some point. He's only a year or two shy of Cooper's age. Sasaki shakes hands, but before he can say anything, Pearce butts in.

'And that's why we're here,' he says. 'Junior's going to copy senior's party piece and make the front pages of all the newspapers.'

'If I had my way,' Walker says. 'I'd be pushing you out a thousand feet above Kakudu. If by some miracle you survived the fall, you can bet the crocs would get you. Either way, the news would *definitely* make the front pages.'

'I'd think twice about doing that with two cops onboard,' Pearce says, giving Walker a wink. 'Takeo here is very much one for rules and regulations. Pretty sure he's not going to let you get away with inflight murder.'

One of the prison officers undoes the cuff from his wrist and flicks it around Pearce's other arm. He gives the key to Sasaki.

'That's not fair,' Pearce says, putting on a hurt child's voice.

'It's the only way you're getting on the plane,' the officer says. 'Orders of the Superintendent.'

'Let's go,' Walker says. 'Pearce in the back with Takeo, Linda up front with me.'

They load their hand luggage and clamber up.

'Cosy.' Pearce wriggles in his seat and beams at Sasaki. 'This is going to be fun.'

In the front, Walker runs through a checklist and performs a radio check. That done, he hits a button and starts the engine. A quick message to the tower, and they have permission to taxi to a runway.

'Lucky I don't get claustrophobia,' Pearce says.

'Just shut up and let Nat concentrate,' Sasaki says, knowing Walker could fly the plane blind drunk and one-handed but wanting an end to Pearce's jokes.

The plane moves off, and in a few minutes, they arrive at the end of the taxiway. The radio squawks out clearance, and the low buzz of the engine changes to a whine and then a roar and Walker guides the aircraft down the runway. In just a few seconds, the plane lifts from the ground, the wings rock, and Sasaki feels queasy in his stomach.

195

Pearce grins across at him.

The aircraft climbs steadily away from Darwin, heading approximately south-south-east on a bearing of 166 degrees. Sasaki only knows this because he can see a GPS display upfront; Walker isn't playing the role of tour guide, and his only words since takeoff have been a grunted 'ETA at Tortilla flats in twenty minutes.'

He needn't even have bothered with the sparse announcement since there's a waypoint on the GPS, and the minutes and distance are counting down.

'Well,' Pearce says. 'This is great. When do you serve the complimentary drinks?'

'Not yet,' Sasaki says.

He runs through the hours ahead. They'll fly down to Tortilla Flats and then head northeast on a bearing determined by the position of the pointing arm. It's nearly two hundred kilometres to the mouth of the East Alligator River and then another seventy to the north coast; beyond that, there's nothing but ocean. Walker wants to land at Kauk airstrip to top up with fuel before they fly the same route back. Allowing for the inevitable circle rounds to check anything they spot, they'll have flown some eight hundred K. Thirty-three years ago, the farthest distance the arms were from the victims was twenty-two kilometres, but Sasaki wants to be sure, hence the route out to the north coast.

He gazes out at the landscape below. The road runs south to Batchelor, a strip of development on either side, beyond red fields and scrub, isolated farmsteads. He's been in small aircraft before, but never *tiny* ones like this Cessna, never flying so low. At one point, they pass over a farmhouse, and a couple of kids in the backyard look up and wave. In a nearby paddock, three horses wheel about and gallop off.

'Just a few minutes, ladies and gentlemen,' Walker says. 'Then we're on a bearing of forty-three degrees at five hundred metres altitude. So keep your eyes peeled.'

'Likely dump sites, remember?' Sasaki says to Pearce. We might not spot a body, but we can return on foot anywhere that looks possible.'

'Could be quite a hike,' Walker says from the front. He taps at something on the dash and moves the joystick to the left. 'Here we go.'

The aircraft banks sharply, turning to the northeast. Sasaki feels a lurch in his stomach as the left wingtip dips. The sensation is over in a moment as Walker levels up and reduces the engine speed. Sasaki leans to his left and gazes down. He can see Ken Royston's ute parked on the track by the crime scene and two large flag markers fluttering in the breeze.

'You're on,' Sasaki says to Pearce. 'And it better be good.'

'If there's nothing to find, then I can find nothing, right?' Pearce turns to his window and looks out.

True, Sasaki thinks.

An hour in, and there's been two false alerts. One: a sheep carcass, flayed of its fleece. From above, the mess of red and pink resembled a body. Two: a human-shaped log shorn of bark and bleached white by the sun. The latter required two low passes to rule out. Aside from that, the journey has been monotonous, and Sasaki is having trouble concentrating. The constant engine noise and the need to lean his head against the window to look out and down has given him a headache. A break can't come soon enough.

When they're an hour and a half out from Tortilla Flats, the Alligator River comes into view, twisting to a mouth of white sand. As they skim over, Pearce cries out.

'There!' He jabs a finger at the window. 'A body!'

Sasaki leans across to look, but at that moment, Walker banks the plane hard to the right, and Sasaki is thrown against Pearce.

'Marking a waypoint.' Walker taps something on the controls. 'We'll go lower for a better view.'

The aircraft loses height as Walker brings it about for a second pass. Sasaki scans the ground but sees only sand, dirt, and scrub.

'There's nothing, boss,' says Malroony. 'Must have been another log or something.'

'The fuck it was a log.' Pearce presses his face against the window. 'It was a woman's body, I'm sure.'

'Can you go around once more?' Sasaki says to Walker.

There's a grunt from up front, and the aircraft circles again. Sasaki peers through the trees and scrub as a huge rocky outlier flashes past below, something pink and vaguely body-shaped lying on top of the grey stone.

'There!' Pearce shouts. Did you see it? We need to land.'

'Impossible,' Walker says. 'There's nowhere to set down here, and the nearest runway is miles away.'

'What about the old prospector camp at the mouth of the river?' Pearce says. 'There's a strip there.'

'You're right.' Walker holds the aircraft steady. 'But it's years since I've used it. No idea what kind of state the strip is in.'

'How far?' Sasaki says.

'Couple of K.' Walker gestures through the windscreen. 'Let's take a look.'

The plane eases forward, gliding close to the mouth of the river, several crocs splashing from the banks into the water. Walker turns a little to the right and then nods. 'We'll do a low pass. Look out for rocks, branches, or anything larger than half a brick.'

The plane loses altitude, and they head towards a bare stretch of earth sandwiched between the river and a marshy area. Sasaki stares down as the ground rushes past. If this is a landing strip, then Walker needs his head examined. Barely ten metres wide and perhaps a hundred long, low scrub has grown up half concealing the earth.

Walker brings the aircraft around again and makes a second pass. Satisfied, he makes a large loop to the right and lines up.

'Buckle up,' he says. 'We'll risk it.'

Sasaki swallows back nausea and checks his seat belt. The ground is close now, small trees skimming past on either side, the earth rushing up to meet the plane.

And then they touch down. A little bump, a larger one, and they're coasting down the strip, the landing as smooth as any Sasaki has had in a commercial jet.

'Fucking A,' Pearce says. 'Respect.'

The aircraft coasts to a stop at the end of the runway, and Walker swings round, ready for takeoff.

'There we go,' Walker says. 'Now you head off while I check things over.'

He pulls a little GPS unit from a locker and enters the waypoint coordinates.

'How far?' Sasaki says as Walker passes him the GPS.

'Eighteen hundred metres. Shouldn't be too strenuous, but look out for crocodiles.'

They clamber out of the aircraft, and Pearce holds out his hands.

'You going to take these off?' He nods down at the handcuffs. 'I can't walk anywhere fast in them for fear of tripping.'

Pearce has a point, Sasaki thinks. He extracts the key from a pocket and unlocks the cuffs. Stows them back in the aircraft.

Malroony comes across and pulls Sasaki away.

'Boss,' she says. She glances across to where Pearce is rubbing his wrists, stretching and stamping his feet. 'Is this a good idea?'

'You're armed, right?'

Yes.' Malroony pats her jacket. 'But that's not the point. When Cooper gets to hear of this, he'll go mental.'

'We don't have much choice.' Sasaki looks at Pearce and then turns in the direction indicated by the GPS unit. 'Keep your weapon drawn and maintain a good distance from Pearce at all times. Don't hesitate to shoot if he does anything untoward.'

'You mean that?'

Sasaki nods. He's never fired his own gun in anger and has a reputation as a pacifist, but out here, something feels different and unsettling. The wilderness is neither good nor evil, but Pearce could use the land to his advantage. The crocs, the heat, the marshland, and the water are all tools he can fashion into weapons. The danger is in underestimating his ability to improvise. Sasaki half smiles. 'As you said, Pearce dismembered three women. Deserves all he gets, right?'

'Right...' Malroony doesn't sound convinced at Sasaki's change of heart, but she reaches under her jacket and pulls out her gun. Checks it over. 'Good to go.'

'That for me or the crocs?' Pearce stands to one side of the aircraft as Walker inspects the undercarriage and flight surfaces. He holds his hands up in mock surrender. 'Because I'm not going to be any trouble, not here. Nowhere to run to, nowhere to hide.'

'No funny stuff, Derek,' Sasaki says. 'If you try anything, you'll regret it.'

The three of them set off. After they leave the river and marsh behind, the terrain is typical bush: low shrubs, small trees, and dry dirt underfoot. Aside from having to weave back and forth through the trees and dodge a thorny plant or two, the going is easy. Sasaki peers at the GPS, where the display counts down the distance remaining.

After twenty minutes, the outlier is visible ahead, a hunk of rock pushing up through the trees and scrub. It's perhaps ten metres tall and gently sloping, something like a miniature Uluru, but made from a harder, greyer rock.

'Far side is the easiest way up,' Pearce says.

Sasaki nods and wonders if Pearce is bossing the situation. He pauses to let Malroony catch up with him.

'Hold back,' he says. 'Make sure you can cover him properly.'

Pearce moves ahead, skirting around the rock until he approaches a gently sloping section. He stops and waits for Sasaki to catch up.

'You go first,' Sasaki says.

'Whatever.' Pearce scrambles up the rock on all fours. For a man in his fifties, he's in good physical condition, Sasaki thinks as he follows Pearce along the curve of the rock to the summit. 'There.' Pearce pushes himself to his feet as he reaches the top. 'I told you so.'

Sasaki scrambles up the last section to find Pearce hunched over the body, hands fiddling with the woman's clothing.

'Stay back!' Sasaki shouts. 'Get away from her, you pervert.'

'My pleasure.' Pearce straightens and turns, something in his right hand. Grey-brown. Metal. A small automatic pistol. Sasaki begins to step back but then realises there's nowhere to go. 'Here.' Pearce gestures with the gun, motioning Sasaki to approach the body. 'And then sit down.'

'Derek, this is—'

'SIT THE FUCK DOWN!'

Pearce has suddenly done some sort of alter ego switch. Spittle flies from his lips, and his whole body tenses while his gun hand gyrates wildly.

'OK,' Sasaki says. He edges forward and sits down next to the dead body.

Except it isn't a dead body. The thing in front of him wearing female clothes has never been alive. It's a mannequin, stiff plastic or plaster, coarse nylon hair, and limbs that only articulate at the hips and shoulders. From the air, it was enough to fool them.

'Takeo?' Malroony hollers up from ground level. 'Is everything OK?'

'Stay there, Linda,' Sasaki shouts out.

'If you want your boss to live, you'd better listen up.' Pearce steps away to the edge of the rock. He faces down but points the gun at Sasaki. 'Throw your weapon out where I can see it, and then put your hands on your head.'

'Don't—'

Pearce fires his gun, the bullet thudding into the mannequin and sending splinters of plastic up in a shower.

'DO AS I SAY!'

A moment or two later, Malroony comes into view as she walks backwards away from the rock. She holds her gun up and then flings it away. Puts her hands on her head.

'Good girl.' Pearce waves the gun at Sasaki again. 'We're coming down, Takeo first. Do anything stupid and I'll shoot him in the back.'

Sasaki gets to his feet and moves to the edge of the rock. Pearce is a couple of paces behind, but if Sasaki tries anything, he won't stand a chance. He eases down off the rock, turning round face on when it gets steeper. At ground level, he drops onto the soil. Malroony's standing there with her hands on her head.

202

'Sorry, Linda.' Sasaki gives a little shrug. 'I should have followed your advice.'

'It's not over,' Malroony says. 'He's not getting out of here, is he?'

'I wouldn't be so sure.'

'That's right.' Pearce slips off the rock and stands several paces away. He waves the gun at the rock and then at Malroony and Sasaki. 'You don't think this is all simple serendipity? A bit of luck that there happened to be a decoy body on top of the rock with a gun hidden beneath it? You fucking idiots.'

'Is Walker in on this?' Sasaki says. 'I should have realised somebody like him would have no morals. What did you have to pay him?'

'Zilch.' Pearce shakes his head. 'You don't get it, do you? I didn't need to bribe a drunkard pilot to fly me out of here. Walker's got nothing to do with this.'

Sasaki wonders if Pearce is crazy. Hiking anywhere from here is impossible, especially considering Pearce's lack of equipment, and it must be forty kilometres to the nearest road. Besides, the chance of hitching a lift on one of the many tracks that crisscross Kakudu National Park is minimal.

'Now, let's get down to business.' Pearce thrusts the gun at them.

For a moment, Sasaki thinks this is it. The end. No escaping from his father's shadow and no making up with Anna. There will be headlines in the papers and a flurry of stories on the evening news. Later, in an obituary in the Darwin newspapers, his father's name will undoubtedly be mentioned, a bitter irony for Sasaki even in death.

He tenses, ready to fight, but then he sees Pearce has a couple of long cable ties in his other hand.

'Going to tie your hands behind your backs.' Pearce approaches. 'You can either wait here for Walker or return to the plane. Either way, you won't be able to move at much more than walking pace, and you won't be able to follow me.'

Pearce drops the ties on the ground and orders Sasaki to bind Malroony's hands behind her. Then he tells Sasaki to kneel and put his hands behind his back.

'I'm going to put the gun down briefly while I put the tie around your wrists. If you want to try something, you have to weigh up the chance of me being able to grab the gun before you turn and disable me. I'd say it's not worth the risk.'

'I'm not going to try anything,' Sasaki says to reassure Pearce.

'Good choice.'

Sasaki kneels and puts his hands behind his back. Feels the cable tie tightening around his wrists, the edges sharp against his skin.

'Job done.' Pearce pushes Sasaki in the back, knocking him forward face down in the dirt. 'No hard feelings, mate.'

Sasaki thuds into the ground and rolls on his side. Pearce is walking away, but before disappearing into the tree line, he turns and stops.

'A piece of advice,' he says. 'If you're going to be a hotshot like your dad, you'll need to be better at maths. Fucking pig.'

And then he's gone.

Malroony is already moving, heading in the opposite direction from Pearce, back towards the landing site. Sasaki struggles to his feet and follows.

'Go, Linda,' Sasaki says. 'Head for the plane. Don't wait for me.'

Malroony sets off at a good pace, with Sasaki following, but as Pearce said, they can't run with their hands tied behind their backs. The ground is too uneven, and scrub and low branches block the way. After a few minutes, Sasaki tells Malroony to slow down.

'He's long gone,' Sasaki says.

'He can't be that far away, sir,' Malroony says. 'Once airborne, we can circle overhead and spot him.'

'And do what?' Sasaki stops for a breather. 'We can't land.'

'We can radio his position in.'

'Somebody must have placed the mannequin on top of the rock with the gun and cable ties, which means he has an accomplice. He's planned a route out of here. No way are we going to catch him.'

Malroony opens her mouth to say something but stops. She cocks her head and a half turns. There's a percussive echo thrumming through the trees. Thud, thud, thud, thud. Louder. And then something black swoops just above the treetops, all spinning rotors, a screaming engine, and a massive downdraught that washes over them, tousling their hair and throwing leaves, debris, and dust into the air.

A helicopter.

~ ~ ~

They're back at the landing strip within half an hour. Walker is waiting, hands outstretched as they approach.

'What the fuck is going on?' he says. 'And where the hell is Pearce?'

'Gone,' Sasaki says. Flown away, quite literally.'

'The 'copter, right? I thought I heard something.'

'Yes.'

'How the hell did he pull a jump on you?' Walker looks across at Malroony and then back at Sasaki.

'The body was a decoy. Someone had secreted a weapon in its clothing. Pearce got to the body first.'

'And who was flying the helicopter?'

'No idea.'

Walker shrugs. Turns and tramps back to the aircraft and pulls a pair of pliers from a toolbox. He snips the cable ties to free them and returns to prepping the plane. Sasaki apologies to Malroony again.

'Not your fault,' she says. 'No scenario I was expecting involved Pearce having outside help.'

'He played us, Linda,' Sasaki says, rubbing his wrists. 'Right from the start back at Alice Springs. This whole thing was a setup.'

'You mean the body at Tortilla Flats?'

'I don't know.'

And he doesn't. If Pearce wanted to escape, why wait thirty-three years to do it?

'Let's go.' Walker stands by the aircraft. 'No point hanging around here, right?'

For a moment, Sasaki wonders about walking off into the bush. Disappearing. The alternative is returning to face the music, and that's almost as unappealing as being left out here with only crocodiles and snakes for company.

'You coming?' Malroony gives an encouraging smile and then climbs into the Cessna.

'Yes.' Sasaki gets in the back and belts up. Watches as the scrub rushes past, and they steal into the air.

An hour and a half later, Walker brings the plane in to land at Darwin, where Assistant Commissioner Cooper has kindly sent a car to meet them.

# Chapter 23

Chase and Green are back in the SCU, and Stafford is inputting some figures into a map on the screen in front of him. Geometry might be his strong point, but even he can't conjure something from nothing.

'Doesn't fit,' he says, pointing at a thick line he's drawn on the map heading northeast away from where they found the arm towards the coast. Also visible are several areas of cross-hatching, which denote bearded reedling habits. 'The nearest misses by at least three miles.'

'Are you sure?' Chase asks. 'I mean, couldn't the arm have moved a fraction?'

'You said there was a black mark showing the correct direction,' Stafford says. 'Whoever placed the arm made the mark to ensure it pointed the right way. Take a line from the body's position to the mark, and the direction is extremely accurate.'

'Shit,' Green says. 'Seems our faith in you was misplaced. Either that or your theory on the bird is all wrong.'

'The bird is a reedling, no doubt about it, but I never came up with a theory; that was you and Jess.'

'It was worth a try,' Chase says. 'But running over it now, it doesn't make sense for the killer to point us to either the place he killed Alison or where he created the voice message.'

'So what's he trying to tell us?' Green leans in past Stafford and runs a finger up the screen. 'And why go to all that trouble when he could just send us a flipping note?'

Chase doesn't have an answer. She squints at the screen, her gaze following Green's finger as it runs along the line. The names of towns and villages jump out at her, but there's no sudden revelation, and when Green reaches the sea, she turns away and retreats to her desk.

She spends an hour tracking down CCTV cameras that might have captured whoever deposited the arm, and she gets promises that the footage won't be wiped and that it will be with her as soon as possible. Then, she reads a report from Pat Kendle. The pathologist has done a rush job on the arm and confirms what they already knew: it belongs to Alison. Kendle adds that she believes the arm was probably placed on the roof at the same time the body was dumped and reemphasises the removal method: *it was cut off with a fine-toothed saw, possibly a bone saw.*

Chase calls the companies with CCTV back and gives them a more specific time window for the footage, and then she listens to the phone message for the umpteenth time.

There's nothing specific about the arm or pointing, but there are a couple of lines about making connections. It's tenuous, but Chase gets up and goes over to Stafford to run it by him.

'How does it help us?' Stafford says.

Chase shrugs. She doesn't know. She was hoping Stafford might come up with something, but he seems to be out of fizz, definitely out of ideas.

Like the rest of us, Chase thinks, glancing around the SCU. They all hunker down for a couple of hours until Stafford pipes up with an idea.

'Better be good,' Green says. 'Or else I'm off for a coffee.'

'I've been running a new search through the database,' he says. 'I think we've been too tightly focused, and we need to include people who, at first sight, might not fit the bill.'

'Is that wise?' Chase says.

'What's the alternative? Sit on our hands and wait for doomsday?'

*Doomsday* is SCU code-speak for Boyle shutting down the unit, which, unless they can crack the case, is moving ever closer.

'OK, what did you come up with?' Chase says, making a theatrical sigh. 'I guess it's a list of nobodies we need to investigate one by one, right?'

'Not exactly.' Stafford hesitates as if he's not sure of what to say.

'Out with it,' Green says. 'Whatever it is can't be worse than what we've got now.'

'I went through the requirements for our suspect and ran some new searches. This time, for each search, I left out several of the major requisites to see who might show up. The database spat out a few different names, and I was able to discount some of them immediately. One suspect stuck out as a possibility, though.'

Stafford leaves them waiting. After a few seconds, he clicks his mouse, and a picture fills the monitor. The man is well groomed with slicked-back grey-white hair. He wears a dinner jacket with a bowtie, a silver badge pinned on one lapel, and a crimson red handkerchief poking from the breast pocket.

Doctor Alan Grainger.

'You've lost it, John,' Green says. 'You've fucking lost it.'

Chase reckons Green has it about right. Stafford must be getting desperate. He's under pressure, but coming out with this sort of crap is unforgivable.

'John,' Chase says with a whispered voice akin to the tone she might use to address a wayward five-year-old. 'Grainger is gay. The Soho Sleeper targeted young men. Women do nothing for him.'

Green isn't finished and isn't so gentle.

209

'This is pathetic. We're supposed to be a team, but if this is all you can come out with, we're better off without you.'

'Do you want to hear the evidence?' Stafford says. 'Or is this your usual display of country boy thicko thinking?'

'He. Is. Gay. That's reason enough for me to dismiss Grainger as a viable suspect.'

'Jessie?'

Chase is stuck in the middle with Stafford and Green waiting for her to take sides. 'You'd better show us your reasoning,' she says.

'For fuck's sake.' Green slams a hand on the desk.

He's behaving like a teenager, Chase thinks. Says: 'Grow up, Nick.'

There's an awkward silence, and Chase wonders if Stafford will sulk, too. After a long pause, he nods to himself.

'If we discount Grainger's sexuality for a moment,' Stafford says. 'Then he fits the bill perfectly.'

'Yeah, but—' Green stops as Chase gives him an acid stare.

'Go on, John,' Chase says.

'Thanks.' Stafford composes himself. 'Grainger has the surgical skills to carry out the insertion of the phone, and Kendle has just restated that the arm was cut off with a bone saw. Grainger has drug knowledge and access to Rohypnol and other substances he could have used to subdue Alison, he knows London well, he has money and time, and he's sadistic. Plus, it's not beyond the realms of possibility that he could have met Alison or Lizzie at some LGBT function.'

'But he's not a killer,' Green says. 'Nor — and this is the clincher — is he heterosexual.'

'First, the profile of our suspect in the Soho Sleeper case, before we confirmed it was Grainger, suggested he could go on to kill. Second, there's no forensic evidence to suggest Alison Madden was sexually assaulted. It's pure sadism.'

'The killer cut away her genitals. That sounds pretty sexual to me. Plus, Grainger got a kick out of inflicting pain on men. Doing the same to women wouldn't give him what he wanted.' Green shakes his head. 'Finally, Grainger was acquitted. You know, not guilty, didn't do it, innocent.'

'You've never said he was innocent before, and I'm pretty sure you don't believe it.'

'Whatever.'

'Come on, Nick,' Chase says. 'We know Grainger drugged and raped those men. Unfortunately, we didn't have enough of the right type of evidence to convince the jury.'

'And you think they'll be convinced by the rubbish John's dredged up?'

'That's it, I'm out of here.' Stafford pushes back his chair and stands. He makes a sweeping gesture towards his computer. 'There's more, so take a look, draw your own conclusions, and we'll discuss an apology later.'

And he's gone.

'Arrogant fuck,' Green says as Stafford weaves away across the open-plan office. 'He thinks he's the only one with brains round here.'

Green returns to his desk, where Chase can see him firing off a few emails. Then he's done, too, not a word as he takes his leave.

'Boys and their willy waving,' Chase says to herself.

Then she goes to Stafford's computer to see if what he says adds up.

It does.

Aside from the information Stafford's just told them, there are a couple more nuggets: One, Alan Grainger's Mercedes was clocked by an ANPR camera crossing Kew Bridge at three AM on the day before Alison Madden's body was discovered. Circumstantial, perhaps, but Chase reckons you can preface that with *highly*. Two, the toxicology from Alison Madden's PM has been completed and shows the presence of Rohypnol and morphine in her bloodstream.

Still, even with the ANPR and tox data, that doesn't mean Grainger's their man. They need more evidence. The problem is Grainger is off-limits. His lawyers made that clear at the end of the trial. If Chase, Green and Stafford so much as breathe within a mile of him, then not only the lawyers but Boyle, the Commissioner, and the Mayor will be on their backs in an instant.

'And since when has that ever stopped us?' Chase says to herself.

An hour later, Stafford returns.

'You're up for this, aren't you?' he says.

'How did you know?' Chase says.

'Because, unlike Nick, you're clever and intuitive. He has a little of each of those qualities, but his main asset is determination, and that won't get you very far unless you can either take directions or someone gives you a map.'

'So, we go after Grainger, all or nothing? Put everything on the line? Our careers, the SCU, the possible future victims if we've got this completely wrong?'

'Have you got a better idea?'

Chase considers Stafford's question for approximately one and a half seconds.

'No,' she answers.

~ ~ ~

212

After some research, Chase discovers Alan Grainger has upped and left London. He's moved from his mews house to the greenbelt near Reigate.

'Pricey area,' Stafford says, standing at her shoulder as Chase brings up a map on her monitor and zooms in on a little cul-de-sac situated on a B road a mile or so from Reigate. 'I wonder how he can afford it?'

Chase switches to a satellite view, and the screen shows a dozen detached houses with extensive gardens, double garages and sweeping driveways. The azure blue of several swimming pools sparkles up at them, and each property is surrounded by thick hedges or substantial walls. Chase remembers the press attention on Grainger at the time of the trial and wonders if the move out to this semi-rural location is due to the media intrusion.

'I doubt he's worried about money,' Chase says. 'That mews house would have been worth a lot, and he signed a sizable book deal.'

'Still to be published,' Stafford says. 'Let's hope it never is because I doubt the SCU will feature favourably. Especially since Grainger lost his job because of us.'

'Well, if your theory is correct, his CV needs updating with his latest surgical skills.'

They spend the rest of the morning trying to get as much information on Grainger's current lifestyle as possible. He still appears to be single and has no permanent employment. He has, as much as possible, kept out of the limelight since the trial.

'We need an *in*,' Chase says. 'We can't just pull him off the street for questioning.'

'Even with the ANPR footage?' Stafford says. 'Proves he drove across Kew Bridge, doesn't it?'

'It's sketchy. Thousands of people drove across the bridge in the early hours of that day, John. There's got to be something more.'

'But there isn't. Boyle will go apoplectic if we suggest questioning Grainger. He'll never agree to it.'

'Let's say we don't ask him.' Chase takes a glance across the office space. 'We go behind his back.'

'Risky.'

'Yes, but if we can trip Grainger up and get a result, Boyle won't care.'

'And if we can't?'

Chase doesn't answer.

~ ~ ~

She decides to go via Grainger's solicitor and arranges for Grainger to voluntarily attend his local nick, where she and Stafford will ask him some questions. No early morning knock. No smashing doors down and dragging Grainger out in cuffs. No aggro.

Much as she'd prefer it that way.

Late afternoon the following day, she and Stafford enter a sterile room deep inside the concrete lozenge that is Reigate Police Station.

Grainger and his solicitor sit on plastic chairs on one side of a Formica table. Grainger looks up as they take seats on the other side.

'Is this about my TV licence?' he says, smiling. He reaches up and scratches his little goatee beard, and Chase wants to smack him right there and then. 'Only if it is, then I think there's been a terrible misunderstanding.'

'Jonathan Bramble,' the man beside him says. Chase notes he doesn't offer a hand to shake. 'Let's hope we can sort this out quickly, hey?'

She remembers Bramble from the trial. He's older than Grainger by a couple of decades, pushing seventy. Grey hair, flared nostrils, watery eyes, a small deposit of wax in his right ear. He has a patrician air about him, as if he expects Chase and Green to tug their forelocks and admit that the whole affair has been a big mistake.

'That depends on your client, Mr Bramble,' Chase says.

'What were you doing crossing Kew Bridge at three AM?' Stafford says, leaping straight in. He pulls out the image of Grainger's Mercedes 4x4 captured by the ANPR camera. 'A long way from home at a strange time, right?'

'Yes,' Grainger says. 'But there's no law against that, is there?'

'An explanation, Mr Grainger?' Chase says.

'Why?' Bramble wants in, too. 'Alan has a right to know what he's being accused of.'

'This is purely an investigative interview, Mr Bramble.'

'It's a fishing expedition,' Grainger says. He taps Bramble on the arm. 'They want to fit me up for something.'

'A woman was murdered and her body dumped near Kew Bridge,' Chase says. 'Your vehicle was clocked crossing the bridge in the hours around when her body was dumped.'

'A woman?' Another smile from Grainger. 'I see. You must be getting desperate.'

More accurate than he knows, Chase thinks. Says: 'So, you were where?'

'I'd had dinner in Hampstead with a friend,' Grainger says. 'Then I wandered.'

'Do you have proof of the dinner?'

'Yes. I paid with my card, but anyway, I'm sure they'd remember me as I go there quite often.' Grainger turns to Bramble for approval, and when the solicitor nods, he continues. 'The Burger and Bucket on the high street. The burger is self-explanatory. The bucket refers to the complimentary bottle of fizz.'

'Some combination.'

'Avantgarde or pretentious, I'm not sure which.'

'And afterwards?'

'We stayed late, probably until after midnight. Then I went for a walk on the Heath, or to be more descriptive, I *cruised*.' The smile turns mischievous. 'Now, in this day and age, I'd be very interested to know if the police have any legitimate business enquiring further into what I got up to.'

Skewered, Chase thinks. Tries not to appear fazed. 'You had sex with somebody you encountered?'

'Not to boast, but more than once. Then I drove home. The route took me across Kew Bridge, round Richmond Park and south to Reigate. I probably arrived back at about fourish.'

'And there you go,' Bramble says. 'An innocent and verifiable explanation. I would like to remind you that my client was acquitted of all charges at the show trial you instigated. He should no more be accused of this appalling killing than anyone else. In fact, given his homosexual proclivities, I wouldn't have thought he'd be anywhere near a list of suspects.'

'You don't know this lot,' Grainger says. 'No wonder the Met's clear-up rates are so low.'

Stafford continues with some more routine questions, and Chase chucks in a couple, too, but it's obvious they're done and need to cut their losses before it all ends in tears. Grainger and Bramble walk out, and there's a parting comment from the solicitor.

'Any further contact or harassment of my client, and we'll see you in court,' he says. 'Understand?'

Then they're gone.

'Fuck it,' Chase says.

# *Chapter 24*

It's two days since Locke's visit to Henrik Mattich's place. After the trip, Locke had some explaining to do to both his wife and his boss at DCI headquarters. Whereas his wife accepted his apology, his boss wasn't so accommodating. She gave Locke a dressing down, and he only managed to escape further censure by mentioning the FBI's involvement and the near certainty that Mattich was responsible for the forest killing, thus neatly wrapping up the case.

'All we need to do now is catch him,' Locke had said.

'And that isn't your job,' the chief had replied. 'Not unless you can verifiably place him in Montana.'

Locke stays in touch with Swanson, annoying the ex-FBI man by demanding updates every few hours. Turns out half a dozen CSIs have combed the property and surrounds, but there's no sign of any other victims.

'I've put all the new details in the database,' Swanson says in response to Locke's latest enquiry. 'Mattich now comes out as ninety-five per cent plus to have done the Lewis and Clarke girl. I can only apologise.'

'No need.'

Swanson says he'll send over anything he finds that links to the Lewis and Clarke case and hangs up.

The FBI man's change of heart highlights the weakness of the serial crimes database: once it flags up a suspect, there's a tendency to narrow in and forget that all systems — machine or human — are fallible. Ever since Seattle, Locke's been wary of that.

He's barely finished speaking with Swanson when his cell rings again.

'Frank Locke,' he says, answering and half expecting Swanson to be back with an update.

But it's not Swanson, just dead air and then heavy breathing like there's a perve getting himself off.

Locke's about to hang up and block the number when a quiet voice breaks through.

'It's Robert,' the voice says. 'He's dead.'

'Karen?' Locke recognises the faint southern lilt. Realises now that the heavy breathing is sobbing as Karen Kell struggles to keep it together on the end of the line.

*End of the line...*

Did she say something about her brother being *dead*?

'They just found him...' Karen's voice fades, and she says something Locke doesn't catch, like she's talking to somebody else next to her. 'Got to go.'

And she does with a click that is final and ominous.

Locke tries to call back but gets voicemail. He leans over his keyboard and punches a couple of keys. Brings up a list of current emergency incidents. There's a fire at a grain store near Great Falls, a multiple pile-up involving a semi and a couple of cars just outside of Butte on the I-90, and an ongoing water rescue at Seeley Lake.

Five minutes later, Locke is speeding north, Leo Sullivan in the shotgun seat, reluctance written all over his face.

'Don't see why you need me along, Frank,' Sullivan says after sulking for a few miles. 'I thought you'd wrapped this?'

'Not yet.' Locke casts a glance at Sullivan but doesn't elaborate.

Fifty minutes later, they rumble down the rough track to the lake. There's a fire truck, officers alongside packing away a rubber dinghy, scuba gear piled in a heap.

Locke flashes his ID as he and Sullivan get out of the car.

'What happened?' he asks one of the fire crew.

'Accidental drowning,' the fireman says, jerking a thumb back at the lake. 'Guy goes out on his boat late last night and takes a bottle of Southern Comfort as his sole passenger. They get friendly, and at some point, the guy gets tangled in some ropes and goes overboard, dragging a length of anchor chain with him. He spends the night curled up on the lakebed rather than in his own bed with his wife.' The fireman glances over at the cabin. Shakes his head. 'And I've seen her and she's a babe. Wouldn't have been my choice of place to sleep with her waiting all soft and warm and wet, you get my drift?'

'Sister, moron,' Locke says, turning away. 'She's his sister.'

Sullivan's down at the dock talking to a local cop. He looks across when Locke approaches.

'Could be suicide, Frank,' Sullivan says. 'Or as good as.'

'How do you figure that?' Locke nods a greeting at the police officer.

'Well, Robert Kell thinks we've got him for the Lewis and Clarke killing. He fuels himself up with liquor and heads out on the boat. Everything seems clearer on the water, and he works through the options. He realises we'll link him to other murders, including those women murdered in New Mexico. One of the women was taken from Lubbock, another from Amarillo; they're both in Texas, a death penalty state. Kell concludes that slipping over the side into the cool blue is the easiest way out. Painless. I suggest we check out his place for a note or something.'

Sullivan's theory is a strong one, Locke thinks. Perps are mostly cowards, and the easy way out often appeals. Except there are a couple of issues. First, because of the cell phone box discovered at Mattich's place, Kell's getting a pass on the Monica Granton killing. Second, Kell arrived in New Mexico *after* the murders had taken place, so it doesn't look like he committed those killings either.

'You trying to find a new angle to get your money, Leo?' Locke says.

'Worth a shot.'

Locke turns and walks away from the shoreline and over to the log cabin. Karen Kell answers his rap on the door. She slumps forward into his arms, and he gently helps her back inside, guiding her to a threadbare couch. He spies a selection of bottles on a sideboard, but, all things considered, perhaps a stiff drink isn't appropriate on this occasion.

The place is one large living area with a few rooms off. On the far side, there's a kitchenette, so Locke heads across and fires up a half-full coffee pot. The brew looks a day old, but it'll have to do.

'What happened?' he says, returning to Karen and sitting beside her. He reaches for her hand and holds it. Not much warmth. A slight shake. Beautiful nails. 'If you're up to telling me, that is.'

For a moment, Locke thinks Karen will lose it completely, but then she steels herself. She makes a little movement with her head, barely a nod, more of an internal affirmation as if she's trying to comprehend something fiendishly complicated.

'He arrived home yesterday evening,' Karen says. 'The first thing we did was talk about you.'

A pause, Locke wondering where this is going, where it will end up.

'I see,' he says.

'Robert didn't trust you, but I said you were an honest guy.'

'I like to think so.'

'Yes.' A tiny smile from Karen. She swallows, tears starting now. 'The discussion became heated, and afterwards,

220

I went to bed, leaving Robert brooding. Then, this morning, I noticed the boat had gone from the dock; only when I went down there could I see it a hundred yards off the shore. It was just sitting there like it was anchored to something on the bottom.'

'Robert,' Locke says, wishing he hadn't.

'I called my neighbour, and he went out on his own boat to check. He found a bottle of liquor and Robert's life jacket in the rowing boat. Said we should phone fire rescue.'

Locke shifts closer and puts his arm around Karen, pre-empting the flood of tears that come within seconds. He doesn't need to ask further questions about what happened because he can visualise the events all too easily: the sirens as the fire truck races down to the water. The officers preparing and launching the dinghy. One officer donning the diving gear and heading down to the lake bed to make the gruesome discovery of Robert Kell, all tangled up in a length of chain and communing with the fishes.

'It wasn't an accident, Frank. He was always so careful.'

But, Locke thinks, how careful can you be when you've half a bottle of Southern Comfort coursing through your veins? On the other hand, if Sullivan's theory is correct, it *wasn't* an accident.

'The autopsy should tell us more,' Locke says, wondering what Doctor Hem will make of the incident. 'And I'll see that everything is properly investigated.'

Karen cocks her head and looks sideways at Locke. 'Robert wouldn't... you know...'

'Wouldn't kill himself?'

'No.' A flat statement with not a moment's hesitation. No doubt in Karen's mind. 'There was no reason.'

But, just like Sullivan said, if you're a bit of a coward, perhaps the cold, numbing waters of Seeley Lake are a more attractive option than being strapped to a gurney in the State Penitentiary at Huntsville, Texas.

'Were you trying to persuade Robert to confess?'

'To what?' Karen's tone is incredulous. 'You've got it all wrong. Robert didn't kill that girl up in the woods.'

'Are you sure about that?'

'I'm one hundred per cent sure, but it sounds like you're not.'

'Why did Robert leave New Mexico?'

'He wanted a change of scenery, new subjects for his pictures. He'd done New Mexico.'

'Very convenient.'

'What do you mean?' Karen shakes her shoulders, wrestling free of Locke's arm.

'Five women were killed, all with the same MO, then Robert heads north, and stuff starts happening up here. Coincidence?'

'The killings took place before Robert went to New Mexico; either way, he didn't kill any of them.'

'How do you know?'

'I just do.' Karen stands and makes her way over to the kitchen area. She picks up the coffee pot and empties the contents into the sink. Starts to make a fresh pot. 'Thanks for your help, but I think you should go now.'

'Right.' Locke eases himself up, cursing at the way he's handled this. 'You'll be OK?'

'I'll phone a friend.' Karen turns and manages to smile.

With that, he's out of there, striding back down to the lake where Sullivan is talking to a local man. Locke lets Sullivan finish up.

'He reckons Robert Kell was a right weirdo,' Sullivan says, his gaze following the man as he strolls away along the foreshore. 'Snooping around the neighbourhood with his camera, travelling all over for god-knows-what. Didn't

222

so much as say "good riddance", but that's what he was thinking.'

'Hearsay, Leo, hardly evidence.'

'You're the one who brought Kell in initially. What changed your mind? You've all of a sudden decided visiting a corpse to take pics for sexual gratification is run of the mill, that it?'

'Perhaps I got it wrong.' Locke swings back towards the car, glancing at the lodge. Karen Kell, he reckoned, was a better judge of character than he was. He'd sensed she wasn't simply standing by Robert because he was kin. She was, however, hiding something. 'Perhaps he really was up in the woods for some true crime story.'

'Fuck it, Frank, you've had your mind turned by that chick.' Sullivan shakes his head as they walk to their vehicle. 'I reckon you owe me a hundred bucks.'

~ ~ ~

Back at the precinct, the chief is on the phone.

'Robert Kell or Henrik Mattich?' she says. 'Which of them did the Lewis and Clarke girl?'

'Not sure,' Locke answers. 'Could have been either.'

'Or perhaps both. The way I see it, Kell as good as signed a confession when he took a swim with the fish. Maybe he and Mattich were partners. Then, when you and the Feds turn up at Snoqualmie Pass, Mattich splits, and Kell kills himself.'

'There wasn't a note.'

'There wouldn't be. Not if he was guilty.'

'So you're saying because there wasn't a note, he *is* guilty?' Locke shakes his head. 'Sounds like the sort of evidence you might get at a witch trial.'

'Don't play silly with me, Frank. Kell and Mattich are shoe-ins for the girl in the woods. Kell is dead, and Mattich is over the border with the Feds on his tail. Could be

Kell killed himself, or it could be that Mattich killed him. Either way, it's a result as far as I'm concerned. I don't understand what your problem is.'

'There's still evidence to gather, people I want to talk to. I believe Kell might have a link to some killings which took place down in New Mexico.'

'New Mexico is a little out of our jurisdiction.'

'So I just leave it?'

'Write it up and pass everything to me. I'll send the whole lot south with your name on it. If anyone down there wants to take it further, they'll know who to contact. Meanwhile, until Mattich turns up, I want you sweating the Billings crack house case.'

Locke takes a moment or two, wonders about protesting, then offers an obligatory 'yes, ma'am,' and hangs up.

~ ~ ~

The Billings crack house case involves a network of rural cook dens, and the investigation comes under one of the state's drug task forces and receives funding from the Rocky Mountain High-Intensity Drug Trafficking Area program. It's a complex multi-jurisdictional inquiry, and Locke has only a small part to play in bringing together some intelligence from local informers. The work is mostly corroborating various statements, deciding on their level of veracity, and scheduling further actions. Tedious is an understatement.

Two hours in and he has eyestrain from too much screen time. He could take a break, but the sooner he wades through the material, the sooner the work will be done.

It takes the rest of the day and most of the next morning. He's on the final couple of statements when Sullivan arrives and drops an envelope on Locke's desk.

'What's this?'

'Pictures of Kell cut open by Doc Hem,' Sullivan says.

'The autopsy is done?' Locke glances at his watch: half-eleven. Kell couldn't have made it to the morgue until yesterday afternoon. 'The chief stick a rocket up Hem's ass or something?'

'He had a free slot, and apparently, Kell was a priority.'

'Yeah, I gathered that. The Chief wants him out the way.' Locke slips a sheaf of papers from the envelope and fans the photographs on the desk. Kell clothed. Kell naked. Kell with his chest slit open and the ribs peeled back. 'If you could summarise.'

'Basically, as we guessed. The high level of alcohol in the bloodstream was indirectly responsible for Kell's death. He got tangled in some ropes — evidenced by markings on his forearms.' Sullivan points at one of the pictures. 'He pitched overboard. A length of chain was enough to provide negative buoyancy, and intoxication prevented him from rescuing himself. I reckon it's fifty-fifty as to whether it was suicide or just an accident. Either way, Kell drank himself into a stupor because he was worried about what happened in the forest.'

'And if he had nothing to do with the girl in the forest?'

'Then I don't know.' Sullivan gives a lift of his shoulders. 'Money problems, women problems. Maybe he thought, even if innocent, that the evidence was against him and being a drunkard loser, he took the easy way out.'

'According to Karen Kell, he hardly touched the stuff except on special occasions.'

'I don't know, Frank.' Sullivan chuckles. 'Perhaps he was fucking Karen and was scared of getting found out. Then again, I'd be keen to play Happy Families if she was my sister. She's—'

'What about the Henrik Mattich angle? Was there any evidence of force?'

'Look, Frank, where do you want to go with this?' Sullivan stuffs the remaining pictures back in the envelope. 'Mattich's not subtle. He wouldn't have the brains to rig Kell's death to look like suicide.'

Sullivan struts away like he's pretty much made his mind up. Locke isn't so sure. He calls Adam Hem.

'Kell was a virtual teetotaller,' Locke says. 'A toast at Christmas was about his limit. The booze in the cabin belonged to a previous tenant. Even allowing for the pressure he was under, there's no way he'd have consumed half a bottle of Southern Comfort.'

'Well, he did. The blood test showed a 0.24 per cent blood alcohol level. He was well and truly intoxicated.'

'Doesn't make sense.'

'That's true.' There's a pause before Hem continues. 'There's damage to two of his front teeth and bruising on the upper palette consistent with something hard being forced into his mouth.'

'Sullivan didn't tell me that.'

'It's in the report. If he chose to ignore it, that's not my problem.'

'So Kell was forced to drink the alcohol?'

'I can only tell you about the damage in the mouth. You'll have to draw your own conclusions.'

'Come on, Doctor Hem, give me a break.'

'Detective Sullivan is convinced Kell committed suicide, and what I observed could have been self-inflicted. If Kell was determined to get drunk as fast as he could and knew he was going to kill himself, then he might have been reckless.'

'But you don't believe that?'

'Surprisingly, it's difficult to hurt yourself deliberately. Your body stops you.'

'Was there any bruising on his arms?'

'Rope marks from the entanglement.'

'Could he have been tied up, and the bottle tipped down his throat?'

'No, I wouldn't say there are any signs to suggest that happened.'

'Humour me, Doctor Hem, let me run a little hypothesis by you. Let's say the killer used a gun and said to Kell drink up, or I'll shoot you. Kell can't do much to resist, but he's clever enough to smash his front teeth and scar the top of his palette, thus leaving a sign to us that this wasn't a suicide. Is that possible?'

'It's possible, but I'd question whether Kell could have had the clarity of thought to carry it off. I don't think most ordinary people would think like that when faced with almost certain death.'

'No, I think you're right there, Doctor Hem. Thanks for your help.'

Locke ponders what he's just learned and how it fits with the investigation. Replace a mystery assailant armed with a gun with Mattich and his bow, and it's unrealistic to believe Kell wouldn't have tried to resist. At close range, a bow is a lot less of a threat than a gun, and Mattich would have to keep the bow drawn while Kell finished the bottle. Plus, the setup doesn't sound like Mattich's way of doing things.

He thinks about Hem's phrase again.

*Most ordinary people...*

Which leads to the conclusion that perhaps Robert Kell wasn't an ordinary person.

# Chapter 25

Back at the station, the tirade doesn't begin until Sasaki and Malroony are in AC Cooper's office. But then he goes OTT. Or, as Malroony says afterwards, MTOTT: More Than OTT. This is vintage turbo Cooper, the AC mainlining on rocket fuel. An empty coffee cup flies across the room and smashes against a wall. A chair is kicked over. Cooper is red-faced, veins bulging in his neck, and Sasaki genuinely fears for the Chief's health as well as his own.

After several minutes of pure bile, Cooper slumps in his chair and puts his head in his hands. The wind has all gone out of him.

'Give me something, detective,' he says. 'Something for the press, something — for God's sake — for the Minister. If you can't, then we're fucked.'

'We've got roadblocks set up on the Arnhem and Kakuda highways,' Sasaki says. 'All patrols on high alert. The RAAF is providing air support, and reservists are on the ground searching the national park.'

'What good are roadblocks against a helicopter? We might as well piss in the wind for all the good it would do.' Cooper looks up. 'What about airports?'

'We're sending officers to every significant landing strip and airport and requesting flight plans for all helicopters. I suggest a media appeal asking for sightings.'

'And how the fuck is that going to look?' Cooper shakes his head. 'Please, members of the public, we've just lost custody of one of Australia's most dangerous criminals and need your help. If anyone has seen a helicopter, might be black, might be white, might have pretty gay rainbows on it, let us know. Kind regards, Detective Dickbrain.'

'There's something else,' Sasaki says. It's clutching at straws, but he might as well bring it up. 'Pearce teased us as he left. He said I needed to be better at maths if I was going to emulate my father.'

'Maths?' Cooper stares at Sasaki. 'Are you joking?'

'No, sir. I was thinking—'

'You can think all you like, Takeo,' Cooper says. He has a smirk on his face now. 'In fact, thinking is all you and Linda will be doing from now on because you're both suspended from active duty pending an enquiry into this shitpit of an investigation. Now fuck off out of my sight.'

Sasaki is about to protest when he sees Malroony move her head, a slow shake back and forth: hold fire, save it for another time. Wars are won using long-term strategy, not short-term tactics.

'Yes, sir,' Sasaki says, and he and Malroony leave the room.

~ ~ ~

Later, he's back at his desk. A cup of coffee and a doughnut on the right-hand side, Malroony perched on the left-hand side.

'What maths?' she asks. 'I don't remember any maths concerning the Tortilla girl.'

'Nor me.' Sasaki reaches for his cup of coffee but then changes his mind and attacks the doughnut instead. He licks a globule of jam from his finger and then searches a drawer for some tissues. 'We didn't do any maths. All we did was follow the bearing created by the position of the arm. I don't know what Pearce was getting at.'

'Me neither.'

'Still, if maths is involved, then we need numbers, right?'

'What do you mean?'

'I'll show you.'

Maroney grabs a cup of coffee for herself, and Sasaki gets to work. He opens a spreadsheet on his computer, and they enter all the data they can think of. The Tortilla girl's age and birth date. Her height and weight. Other body measurements.

'Bust size?' Malroony says.

Sasaki blushes.

'Well, that's the sort of thing serial killers are obsessed with, right?'

'I've no idea.'

They move on and enter other information. The postcode of the area where she lived. A phone number and bank account number. Soon, the spreadsheet has dozens of rows, but nothing pops out at them.

'This is no good,' Sasaki says. 'Perhaps Pearce is just playing with us, trying to lead us down a path that will take us away from the answers.'

'If so, then why be so obtuse? So far, this is wasting our time, but it isn't leading us in the wrong direction.'

'It's not leading us anywhere.'

Another round of coffees. More data heads into the spreadsheet.

'Wood and trees, boss,' Malroony says. She brushes a hand against the computer screen. 'We've too much to see anything now.'

Malroony is right. Sasaki stares at the figures on the screen, and they swirl and blur, and he can almost hear his father's voice chiding him for his stupidity.

'What's this then?' Kieran Lamb leans into the office. 'Finally getting round to doing your expenses?'

Sasaki explains what Pearce told them, what they're up to and the problems they're having.

'I don't remember anything to do with maths with the BUK. The arms were some distance from the bodies and pointing to the previous victim, but a compass bearing was the only number I remember.'

'You were the CSI? I 'Sasaki says.

'No, not the main CSI. I was just a pup in training, following old codger Henry Smith round, snapping at his heels, eager as anything.' Lamb smiles. 'Thirty-three years later, and I'm the old codger.'

'And what did the pup learn?'

'Not much, to be honest.' Lamb reaches up and taps a finger to his temple. 'And being of the age I am, I can recall even less. Your best bet is to find the original paperwork, especially the map showing the locations of the bodies relative to each other.'

'In the document store?'

'If that's a fancy name for the detritus in the basement, then yes. It was all on paper back then, and I don't think the old stuff's been digitised.'

'Well, how about it, sir?' Malroony says. 'As we're suspended, we've got nothing better to do, have we?'

They don't, so after a brief lunch, Sasaki and Malroony head down to the basement. Lamb's little workshop is situated in a cubbyhole under the stairs, but the rest of the space is utilised for general storage and is a complete mess, a vast dumping ground for equipment that is no longer needed. There's a pile of old riot shields in one corner, while against one wall, there are various promotional displays that have figured in PR drives over the years. The document store is behind a wire cage stretching the room's width. There's swipe-card entry through a locked mesh door. Inside, metal shelving bends under the weight of stacks of files, cardboard boxes are piled several high and in danger of toppling over, and loose sheets of paper are scattered liberally on the floor.

'Record keeping should be more than just keeping records,' Malroony says as she swipes them into the store with her ID. 'This is a shocker.'

Sasaki nods. A shocker is what it is. When the police moved first to computers and then to entirely online, the rush to eliminate paper meant it was easier to just get everything out of sight and out of mind. He'd even heard AC Cooper talk of disposing of all these records. Sasaki knew the only thing stopping him was the thought that every document would need to be first digitised and then shredded.

An hour in, and the mess is no clearer.

'I've come across cases from thirty years ago,' Sasaki says. 'But nothing to do with the BUK.'

'Do you think somebody has taken the files?' Malroony says as she shifts a large box of photocopies to a nearby table. 'Perhaps for shredding?'

'Cooper has been threatening to get rid of all this stuff for years, but it would be strange if he suddenly decided to do it now.'

'Strange or suspicious?'

'What are you suggesting, Linda?'

'I don't know.' Malroony pulls a stack of photocopies from her box and spreads them on the table. 'Just what I said, I guess. Suspicious. Of course, it might not be Cooper. It could be someone else.'

Sasaki returns to shifting some boxes, trying to remember to bend his knees as he lifts so as not to do his back in. They work methodically, going through each shelving unit shelf by shelf. Sasaki takes a marker pen and ticks the side of each box as they go, and by late afternoon, there are more boxes with crosses on than without.

Then Sasaki finds the BUK files.

'Three boxes,' he says. 'No labels, just a heap of paperwork piled inside.'

They clear the table and disgorge the paper onto it. It's still a mess, but at least it's manageable, and page by page, they sort the case notes and official records. In another hour, it's done, but they're missing something.

'There are no crime scene maps,' Sasaki says. 'Details on the forensics, autopsies, but nothing about the positioning of the bodies or the arms.'

'Could your dad have kept those notes for some reason?'

'No.' Sasaki knows his father was a stickler for procedure and would never have taken anything official home.

As they're re-examining the stacks of paperwork to see if they've missed anything, boots clomp down the stairs, and an officer dumps a broken office chair in one corner. He acknowledges them and leaves. Sasaki stares after him. The cage and card access provide only nominal security, and anyone with a card could have come down here and removed the maps. The question is, why?

They order all the paperwork, stack everything back in the boxes, and resume searching for the missing files. By late afternoon, having had only two short breaks, they're on the final set of shelves.

'Remember that petition on domestic violence handed in last year?' Malroony says, delving into yet another box. 'Calls for increased measures and longer sentences?'

'Of course,' Sasaki says. How could he forget? Anna had been one of those who'd started the campaign.

'Well, conspiracy theories or not, I've found the map files in amongst all those sheets of signatures.'

Malroony pulls out a flimsy cardboard ring binder, takes it over to the table and opens the front cover. Several large sheets of paper have been folded to fit into the binder, one edge hole-punched. She clicks open the binder and takes out the maps one by one. Sasaki begins unfolding them.

'Girl A's body location,' he says. 'And the next is Girl B.'

Then comes Girl C and some aerial shots of all three crime scenes. Several very large-scale maps reveal the precise position of the bodies and items found nearby, and a map of the Northern Territory shows the three crime scenes in relation to each other.

'We're missing something,' Sasaki says. 'There should be a medium-scale map that would show the position of the arms relative to the three bodies, but it's not here.'

'Boss?' Malroony inspects the ring binder and removes the remaining sheets. She points down at the rings. 'Look.'

Sasaki leans over and peers at the rings. There's a sliver of paper with a jagged edge and two neat semi-circular holes. Someone has ripped a sheet from the binder.

~ ~ ~

The following day, Sasaki is in early. Before Cooper, Anderson and nearly everyone else. Not before Kieran Lamb, though.

'Knew I'd find you here first thing,' Sasaki says as Lamb looks up from his computer. 'I need to ask a favour.'

'Don't you always?' Lamb says with a smile. 'Go on, shoot.'

'We found some material to do with the BUK, including several maps, but not the precise one we need. I think somebody has taken it and, by the looks of things, recently.'

Lamb, always the one for cold, hard evidence, wants to know why.

'The map file had been moved,' Sasaki says. 'It had been placed in a box of petition signatures only dumped in the store last year. There are signs a page has been ripped from the file.'

234

Sasaki shows Lamb the file.

'I want to know who accessed the document store in the last few weeks. We have to scan in and out, right? — so there must be a record somewhere, and I can't see any reason it would be secret.'

'It's called an evidence trail, and no, it's not secret.' Lamb turns back to his computer and taps a couple of keys. 'As nearly everything is now digital, there shouldn't be many people on the list. I'm in my cubbyhole a fair bit, and hardly anyone comes down there, let alone goes into the doc store.'

Sasaki stands at Lamb's shoulder and watches a handful of names pop up on the screen. There's Lamb himself, Sasaki and Malroony, two civilian administrators, a local lawyer and Ken Royston.

'That good enough for you?' Lamb hits a key, and a nearby printer begins to whirr into action.

'Yes,' Sasaki says.

He grabs the sheet from the printer and goes outside, where the early morning sun is just beginning to give some heat. He looks at the names, and it's Royston who stands out since the date he accessed the store was just a few days before the Tortilla girl was found.

*Before...*

How does that work? Sasaki asks himself. Why would Royston tamper with evidence linking the BUK to the Tortilla murder when the crime hadn't even been committed?

There is only one way to find out.

He heads out of town, driving south towards Tortilla Flats, once again sans Malroony.

'Sorry, Linda,' he says to himself as the suburban sprawl gives way to countryside. 'I need to do this by myself.'

After an hour of driving, he slows at the junction for the flats and pulls in. Stops the car for a minute or two. Then he turns around and drives back towards Darwin for a few miles before taking a left signposted *Batchelor*. This isn't about now, about what happened at Tortilla Flats, it's about what went on thirty-three years ago, and Ken Royston, one of Endo Sasaki's contemporaries, might just have a story to tell. Royston, Sasaki knows, left Darwin shortly after his father had caught the BUK, giving up a promising career as a detective to return to uniform in the sleepy town of Batchelor. Sure, everyone has to make choices in their lives, but to Sasaki, it seems like an odd one.

The countryside around Batchelor is low scrub and sparse woodland, lusher than the dusty fields a few miles away at Tortilla Flats. He follows the road through tall trees to where the police station sits behind a wire fence with palms and a neat-cut lawn out front. Sasaki pulls into the driveway and parks beside Royston's ute. It's a warm day, the temperature up in the high twenties, and Sasaki has been driving with the aircon off and the windows down. The cool inside the building is welcome as he pushes through the door into the reception area. Ken Royston sits at a desk behind the counter and looks up as Sasaki enters.

'Takeo?' For a moment, Royston is confused. He springs up, alarmed. 'What are you doing here? It's not...?'

'Morning, Ken,' Sasaki says. 'Not what?'

'Nothing.' Royston grimaces. 'I don't know. For a second, I thought there'd been a family tragedy and they'd sent you to tell me. Doesn't make much sense, but there you go.'

It doesn't make much sense at all, Sasaki thinks.

'What can I do for you?' Royston says, the grimace replaced by a wry smile. 'Aside from keeping a lookout for Derek Pearce, of course. Mind you, you can't switch on the

TV without seeing his ugly mug, so I can't see him getting far.'

'Let's hope not.'

Sasaki holds Royston's gaze for a few seconds, letting a silence build, the only sound a bird singing, the song drifting in through an open window.

'So?' Royston spreads his hands. 'Something to do with the Tortilla girl, right?'

'You were my father's right-hand man back when all this started.' Sasaki walks to the far end of the counter, lifts the flap and moves into the office area. There are three desks with workstations, and he pulls out one of the chairs and sits. Gestures at Royston to do the same. When he returns to his desk, Sasaki continues. 'You were at the crime scenes and helped my father on the case.'

'Sure, but I can't take credit. Endo did all the work. Clever, your dad. Very clever.'

'So why did you walk away when it was all over? You could have stayed in Darwin and risen the ranks. Instead, you put the uniform back on and moved here.'

Royston shrugs. 'Lifestyle. Change of pace. The pressure around the BUK killings was enormous, and I couldn't cope. Out here, we don't have to worry about things like that. At least not until a couple of weeks ago.'

'And that was the only reason?'

'Yeah, of course.' Royston squares his shoulders. 'What are you suggesting, mate?'

'There was pressure, yes, but I don't think the media or your superiors caused you to quit Darwin. There was something else.'

'You don't know what you're talking about, Takeo. You were barely out of nappies.'

'I was seven, but it's a fair point, although I'm a long way from nappies now.' Sasaki nods. 'And while I'll admit I don't have my father's intellectual ability, like him, I'm a good judge of character.'

'Are you accusing me of something?'

'Quite the opposite. Endo wouldn't have had you at his side had he not trusted you. I'm sure he was devastated when you quit Darwin, and he was left surrounded by brutes like Cooper, Anderson and the other racist cronies.'

'They were different times, Takeo. A different world. You can't blame people for their upbringing. Hell, I'm not clean in that regard. Even I tell the occasional off joke, but it doesn't make me a Nazi.'

'Sure, and you're not.' Sasaki holds up the folder he's brought with him. 'But you might be a thief.'

He places the folder on the desk and opens it. It's the file with the selection of maps, and Sasaki flips through until he gets to where a page has been removed, and there's only a thin strip of paper left behind. When he looks up, he's met with a stare from Royston, the colour all drained from his face.

'You came up to Darwin last month, and while there, you scanned yourself into the document store. You probably don't realise, but every card swipe is logged, so it's no good denying it.'

'I needed a piece of paperwork for a case here in Batchelor.'

'Which case? Show me.'

'I... I couldn't find it. I left empty-handed.'

'My father would be disappointed in you because you're better than this.' Sasaki flicks the pages in the file back and forth. 'The missing page, as I'm sure you know, is a map showing the precise locations of the bodies and, more importantly, the severed arms. My father used the map somehow to work out that it was Pearce who'd killed the women.'

'It's history, Takeo. Why can't you leave it alone?'

'Because a woman died out at Tortilla Flats. That tells me it's not simply history.' Sasaki pauses again. More silence; this time, there's no bird song, only the tick of a clock on the office wall. 'I need the map, Ken.'

'I was threatened,' Royston says. 'Not just me, my family. My children and grandchildren.'

'How?'

'A letter.' Royston swivels on his chair and opens a drawer. He pulls out a sheet of paper and hands it to Sasaki. 'Gave me instructions to retrieve the map from the document store and destroy it, or else one of my grand-daughters might be involved in a traffic accident.'

The A4 sheet is printed in large block capitals, and as Royston says, it lays out what would happen if he didn't do as he was told.

'So someone knew the map was in the store but either didn't have the right access rights or, more likely, didn't want to leave a trail.'

'I guess.' Royston shrugs. 'From the dust on the file, no-body had touched it for years, and I didn't see how it could matter, as it was so long ago. Whoever wanted it removed was probably someone who fucked up back then and didn't want the information to come out.'

'Bullshit. When I first came out to Tortilla Flats, you told me explicitly the new case was related to the BUK killings. You must have realised the map was important, and it wasn't simply about somebody protecting their reputation or pension. Besides, you removed the maps *before* the Tortilla girl was killed. When you went to the crime scene and discovered the severed arm, you knew you'd been set up, yet you didn't tell me.'

'But that's the point. When I took the file, I knew I was doing something wrong, but nobody had been murdered. I wasn't covering up anything.'

'You were perverting the course of justice.'

'Takeo, they threatened my grandchildren.'

'So come to me about it or talk to AC Cooper.'

Royston makes a huffing sound and shakes his head. 'Cooper's up to his neck in shit.'

'Are you accusing the AC of something?'

'The whole force has been mired in crap for decades. It's why your father was a breath of fresh air. He was guided by morals rather than cash, his dick, or a quick promotion.

'But Cooper?'

'Not the letter, no.'

'So, who do you think?'

Another shrug. No answer.

'Look, Ken, I'll have to push you on this. If you don't co-operate, then I'll need to ask you to come back to Darwin with me. We'll have to get AC Cooper involved.'

'And the threats? If I'm seen helping you, my family could be at risk.'

'I'll arrange protection.'

'I've got two daughters and a son. Between them, they've given me five grandkids. Are you going to lock them all up somewhere?' Royston shakes his head. 'Sorry, no can do, mate. It's not going to happen.'

'There's a killer out there, and now he's teamed up with Pearce.'

'And who's fault is that?'

'Ken, just give me something I can work with. A name. Because if you don't and they kill again, it's on you.'

Royston gives Sasaki a long, hard stare. Then he turns back to the drawer and pulls something else out.

'I'll give you this.'

Royston hands a sheet of paper across, and Sasaki stares down. Roads and rivers and towns and villages. Scribbled markings and circles and arcs and lines. Adorning it all are several columns of Japanese characters.

'You see,' Royston continues, 'I destroyed the original map just as I was asked to, so scout's honour, I could swear I'd complied with the letter's demands. However, I thought it might be prudent to take a copy.'

# Chapter 26

Chase is kicking her heels. It's a couple of days after the interview with Alan Grainger, and Green and Stafford are off following a lead involving a sex offender who's missing from the register. He's a knife fanatic, served fifteen years for rape and is out on licence. Only he's gone AWOL, and a call to his probation officer indicates he might fit the required profile.

But Chase isn't feeling it.

She thinks back to the interrogation. She was surprised Grainger had been so confident because even someone innocent usually displays some anxiety. It was as if he *knew* they had nothing on him.

But they did have something: the ANPR camera had snapped his car crossing Kew Bridge. Which suggests Grainger's confidence came not from the lack of police evidence but his knowledge that the evidence made no difference. His alibi was watertight. Or so he thought.

She fires up a map on her workstation and zooms in on London. She eyeballs the route from West Hampstead, where Grainger had dinner, to Reigate. The obvious way is south through Kensington, crossing the river at Putney and heading down past Wimbledon Common to Epsom and Reigate. When she plots the start and destination into the map, the shortest route does turn out to be that way, but the quickest, although nearly twice the distance, is out along the A40 to the M25 and then anti-clockwise round London to Reigate. An alternative route, only a few minutes longer at three in the morning, does cross the river at Kew Bridge, but it seems the most unlikely choice. However, it would be hard to argue the Kew route would have taken Grainger far out of his way.

She drums her fingers on the desk. Earlier, she'd sent two DCs — Nikki Ghosh and Kyle Willem — to West Hampstead to check Grainger's booking at the *Burger and Bucket*. She doesn't expect anything but a confirmation that he was there, but when the call comes through, DC Ghosh produces a nice little *gotcha*.

'He was there that evening,' Ghosh says. 'The manager showed me the transaction on their system. The bill was for fifty-three pounds and seventeen pence. Grainger rounded it up to sixty.'

'Right,' Chase says, disappointed. 'And the times match?'

'Yup. The transaction time was eleven fifty-three.'

'Shit.' Chase stares at the screen where West Hampstead is plum centre. She imagines Grainger leaving the restaurant, having a drink with his companion at a bar on the high street, parting and then going on to meet someone for casual sex, driving back to Reigate via Kew Bridge. 'Well, never mind, Nikki, we tried.'

'There's something else. When I looked at the bill, I figured it was cheap for two. Fifty quid for a meal with a drink? In a posh place like that? No way. So I asked to see the breakdown, and there was only one starter, one main, two soft drinks and one coffee. Just to be sure, I checked with the manager and Grainger ate alone. That doesn't make sense, does it?'

Chase congratulates Ghosh on her good work and hangs up.

Driving from Reigate to North London to eat alone doesn't make sense at all. Grainger knew that, so he slipped in a lie about eating with a friend, thinking all that mattered was the proof he'd been at the restaurant. But, in Chase's experience, one lie usually leads inexorably to others.

'Got you, you fucker,' she says.

~ ~ ~

An hour later, she has cause to repeat the exact words as DC Sam Hastings beckons her over.

'Result,' he says, pointing to his screen. 'A clear shot of Grainger's Merc passing a security camera at the apartment block at Kew.'

Chase leans in. A black and white image shows a Mercedes 4x4 heading down the slip road on the north side of Kew Bridge. She notes the time code at the bottom of the picture: one thirteen am.

'What's down there?' Chase says.

'A bar and the marketing suite for the apartments. Car parking for the local business under the arches.'

'Access to the river?'

'Yes. Steps down to the mud at low tide.'

'Do any cameras cover the parking closer to the river.'

'No.'

'What do you think, Sam?'

'Um...' Hastings looks at the screen for a moment. 'Grainger eats at the restaurant and then goes to a nearby bar for a drink. He drives to Kew and parks up beside the river. He's already got the body in the back of the 4x4, so he unloads it and takes it down to the mud. He's reconnoitred the area earlier and knows the houseboat just upstream has a tender, so he nicks that and loads the body. He ferries it across and dumps it. Then he comes back and picks up the already severed arm, takes it up to the top of the apartment block, and leaves it on the lift shaft. After all that, he drives off, and the ANPR camera on the bridge clocks him at three eleven AM as he heads back to Reigate.'

'Very good,' Chase says. She turns from Hastings and spots Stafford waltzing across towards the SCU. 'Now let's see what John thinks.'

Stafford is enthusiastic, which is hardly surprising since he was the one who suggested Grainger in the first place. Plus, the knife-play suspect he and Green were after has turned up and has a cast iron alibi.

'Nick's gone off in a sulk,' Stafford says. 'Refuses to believe Grainger can be involved.'

'Well, the new evidence says he is,' Chase says.

'I agree, but what are we going to do about it? There's no way we can call Grainger in for a second round of questioning without alerting Boyle. We're on our own.'

Which explains why, two hours later, she and Stafford are sitting in Stafford's car parked near the entrance of Littlewood Close, a cul-de-sac on the outskirts of Reigate. There's a short white picket fence on either side of the road and a neat area of mown grass. A *Private Road* sign makes it clear that if you don't have business with the residents, then you're not welcome.

Sleepy doesn't even begin to describe the area, Chase thinks. A couple of cars have driven along the B road, but there hasn't been any sign of life from Littlewood Close. If they're to discover anything about what Grainger is up to, they need to get nearer.

Stafford starts the car and pulls into the close. He cruises down and slows as they pass *Wyndhams*, Grainger's house. A huge leylandii hedge blocks the view of the garden, but they can see through a set of tall, wrought iron gates. The house is a post-war imposing brick structure. A garage is tacked onto one side, and Velux windows in the tiled roof show the loft has been converted into bedrooms.

'He's out,' Stafford says.

245

What Chase believes at first to be a fantastic feat of clair-voyance turns out to be nothing more than a logical deduction: To one side of the gate is a metal letterbox in a brick pillar, and several letters are visible in the slot. An Amazon parcel lies on the ground by the gates, the card-board darkened and soggy from overnight rain.

'Let's ask the neighbour,' Chase says as she spots a car cruise past and turn into the next-door property, auto-matic gates opening to let the vehicle in.

The neighbour is a well-to-do woman in her early forties, and she looks alarmed as she gets out of the car and spots Chase and Stafford slipping in through the gates before they close.

'No need to worry,' Stafford says. As they approach, he pulls his warrant card from his jacket and shows it to the woman. 'We're the police.'

'Police?' she says worryingly, reacting like all people who've never broken the law. 'Is there something wrong?'

'Not at all. It's just about your neighbour, Mr Grainger. We've had a call from someone concerned with his mental health.'

'Really?' The woman looks flushed and then relieved. 'That can't be right. I saw Alan yesterday morning before he left for a holiday abroad. A bit last minute, he said, but it was a bargain apparently.'

'A holiday?' Chase says, wondering if the interview ses-sion had stirred Grainger into action. 'Did he mention where he was going?'

'No, just that it was somewhere hot. He told me he'd be gone for a couple of weeks.'

'Are you sure about that?'

'Quite sure. You see, I promised to collect his post and pop it inside for him. To feed his cat, too.' The woman turns her head and looks towards Grainger's house. 'Only

246

last night I came back late. I fed the cat, but I must have missed the parcel in the dark.'

'Right.'

'And he won't be back for two weeks?'

'That's what he said.'

Chase is aware of a tingle forming in her fingertips.

'I wonder if you could let us into Alan's house so we can check everything is all right?' Chase gives a little smile. Innocent. Meek. 'Just to be on the safe side.'

The woman shifts from foot to foot, one hand clasping another.

'You can verify our identities by phoning New Scotland Yard,' Stafford says, handing over a business card. 'Ask for the Serial Crimes Unit.'

The woman takes the card and stares down at it. She turns and gazes in the direction of Grainger's house.

'Serial Crimes Unit?' She gives an involuntary shiver as if she's been made aware of Grainger's infamy for the first time. 'No, that won't be necessary.'

Two minutes later, armed with the remote control for the front gates, a set of keys, the code for the burglar alarm, and instructions on where to find tins of cat food so they can feed the moggy, Chase and Stafford are back outside Grainger's property.

'Risky,' Stafford says. 'If she phones to check, if she tells Grainger, if Grainger isn't the killer, if he comes back unexpectedly. Four ways to lose, and those are only the ones I can think of off the top of my head.'

'You got us into this,' Chase says as the gates swing open, and they walk down the driveway to the front door.

'Thanks.' Stafford takes the keys and unlocks the door. He steps inside and punches the alarm code into a panel to the right.

247

Chase follows and swings the door shut behind them. A tick-tock, tick-tock comes from a Grandfather clock in the hall. Otherwise silence.

'Do you think he's done a runner?' Chase says. 'Spun the holiday story to his neighbour as a diversion?'

'It's possible,' Stafford says. 'But there's only one way to find out. I'll take the ground floor. You go upstairs.'

'Right. And remember what we're looking for: Scalpels, suture thread, chloroform, the odd bone saw, and a bird cage with a bearded reedling singing sweetly. That sort of thing.'

Stafford laughs and moves away down the hall towards an open door, the kitchen beyond. Chase turns to where a wide wooden staircase rises and curls around three walls to a landing. Brass stair rods hold a rich ochre carpet in place, and as she climbs the stairs, each step creaks in response. At the top, she pauses. There are at least half a dozen doorways off the landing. Four or five bedrooms, she thinks. Then there could be a family bathroom and a study, perhaps a storeroom. She eases down the landing to the first door. It stands ajar and she pushes it open. Bingo. First time lucky. The master bedroom.

Grainger's taste in furnishing is ostentatious and lurid. The subtle ochre carpet of the landing gives way to a swirling purple pattern in here. The bed is a four-poster with yet more purple material as a canopy, white sheets on the bed itself, and oversized pillows fluffed up against a padded crimson headboard.

Where to start? There's an antique rolltop bureau, a chest of drawers, a bedside cabinet, and a built-in wardrobe. And, at a second glance, something metal wrapped around one of the bedposts.

Chase walks across. She stares at the length of chain with a manacle welded to each end. It looks like Grainger forgot to put away one of his toys. The bedside cabinet reveals another pair of manacles, a large veined dildo and a rubber ball gag. There's nothing wrong with a little sex play, Chase thinks, but taken in the round knowing what Grainger has got up to in the past, it's more than a little disturbing.

She's about to kneel and check under the bed when she gets an overwhelming sense she's not alone. To her right, in her peripheral vision, the door to the ensuite moves a fraction. Then a little more. Chase prepares to go for the heavy marble lampstand on the cabinet. She just needs to get her timing right and make the move at the exact moment she's attacked. She keeps her back to the door, listening for a creak of a floorboard or the slide of a foot on the carpet.

Nothing.

And then fingers brush against her ankle.

She leaps sideways and lunges for the lampstand. Grabs it, turns, and raises it to smash into Grainger's face...

But he's not there.

A sleek Persian cat stands beside her, tail straight up, the tip twitching. The cat purrs and rubs against Chase's leg.

'Jeez!' She bends and strokes the cat. 'You scared me.'

The cat mews and saunters across to the doorway. Chase follows and shouts downstairs to warn Stafford about the cat and goes back to searching the room.

There's nothing else of note in the bedside cabinet, while the wardrobe contains only clothing. Which leaves the rolltop bureau. The cover slides up to reveal an inlaid green leather writing surface and a dozen small drawers. Chase works methodically from top to bottom and left to right. There are bank statements going back several years, bunches of till receipts held together with paperclips, some letters from Grainger's sister, a drawer full of pens and pencils, a couple of wristwatches and various other items of no consequence.

She gets excited momentarily when she comes across several pictures of Grainger clad head-to-toe in leather, but they turn out to be a series of images taken at some glam fetish party full of celebrities. She supposes Alison and Lizzie could have been there, but if so, there's no photographic evidence.

Fuck, Chase thinks as she pushes the last drawer closed. There are a couple of vertical letter slots containing several postcards. She pulls them out and examines them, but they appear to be from casual acquaintances and nothing more than the usual 'wish you were here' greetings. She returns the postcards, but as she slides the final one in, it stops, snagging on something in the slot. Chase reaches in and pulls out a passport. She opens it and flicks through until she comes to Grainger's ugly mug shot.

'Abroad, my arse,' Chase says.

# Chapter 27

More work from the Billings job lands on Locke's desk, and he doesn't think about Kell and Mattich and the poor girl from Lewis and Clarke for a while. There's no word from Jim Swanson on the search at Snoqualmie Pass and how the hunt for Mattich is going. No call from Karen Kell. Nothing new from Kerri Dunstan or Adam Hem.

At the end of the day, when everyone else has left the office, Locke reviews all the material, hoping for some kind of revelation. As he clicks through various documents, he comes to the conclusion that the patron saint of investigators must be on vacation because there's a severe shortage of anything approaching a decent lead or a clue.

Frustrated, he calls Jim Swanson for an update on the search of Mattich's place. With all the resources and tech the agents will have used, they'll surely have discovered something. However, the call goes through to voicemail.

*I'm sorry I can't—*

He doesn't even bother to leave a message. Instead, he shuts down his computer and heads for home. He has a few rest days scheduled, and it's time to take a break and let someone else deal with all the shit for the next forty-eight hours.

Locke and his wife own a plot ten miles northwest of Missoula. Nearest neighbours a couple of hundred yards away. The way Locke likes it. A significant change from Seattle, where they lived in an apartment downtown for most of their time there. Noise, bustle, disturbance. People top, bottom, left and right, but in truth, he hadn't known any of his neighbours more than to nod to in the elevator.

A short gravel road curls away from the highway and up to Locke's place. There's a substantial garage off to the right with enough room inside for two cars and a workshop. In his downtime, Locke likes making things: woodwork, metalwork, any kind of work where you create something from scratch. The results are scattered round the yard and inside the house. There's a swing seat on the front lawn, a sundial close by, and a sculpture of a wildcat made from old motorcycle parts that guards the approach to the driveway. In the house, the kitchen cabinets are all Locke's work, as is a rustic coffee table hewn from a massive fallen oak tree.

To the left, there's a stable block where his wife keeps her horses. The house is a new build, snug in the winter and cool in the summer. The big enclosed veranda lets them entertain whatever the season. The house is cosy for two, but Locke likes it that way. When the kids come to visit, they bed down in a spare room. Sure, there'll be grandkids someday, but Locke has plans to build a guest chalet to house them all.

A pair of floodlights flare from the stable block and the garage, but no light from the house itself, and Locke remembers his wife is out this evening. He parks up, but before he gets out, he checks his shoulder holster.

'Can't be too careful,' he says, pulling out his weapon as he climbs from the car.

He stands for a moment and breathes in the mountain air. Seattle this isn't. Then he walks across and climbs the steps, pushing at the veranda door. Stops and swivels on the veranda and peers out into the night. A glow from down the valley marks his neighbour Earl's house. Another half a mile to the west is the next-door property but one. He glances at the gun in his hand. Shakes his head. This is why they moved out here, away from all the crap in the city. Not having to bolt the door. Not worrying you're going to get carjacked. Not being suspicious of every stranger you encounter.

'You're getting paranoid, old man.'

He takes another deep breath, the cool night air biting his lungs. A few wisps of snow drift down into the light from the floods. According to the weather forecast, there'll be more tonight, and spring will be forestalled for a week or so. The passing of the seasons is something Locke has grown to appreciate with every year he spends in Montana. Each contains its promise and will arrive with an inevitability whatever else happens in the world.

Locke is about to turn back to the door, but his gaze follows a snowflake as it falls in front of the garage. A crack between the doors reveals a slit of light as if he or his wife have forgotten to turn a switch off. He steps back off the veranda and walks over, stopping a few paces from the doors as the light flickers. He reaches for the handle and eases the door open, but he realises he was wrong about leaving the light on because the light *isn't* on. The flickering comes from a dozen candles arranged in a rough circle on the workshop floor. They gutter in the draught from the open door, and for a moment, Locke is utterly confused.

He steps through the doorway and slips inside, his gun held up and ready. As he approaches the candles, a copper taste hits the back of his throat.

*Blood.*

Something is lying in the centre of the circle of light.

*Something* or *someone*?

Not someone, because it's too small to be a person.

Locke moves closer. Squinting in the dark, he can make out a pink mass of meat like a chunk of steak or a whole chicken. He turns to the right. Just outside the circle of light is a bundle of fur belonging to the skinned creature. Black with a hint of white and tan.

And Locke and his wife own two cats, Yin and Yang. Yang is white with a few black splodges. Yin is...

Locke lunges for the side of the workshop, where there's a heavy workbench. He ducks behind it and pops his gun forward, covering the rear of the garage. His gaze flits around, trying to penetrate the shadows. As best he can tell, there's no one in here. He swings his aim back to the doorway. Outside, snow has begun to tumble down in the light from the flood above the door.

This butchery is Henrik Mattich's work, for sure. But is he out there waiting, or has he long fled, the corpse of poor Yin a marker of his deranged state?

Locke doesn't know.

*Work the numbers, Frank,* he says to himself.

One, Mattich killed Yin as a warning to Locke. Stay away from the case or else. Only the FBI has presumably been swarming around Mattich's place, so as a warning, it isn't going to work. Two, Mattich slaughtered the cat as an act of revenge. But, like option one, that doesn't make sense; Mattich would want much more than the death of a pet as payback. Finally, three, Mattich was waiting to kill Locke, but Yin — always the friendliest of the two felines — crossed his path; Mattich simply killed the cat because he enjoyed doing so. He couldn't help himself.

*So he's out there...*

Locke emerges from behind the workbench. He takes slow steps towards the doorway, pausing every so often. He looks around. Listens.

Nothing.

At the door, he stops again. The driveway between the workshop and the house is already white-over with snow, flakes whispering down, the fall heavier now. Locke reckons he could make it to the car in a couple of seconds, but it will be five seconds or more to get to the house. When he reaches the verandah, he will be a sitting duck for a moment.

'I know you're here, Henrik,' Locke hollers into the night. 'You killed the girl up in Lewis and Clarke, and I'm certain you killed the women in Seattle. Whatever happens to me, you're going down for multiple homicide.'

'Whatever happens to you...' His words come echoing back.

Locke recognises Mattich's characteristic rasp and instinctively ducks behind the workshop door. As he checks his weapon, there's a sharp *hiss* and an arrow thuds into the wood cladding beside the door. Locke stares at the arrow; Mattich is highly skilled with a hunting bow, and if he'd wanted, he could have hit Locke before he announced his presence. Which can only mean he has something else planned.

'I don't appreciate the little surprise you left me, Henrik.' Locke checks he can't be targeted through the half-open door and readies his gun. 'What do you want?'

'I want to gut you like I filleted those girls in Seattle. I'll flay you, too, even while you're still breathing.'

Locke tilts his head as the voice, muffled by the snowfall, floats across the yard. It's hard to be sure, but he reckons Mattich is over by the corner of the house.

'Sure, but what's the endgame, Henrik?' Locke shouts. 'You kill me, then what? It's not like you'll get away with it, so why risk everything to do this?'

'I have no choice,' Mattich says. 'Instructions have been handed down, and I'm compelled to carry them out.'

It's the old *voices in my head* routine again, Locke thinks. God or the devil or some other entity providing all

255

the excuses Mattich needs to embark on a fresh spree of murders.

'Well, if you're going carry out your master's wishes, then you'll have to come in and get me,' Locke says. 'How about that?'

For a moment, there's no response, but then Mattich's voice comes again. 'Did you know there's more than one way to skin a cat?'

As the words are choked by the snow, a flare of yellow light comes spiralling in an arc through the darkness. Locke leaps back as a Molotov cocktail explodes at the entrance to the workshop, a wash of flame igniting the doors. In seconds, the cladding at the front of the shop is on fire, sparks crackling in the night air. Locke steps away from the doors and retreats into the depths of the workshop. It will take only a minute or two for the fire to catch hold and begin to devour the building, but escaping through the doors into the yard doesn't hold much appeal; Mattich will pick him off the moment he emerges. He thinks about getting hit by an arrow, the wound probably not fatal, Mattich then free to carry out his threat of skinning Locke alive. If the heat wasn't already so intense, he'd shiver at the thought. As it is, he needs to move fast.

At the rear of the workshop, there's a single door that provides another exit. Unfortunately, it is padlocked from the outside. Mattich, ever careful and precise when it comes to his trade, will have checked the door out and knows Locke can't escape that way. What he doesn't realise is that Locke won't give up so easily. He moves quickly over to the bench, where there is an array of storage bins. He reaches for an impact driver and runs to the door. It takes but a few moments to remove the eight screws holding the big flat hinges, and then the door is free. Locke drops the driver and grabs hold of the handle to prevent the door from falling outwards. He carefully manoeuvres it open enough to squeeze through and then lets the door hang on the padlock.

The fire is intense now, consuming the workshop in an ever-growing inferno. Flames ripple into the sky and meet the falling snow. Locke edges away from the workshop and skirts round towards the house. The light from the fire is strong enough to cast deep shadows, and Locke is confident that Mattich can't see him as he runs up a fence line and reaches the far side of the house. He circles the building, his gun drawn and ready. Sure enough, when he comes back round to the front, he can see Mattich standing at the corner facing the workshop. He holds a compound hunting bow, an arrow already nocked and the trigger release in his hand.

Locke moves to within a few paces, steadies himself and takes aim.

He whispers: 'Henrik...'

Mattich whirls around, drawing the bow as he does so. The fire silhouettes his head, but Locke sees a flash of white teeth as if Mattich is smiling.

Then Locke pulls the trigger on his gun.

At close range, he can't miss, and the bullet hits Mattich somewhere to the right of his nose. The arrow releases but flies over Locke's head. The bow flops uselessly to the ground as Mattich spins sideways and falls into the snow.

Locke steps forward as Mattich coughs once and then lies still. Locke aims down with his weapon and considers putting another couple of rounds into Mattich's head. Just to make sure. Doesn't. Instead, he walks round to the front of the house, where a white cat with one black ear emerges from the crawl space. Locke holsters his gun and bends and picks up the cat.

~ ~ ~

'Couldn't you have subdued him or something?' Leo Sullivan says when he arrives. 'Was it really necessary to kill him?'

Locke doesn't answer immediately. He stares over to where several of the fire crew are tamping down the grass round the edge of the workshop. There isn't much more for them to do since the building has all but burned to the ground. Before they arrived, Locke went to the stables and released his wife's two horses into the paddock. Then, he'd done his best to douse the blaze with a hose, but it was futile. He stored fuel, paint and other flammables in the shop, and once they caught fire, there was only one outcome. Luckily, the cold weather and covering of snow have stopped the fire from spreading beyond the immediate vicinity, and there's not much the fire crew can do other than help the police sift through the debris. A hose snakes from the fire truck to a man who is playing the jet on the workshop. The roof has collapsed but two of the four walls are still standing.

'Of course it was necessary,' Locke says eventually. 'If I hadn't fired, I'd be lying on the ground with my skin beside me and my intestines wrapped around my neck. Mattich would have done half of Adam Hem's job for him.'

'But—'

'I know, Leo, we're not going to get much out of him now.' Locke gives a dip of his shoulders. 'But what was I to do? Talk nicely to him?'

As far as Locke is concerned, this isn't a bad result. The families of the Seattle victims sure as hell aren't going to be disappointed, and assuming Locke can get some more evidence to link Mattich to the death of Monica Granton, then there's justice for her, too.

He looks over to the corner of the house where two of Adam Hem's orderlies are trying to get Mattich's body into a body bag without bringing a whole heap of snow along for the ride.

Hem strides across to Locke and Sullivan.

'There's a lot of blood in his airways,' Hem says. He narrows his eyes and grimaces. 'He took several minutes to die. Didn't you realise he was still alive?'

'No,' Locke says. 'I was more concerned with trying to contain the fire and save my wife's horses. Then there was the cat.'

'The cat?'

'It needed comforting.'

'You had a duty of care to the suspect in your custody.'

'What was I supposed to do? Administer first aid? Give mouth-to-mouth resuscitation?

'He suffered,' Hem says, looking pained. 'That's all I'm saying.'

'To be honest, Doc,' Locke says. 'I can't say I'm sorry.'

# Chapter 28

Chase checks with the Border Force and confirms Grainger hasn't left the country, at least not officially.

'Not wanting to be a party-pooper,' Green says. 'But I think he's long gone.'

'If he's left the UK, he'd have taken his passport even if he'd slipped out,' Chase says. 'You're just jealous we found something.'

'Correction, you didn't find anything. At least not anything that links Grainger to Alison or Lizzie.'

Green is correct. All they can say for sure is Grainger lied to his neighbour about going abroad. For all they know, he could be in a holiday cottage in Scotland, watching the rain cascade down.

After Chase and Stafford had gone through the house, Stafford suggested calling in a search team. The problem was Boyle. No way in a million years would he authorise ripping Grainger's place apart on the evidence of a passport and a set of manacles wrapped round a bedpost.

'I reckon DCS Boyle's missus locks him up in his own cuffs,' Green had said when they arrived back in the SCU with pictures of Grainger's set-up. 'Spanks his bare bottom with a wooden spoon until it's as red as his face.'

That's an image Chase doesn't think she'll forget in a hurry.

Chase and Stafford spend the morning delving further into Grainger's life, while Green focuses on Alison and Lizzie and tries to link the pair to Grainger. Between them, they come up with a big fat nothing.

'Grainger,' Green says when they convene at lunchtime. He shakes his head as if still disbelieving Stafford's original hypothesis. 'It simply doesn't make any sense why a man attracted solely to other men would change his spots and abduct two women. We know it wasn't sexual, so why choose them?'

'Alison and Lizzie were gay,' Chase says. 'But it's hard to imagine them frequenting the same places as Grainger.

'And they lived outside London,' Stafford says. 'Plus, as far as we know, they weren't in the scene.'

The statements drift between the three detectives, meandering, taking them nowhere. Still, Chase thinks this is better than sitting behind a screen and hoping something might come up. It only takes a tiny spark of an idea to generate a lead that could take them to Grainger's motive and, from there, to the man himself.

But after an hour of back and forth, there's not even a flicker.

'I'm going to ask Boyle for a search warrant for Grainger's house,' Chase says.

'But we've searched the place,' Stafford says. He holds up his hands. 'Nothing found.'

'It was cursory at best. We need a full search with a forensic team. We'll not get anywhere until we have proof that Grainger is connected somehow.'

'Good luck with that,' Green says.

Chase finds Boyle deep in conversation with the deputy commissioner of the Met. There's been a result on the Croydon job, and three men have been arrested on suspicion of murder. The DCS is buoyant and flushed with success, and there's a sneer on his lip as he sarcastically asks Chase where the SCU are up to on the Alison Madden case. The deputy commissioner, a woman Chase respects, wants the lowdown too, and Chase wonders if Boyle hasn't set a little trap she's about to walk right into.

Well, in for a penny...

'We need a search warrant for Doctor Alan Grainger's place,' Chase says. 'He informed the neighbour he was going on holiday abroad, but the Border Force has no record of him leaving the country.'

Chase continues to argue her point, highlighting the CCTV and ANPR footage and Grainger's misdirection concerning his solo meal at the posh burger joint, until Boyle raises a hand.

'I think we've heard enough,' he says. 'A warrant is out of the question and would be pointless since Grainger did not murder those women.' He turns to the Commissioner. 'Ma'am, it might be worth considering the lack of progress made by the Serial Crimes Unit and whether its continuation is the best use of scarce resources. The investigation would be better handled by one of my Major Investigation Teams. As demonstrated by the arrests this morning, we have the experience, expertise, and attitude to get this done and wrapped where the SCU has failed.'

Chase steels herself as a smirk begins to form on Boyle's face. This is where the SCU gets canned, and Chase, Green, and Stafford return to their regular jobs.

'Tell me, DI Chase,' the Commissioner says, dismissing Boyle's statement with a wave. 'Explain why we should risk our reputation by going after Grainger.'

So Chase does precisely that.

Ten minutes later, she's back on the SCU floor, striding over to the nest of cubbyholes with a massive grin on her face.

'You didn't get it?' Green says.

'I did,' Chase replies.

~ ~ ~

The following morning, Green coordinates the hunt for Grainger. Chase and Stafford head out to Reigate armed with a newly minted search warrant and accompanied by

262

half a dozen officers all too eager to ransack Grainger's house. Luckily, there's a police search advisor along for the ride, and Chase hopes he can keep the officers in line because if this doesn't work out, Grainger will be suing for every boot print, every crushed blade of grass and every ruffled bedsheet.

This time, it's PPE all around. Hairnets and masks and Tyvek suits, latex gloves and little booties. Chase thinks the cat is going to have kittens.

Inside, the forensic team get to work looking for trace evidence from Alison Madden or Lizzie Thomkin while Chase, Stafford and a couple of other officers search every available cupboard and drawer. Lift every mattress. Remove every book from the extensive bookshelves. Pull back the carpets. Search the fridge and freezer. Send the smallest, lightest officer up into the loft space.

They find several sex toys and another set of handcuffs in a box hidden at the back of a built-in wardrobe. A pillbox labelled as vitamin C comes from a kitchen drawer and contains a dozen poppers, while a polygrip bag holds a decent amount of speed.

'Quite the party animal, our Mr Grainger,' Stafford says as he sorts through the sex toys, placing each in a separate bag and labelling them. He holds up a piece of hard rubber with several bulbous protrusions. 'What would you use this for?'

'I wouldn't use it for anything,' Chase says. 'But be my guest.'

'Looks rather painful, so think I'll pass.' Stafford scribbles on the label and places the bag to one side. Stares at the piles of bags. 'Not really getting anywhere, are we?'

Chase shakes her head. Stafford is right. So far, they've found nothing linking Grainger with Alison and Lizzie, and unless the CSIs can locate a rogue hair, blood spot, or fibre sample, Chase and Stafford will be in deep trouble. Boyle will, perversely, be delighted. It's another nail in the coffin, another hole below the waterline, perhaps the straw that breaks the SCU's back.

'Fuck it,' Chase says as the cat comes across and rubs itself against her legs before joining Stafford amid his toys. 'This is a dog's dinner.'

'Sorry,' Stafford says as he gently lifts the cat away from the evidence bags. 'I bet you're regretting going along with my hypothesis.'

Chase notes how Stafford uses the word *hypothesis* where she would use *hunch*, but the terms are not interchangeable, and Stafford doesn't do hunches. He doesn't guess, he calculates.

'Could you remove the cat?' Stafford says, disturbing Chase's thoughts. 'Put her outside or something?'

Chase goes across and bends to pick up the cat. She looks at the evidence bags and the sex toy Stafford has just shown her.

'Did that one come from the box in the wardrobe?' she says.

'Huh?' Stafford glances at the black rubber toy. 'No, someone found it in the spare bedroom.'

'Get a CSI up here now!' Chase says. 'Tell them to look for hairs on the carpet in the spare room.'

'You think Grainger kept one of the girls locked in there?'

'No, but he did lock someone — or rather something — in there.'

'Some... *thing*?'

'I don't think this is a sex toy.' Chase picks up the evidence bag, the rubber squishing against the polythene. The thing is shaped like a five-pointed star and covered with little nodules. She can't imagine using it in any form of sex she's ever tried, wanted to try or heard of. She looks

264

down at the cat and smiles. 'That's one clever kitty. This toy belongs to Max, Alison's dog.'

~ ~ ~

When they arrive back in the SCU, the relief is palpable.

'Always said Grainger was involved,' Green says. 'From day one.'

'Fuck off.' Stafford flicks his middle finger and settles down at his desk. 'You owe me an apology.'

'Sure, the next meal out is on me.' Green nods. 'But only once we've caught Grainger.'

To which end, the presence of the dog, Max, at Grainger's place — confirmed by the discovery of short, white hairs in the spare room — doesn't get them any closer to an arrest. It's DC Ghosh, going through a box file of documents retrieved from Grainger's study, who does.

'There's this,' she says, holding several sheets of paper. 'It's from a solicitor and concerns the purchase of a property.'

An accompanying letter from an estate agent and a document from the Land Registry is attached to a set of house particulars. Chase reads the material.

'A *water tank*?' she says.

'An unfinished conversion project.' Ghosh points at the property details. 'The agent calls it a bargain for someone with the necessary creative imagination to turn it into a unique home.'

Chase reads on. The water tank is like an underground concrete bunker. It's soundproof, isolated and ripe for development. But development into what? She gets a flash of some dank dungeon, Grainger there dangling a pair of manacles in front of him.

'Jeez,' she says. 'Not sure I'd fancy being Grainger's first guest at his housewarming party.'

265

'Where is it?' Stafford asks, the map showing the location of the severed arm popping up on his screen. 'Any chance the line hits it?'

'No.' Chase looks for the location and reads out the postcode. 'It's over in Kent near the mouth of the Thames.'

'Shit.' Stafford puts a hand to his forehead before typing the postcode into the search box at the top of the map. A smile comes to his face when the map shifts to centre the new location. A single click and the familiar crosshatching appears. 'Not on the line from the body to the arm and beyond, but right in the centre of a wetland haven for birds.'

'The bearded reedling?'

'Exactly. The phone call was made from there.'

'We could be there in an hour and a half.'

'I'm in,' Green says.

'The johnny-come-lately Grainger fan?' Chase mocks.

'That's me.'

'Forget it.' Stafford pushes back his chair and stands. Points at the screen. 'You concentrate on the Alison and Lizzie angle because we're still missing the link from them to Grainger.'

Chase hadn't factored in roadworks on the M25, and it takes them close to two hours before they are over near the Kent coast on the Hoo Peninsula, a weird claw of land that separates the Thames from the Medway. They cruise down a country lane searching for the water tank and drive through an area of flat fields and cows in sodden pastures, drainage ditches crisscrossing the landscape and only the occasional hamlet to break the monotony.

'Not surprised the previous owner pulled out,' Chase says. 'Can't say I'd want to live round here.'

'Perhaps you would if you were a sadist with a noise problem,' Stafford says.

They take several wrong turns before spotting a low grassy rise surrounded by sagging chain-link fencing. A stony track leads across a field to the rise.

'This is it,' Chase says after a glance at the estate agent's particulars. 'Described as having huge development potential. What the fuck are these guys on?'

'Probably a hundred K a year with the commission.' Stafford drives past the end of the track and pulls into a layby a little farther on. 'Beats coppering for a living.'

They get out, stand by the car, and argue about what to do. Chase wants to go in, whereas Stafford suggests calling for backup.

'Suppose he's chopping up his next victim as we speak?' she says. 'Waiting simply isn't an option.'

Stafford doesn't have much of a response to that, so they climb a nearby fence and squelch across a muddy field towards the water tank. They skirt the grassy mound to where a stack of blocks and a large dumpy bag of sand stand, a testament to some sort of construction work having once gone on, but there's no other sign this is currently a building site.

The mound is about ten metres square, perhaps two high, the grass sloping up at a forty-five-degree angle on all sides. The chain-link fence surrounds the tank, but there are several places where it curls away from the metal supporting posts; getting through won't be a problem.

'If he's here, then he must be inside,' Stafford says, stating the obvious because the flat countryside provides no hiding place. 'The question is, how does one get in?'

'Up top.' Chase approaches the chainlink and pulls back a section for Stafford to slip through. 'They'll be an access hatch.'

'How do you know?'

'I saw a property renovation show that featured one of these. *Crap Designs* or something.' Chase follows Stafford through the gap. 'Before you cut a hole for a front door, the only way in is via a hatch and ladder.'

Chase moves to the grassy slope and clambers up to the top. It's bowling-green flat aside from a couple of mushroom vents and a raised brick plinth where a cast iron cover has been removed and lies to one side. Stafford joins Chase, and they both stand listening. There's nothing but the cry of gulls wheeling over a nearby field and the low rumble of a distant tractor working somewhere.

They pad carefully up to the opening and stare down. A column of daylight illuminates a pale interior, and inside, it looks and smells as dank as Chase feared.

Stafford hesitates, but Chase moves to the brick-lined shaft, where an iron ladder is bolted to one side. She turns and lowers herself into the hole, descending rung by rung into the gloom. She drops off the final rung into a pool of shallow water that spreads into the darkness. The light from above reveals new blockwork dividing the chamber into separate rooms. How anyone could have dreamed this could be a place to live, she can't imagine.

'Anything?' Stafford splashes down beside her.

'No,' Chase says. She pulls out her phone and turns on its torch. 'Let's go that way.'

They move slowly, their feet sloshing in the water. There's a block wall ahead with an opening and, to the right, a narrow passage.

This isn't a set of *rooms*, Chase thinks, it's a *maze*. Perhaps that's what the original builder intended, or maybe Grainger has done this work himself.

'Be careful,' she whispers as Stafford gets out his phone, takes up point and inches down the passage. Chase follows, and the corridor turns left and ends at a metal door.

Stafford pushes the door open and shines his phone torch in.

'My God.' He steps to the side so Chase can see.

In the centre of the space, several scaffold boards sit atop a pair of metal trestles. A tangle of ropes at each end. Red-brown liquid has pooled and congealed on the boards, and several scraps of clothing lie bundled on the floor. A work-bench to the side is laden with a tray of surgical instruments: scalpels, forceps, needles and thread, while in one corner, there's a shelving unit containing smoke-brown bottles of chemicals. An overhead light on a boom contraption completes the horror show.

'Grainger's DIY operating theatre,' Chase says. 'He can do whatever he wants here, and nobody will know. There's no treatment plan to stick to, no GMC to answer to, no one suing because the procedure went wrong.'

'Yes,' Stafford says. 'But why Alison?'

Chase looks at the dried blood on the scaffold boards and remembers the pathetic form of Alison Madden lying in the dirt on the bank of the Thames. Doesn't have an answer.

~ ~ ~

Within two hours, a hoard of police officers arrive. There are uniforms, CSIs, detectives, a PolSA, a search team complete with dogs, and a Chief Superintendent from the local force. The Super gets all stroppy that Chase and Stafford are on his patch until Boyle turns up keen to share the limelight. He namedrops the commissioner and the Mayor half a dozen times, and eventually, the CSupt gets the message and buggers off.

Even with the evidence before his eyes, Boyle wants to know if this is a bona fide result.

'Christmas Day with all the trimmings?' he asks Chase. 'No doubt about it?'

'Yes, sir,' Chase says. She breaks down the evidence bit by bit, starting with Alison and the Rohypnol, moving to the severed arm, the presence of Max the dog at Grainger's place, the purchase of the water tank, and finishing with a description of the room of horrors lying beneath the green turf not a hundred metres away.

'I'll never understand these nutters,' Boyle says. He stares at a nearby patrol car, its blue light strobing, then stalks off toward the water tank, spends ten minutes inside annoying all and sundry, and then heads back to London.

This means he's long gone when two unlucky PCs come across the half-clothed body of a woman a mile from the water tank.

~ ~ ~

She's lying in one of the many drainage channels that crisscross the flat fields surrounding the water tank. A sheet of rusty corrugated iron has been pulled over the body, and when the sheet is removed, ID is all but confirmed.

'Lizzie Thomkin,' Chase says, staring down at the battered corpse. Cut marks and bruises cover the exposed skin, the rage in the assault apparent.

'You sure it's her?' Stafford says as he turns his face away.

'Brown hair, slight build, a matching dolphin tattoo on the arm? Yes, I'm sure.'

'I don't get it. A medical procedure with Alison, some kind of method in the madness; this is a complete lack of control. Like a madman attacked her.'

'You're right. Alison was posed, and there was the complexity of inserting the phone and the risk of placing the arm on top of the apartment block. And yet Lizzie was dumped here with no ceremony.'

'Two different people working together?' Stafford says. 'Grainger does the first girl, someone else kills the second?'

'If one had been shot and the other stabbed, and the method was the only distinction, that theory might fly, but it's more than simply how they were killed.'

'A split personality? Grainger as a top medic and Grainger as an out-and-out psycho?'

'It's called dissociative identity disorder, and there's no evidence to suggest he's affected.'

'The victims then. He was minded to do the things he did to Alison but not to Lizzie. Perhaps he targeted Alison, but circumstances meant he had to kidnap Lizzie, too. She was simply in the wrong place at the wrong time. She was an afterthought, accidental.'

Chase nods. She steps back to allow a CSI to approach the body.

*An afterthought.*

It's about as sad and pathetic a eulogy as she can imagine.

# Chapter 29

Locke wakes to a heavy fall of snow, the white blanket silencing the landscape and hiding the blackened remnants of the workshop, the canvas wiped clean, like Mattich and what happened last night was no more than a bad dream. He stands at a window and looks out, spying a set of his wife's footprints leading to and from the barn where she keeps her horses. You try to follow a trail, he thinks, but it turns upon itself and heads back the way it's come, leaving you no wiser. Mattich was the obvious suspect, but then what part does Robert Kell play in all of this? Was he the kind of man to be involved with a sick fuck like Mattich? And with both Kell and Mattich dead, is the whole thing over? There are still the murders in New Mexico to consider, but for now, it looks like Locke has wrapped up the Seattle killings and solved the mystery of the girl in the forest.

Locke remains at the window even as his wife places a cup of coffee in his hands. He sips and stares and stares and sips, but by the time the cup is empty, he's still no nearer to an answer.

'A penny for them,' Elsie says when he comes over to kiss her goodbye before heading off to work.

'Something doesn't feel right,' Locke says as he pulls on his shoulder holster. 'But quite what it is, I can't figure.'

'Something about Henrik Mattich?'

'Mattich is like a horror-movie psycho: persistent, eternal, keeps coming back. And those types of killers are, to a large extent, cowards. Why take the risk of coming here to kill me?'

'You said he told you he had divine instructions. Wouldn't that explain it?'

'Yeah, I guess. Still...' Locke puts a jacket on and then gestures over at the coffee table. Two empty cups, a copy of the local paper and his spare Glock. 'You going to be OK?'

'Henrik Mattich is dead, sweetheart. But even if he wasn't, that's a dumb question.' Elsie reaches out and takes the gun. Ejects the mag, checks it and clicks it back in place. 'I'm a Montana girl. You know my pa taught me to shoot before I could walk? I was playing with guns instead of dolls. Got a rifle for my eleventh birthday and shot my first squirrel that very morning. Skinned it and pinned out the pelt before I opened the rest of my presents.'

'You and Mattich were separated at birth.' Locke laughs. 'Shit, I should have got hitched to one of those nice sophisticated Seattle women. Guess it's too late for a divorce, right?'

'Don't even think about it.'

Locke gives Elsie another kiss and then leaves. He's not worried about Elsie's safety, but he nevertheless detours to his neighbour's place and asks him to watch out for anything suspicious.

'Like the odd building on fire?' Earl says.

'Yeah, that sort of thing.'

It was Earl who called fire rescue, and his quick thinking probably saved Locke's house. Locke has already thanked him, but he does so again and is met with a shrug.

'We're neighbours,' Earl says. 'We look out for each other. This isn't like the city where people cross over the street to avoid trouble.'

From Earl's place, Locke takes the road into Missoula but barely goes a mile when he becomes aware of a vehicle behind. Lights flash and there are a couple of beeps from the horn.

'Avoiding trouble would be handy right now,' Locke says as he tenses, slows, and flicks a glance in the rearview mirror. He gets ready to either swerve out of the way or accelerate off. 'Who the fuck are you, and what the fuck do you want?'

The vehicle is a pickup, with someone behind the wheel wrapped up against the cold, a hat pulled down, and a scarf across their face. Either wrapped up or not wanting to be recognised.

Locke reaches up and taps his shoulder holster, feeling the reassuring solidity of his gun. He slows some more and indicates, pulling into a turnout and stopping his vehicle. The pickup does the same and comes to a standstill a car's length behind. The door opens and the driver gets out. Long coat, fluffy scarf, fleece hat. Fierce brown eyes in the slit between the hat and the scarf.

Locke notes this all in the mirror, and as the figure draws close, he sees more: black, calf-length boots; empty hands out in plain view, the nails red; a hint of mascara on the eyelashes; more red in a wisp of hair that has escaped the hat.

He operates the window, and as it glides down, he leans out and turns his head to look back.

'Mr Locke,' the soft voice says from behind the scarf.

'Karen Kell,' Locke says.

~ ~ ~

Fifteen minutes later, they're sitting in Locke's vehicle, parked on a mountain track well out of sight from the main road. Out of sight because that's the way she wants it. There is no explanation. She just says she wants to talk.

The heater is on, and the demist blasts air to prevent the windows from steaming up. Considering Locke's wandering thoughts the other day, which subsequent events have made him ashamed of, he feels that's a good thing.

274

'So talk,' Locke says, wondering if he's going to get another spiel on how Robert was an absolute angel and wouldn't hurt the proverbial fly, let alone do unmentionable things to a sex worker he'd abducted from Salt Lake City.

'Look, I'm sorry about your place,' Karen says. 'I kinda think it was my fault.'

'Your fault?' Locke takes a glance at Karen. 'Explain?'

'Here.' She reaches into her pocket and pulls out a little plastic ID wallet. 'I don't normally carry this with me for obvious reasons, but I figured I might need it today to persuade you of the truth.'

'About Robert?' Locke says. 'The truth, Karen, is we don't know yet. The evidence, either way, isn't conclusive. Nothing you can say will—'

Karen flips open the wallet and places it on the dash. Locke stops mid-sentence and tries to take it all in.

The *Department of Justice* label at the top. The picture of Karen Kell that, aside from the eyes and nose, doesn't look much like her. The letters *FBI* in large type across the centre of the card, a crest to the left, and below the words *Special Agent* followed by a name: *Karen Holsworth*.

'Where did you get that?' he says, picking it up and examining the wallet. 'You know it's an offence to impersonate an official working for a government agency?'

'Sure,' Karen says. 'But I'm not impersonating anyone apart from Karen Kell.'

'Sorry, this is serious. I'll need to take you in to make further...'

Locke stops as Karen reaches out and puts her hand on his forearm.

'We're not going anywhere, Frank.

'But...' Again, he hesitates, beginning to feel stupid.

'I'm special agent Karen Holsworth. Robert Kell wasn't my brother; he was also with the FBI. The two of us are — were — on a deep cover operation to track down the killer responsible for the murders in the vicinity of the White Sands missile testing range. The so-called X-Mex Slayer. Certain clues to do with the tampering of evidence led us to believe the killer is a member of a law enforcement agency. We moved north following a trail we'd picked up in New Mexico.'

'I know Kell was an agent. He was kicked out of the service because of sexual harassment charges.'

'Against me,' Karen says. 'And the charges were entirely fictitious. It was a way for us both to leave without causing suspicion. Robert kept his identity. I took a new one as his sister.'

'Hold on,' Locke says, increasingly confused. 'Can you start from the beginning, step by step?'

'Sure thing.'

And Karen Kell — *Holsworth* — starts from the beginning.

~ ~ ~

Last year, she tells Locke, the FBI serial crimes team was approached by police in New Mexico to help investigate the X-Mex murders.

'All women, all Mexican.'

'Illegals?'

'Yes. Five in all, and they were all sex workers. The fact they were illegal immigrants meant it was hard for the local police to get any traction on the case. Nobody wanted to talk.'

'And you and Robert were in on this investigation?'

'Not me, not initially, but Robert and several other agents visited New Mexico and reviewed all the evidence. Initially, they worked on the possibility that the offender

276

could be in the military, but extensive inquiries failed to find any meaningful leads. They broadened the search but still came up blank. After several weeks on the ground, Robert and the others shelved the investigation and moved on to other more pressing cases.'

'The victims were Mexicans.' Locke nods. 'I get it.'

'They were women with no identities, no legal status, sometimes nothing but a first name. They may have had children or relatives, but they weren't paying taxes, and they weren't voting.' Karen shrugs. 'Still, this is where I come in. Shortly after Robert returns, I'm summoned to a meeting with the Deputy Director. Robert is there, too, but there is no agenda, no note-taking, and no entry in the diary. The DD tells me this is hush-hush and off the record. Turns out the lack of progress on the X-Mex Slayer isn't so much a lack of evidence as a confusion of evidence.'

'What do you mean?'

'During the investigation, Robert became convinced that X-Mex worked in law enforcement since various pieces of evidence had been obfuscated. The record-keeping, such as it was, was all over the place. He was sure that at some point in the mass of information that various agencies had collected, the data had been tampered with. This led him to conclude that X-Mex was either in the police, the CIA, NSA, ATF or even the FBI itself.'

'Shit.'

'Exactly. Wisely, so as not to let on or compromise his hypothesis, Robert decided to go straight to the top and speak to the Director. After he'd done so, the Director, the Deputy Director and Robert conceived an operation to run alongside the standard investigation. Enter me as part of the initial setup and as a partner for Robert once we'd left the Bureau. I left on compassionate grounds with a substantial settlement, and Robert was kicked out in disgrace.'

'So what led you up to this neck of the woods?'

'A phone call made from a mobile one of the Mexican women had owned. She'd just bought the phone and hadn't even charged it. The thing was brand new and boxed, but we know she bought it because a friend was there when she did so.'

'I found the box at Mattich's place.'

'And the phone itself was inside Monica Granton.'

'How...?' Locke smiles. 'Of course, you could access the post-mortem report via the FBI.'

'Yes.' Karen nods. 'But to back up a little, Robert and I were undercover in San Diego, chasing a non-existent lead when a flag on the phone number came up a few days ago. It was the first time it had been switched on, months after the killing, and when we checked the location, we had a rough fix somewhere in the mountains northwest of Seeley Lake. We headed here, rented a holiday lodge, and began searching.'

'Needle in a haystack.'

'Not quite, but close. We knew the phone had connected to a cell mast from one of three possible locations, so we spent days searching the woodland with a drone, not knowing what we'd find. Then, we discovered a shred of clothing near the trail, and I stumbled across the body that afternoon. I returned to Seeley Lake, and Robert headed out to take a look. Which was when you encountered him.' Karen gives a smile that turns into a sad frown. 'And you know everything from then on.'

'So Robert allowed himself to be a suspect so as not to blow the operation?'

'Yes. For all we knew, the killer could have been in law enforcement in Montana. Could have even been you.'

278

'Well, somebody was on to you and Robert.' Locke turns to the windshield, where a flurry of snow is accumulating, starting to obscure the view. He flicks the stalk, and the wipers creak across, clearing the flakes. 'Where does Mattich fit in? He's not in law enforcement, but it looks like he killed the girl.'

'That's what I don't understand. He has to have had an accomplice.'

'Figures. I can't see Mattich being clever enough to kill Robert and make it look like suicide, at least not off his own bat.' Locke glances at Karen. 'But why didn't they kill you too?'

'Circumstance, serendipity.' Karen shrugs. 'Perhaps they didn't penetrate my cover. I don't know.'

More snow on the windshield, flakes swirling. Locke thinks about Robert Kell, shivering as he died in the cold water.

'Mattich said something to me about acting on instructions. I thought he was delusional, but if he has an accomplice, then he might have been telling the truth.'

'So the accomplice tells Mattich to kill Robert and then you in order to frustrate the investigation? That would fly.'

'Yes, but I still don't understand why Mattich murdered the girl in the forest. He goes down to New Mexico to commit crimes where he isn't known, gets away with the killing, but then comes back here and lands himself in it by pooping on his doorstep? Like a lot of things in this case, it simply doesn't make sense.' Locke stares through the windshield again at the surrounding countryside. Mountains and forests and the blue of a lake. 'And why here in Montana?'

'There's the girl ethnicity, too,' Karen says. 'She's white. No racial motive there.'

'You know about Mattich's history?'

'I got up to speed this morning, but he was already on our long list of suspects for the X-Mex killings.'

'How come?'

'The Mexican women, the ones murdered around White Sands...' Karen pauses, a shudder passing through her. 'They were skinned.'

'*Skinned*?' Locke draws in a deep breath. 'But why the hell weren't those killings linked to the ones in Seattle? Surely, if they'd been in the database, a connection should have been flagged up?'

Another pause. This time, Karen is the one staring through the windshield.

'That I don't know,' she says.

# Chapter 30

Sasaki is at Kieran Lamb's house. First-time invite. It's a single-storey dwelling on a small plot. Everything neat and ordered. A well-manicured lawn. Freshly painted railings. A line of solar panels on the roof. A cool, Scandi-style open-plan interior. Sasaki, Malroony and Lamb are seated at a big ash table, hunched close to a laptop. The copy of the map Sasaki obtained from Ken Royston is to one side, and a sheet of paper with Lamb's spidery writing sits next to the map.

Meeting here was Lamb's idea. Away from prying eyes, he'd said when Sasaki told him he had the map.

Prying eyes? He's unsure if Lamb is prescient or ultra-cautious, but either way, it suits Sasaki; Cooper will blow his top if he discovers Sasaki and Malroony are still working the case.

'Pearce said I needed to be better at maths,' Sasaki says. 'Which implies some sort of calculation involved in the location of the bodies back in the original BUK murders.'

'Like I said before, that's news to me,' Lamb says. 'If you look at the map, you can see the three locations are in a rough triangle, but that would be the case with any three points. What does your dad say?' Lamb nods to the Japanese characters Endo Sasaki wrote on the map thirty-three years ago.

'Well...' Sasaki's Japanese isn't so good. His dad insisted his son and daughter learn English as their primary language, and while Sasaki can understand spoken Japanese a little, his knowledge of the written form is lacking. Still, he can make out a couple of points. 'There's something here about a relationship. Next to these numbers, see?'

His finger points down at the map. Several sets of numbers are jotted on the page, but they look random to Sasaki.

'Relationship?' Malroony shakes her head. 'The files don't mention a relationship between the three women and Pearce, nor did they know each other except in passing.'

'Let's go over this again,' Lamb says. 'The arms were removed after death and pointed one after the other to the location of the *previous* victim. That makes sense because they could hardly point to the next victim unless Pearce had decided in advance where to dump the body.'

'And the first arm?' Malroony asks.

'It pointed to where Derek Pearce lived.'

'*What?*' Sasaki says.

'Didn't you know?' Lamb touches the map, his finger placed on a Darwin suburb. 'That dot is Pearce's house.'

Sasaki stares at the map. The dot is twenty kilometres from the first victim, and an imaginary line drawn to the dot would bisect dozens, if not hundreds, of houses.

'I get how my father could deduce that the third victim's arm pointed to the second, the second to the first, but I how he could find Pearce merely from the direction the final arm was pointing in?'

'I don't know,' Lamb says.

'There's nothing in the files,' Malroony says, 'No mention of it in the trial transcript either.'

'Anyway, it doesn't make sense. Why would Pearce give the game away and lead the police to his front door?' Sasaki nods at Malroony. 'And, as Linda said, nothing about this came out then. The fact that the arms were served, yes, but not a hint of the meaning.'

Sasaki and Malroony continue to talk, batting ideas back and forth. It's not until a few minutes later that Sasaki realises Lamb hasn't spoken for a while.

'Kieran?'

'You said the Japanese mentions something about a relationship,' Lamb says. 'But I think it's not a relationship between two people. Your father is talking about a relationship between the arms and the bodies. In other words, a ratio. Look.'

Lamb is working the touchpad with one hand, and the pen and paper with the other. He scribbles down figures on the paper and taps numbers into an onscreen calculator.

'I don't...'

'The distance from the third victim to the second victim was eleven point three kilometres. The distance from the third victim to the third victim's *arm* was thirty-four point two metres. A ratio of three hundred and thirty to one. From the second victim to the first victim, seven point five K. From the arm to body, twenty-two point seven. Ratio: three hundred and thirty to one. From the first victim to Pearce's place, twenty point eight K. Arm to body, sixty-three point zero three. Ratio... have a guess?'

'Three hundred and thirty to one,' Sasaki says.

'Fuck.' This from Malroony. 'Your dad was the only one who realised that.'

'Too late, though,' Sasaki says. He remembers the night he crept onto the landing and saw his father crying.

*Three... It never should have got to this.*

'Too late for what?' Malroony says.

'Nothing.' Sasaki points at the map. 'But who cut off the arms and made them into clues? It just doesn't make sense.'

'No,' Lamb says. 'And why didn't whoever it was simply call the police or leave a note? The manner was so obtuse it went under the radar for everyone but your father.'

'We're missing something,' Sasaki says.

'It might not matter.' Lamb is back on the laptop, bringing up a map of the Northern Territory. 'We can put the ratio in and see what pops out.'

Click, click, and Lamb has loaded an overlay that marks out the position of the Tortilla Flats victim and her arm.

'Three hundred and thirty,' he says, clicking again and drawing a line from the body to the arm and beyond. He stops to load up the calculator. 'The arm was three hundred and ninety-three point nine three metres from the body, which times the ratio gives us darn close to one hundred and thirty K.'

Lamb drags the line out across the map, stopping some way short of the coast.

'That's still sixty K from where we found the dummy body near the East Alligator River,' Sasaki says. 'The calculation must be wrong because there was nothing there.'

'The calculation is correct, so perhaps you missed the body,' Lamb says.

'If there *was* a body, then it's possible but unlikely. The terrain on that part of the trip was open, and with four pairs of eyes, I think we'd have spotted anything in the open.'

'Three pairs, sir,' Malroony says. 'You can't trust Pearce, considering what happened.'

Sasaki leans back from the table. He has a mild headache, something he's sure his father never suffered from. Of course, Endo's suffering now, and for a brief moment, Sasaki wonders about going along with Malroony's suggestion about visiting. Is it possible his father could have some valuable information?

He remembers the last time he saw him. The vacant eyes. A smile when he sipped a cup of sweet tea, but the newspaper Sasaki brought him had been pushed to one side, more interest shown in a TV blaring in one corner of the room, the colourful movement of a kids' cartoon of far more importance than his son's clumsy attempts to communicate.

'Let's take a stroll,' Sasaki says to Malroony. 'Leave Kieran to double-check the maths.'

Outside, they walk up the street. Afternoon heat. Few vehicles. Malroony keeps silent, her usual chitchat absent. Or perhaps she knows it's not wanted.

'I'm trying to figure out why my father kept all this quiet,' Sasaki says after a while. 'Was he so conceited he wanted it to be a mystery as to how he found Derek Pearce?'

'From what I've heard, that doesn't sound like Endo,' Malroony says. She gives a half smile. Holds up her hands. 'Sorry, I know you hate the hero worship.'

'That's OK. I'm used to the hagiography by now.'

'There had to be a reason he didn't let on about the ratios. Did he want to protect Pearce in some way?'

'Protect him from what? Appearing so dumb as to shop himself to the police?' Sasaki shakes his head. 'No. My father had nothing but contempt for men like Derek Pearce.'

'So why not mention the ratios?'

Malroony leaves the question hanging, but Sasaki doesn't have an answer for her. His father's behaviour in this matter, as in many areas of Endo's life, is a mystery to him. He looks down at his feet as they continue walking around the block. Pace, pace, pace.

'The critical questions are,' he says to Malroony. 'One, who arranged the arms all those years ago? Two, do they have anything to do with what is happening now? If they do, they're probably the killer; if they don't, the killer must be somebody else who knows about the ratios.'

'But Kieran's just proved the ratios are wrong when applied to the Tortilla Girl.'

Malroony's right. 'I don't know then,' Sasaki says.

They've come full circle and are back at Lamb's place, none the wiser. Such is life, Sasaki thinks. At the end of the road, what have you got? He thinks of his father again. Kids' TV programmes and an unread newspaper. Some faded memories, some so distorted that he can't even remember his own son. He wonders if Endo's past glories are any compensation to the old man in his current state.

Inside, Lamb's mood is the opposite of Sasaki's melancholy. He's popped open a can of VB, and another two stand on the table, condensation misting the cans' green, blue and gold surface. He turns from the laptop, all smiles.

'Grab a drink and pull up a chair,' he says. 'I might just have cracked it.'

~ ~ ~

With the two remaining cans of bitter opened and Sasaki and Malroony seated on either side of Lamb, the CSI begins.

'While you were walking, I got to thinking,' he says. 'What if the ratio isn't wrong, but we simply misapplied it?'

'Right,' Sasaki says.

'So, it's thirty-three years since the BUK, and the ratio your father discovered was three hundred and thirty to one. Don't ask me why, but that can't be a coincidence. The killer is obsessed with that number, so I figure he will use thirty-three somewhere along the line, excuse the pun.'

Both Sasaki and Malroony nod.

'Here.' Lamb taps the laptop screen, where, once again, there's a map of the Northern Territory. With a couple of clicks, he zooms in on Tortilla Flats. A couple more, and he creates an extending line to the northeast. He zooms out and drags the line past the entrance to the East Alligator River. 'This is the line we flew down, spotting nothing. Could we have missed a body? Sure.'

'So we need to go back and search?'

'No.' Lamb drags the line on the map until it extends into the Arafura Sea and ends up in the centre of Papua New Guinea. 'Our original distance of just under four hundred metres times a ratio of three thousand three hundred lands us here in the rain forests of Papua. Could there be a body there? Possible, but let's continue.'

'Sorry, Kieran, I don't see where you're going with this?'

'Wait.' Lamb raises a hand and then reaches for his can. Necks the remaining beer. 'We proceed.'

He resumes dragging the line out beyond Papua New Guinea, across Micronesia and into the vast emptiness of the North Pacific, arcing into a graceful curve.

'It's not straight,' Sasaki says.

'No, the line is called a great circle,' Lamb says. 'The shortest distance between two points on a sphere. However, our original bearing from the body is unchanged.'

Sasaki doesn't fully understand but keeps silent as the little icon on the screen counts up the kilometres, hitting twelve thousand two hundred when the line hits the North West coast of the US. Lamb drags the icon into Washington State, over Seattle, and into Montana. The line slips past Missoula, and Lamb finally clicks to a stop in the Lewis and Clarke National Forest as the counter reaches thirteen thousand kilometres.

'I was just playing around and using a ratio of thirty-three thousand to one, and that's where we end up.'

'Fascinating,' Sasaki says. 'But I thought you said you'd found something?'

'Yes. I played around with the map and then did a quick web search.' Lamb ignores Sasaki. His finger jabs at the curving line on the screen. 'I mean, why not? After all, you might find a pot of gold at the end of a rainbow, right?'

Lamb clicks once more, and the map disappears, to be replaced by a browser showing the webpage of the *Independent Record* newspaper.

'Going for another beer,' Lamb says, pushing back his chair and rising. 'Take a read.'

The *Independent Record* is based in Helena, Montana, and the page Lamb has found details a story about the body of a woman found in a forest. The Division of Criminal Investigation is in charge of the case, and murder is suspected. The public is urged to be vigilant, and anyone with information is asked to contact detectives at DCI.

There's a fizz from behind Sasaki's left ear as Lamb pops another can.

'You see, mate, as far as I can tell, this woman was found in the Lewis and Clarke National Forest in exactly the right location to make our ratio of thirty-three thousand to one bang on a hundred per cent correct. That's got to be more than just a coincidence, right?'

~ ~ ~

'Got to be, boss,' Malroony says as they drive away from Lamb's place. 'I mean, what are the odds otherwise?'

Sasaki doesn't know, and since he's had enough maths for one day, he won't even go there.

'There was nothing about how she died,' he says. 'I'll have to give them a call.'

'You going to clear that with AC Cooper?'

Sasaki ponders the question for a few moments. Cooper isn't going to want to spread the net wider than it already

288

is. The possibility that their killer is crossing borders at will and can escape Australian law enforcement so easily will only serve to point the finger of blame at Sasaki once again.

'No, I don't think so.'

The man on the switchboard at the Montana Department of Justice Division of Criminal Investigation has trouble understanding exactly who Sasaki is and what he wants. Initially, he thinks Sasaki is a foreign press ghoul after a garish story.

'I'm a police officer with the Northern Territory force in Australia,' Sasaki says for the fifth time. He gives his rank, number, and contact details and implores the switchboard operator to find someone dealing with the case to call him back.

Half an hour later, somebody does.

~ ~ ~

'Open and shut. We found the guy who did it. He tried to go out in a blaze of glory, but my colleague took him down.'

The cop on the end of the line from Missoula, a detective called Leo Sullivan, isn't much help. He seems to think they've solved the murder, and he can't understand Sasaki's story.

'You've got a girl all cut up, and you're saying she must be connected to our case?'

'Yes, exactly.'

'We must have half a dozen murders like that every week here in the US, and yet I'm not getting phone calls from out-of-state cops trying to link their homicides to ours.'

'She was pointing,' Sasaki says feebly. 'In the direction of Montana. When we followed the line, it ended in the Lewis and Clarke National Forest.'

'Pointing? Like with a finger?' There's a huff and then dead air. 'Listen, fella, if this is a fucking windup, then I've got better things to do than talk to some mad Crocodile Dundee type.'

'There was a phone inside the girl,' Sasaki blurts out. 'Plus, her arm was cut off.'

He'd meant to keep those facts to himself to separate the actual perpetrator from the cranks.

'How did you know that?'

'So I'm right. The cases are connected.'

A pause. More dead air.

'Listen, pal, I'm not up to speed on all this. Whadaya say your name was?'

Sasaki gives his details once more, and the cop hangs up.

This time, the wait is longer, and it isn't until mid-morning the following day that his phone lights up with an incoming call from overseas.

'Detective Senior Sergeant Takeo Sasaki,' he says as he answers.

'Locke,' comes the reply. 'Detective Frank Locke.'

# Chapter 31

A silence hangs over the SCU the following day. Everyone is shell-shocked. The truth is, Chase hadn't expected to find Lizzie Thomkin alive, but the manner of her death and the casual way her body was dumped in some strange way made the whole thing worse.

Locating Doctor Alan Grainger has become the SCU's number one priority, and Boyle, as unhappy as ever, concedes they need help in the form of the Met's not-inconsiderable resources.

'But all the officers in the city won't help if he's left the country, will they?' he says.

Stafford counters by redoubling his efforts with the Border Force and the security services.

'With the proviso that you can't prove a negative,' he says after hearing back, 'Grainger hasn't left the UK by any legal means. He hasn't passed through any major airports or sea ports.'

'False passport?' Chase says.

'Possible, but the facial recognition systems aren't showing a match in the last month.'

'So,' Green says. 'Grainger kills Alison and Lizzie. He arranges Alison's body in a weird way, placing her arm on top of a nearby building. Conversely, he dumps poor Lizzie in a ditch. Considering the setup at the water tank, he obviously planned the whole thing meticulously. The question is, why?'

'I don't know,' Chase says. 'We're struggling for motive here.'

'Motive, yes. Opportunity, no. Evidence, no. And the latter trumps all, right?'

Chase nods in agreement, albeit reluctantly. Without motive, they can't get a grip on the case, and they can't predict what Grainger might do next. That could make finding him almost impossible.

Except, half an hour later, Stafford *has* found him.

'Just maybe,' he says, holding up his hands to calm Chase and Green's excitement. 'With the evidence at the water tank all but proving he's involved, I managed to get access to his bank accounts. I discovered a payment to AirBnB made a couple of weeks ago.'

'For his holiday abroad?'

'For a holiday, yes, but the property isn't abroad.'

'Where?'

'A charming country cottage.' Stafford shakes his head, his expression downcast. 'We've boobed, Jess. It's on the Hoo Peninsula close to the village of High Halstow and less than three miles from the water tank.'

'He's been there all along?'

'The owner lives in the north of England, but I've been in contact with her, and she says Grainger rented it long-term while he supervised the water tank build. I guess he used it to save commuting back and forth.'

'Or, considering he doesn't live that far away, it was conceived as a bolt-hole from the start.' Chase looks over Stafford's shoulder at the AirBnB page. 'Is he there now?'

'The owner doesn't know. Grainger didn't want a weekly clean of the property and said he'd do it himself. He plainly didn't want to be disturbed.'

'Well, he's going to be disappointed,' Chase says.

Chase gets Green to take her while Stafford remains behind to see what else he can dig up. Green's previous misgivings concerning Grainger are history, and now all he wants to do is inflict some serious violence on the man.

'I keep thinking how I can hurt him and get away with it,' he says as they drive out of London. 'Hypothetically, of course.'

'If he's there, we're going to question him, that's all,' Chase says. 'A jury will establish his guilt, and retribution we leave for the judge first, God eventually. So try to remember that before you beat him to a pulp.'

'Yeah, sure.' Green holds the wheel tight as he guides the Land Rover into a sharp bend. 'The trouble is I'm too often disappointed by the choices juries, judges and gods make.'

'You'd be happiest being a not-so-benign dictator, right?'

'You nailed it.'

They follow the same route as before, passing Dartford and Gravesend and taking a left before Rochester. Then they're heading out onto the Hoo Peninsula, first on main roads and then weaving through country lanes from the village of High Halstow. Chase is looking at a map on her phone and giving directions while Green is trying to follow his satnav, and eventually, by combining their efforts, they come upon a wooden five-bar gate with a ceramic pottery sign attached to the top bar.

'Sandpiper Cottage,' Green says. 'What happened to the bearded reedling?'

Chase gets out and opens the gate. Beyond, there's a field, and for once, the Land Rover comes in useful as Green bumps the vehicle through the gate and along a track awash with puddles. In the distance, the only thing taller than the low rushes is a pretty red brick cottage with a dark slate roof and, parked beside it, a Mercedes 4x4.

Green pulls up next to the bump of a grassy sea defence and kills the engine.

'If he's in there, he'll have seen us,' he says. 'And forewarned is forearmed.'

'Do you think he's got a weapon?' Chase says.

'No idea, but let's be careful.'

As the engine dies, the silence is broken only by the whispering of nearby rushes and the faint tweet of a bird in the distance.

'Before you ask,' Chase says, as they get out, 'that's a blackbird.'

'Pity.' Green clicks the driver's door closed and gestures to the house. 'I was going to suggest one of us goes round the other side, but there's nowhere to run to, right?'

Chase turns and takes in the barren countryside of muddy fields and salt marsh, flat as far as the eye can see. Even if he nips out the back, Grainger won't get far.

A half-glazed door stands beneath a small porch, and a knock on the glass echoes in a bare hallway. Chase peers in, spying a coat on a hook on a wall, a pair of Wellington boots beneath. The place looks neat and unlived in. A typical holiday cottage. She tries the door knob, a little surprised when it turns, and the door slips open.

'Mr Grainger?' Chase says, raising her voice. 'Alan?'

Nothing.

'The door was open,' Green says. 'And we're investigating an ongoing crime. There could be a victim in here.'

Green is spelling out their right to enter the property, something for a later report. It clarifies what Chase already knows, but even if he hadn't said anything, there's no way she's staying outside. She edges into the hall. On the left, there's a door to a cosy living room. Bookcases on either side of a fireplace and a sofa with a floral-patterned throw. A low table with a coffee cup and a mobile phone.

Chase moves across and enters the room. There's a thin layer of scum on the dregs of coffee inside the cup. She pulls out a latex glove and slips it on. She picks up the phone, but the battery has died, and repeated presses of the power button do nothing.

'Jess.' Green's voice comes low and in a whisper. Chase turns to see him pointing at the staircase. 'Blood.'

A thick white carpet runs to the top of the stairs, and halfway up, a large brown stain spills down the face of a riser. On the first step, a fainter mark could be the outline of a boot or shoe.

Green eases towards the stairs and Chase follows. A creak from the bottom step. Another from the next. Chase holds back and gives Green room. He's halfway up now, avoiding the stain, and she begins to climb, too. He reaches the top, stops, and waits until she joins him. He gestures at a door at the end of a short landing area and holds a hand up to his right ear, miming.

*Listen.*

Nothing.

They stand motionless for a second, and then Green steps to the doorway and looks in. Chase is right behind.

The bedroom is tiny, with a window facing the sea, but the curtains are drawn closed, just a narrow slit of light cutting across to a double bed that takes up most of the space. In the shadows, Chase can make out a figure lying atop the bedclothes. Green reaches in and flicks the light switch.

'Jesus,' Green says. 'He's back on male victims again. If he ever stopped.'

On the bed is the prone form of a man wearing an enormous rubber gas mask. A white shirt is stained with red while the man's left arm is curled over his chest. There's an iron tang in the air and a smell of shit and piss.

'I'm not sure,' Chase says, squeezing past and approaching the body. She leans over and peers at the gas mask.

The two glass eyepieces make the man resemble some alien creature, but when she moves up close, she can see through the glass to the face behind. 'This isn't one of his victims.'

'I don't get you. Are you saying Grainger didn't do this?'

'Definitely.'

'How do you know?'

Chase slips her hands down to the mask and releases the straps. Gently removes the mask.

'Because this *is* Grainger,' she says.

For a moment, Green stands there, perplexed. But there's no mistaking Grainger's rounded face and little goatee beard, and eventually, he nods.

'Result then,' he says. 'Saves on a trial. No need for me to worry about the jury or the judge. As for God...? Well, Grainger's face-to-face with him right now, and I don't think there's much upside for the man.'

'We've still got to catch whoever did this.' Chase puts the mask to one side and steps back. 'And...'

She cocks her head, squints in the gloom, and then puts a hand out and touches Grainger's chest. Pulls it back when she senses warmth on her fingertips.

'What?'

'He's not dead.'

~ ~ ~

Grainger's unconscious but breathing, so they leave him where he is and head outside. Green calls an ambulance while Chase gets on the phone to Boyle. The DCS wants the lowdown on Grainger's condition.

'Is he going to pull through and stand trial, or — and I'm offering a little prayer here — is he not long for this world?'

'He's not in a good way, sir. Aside from the blood loss, he's seriously dehydrated. He's been lying on that bed for days.'

'Will he regain consciousness?'

'No idea.'

'Well, assuming he lives long enough to get to a hospital, if and when he does wake up, I want you there. We need a confession before he pegs it. As to who attacked Grainger, I'd give them a medal.'

'We've found a knife by the bed, sir. And the blood came from a slit on his wrist. Looks like he tried to kill himself.'

'Then that's all the more reason to ensure you get something out of Grainger. Once you do, it's case closed, right?'

Boyle hangs up, and Chase has visions of him skipping up to the commissioner's office, bearing the good news with a smile on his face, the two of them preparing a press release, Boyle likely downplaying the part the SCU played in catching Grainger and emphasising his own invaluable contribution.

Thirty minutes later, a siren heralds the arrival of an ambulance, and Grainger is taken away more dead than alive, the paramedics unable to give Chase much of a prognosis. Several CSIs turn up and pile into the house, while the bolshy local Chief Superintendent is back too. He watches while half a dozen of his officers fan out and fingertip search the surrounding fields.

'After this, are you done?' he says to Green. 'Because, if you don't mind, I'd like to get my guys and girls back to normal policing.'

Chase, a few steps away, hears Green mutter something noncommittal, something about 'important work' and 'keeping the community safe', and she turns and walks across to the garden fence and stares out across the barren landscape. A curlew, startled by the search team, takes flight, its distinctive warble fading as the bird flies into a thin mist, leaving Chase feeling as flat and deflated as the surrounding countryside.

~ ~ ~

The next day, Chase is on hospital duty, stuck in a tiny cubicle around the corner from where Grainger lies in a bed in the high-dependency unit. Inside the unit, machines bleep and flash and extrude tubes that bend and coil into Grainger's body. Nurses frown at Chase every time she presses her head to the glass to see if there's any change in Grainger's condition. Another patient, greyer and closer to death than Grainger, occupies an adjoining bed, and relatives come in and hold the man's hand, whispering final messages of love. No justice there, Chase thinks when a nurse tells her Grainger appears to be hanging on and is out of immediate danger.

Green keeps pestering her with constant messages asking if she's found a wealthy male doctor to hit on and how many cups of coffee she's consumed. By mid-afternoon, it's no to the first question, half a dozen to the second.

Grainger doesn't stir. His chest rises and falls in response to the machines, and his eyelids flutter occasionally, but that's it. She asks a passing doctor if there's any chance Grainger will regain consciousness soon, and she's met with a noncommittal shrug.

By early evening, she begins to think she's wasting her time. She moves to the doors to take a final peek before leaving for home. Grainger's in there, lying still, breathing regularly. But his eyes are wide open.

Chase pushes in through the door and approaches the bed. There's no nurse present — the monitoring station is down the hallway — so she drags a plastic chair over to the bed and sits. Grainger moves his head slightly, his gaze alighting on Chase.

'You,' he says, his voice gravelly and faint. 'Harassment, that's what this is.'

298

'You should be thankful, Alan,' Chase says. 'If we hadn't turned up, you'd be dead.'

'Thanks for nothing.' Grainger blinks and resumes staring at the ceiling.

'At least you *are* alive, not butchered like Alison and battered to death like Lizzie.'

Grainger closes his eyes and the muscles in his neck tense. He gives a slight shake of his head.

'No, you didn't do it, or no, you regret it?' Chase waits, but there's no answer. 'The latter, I'll accept, but the former won't wash because we have enough evidence to convict you this time. There's DNA, witnesses, CCTV, Lizzie and the scene at the water tank, and Alison's dog at your house. No chance a jury will acquit.'

Silence, the eyes resolutely shut.

'Why did you do it, Alan? What had Alison and Lizzie done to deserve what you did to them?'

Still no response, Grainger's expression blank as if he's dozed off.

Chase tries a different approach. 'When you slit your wrists, we weren't on to you, so I guess it wasn't fear of being caught that made you try to commit suicide. That suggests you may have some regret or guilt for your actions.'

There's a pause and a wheeze, and Grainger opens his eyes.

'You wouldn't understand.'

'Try me.'

'There's a nutcase,' he says. 'A madman. A total psycho. He's the one who's responsible for Alison's death.'

Here we go, Chase thinks. Grainger is distancing himself from the act by talking about himself in the third person. Next will come some sort of justification and an attempt to play the mental health card. Still, she'll let him talk and

299

give him enough rope to hang himself. Second time around, no jury will allow Grainger to walk free.

'This nutter,' Chase says, playing along. 'Why did he want to kill Alison?'

'I don't know. He just told me to do it. I had no choice. And he wanted me to kill again. It's why I tried to top myself. Suicide was the only way out.'

The way Grainger is speaking, Green's suggestion of dissociative identity disorder doesn't seem so far-fetched now. Only Chase doesn't buy it. Grainger is well-versed in medical terminology and knows how to put on a show that'll convince many he's got severe psychological problems. It's not going to work with Chase, though.

'Was this a voice in your head? Or perhaps you had a dream? Maybe clouds formed in the sky telling you what to do?'

'Don't mock me, detective. I'm not mad.'

'No, sorry.' Chase bites her lip. And yes, he is mad, self-evidently. But as hard as it is, she needs to go along with Grainger's fantasy so he'll come clean. 'Carry on.'

'As I said, I was forced to kill Alison. I didn't want to kill her, but I had no choice.

There's always a choice, but Chase lets that lie. 'How did he force you?'

'He knew things about me that would put me back before a judge and jury. Evidence that didn't come out at the trial. He said he'd make sure all the details got into the right hands if I refused to cooperate.'

Perhaps Grainger really is crazy. Chase can see his face is flushed, and pinprick beads of sweat pepper his forehead. It's as if he's genuinely frightened. But who of? *Himself*? Are there two Alan Graingers, one of whom would pass evidence to the police?

'You killed two people because of a simple *threat*?'

'Not a threat, blackmail. This nutter knew something that would make the Soho Sleeper case against me one hundred per cent watertight. He sent me a copy of new evidence the cops hold.'

'You were conned. There is no such evidence. Don't you think we'd have used it against you if there were?'

'He had all the facts, details only the police could know. All the minutiae of my life. Things like where I'd been driving, the CCTV footage of me cruising the bars, all the stuff you presented at the trial, and lots more detail.

'And what was this new information he threatened you with?' Chase is sceptical, and she wonders if this is just some crazy story Grainger invented to try to justify his actions. 'Prove to me this isn't a figment of your imagination, possibly brought about by the drugs you're on.'

'I was sent several letters, each more explicit. The final letter detailed the information this psycho would release to the police if I didn't do exactly as he wanted.'

'Which was to kill Alison?'

'Not her specifically, but he told me what to do and where to place the body.'

'We didn't find any letters at your place.'

'I destroyed them—'

'Pathetic.' Chase has had enough. 'Your attempt to convince me you're mentally ill isn't working, and it won't play with a judge and jury, however many wild stories you come up with.'

'You've got it wrong,' Grainger says. 'I'm not mentally ill, and this isn't a story. I was trying to say I destroyed every letter but the last one. If you read it, you'll understand.'

'So where is it, this mystery letter?' Chase calls his bluff. Waits for some excuse as to why the fictitious document can't be produced.

'My house,' Grainger says, raising his head and leaning forward. 'There's a pond in the garden. I put it in a water-tight container and placed it under a large rock at the bottom of the pond. Go and find it and tell me I'm lying.'

'You're not making sense. Just tell me what you put in the container.'

'The evidence to convict me in the Soho Sleeper case.' Grainger reaches out to where a red plastic handle hangs from a cord close to the bed. He tugs it, and his head nods back onto the pillow. 'Now leave me alone.'

'But...'

Chase turns as a nurse enters the HDU. He stalks across and stares at Chase like she shouldn't be here. She stands and holds up her hands in apology.

'I'm just going,' she says.

# Chapter 32

'There's been a development,' Locke says when he calls Karen Kell. 'To put it mildly.'

'Tell me,' Karen says.

So Locke fills her in on the phone conversation he had last night with a cop on the other side of the world.

'Interesting,' she says. 'Are you taking it further?'

'Of course. Do you want in?'

'No. I need to stay undercover for the moment, but keep me informed, OK?'

Locke says he will and then goes in search of Leo Sullivan.

'So, did the nip tell you anything, Frank?' Sullivan says. 'Or was he full of shit?'

'He was most informative,' Locke says. 'Got a similar case to ours.'

'Yeah, sure, but this guy's an *Australian* nip, right? Have you ever heard of that?'

Locke doesn't understand why there should be a problem with an Australian of Japanese descent but knows better than to discuss the matter with Sullivan. Sullivan is old school in a bad way. If good-ol-boy Leo can crack a racist or sexist joke, he will, and he'll see no shame in it. If he pulls over someone who's not Montana snow white, he'll draw his weapon and let them know who's boss. And if one of his mates crosses the line, Sullivan will either look the other way or take a fistful of ten-spots as a payoff.

Locke ignores Sullivan and gets to work. Takeo Sasaki has suggested a *Teams* meeting between the Darwin force and Locke and co., but since Locke doesn't know one end of a microphone cable from another, it's down to Kerri *Helluva Thing* Dunstan to step in and sort the technical side out. She finds an empty meeting room and sets up cameras and microphones. They've done this sort of thing before during the pandemic, but Locke has never liaised on a case with cops from the other side of the world. One difficulty has been finding a suitable time for their online meeting, but they finally settle on eleven PM UTC. That's five o'clock in the afternoon Montana time, eight-thirty in the morning Darwin time. That's eight-thirty in the morning *the next day.* Locke is struggling to get his head around that, and when the screen flashes with the incoming call at a little after five, he can't help but think the disembodied voice saying *hello* is somehow coming from the future.

And, given the circumstances, perhaps that's appropriate.

The screen fizzes into a picture. There's a table facing the camera and three people sitting behind it. Little nameplates perch on the table. Behind the one labelled *Linda Malroony* sits an aboriginal woman. She has strong features and jet-black hair, which gives a no-nonsense look to her. On the right, the nameplate says *Kieran Lamb*. Behind it is an older guy with tanned and sun-worn features and dusty ash-blonde hair. Between Lamb and Malroony, the name says *Takeo Sasaki*. Japanese. Dark hair, a round face, and an engaging smile when he realises the connection is stable.

Locke hadn't thought about nameplates or anything. But, of course, with the vast wilderness distances in Australia, the Darwin force must have done it this way even before COVID. Locke introduces himself, Sullivan, and Dunstan, and there are a few minutes of chitchat. Then Locke decides they'd better get down to business.

The cops on the other side of the world set out what they've got. There's a woman sex worker with a severed

304

arm, a cell phone stuck inside her, and a voicemail message on the phone.

Locke tells them to back up. Asks them to play the message. There's a momentary pause, but the Australians aren't phased and have everything ready. After a few seconds, the familiar distorted sound travels from the far side of the world to Missoula and crackles out of the desktop speakers.

*Let's play a game. A game with numbers. Shall we start with three?*

'Jesus, Frank, that's a helluva—'

'It's the same message,' Locke says, cutting off Dunstan. 'The same words, the same voice, the exact same recording.'

'And you have a similar MO over there?' Takeo Sasaki says. 'A female, violently killed, with a severed arm placed at a distance from the body?'

'Yes.' Locke scrabbles among some papers on the desk and finds a photograph. He holds it up. 'Although we haven't found the arm.'

In truth, Locke thinks, they didn't search more than a few paces from the body. The forest was so dense, the terrain so rough that he assumed the body had simply been dumped sans arm. Now, he realises there is more to it than that. A whole lot more.

The Australians are controlling the meeting, quickly moving on to a presentation. Their faces pop into a little window on the top right of the screen, and various maps and documents fill the remainder. Sasaki tells them of a historical case with three bodies and three arms, the arms of each victim pointing to a previous murder. The police found the killer when detectives realised the first victim's arm pointed to his house. The implication, to Locke, is obvious.

305

'So we've got to find the arm?'

'Yes,' Sasaki says. 'That's how we discovered your murder.'

'But...?'

'Is it the same murderer?' Sasaki and the others suddenly pop full screen again. 'That's what we don't know. We don't have a suspect here.'

'And the man behind the original killings?'

'Moot point. He was in prison but is now on the run. However, he didn't commit the killing here because he was behind bars at the time. What about at your end?'

'We had a suspect, but as far as I know, he had no interest in travelling abroad. I very much doubt he's ever been out of the US. Plus, he is now deceased.'

'So perhaps he's not your man?'

Sullivan nudges Locke and lowers his voice to a whisper. 'Fucking smart alec, right?'

'No, not necessarily,' Locke whispers back. 'Not if we're wrong.'

'There's one killing here,' Sasaki says. 'One in Montana, and — if our historical case is anything to go by — one or more somewhere else. It's vital you find the arm so we can track down the next victim.'

'Right, we'll get on it,' Locke says, thinking he has no idea exactly *how* they'll find the arm in the dense trees of the Lewis and Clarke National Forest. 'And we'll double check whether our guy left the US recently.'

There are a few more minutes of back and forth, the Australians explaining they'll share all the case files and requesting the same from Locke, and then it's over.

'They fucking bossed us, Frank,' Sullivan says as the screen blinks to grey. 'Talked down to by a nip, a darkie and an old codger on the world's underbelly. What the frig is it coming to, hey?'

Locke isn't listening. He's thinking about Jim Swanson and the Global Serial Crimes Database and wondering how many cases of severed arms there might be... worldwide. Wondering also how the X-Mex killings never got linked to Henrik Mattich. The women were skinned, for God's sake. How they failed to get connected to the Seattle case is something he needs to take up with Swanson urgently.

'It's going to be a helluva job, Frank,' Kerri Dunstan says, interrupting his thoughts. She has opened her laptop, a map of the Lewis and Clarke forest onscreen. She's zooming and clicking and dragging and huffing. 'In that terrain and in this weather? We're going to need some help.'

There's been another dump of spring snow overnight and flurries throughout the day. A few CSIs tramping about in the woods aren't going to find jack shit.

'You're right, Kerri,' Locke says. 'I'll make some calls.'

~ ~ ~

Locke gets on the phone. Blitzes it. He calls on forest rangers, the National Guard, air support in the form of a National Parks' helicopter, and as many uniformed officers as can be spared. Dunstan has been busy, too, and brought in the services of a Seattle tech startup that specialises in searches using drones.

'The icing on the cake,' she says. 'Even though searching by drone is experimental, they could make all the difference.'

Let's hope so, Locke thinks, because, with all the new expenditure, his arse is on the line if they don't find something.

They start at first light the next day. They set up a control centre beside the track close to where the body was found. Dunstan erects a pop-up forensic tent to act as a shelter against a persistent rain that has displaced the snow of earlier, and she sits behind a table ticking off items on a checklist and passing out instructions. Locke talks to the techies who've driven overnight from Seattle, their truck packed with drones.

'We send them up, they swarm across the search area, and an AI carries out real-time analysis of the pictures they send back,' one of the startup's founders, a long-haired guy who doesn't look long out of college, tells Locke. 'The AI can distinguish between a body or body parts and something non-organic. It can also highlight clothing or other discarded items that might be of interest. Then, if anything gets flagged for further investigation, we can send a single drone in for an ultra-close look. If that seems promising or indeterminate, someone can go in on foot to check it out.'

'And the trees?' Locke waves a hand at the conifers clustered on the mountainside. 'Won't they prevent the drones from getting a decent view from above?'

'You just wait.' The man gives Locke a wink and goes back to unloading the truck.

Half an hour later, Locke returns to find two rows of drones lined up on the track. Must be fifty or more, but before he's done counting, the man gives a signal, and the drones whirr into life. The noise as they rise from the ground is like a mass of angry buzzing insects, and for a moment, they hover at waist level before an unseen command tells them to move. They slide forward and swarm beneath the canopy of trees, somehow avoiding the tree trunks and low-hanging branches. Locke stands there open-mouthed.

'The next thing is Robocop, right?' Kerri Dunstan says, staring after the departing drones, a smile on her face. 'And then we'll be out of a job.'

Locke turns away, wondering if that's true. He can't see a drone or a computer getting angry in the same way as he's done when he has found the body of some unfortunate woman killed in appalling circumstances. Then again, perhaps they can program emotion in too. Perhaps in the future, some robotic cop can collect evidence, ascertain guilt, and carry out an appropriate sentence all on its own. And that might just make the criminals think twice.

Three hours into the day, the future of robotic policing looks in doubt. Several of the drones have succumbed to the weather. But then, in the early afternoon, the sun peeks through a gap in the clouds, and one of the drones comes good.

The tech guy beckons Locke over to the back of his truck. Inside, there's a host of electronic equipment and a couple of operatives sitting in front of screens.

'We've got something,' the man says. 'Or rather, the AI reckons we've got something.'

Locke clambers into the back of the van, and one of the operatives shows him a screen.

'Run the footage, Jennifer.'

The operative clicks a mouse button, and a video plays on the screen. It's a low-level POV shot, the drone gliding beneath heavy vegetation until it reaches a pile of dead brushwood. Something pale is visible just to one side, but the drone can't get any closer due to overhanging branches. The operative pauses the video and zooms a section of the picture.

'The computer is flagging a colour match,' she says. 'Caucasian skin with the correct decay rate compared to your victim and taking into account the average ambient temperatures around here.'

'You can tell that from the information on the screen?'

'The AI can. There's no way we can look through all the footage from all the drones, but the AI searches through the keyframes and analyses everything. It compares what it finds with examples stored in the database, and machine learning means it gets better and better.'

Definitely Robocop, Locke thinks again.

'You'll need to go out there to be sure,' the head techie says. 'But the computer calculates there's a seventy-eight per cent chance that what we are seeing is human flesh.'

'What's the position?'

'A little over two thousand metres out from the dump site.' The techie points into the truck at another screen. There's a map with the target icon at its centre. 'Bearing one one six.'

Locke thanks the tech guy and goes to find Dunstan.

'Looks like us humans are still in the game,' Locke says. 'A seventy-eight per cent chance anyway.'

They clamber into Dunstan's vehicle and set off. To get to the drone's location, they must take a long detour round the side of a valley. The forest track starts as a decent gravelled surface but soon changes to a mess of mud, ruts, and fallen branches. Locke hangs onto the dash as Dunstan swings the truck around, showing zero respect for government property. After a few miles of back-jarring driving, Dunstan halts the vehicle at the edge of a steep ravine.

'Down there,' Dunstan says. 'Half a click.'

She grabs her kit and Locke pulls on his waterproof. They follow a narrow stream down a gully until the terrain flattens out. Dunstan glances at her GPS.

'North,' she says, plunging into a thicker area of woodland where the pine branches hang low.

Locke pushes after the CSI, surprised the drones managed to get this far. A tangle of branches is ahead, pine needles brushing his face as he stoops to pass. Then, Dunstan's GPS unit gives a celebratory *beep*.

'We're here,' Dunstan points at a thicket where, to one side, a black drone sits on the ground. A green light blinks atop the drone. 'Clever little fellow.'

They move closer, careful where they step. Dunstan takes a stainless steel rod and prods at the undergrowth where there's something pale and white and eighteen inches long. It's the victim's arm, no doubt about it. Bits of stringy flesh at one end where the upper arm has been severed from the body. At the other end, three curled fingers, one extended, the hand pointing.

Locke shivers. The dampness has worked inside his jacket, and the cold has slipped into his heart. He steps back and scans the area. The light is growing feeble, the drone's LED ever brighter. There's little chance of being able to get a search team in here now, but Locke doesn't think they'd find much anyway. His best guess is the arm is all there is.

'Direction?' he says to Dunstan.

'East or thereabouts,' Dunstan says. She looks at the GPS screen. 'Two thousand one hundred and ninety-eight metres from the body.'

The CSI extracts a large bag from her rucksack and pulls on gloves. She reaches into the undergrowth and drags out the arm. There's an odour, a faint sweet smell of rot and decay. If the weather had been any warmer, the arm would have been blown with fly eggs, maggots would have hatched, and there'd be nothing left but bone. As it is, the thing is intact, limp and floppy, and if Locke didn't know better, he'd assume it was a Halloween prank body part or a prop gone AWOL from a zombie apocalypse movie set.

Dunstan carefully bags the arm before turning to Locke.

311

'Don't know if we'll get anything from it,' she says. 'But it's worth a try.'

'And what about Takeo's idea?'

'He's been right so far. We just need to get back to base, work out all the figures, and plug them into a map. Then we'll know where.'

'And where do you think?'

'If the ratio he gave us is correct, it doesn't make sense.'

'How come?'

'Two K times thirty-three thousand? You do the math.'

Locke does and Dunstan is right. It makes no fucking sense at all.

~ ~ ~

They don't return to Missoula until late that night. Locke has already messaged Sasaki about the discovery, but he holds back the information Dunstan has given him. He wants to wait until the morning so they can work through the numbers and see if the CSI's hypothesis is correct.

*It doesn't make sense...*

The number is too big. Never mind the jump from the Northern Territory to Montana; this takes them around the globe several times. Something is wrong.

Locke is in early the next day, keen to get on, but Dunstan says she needs breakfast. She heads off to grab a coffee and doughnut, and it's another half an hour before they're seated at Dunstan's workstation.

The CSI brings up some mapping software and tells Locke the highly-detailed base map only covers Montana and the surrounding states.

'Look,' she says, 'I've been thinking. Suppose the killer got the math wrong?'

'Explain.'

'For some reason, they got messed up and put in an extra zero when leaving the arm. If that's the case, then our two thousand and something metres becomes a much more reasonable two-twenty. That's much closer to Takeo's four hundred for his body.'

'Try it.'

'Sure.' Dunstan's fingers tap the keyboard as she enters some figures. 'Here's the bearing and the distance worked out using Takeo's ratio but with a zero knocked off.'

Dunstan clicks and the map zooms out in stages to show them where the endpoint is.

'What the fuck?' Locke stares at the line as it arrows across the Atlantic.

London,' Dunstan says, adding unnecessarily, 'England.'

# Chapter 33

The cops in Montana have found the arm and sent through the all-important bearing and measurement. Sasaki and Malroony watch as Kieran Lamb plots the figures into his map, confirming Frank Locke's guess.

'The UK,' Lamb says. 'Bang in the middle of London.'

'So where does that leave us?' Malroony says. 'Are we at the centre of this or the periphery?'

'The link with the Black Ute Killer suggests whoever is doing this started here,' Sasaki says. 'They used the ratios from the killings to set all this up: the murder here pointing to the one in Montana, which, in turn, presumably points to another in London.'

'And another after that?' Malroony shakes her head. 'Where the hell does this nutter stop?'

Sasaki doesn't know.

'And who is he?' Malroony is agitated. 'An airline pilot? An international business traveller? A rich tourist?'

Sasaki doesn't know that either. He's never heard of a serial killer working across continents, but how would the authorities find out if one was?

'We need to focus on the here and now,' he says. 'Ken Royston was made to remove the map from the document store shortly before the first murder took place. Whoever blackmailed him is either the killer or knows who the killer is, so finding the blackmailer is our priority.'

'And Royston's not telling?'

'He claims he doesn't know, but I suspect he has a good idea. He left Darwin when the BUK was caught all those years ago, but why? My guess is that he suspected that others were involved beyond Derek Pearce.' Sasaki turns to Lamb. 'Do you think you could have a word? After all, you are cohorts from the same era.'

'You make me sound like a dinosaur,' Lamb says.

'With age comes wisdom,' Sasaki says, seeing Malroony conceal a little smile. 'And it could be he trusts you more than me.'

'I can try,' Lamb says. 'But I'm not promising anything, and I don't want to cause trouble.'

'For fuck's sake!' Malroony turns on Lamb. 'At least two women are dead, and you're worried about office politics?'

'Linda.' Sasaki holds up his hands. 'He'll do his best, won't you, Kieran?'

After a lengthy pause, Lamb gets up, nods, and walks off.

'That doesn't exactly fill me with confidence, sir,' Malroony says. 'Do you think he could be involved somehow?'

'No,' Sasaki says, although, in truth, he isn't sure of anything any longer.

~ ~ ~

A few minutes later, Lamb passes Sasaki in the corridor.

'Royston will text you,' the CSI says. 'But he was at pains to tell me he's not accusing anyone, not doing anything other than raising questions floating about at the time of the BUK murders. Also, you didn't get it from him.'

And Lamb spins, trots away and is gone.

~ ~ ~

A vibration on Sasaki's phone comes within the hour. He lifts the phone from the desk and looks at the notification. Unknown number. Two capital letters. Nothing else.

KA

Sasaki takes only a second to resolve the initials into a name: Kevin Anderson.

He takes a deep breath and closes his eyes.

315

Anderson was a young cop at the time of the Black Ute Killer, and Sasaki still vividly remembers that ride home when the third body had been found:

*She was cut up, Japboy. Slit, slit. Understand?*

*Sasaki, trying to enjoy the ride in the police car, ignores Anderson, but the officer persists.*

*Slit, slit, slitty eyes. You think I'm funny, right?*

*Not funny. Sasaki stares out the window.*

*She was a bad girl, Jappy, bad, and that's what happens to people who don't behave, who don't do what they're told and don't know their place. You remember that. You and your people.*

*Sasaki's face is pressing against the glass now, Darwin streets rushing by. Left, right, and only a couple more minutes before they're home. A couple more minutes of Anderson ranting.*

*There won't be many crying. Like they didn't cry when the bombs dropped on your lot. Boom, boom. Gone. A hundred thousand vapourised and good riddance. That's what people think then and now. You remember that, Jappy. Call it a free life lesson from Mr KA.*

*Anderson pulls the car to the side of the road, and Sasaki opens the door and sprints for the front gate.*

*Say thank you, you ungrateful fucking prick.*

*But Sasaki is round the side of his house, not looking back and certainly not saying thank you.*

That Anderson is an unpleasant excuse for a human being isn't in doubt, but does it put him in the frame for anything approaching serial murder? Sasaki isn't sure. He checks out Anderson's police record. Not a high-flyer, he's remained in uniform and managed to make sergeant, but no further. In his twenties and thirties, there were several complaints against him, primarily accusations of racism, but back then, there wasn't an urgency to investigate, and they were left 'on file' as the euphemism for doing nothing went. He's been married and divorced twice, no children, one brother.

Speaking to Royston again is probably out of the question; AC Cooper wouldn't be a good idea either. There's only one other person who was a contemporary of Anderson and is still in the force.

Sasaki finds Lamb outside in the car park, packing boxes into the back of his vehicle. Could Sasaki have a word or two about Kevin Anderson?

Lamb sighs and dumps a box at Sasaki's feet. 'So Royston's been in touch?'

'This is nothing to do with Ken Royston, understand?' Sasaki takes a glance around. There's nobody out here but himself and Lamb. 'Tell me anything you remember from when the BUK was first active.'

'Are you talking facts or gossip? Because...' and here Lamb nods at the pile of equipment in the van '...in my world, only facts matter. I've spent my whole life lifting prints, taking swabs, and tweezering fibres. Facts don't lie, don't bear grudges, don't fuck each other over to come out on top.'

'Sure, I understand. Facts to start with, gossip if it helps paint a picture.'

'Kevin's an A-hole,' Lamb says. 'First rate. But then many cops who started when he did are. Thankfully, most have moved on.'

'I remember him being an out-an-out racist when I was a kid.'

'He was that. Misogynistic as well. Female officers didn't like being alone with him because of his behaviour. Still don't, to be honest.'

'Anything particular to do with the BUK case?'

Lamb pauses for a few seconds. Shifts one of his plastic boxes with his foot before looking at Sasaki. 'Kevin was mates with Derek Pearce.'

'That's not in the files.'

'The chief at the time — Ron Bassford — encouraged detectives to overlook the friendship. He said it added nothing to the case for or against Pearce, and I guess it didn't.'

'How friendly were they?'

'Drank together, fished together, chased skirt together.'

'And the chief didn't think the fact they were friends was relevant?'

'Anderson was in Sydney on some force exchange course during the second and third murders. Whatever Pearce did, it was off his own bat. They might have been a bad influence on each other, but as unpleasant as Anderson was back then — still is — he wasn't a killer.'

'Yet it could be he's helping a killer now.'

'We don't know for sure.'

'True.' Sasaki taps his foot near one of the plastic boxes. 'We're going to need evidence for that.'

~ ~ ~

Kevin Anderson lives outside Darwin on a beat-up small holding a stone's throw from the Stuart Highway. According to Lamb, Anderson inherited the place from his dad but has done nothing with it other than watch the buildings decay into dust. The journey is an easy drive thirty kilometres down the dual carriageway, and with few vehicles on the road, Sasaki tries to relax. He lowers the windows and enjoys the breeze. He thinks about what he's going to ask Anderson.

He's so focused that the sudden rush of red and white in the air startles him, and it takes a second to register the shape of a helicopter as it skims away to the east, barely above ground level. A moment later, Sasaki spots a road sign for the Sandford airstrip and, clustered around it, advertisements for various businesses at the airport. One ad has a logo that shows a fish with rotor blades in place of a dorsal fin below the company name: *Copter Catches*. It's a helicopter fishing outfit that takes clients to remote locations to catch fish and photograph wildlife. Sasaki almost drives past, rationalising that the helicopters at the Sandford strip and Darwin airport have been checked to see if they have the right skids to match the marks out at Tortilla Flats, but something makes him take the turn.

Kevin Anderson's place is only a couple of K away, and it was Anderson, because he lived so close and could do it at the end of his shift, who was the officer designated to visit *Copter Catches*. His check came in negative like all the checks so far had.

But if Anderson is involved...

It's a five-minute drive to the strip. A dirt road leads to a string of prefab buildings and a dozen planes scattered round a beat-up length of asphalt. The bright logo of *Copter Catches* sits on the side of a cavernous hanger, and out front are three large circles, each with an H in the centre. Two are empty, but a black helicopter stands on the third. Sasaki pulls up in front of the hanger and pops the glove box. There's tape measure inside, handy at crime scenes, handy, too, for measuring helicopter skids.

He's down on his hands and knees, extending the tape underneath the helicopter, when a female voice comes from behind him.

'Can I help you?'

Sasaki reads the tape measure and then turns to see a woman in cut-off jeans and a revealing halter top standing by the entrance to the hanger. He stands, pockets the tape measure and pulls out his ID.

'Takeo Sasaki,' he says. 'Routine safety check.'

'Your ID says you're police, not CASA.'

'CASA?'

'Civil Aviation Safety Authority. If you had anything to do with aircraft safety, you'd know that.'

Sasaki nods. The woman's apparel — likely chosen to appeal to the primarily male fishing clients — belies her intelligence; she isn't as stupid as she looks.

'Where's your boss?'

'I'm the boss.' The woman gives a laugh tinged with irony. 'Now, would you tell me what you're here about?'

The woman turns out to be the daughter of the guy who set up *Copter Catches*, Mike Keelan. Vicky Keelan took over the business when her father unexpectedly decided to retire and sail round the world. She's taken it from one aircraft to three and expanded the business into other areas, such as weddings.

'Quite something when the bride turns up in our black beauty rather than a limo,' Vicky says, gesturing at the helicopter Sasaki has been measuring. 'More lucrative than taking a couple of blokes fishing, and we can do three a day.'

'Do you fly?' Sasaki asks. He turns to the helicopter. 'This one, for example.'

'Yes. I fly all three when I get the chance.' She looks baleful for a moment. 'Which unfortunately isn't very often because there's always something urgent to do on the admin side of the business.'

'Do you have records of which helicopter flew where on which days?'

'We have flight plans, but they're subject to change. Clients cancel, or the weather means we choose alternative fishing spots. That sort of thing. Luckily, as long as we stay out of the Darwin area, we can pretty much fly where we want.' Vicky cocks her head. 'Is this leading somewhere? If so, I'm wondering if I should contact my lawyer.'

'No, you're fine.' Sasaki takes a couple of paces as if to walk off. 'Just one further question. Who, aside from you, flies for the company?'

'We've got a rota of pilots, five in all.' Vicky pauses. Shrugs. 'I guess you could ask in the bar down the road, and someone would tell you.'

'Perhaps, perhaps not,' Sasaki says. 'Likely, if I walk into the place down the road, I'll get dozens of stares and no answers. It would be an awful lot easier if you told me.'

The names trip off Vicky's tongue. Five men, the last one Pete Anderson.

'He wouldn't be related to my colleague in the Darwin police department, Kevin Anderson?' Sasaki asks.

'Sure,' Vicky says. 'Pete is Kevin's brother.'

~ ~ ~

Back in the car, Sasaki makes a quick call to Lamb to double-check the measurements for the marks out at Tortilla Flats.

'Two point four five metres width,' Lamb says. 'An eighty-five millimetre tube.'

The black helicopter is an exact match.

The scales, Sasaki thinks, are beginning to tip one way more than the other. Kevin Anderson was supposed to check the helicopters at the Sandford strip, so either he was lazy and didn't bother, or there's another reason he didn't report the black helicopter as a match. The fact that his brother, Pete, is a pilot for *Copter Catches* suggests the latter.

Sasaki doesn't tell Lamb where he's been or that he's found a match, merely that there's been an interesting development and he'll get back to him. The next step is to speak to Kevin Anderson and see if there is some kind of innocent explanation. Then he needs to get a crew roster and diary of flight plans from Vicky Keelan, do forensics on the helicopter, and then...

He's getting ahead of himself. First, Anderson, and luckily, his house is only a five-minute drive away.

The property is set back a little from the main road, with palms and scrub surrounding a mismatch of containers, shacks and abandoned vehicles. In the centre of the mess, there's a single-storey dwelling with a tin roof. The roof is speckled with rust, while the windows and front elevation look like they could do with a lick of paint. Sasaki pulls off the Stuart Highway just after the house and parks. He gets out and walks back.

A police ute sits at one side of the house, and Sasaki moves to the ute and then towards the front door. As he's approaching, a curtain billows out from an open window, sucked through by a gust of wind. Sasaki catches the distinctive smell of weed in the air. It surely wouldn't be Anderson smoking dope, he thinks. Random drug testing in the police force means he wouldn't risk even a single toke on a spliff. So there's someone else in there with Anderson. Sasaki moves closer to the window, and a smatter of conversation confirms his hunch.

He raises his head to the sill to listen in.

*... he's fucking coming here. All the way from the US of fucking A. How about that?*

*He's got a fucking cheek after what he made me do.*

*Look, mate, it was necessary, right? Got me out of Alice, didn't he?*

*I think you'll find I was the one who sorted it. If I hadn't killed that slut hooker and arranged the stuff out at the Alligator River, you'd still be locked up.*

*Sure, and I'm obliged, and I promise I'll see you right once I get out of this stinking shithole.*

*What are you saying about my place?*

*Not here, Kev. Not this house. I mean this country. The only way I could remain in Oz and stay ahead of the cops would be to live out in the bush like a hermit. That would be worse than prison.*

*So I've got to remain here and take the flack? You pick a Get Out Of Gaol card while I Do Not Pass Go and head the opposite way?*

*Don't worry, mate, you'll be fine. Give it a few weeks or months, and they'll wind down the search. In another year, you'll be signed off and get your pension. Then you can come to South America and hook up with me. There's some sweet pussy down there. Hot chicks, know what I mean?*

*What are you going to do for money? One thing I know about hot chicks is that they cost plenty of dough.*

*He's going to set me up with something. A bar or a little beachside café. Perhaps a couple of apartments I can rent out. It's a perfect place to retire. I can see it now: a sundowner each, some big-bottomed Brazilian women fawning over us, waves lapping gently on the sand. It's going to be cushy, mate; you wait and see.*

*You've settled on Brazil, then?*

*Brazil, Argentina, Chile. All the fucking same, right?*

*You could be extradited.*

*I'll have a new identity. He'll sort that, no problem. Goodbye Derek Pearce, hello Kendal Rushton.*

*That's it? Your new name?*

*I don't fucking know, mate. I just made it up. Now, why don't you rustle us up some nosh? He'll be here soon.*

Sasaki slips away from the window and rounds the side of the house. He leans back against the gable wall. Derek Pearce and Kevin Anderson. Birds of a feather, buddies

323

reunited after all these years... or is there another explanation?

He steps a couple of paces to the rear of the house and then trots over to a clump of scrub and ducks behind it. Anderson and Pearce are oblivious in there, but that's because Pearce has played a blinder. Who in their right mind would search a cop's house for signs of a fugitive?

Sasaki reaches for his phone. He's close enough to Darwin that there's decent network coverage out here. He just needs to make a call to bring a hoard of officers swooping in to arrest Pearce and Anderson.

And yet...

*He's fucking coming here. All the way from the US of fucking A. How about that?*

No doubt about it, whoever Pearce is talking about is linked to the killing in Montana. If Sasaki makes the call, whoever it is will be scared off. Better to wait and watch and see if he can tail whoever turns up.

*He'll be here soon...*

Sasaki glances at his watch and then moves back to the corner of the house and peers round.

'The hell you doing here?'

Kevin Anderson is standing two paces away, holding a shotgun trained on him. Derek Pearce bobs out from behind Anderson, a cricket bat in his hands.

'The Japanese detective,' Pearce says. 'What a surprise.'

'Bloody chink.' Anderson thrusts the shotgun forward. 'Now what the fuck are we supposed to do?'

Sasaki moves his arms slowly out from his sides. His gun is in a shoulder holster, but he doesn't fancy his chances against Anderson and the shotgun.

'Steady,' he says. 'Let's not do anything stupid.'

'Who the fuck are you calling stupid?' Anderson is bouncing on the balls of his feet, nervy, pent-up.

'Give me your gun, Takeo,' Pearce says. 'Use your finger and thumb. Try anything, and Kevin will put a big hole in your head.'

Sasaki isn't the hero type. He's about average when he does his yearly firearms assessment. Anderson, on the other hand, is a gun nutter. He brags about his scores and regularly goes on water buffalo and wild boar hunts, flashing the pictures of his trophies to the squad room. He's not going to miss from two metres with a shotgun.

The gun emerges slowly, Sasaki holding the grip between his finger and thumb.

'Put it on the ground,' Pearce says. 'Then step back.'

Sasaki does as he's told.

'This isn't going to work,' he says. 'There are roadblocks everywhere. You haven't got a chance of driving out of here.'

'You're lying. There aren't any roadblocks.' Pearce smiles. 'And even if there were, who said anything about driving?'

Then he steps towards Sasaki and swings the cricket bat. Sasaki raises his arms in defence, but Anderson is there too, flipping the shotgun and slamming the stock into the side of his head. A blinding flash flares like lightning, and Sasaki crashes into the building and slumps to the dirt. The sky does pirouettes, the two faces of Anderson and Pearce circling above him. Pain comes again and again as the blows rain down.

Stock, bat, stock, bat, stock, bat.

The pattern repeats over and over until...

...nothing.

# Chapter 34

Chase arranges to rendezvous with Green back at the SCU, and the two of them head out to Grainger's house. Green, as Chase might have guessed, isn't convinced. He wants to know:

'One, what evidence could there possibly be that we missed the first time around?' Green shakes his head. 'Two, if there is such evidence, who could get access to it? Three, why would they blackmail Grainger to kill for them?'

'No idea,' Chase says. 'But the answer might lie in the muddy depths of Grainger's garden pond.'

'What, nestling among the lily roots and known only to a few inquisitive water snails? Bollocks. I don't buy it, Jess. Not at all.'

'Well, let's see, shall we?'

At the house, they once again make themselves known to the neighbour. She's seen the news and informs Chase she's already had to shoo several reporters from the private road.

'Scum, looking for shit,' she says. 'That's my view.'

Chase agrees. She tells the woman the cat will need a new home, but the woman explains she owns a dog, and the two wouldn't get on. Green mentions the RSPCA and euthanasia, and the woman holds her hands up in horror, and, for some reason, mainly so they can get into the garden and get on with the job in hand, Chase promises she'll take the cat.

'There are too many animals in this investigation,' Green says as they open the gates to Grainger's place. 'Alison's dog, Grainger's cat, the bearded reedling.'

They're round the back now, and as they stand beside the pond, several koi carp cruise back and forth, looking like submarine carrots. The pond is set into a rectangular patio, about ten paces long by four wide. Chase stares at the koi, thinking they can add fish to the menagerie, while Green finds a garden rake and prods the depths.

'Bloody hell, that'll be up to my waist,' he says. 'I'm not going in there. We need a specialist diving team.'

'You wimp,' Chase says. 'Poke around some more and see if you can locate a rock. Otherwise, you're getting wet because Grainger told me it's in there.'

Green swirls the rake back and forth, covering the pond bit by bit. Halfway along the length of the pond, he stops.

'There's something here,' he says, reversing the rake and using the handle to probe. 'Feels like a brick or a concrete block.'

'Try to shift it.'

Green manoeuvres the rake, crouching to get additional leverage. He pushes and prods and curses, and then the water boils, and a plastic sandwich box bobs to the surface. Chase moves to the edge and reaches for the container.

'Let's see what mystery Grainger has served us,' she says, shaking water from the box. 'And whether whatever it is could be worth killing for.'

The container is covered with slime and weed, and Chase wipes it clean and throws the weed back into the pond. Her fingers close round the lid and gently peel it off. Inside are two pieces of paper folded in half. She opens them up and hands one to Green.

'Fuck.' Chase stares at the streaks of black spidering across the page. Water has leaked into the box and soaked the paper, and the ink has run everywhere. She shows Green the paper. 'This one is in a right state.'

'Can you read it?'

Chase peers down and skims through. It's some sort of pre-printed form. Boxes with code letters and numbers. Scrawls of writing in various places. A department and address on the top right.

'It's a lab report,' Chase says. 'But like none I've ever seen.'

'Hey?'

'It's from the New York State Police Forensic Investigation Center. Something about multiple DNA samples. There are various references and a supervisor's name. Nothing about where the samples came from.'

'Is there a date?'

'Yes. June year before last.' Chase looks up. 'And yours?'

'Similar. It's an NYPD report concerning an arrest for the possession of Rohypnol. Care to guess the name of the suspect?'

'Grainger.'

'Yup. The same month, and that's when Grainger was away from the UK. Remember the rapes stopped while he was absent?'

'Except they didn't stop, Grainger carried on while he was on sabbatical.' Chase takes the sheet back from Green and carefully places both pieces of paper back in the plastic box. 'So we have a DNA report likely from semen samples swabbed from male rape victims, plus an arrest sheet showing Grainger with Rohypnol, but for some reason, he wasn't charged.'

'Perhaps the two things were never linked together.'

'That's the only conclusion. However, *someone* linked them together and blackmailed Grainger, knowing that the evidence would likely either result in a retrial here or his extradition to the US.' Chase shakes her head. 'Seems like he was telling me the truth in the hospital.'

'He killed because of this?' Green stares at the box. 'Sorry to be forever sceptical, but I don't believe it.'

'Why not? Grainger would be facing his original twenty-five-year sentence here, longer in the US. I can well believe he was willing to do exactly what his blackmailer said. And remember, Grainger isn't some meek innocent; he's an aggressive and violent sexual predator.'

'So he kills Alison and Lizzie and then tries to take his own life? That doesn't make sense.'

'He told me the blackmailer came up with new demands, and he realised the situation was hopeless. Perhaps he also knew we were on to him.'

'So, if you're correct, we need to track down whoever is doing this.'

'Yes,' Chase says. 'Easy, right?'

~ ~ ~

Except it isn't easy. Obtaining information from US law enforcement proves to be akin to squeezing blood from a stone. In other words, impossible.

'Fucking Yanks,' Green says after a dozen fruitless phone calls. 'Cooperation just isn't in their lexicon.'

'That's actually not true,' Stafford says. 'There's the GSCDB, remember?'

'The *what*?'

'Didn't you do any homework before you joined the unit?'

'Yes, but not the boring kind you get excited over.'

'The GSCDB is a global database of serial crimes created by the FBI. It was designed to spot patterns of offending behaviour so as to be able to predict possible serial offences based on the data entered matching existing patterns in the database. A secondary benefit was the tracking of crimes across national boundaries, ensuring if patterns in one country were repeated in a second country, they'd still be picked up. It was a brilliant idea in theory but hard to implement in practice.'

Stafford explains that persuading individual forces to share information has proved difficult. Police forces in some countries have cooperated, whereas others haven't, leaving gaps in the data.

'We were one of the first countries to get on board with the idea. Most of Europe is now involved, but it's patchy elsewhere.'

'Trust you to know about this, John,' Chase says. 'But how does it relate to Grainger?'

'He's in there. I entered all the details of the Soho Sleeper when the case first came up, and when Grainger became a suspect, I added him, too. If there were multiple male rapes in New York, then those offences should have been recorded too.'

'But they weren't?'

'Obviously not.' Stafford pauses for a moment. 'Or rather, if they were, there weren't enough common data points to link those crimes to Grainger.'

'Do you have access and can you find out?'

'Yes, of course.'

Stafford hunches over his keyboard, and Chase and Green leave him to it. Thirty minutes later, he raises his head.

'You were right, Nick,' he says. 'Fucking yanks.'

'Problems?' asks Chase.

'All the info I entered on the Soho Sleeper and Grainger is there, but there's nothing on the male rape victims in New York.'

'And yet we have a forensic report with multiple samples from the NYPD.'

'Well, the lazy cops over there didn't enter the information.'

'Or it was entered, but somebody prevented it from being linked in the same way as Grainger's arrest for possessing Rohypnol wasn't flagged up.'

'Well, let's find out,' Stafford says.

He leans over his keyboard once more and fires off an email to a contact in the FBI. A few minutes later, he receives a short, curt reply saying the matter will be looked into.

With zero input from the FBI and more questions than answers, the three of them decide on an intensive session of *what the fuck is going on?*

The session begins, as usual, with a food delivery, and soon, they're clustered round a desk bearing several foil trays of take-out curry. They've also got bhajis, samosas, naans, papadums, raita, and mango chutney. 'Brain food', Stafford calls it, and if the way the platter is disappearing is anything to go by, they'll crack the case within the next thirty minutes.

Except Chase doesn't think they will.

'Someone gets Grainger to commit a bizarre murder,' Chase says as she dips a bhaji in some raita. 'But for why?'

'Has to be something in Alison's past,' Green says. 'A spurned lover, for instance. That would explain why Grainger killed Lizzie in an entirely different manner.'

'A spurned lover with access to US law enforcement databases? Unlikely. Doesn't explain the message or the arm, either.'

Chase and Green carry on a back-and-forth for a minute, and then Green asks Stafford if he has any ideas.

'Why do you always expect me to have the answers?' Stafford dips a piece of naan in his rich red-pink masala.

'Oh wait, it's because you're a thick West Country boy, and you can't come up with any yourself, right?'

'That'll be it.' Green looks at Chase again. 'If you don't like my take, then let's explore alternative theories as to who the killer could be.'

But by the time the foil trays are empty and every last morsel gone, they're none the wiser.

Then one of the office phones rings, and Stafford puts it on speaker, and an American accent echoes out, and all of a sudden, everything is completed and utterly fucked.

~ ~ ~

The call isn't from Stafford's contact within the FBI, and the news it brings proves much harder to digest than the curry.

A killing in the US state of Montana.

A killing near Darwin, Australia.

Both victims sex workers with a weird message left on a phone inside them.

Both having severed arms pointing to another victim on a different continent.

Detective Frank Locke from the Montana Department of Justice Division of Criminal Investigation does his best to explain, but Chase still can't get her head around it even though he's been kind enough to send through a complete dossier. There's plenty to think about, so they adjourn to the pub and wash the curry and the news down with a couple of pints and a second round of *what the fuck is going on?*

It's early evening, and there's a buzz in the pub. Some DI is getting married and very sensibly leaving the force at the same time. Gas-filled balloons bounce on the ceiling, bottles of fizz pop open, and a chorus of raucous but good-natured singing rings out. Officers retell arrest stories;

like fishermen's tales, they grow more unbelievable by the minute.

But Chase, Green and Stafford sit in one corner, oblivious to the celebrations.

'They've got a suspect in the US for their killing, but he's dead,' Chase says. 'Like Grainger, he never left the country. Like Grainger, he may have been coerced.'

'But in Australia, no suspect so far, right?' Green takes a deep sup of his bitter. 'But a case with a similar MO from decades ago?'

'Yeah,' Stafford says. He's holding his pint with one hand, flicking through a sheaf of printouts with the other. 'Arms chopped off and moved to point to other murders. Something about bearings and ratios.'

'And Alison Madden's arm, where does that point to?'

'Just south of Darwin, Australia.'

'No, it doesn't. The line went northeast out towards Suffolk.'

'It's a Great Circle.'

Stafford doesn't elaborate until Chase asks.

'You've been brought up on maps stuck on the wall of a classroom or the screen of your phone. The problem is they are a two-dimensional representation of a three-dimensional object.'

'What?'

'The earth is a globe. On a conventional "flat" map, the shortest distance to Australia might look as if it's heading southeast or something like that, but on a globe, the shortest route goes towards Harwich, then north of Amsterdam, Does Poland, passes over Moscow and heads down over Kazakhstan and China. It ends up at Tortilla Flats, where the Aussies found their body.' Stafford shrugs as if no more explanation is needed. 'If we had a football or similar, I could show you it's a straight line. But we don't.'

Chase looks at Green and can see he doesn't understand either.

'Right...' Chase says. 'Still doesn't answer why?'

'Fuck knows.' Stafford throws the printouts down and shakes his head.

'Nutters, Jess,' Green says. 'You can't fathom their motives. We call them lunatics because they bark at the moon, and nobody can understand them, right?'

Chase thinks not being able to understand is concerning. Especially given the breadth of this case. She wonders what resources a cop in rural Montana can access and what the Darwin Police force can contribute. She looked up Darwin earlier and discovered it has a population of a hundred and fifty thousand, about the same size as Blackpool or Peterborough. Hardly set up to deal with a complex murder investigation. She puts her worries to the other two.

'We're the SCU,' Green says. 'A crack investigation team. We'll solve this, don't worry.'

Silence until Stafford nods at their half-finished pints. 'Better drink up then,' he says.

# Chapter 35

Things are moving fast, Locke thinks. The Brits are now in on the action and appear to know what they're doing. Everything has played out just as Takeo Sasaki guessed it might do, and DI Jessica Chase and her team have confirmed they have a murder almost identical to the killing near Darwin and Locke's girl-in-the-forest case.

But there's something of a crisis occurring in Australia.

Senior Sergeant Takeo Sasaki has gone missing.

Locke doesn't know what the fuck is going on down under, but it's really not his problem. Anyway, what can he do to help find a missing officer when he's eight thousand miles away?

Nothing, that's what.

Instead, he heads back to Henrik Mattich's place. More miles under the wheels. More gas in the tank. More crap food to keep him from getting bored on the journey. Another six hours in his own company. Wanting to be distracted, he tries a couple of stations on the radio before giving up and sticking with his thoughts. Driving back to Taxidermy Central was not what he'd planned to do, not after hooking up with the guys in London. But there are issues. The British detectives are sure their suspect killed himself, and he did so after being blackmailed into murdering a sex worker. And then they dropped a bombshell.

'By somebody with access to US police records,' the thin guy with the tweed jacket had said. John Oxfordshire? Staffordshire? John Something, anyway. 'We think there's information about Alan Grainger that you guys haven't been sharing with us.'

Turns out their suspect had made a trip to the US, where he was caught in possession of a date rape drug, but the details were never passed to the British police. Also, there's a DNA match to several sexual assaults in NYC.

Which leads Locke to call Jim Swanson, AKA Mr Global Serial Crimes Database. If anybody should know what the fuck's going on, he should.

'Jim, Frank.'

'Frank.' Swanson's quiet for a couple of moments, and there's a buzzing on the line. 'You OK? You did good with that Mattich fella. Real good. I hope you're not feeling any heat from the incident. Excuse the pun.'

'His death was chalked down to self-defence, so I'm fine,' Locke says. 'Got a couple of questions about the serial crimes database. Is that OK?'

'I told you, I no longer have much to do with it. I let the kid coders work their magic these days.'

'But you created it. You know how it works, right?'

'Of course. What do you want to know?'

Locke gives Swanson a rundown of the case of the Brit, Alan Grainger. He explains about the blackmail and the incident Grainger was arrested for, his possession of Rohypnol and his subsequent release, and the DNA match that was never followed up.

'The semen samples go to the New York lab but never get connected to Grainger in the GSCDB. Likewise, he's arrested for having Rohypnol, but the information isn't acted on. It looks as if the details weren't shared globally, meaning law enforcement in the US and worldwide couldn't use the data.'

Silence. The line breaks for a moment, and Locke stares at the screen. In the mountains, reception is patchy, but the signal looks good, and there shouldn't be a problem.

'You there?' he says.

'Yes,' Swanson says. 'Lost you for a moment.'

'I was asking about the sharing of information.'

336

'I don't know what happened,' Swanson says. 'Not everything is shared. Sometimes, a review finds the data are not of sufficient quality, or occasionally, information is withheld for national security reasons. I'm unaware of the details in this case.'

'But somebody *does* know the details,' Locke says. 'Somebody accessed the record and used the information to blackmail Grainger. Moreover, had the information been available back at his trial in the UK, the jury almost certainly would have reached a different verdict. Then there are the X-Mex killings. The MO was so similar to the Seattle murders that there should have been some sort of flag to highlight Mattich as a suspect. It's possible Mattich was blackmailed to kill, too.'

'Frank, I designed the thing. I don't spend my days trawling through the millions of records in there.' Swanson chuckles. 'I might be as good as retired, but I've got better things to do with my time than look for connections between disparate pieces of data.'

'I understand, but we'll have to do some digging, and afterwards, we'll need to debrief the whole way the database works. Is it OK if I send you the details?'

'Sure, send away, but I don't see it's our problem that some evidence got mislaid. The Brits should have been able to build a better case based on evidence they collected in their own country. As for the X-Mex thing, perhaps Mattich fell off the radar because he was found innocent in Seattle. Have you thought of that?'

Locke doesn't answer the question. Instead: 'I'm on my way to Mattich's old place now. Anything I should know?'

'Not particularly, but it's good you'll take a second look. Really good. Give me a call when you're finished. Let me know what you think.'

337

And that was that. Had Swanson tried to be helpful, or was there a touch of him running a defensive play? If there was a flaw in the software or a security breach, his reaction was understandable but not forgivable. It still left Locke not knowing who had managed to get the information from the database.

Locke's done the boring bit of the drive, and he's approaching Ellensburg, the mountains rising in the background. In less than an hour, he'll be at Mattich's place. He's unsure what he expects to find, but a piece is missing from the jigsaw, and Locke feels as if he's letting the others down with the lack of progress.

When he turns off the I-90 into the forest, he can sense a change. It's not simply that Mattich is dead; there's also been a shift in the weather, and a sudden warmth has banished the last snow. The peaks are still white, but down here, the winter is over, and spring is in full progress. Swarms of insects cloud the air, birds flit back and forth, and carpets of flowers brighten the verges.

'You daft old bugger,' Locke says to himself. 'You're just seeing everything in a different light.'

But as he leaves the blacktop and drives up the track, he swears the light *is* different. A yellow glow filters through the trees, fingers of sunlight caressing the earth into life. And it's not just the insects and the birds; with the car windows down, the arrival of spring is heady in the air.

As he approaches the cabin, he's no longer fearful of a stray shot from Mattich's bow. Nevertheless, he takes the side track once more, hiding his car from view, before walking the last quarter of a mile.

*Old habits...*

Locke is expecting a cross of police tape over the front door, perhaps an official-looking FBI notice. But when he arrives at the house, there's nothing. He opens the door and steps in.

A swirl of dust floats in the air as he closes the door behind him and stands for a moment, surveying the scene. If the FBI or the local cops have searched, they've been tidy about it because little appears to have changed since Locke was last here. He pulls out his phone and takes a couple of snaps to show Swanson. It's likely the FBI man left the team unsupervised, and he'll want to know if the search was below par or even — as it looks to Locke — abandoned uncompleted. He checks the cell for a signal but isn't surprised when there's none. As soon as he gets back to the main road, he'll call Swanson and check what's going on. In the meantime, he'll carry out a brief search himself.

He starts with a big pine cabinet that sits against one wall. Doors open to a host of tiny box drawers, and when Locke begins pulling them out, he finds screws and nails and hinges. There are drawers containing thread and needles and razor blades. One is stuffed full of rolls of bandages, while another has a dozen empty snail shells. If there's something hidden here, he thinks, it will take him hours to find it. He perseveres and, after half an hour, opens a larger drawer crammed full of receipts: Grocery stores, a hardware supplier, gas stations. Must be several hundred going back years. He moves the pile to a small table and spreads the receipts out. Shakes his head. To make any sense of them, he'll need to take the lot back and file every single one. Then, something catches his eye — a gas receipt and the words *Truth or Consequences*. The receipt comes from a Chevron gas station in Truth or Consequences. The town's name is not easily forgotten, and Locke remembers it from the information he read about the women killed in New Mexico. Looks like solid evidence that Henrik Mattich *did* pay a visit south after all.

He scrabbles through the pile and finds a couple more receipts from places in New Mexico. Mattich has bought gas, paid for a motel, and eaten out at a diner. There's a definite trail to follow here, and he wonders why Swanson didn't alert him. Why was none of this information in the Serial Crimes Database when there was direct evidence? And yet Locke remembers Swanson categorically stating that Mattich hadn't been to New Mexico and thus could not be implicated in the murders. But with the receipts and the phone that Karen Kell said belonged to one of the victims, there is now unassailable evidence linking Mattich to the X-Mex killings.

Locke stares at the pile for a few minutes before returning to the pine cabinet. He's only looked in about a quarter of the drawers. It's time for a break, he thinks. Time for a change of scenery.

He heads for the open staircase that crabs up and round two walls to a mezzanine level that hangs over the main room. There's a bed next to a round window, a small wooden storage chest, a decrepit chair and a little potbelly stove. In one corner close to the stairs, a rancid smell of sweat and other bodily fluids rises from a pile of bed sheets, while over the bed itself, there's a sleeping bag. Locke strolls over to the bed, glances back at the bedclothes and then at the sleeping bag. He reaches out and touches it, bends, and takes a sniff. The bag looks and smells brand new, as if it's recently come from an outdoor supplier. Sure enough, when Locke steps back, he spies a sliver of white card beneath the bed, the words *North Face* printed next to the company's logo. Unless Mattich bought this just before he died, it looks like Goldilocks has come to stay.

Locke returns downstairs and moves to the rear of the large room, where a door opens onto a tiny storage area. There's another door to the outside, and just to the right stands a metal trashcan. A lift of the lid reveals several pieces of fast food packaging, a couple of empty beer bottles, and an empty gum packet. He pokes at the food waste. There's a corner of a fresh burger bun, and when he picks out the gum packet, he notes the brand: *Airwaves*. Not Goldilocks, then. *Airwaves* is the brand of menthol-flavoured gum Leo Sullivan buys.

It's the menthol that saves Locke's life because as he steps back into the main room, he bends his head to sniff the packet once more, and as he does so, something thwacks into the wall behind. The sound from the gunshot and the window shattering comes a microsecond later, and Locke is already diving to the floor and rolling to his right, finding cover behind the big oak table. He pulls out his weapon and double-checks it. Adjusts his position and, in one fluid movement, rises and fires off two rounds at the window while sprinting to the back door. He glances out, sees the coast is clear, and edges through the door and along the back wall. At the corner, he peeks round just in time to see Leo Sullivan step into view.

Good ol' Leo Sullivan. A couple of beers. A night out at Fat Tams. Enjoys his NASCAR and his hockey and a spot of ice fishing. The patsy at Locke's regular poker nights who always thinks he ends the evening well up even though he's well down. Likes telling you a joke he's told you a dozen times before.

'Leo.' Locke pushes out so Sullivan can see him. 'It's—'

Sullivan swings sideways, his right arm straightening, the weapon coming to bear.

Sullivan's vision is better than 20-20; he's always boasting about it. *Eyes like a hawk*, he's been known to say.

There is no way he can fail to recognise Locke at this distance.

Locke's finger tightens on the trigger, but instead of firing, he dives forward, tumbling down behind a large stack of cords. The wood pile is as high as a man and twice as long, giving solid cover from Sullivan's gun.

Above his head, a cord explodes in a burst of splinters, and Sullivan walks forward and fires again. The angle between him and Locke opens, and the cover from the wood pile becomes less and less.

'Leo!' Locke shouts again. 'It's me!'

Five strides and Sullivan will be there, but Locke stays low and crawls to the end of the pile. He scrabbles around the end, and now Sullivan is sideways on. He spots Locke out of the corner of his eye and wheels round, the gun outstretched, his finger squeezing.

Then Locke whips his gun up and fires before Sullivan can react.

20-20 vision, eyes like a hawk, but the one thing Locke remembers from their times on the range is the man's lousy reaction times. Good ol' Leo Sullivan.

Sullivan tumbles backwards and slumps against the wall of the house. Locke walks over, covering him with his gun.

'Frank,' Sullivan croaks. Locke's hit him in his right shoulder. If the bullet missed Sullivan's heart, there's a chance he'll live. If not, he's a goner. 'You bastard.'

'What the fuck do you mean?' Locke bends and picks up Sullivan's gun from the boardwalk.

'You're the killer, Frank. You butchered the girl and killed Robert Kell. Now he's out of the way, I guess your next victim will be the lovely Karen. Clever, very clever.'

'You're talking crap, Leo.'

'Am I? You're a shoo-in as far as I'm concerned.'

'So why didn't you simply confront me at the precinct? You could have arrested me there where you'd have had plenty of back-up.'

'It was down to the Feds. They told me we needed to go hush-hush so as not to scare you off. According to the Feds, the GSCDB says you're fifty-eight per cent likely to be the killer, but if you turned up here, that probability would rise to over ninety per cent because you were coming back to frame Mattich. I was sent here to stake the place out and wait for you.'

'When you say the Feds, you mean Jim Swanson?'

'Yeah. The FBI are all over you, buddy. You haven't got a cat in hell's chance. They'll be swarming round this place soon. Going to be like Ruby Ridge, only you ain't getting out.'

'I don't know what Swanson's playing at, but he's mistaken. The database has got it wrong.'

'No, Frank. What you don't know is that Robert Kell was a Fed, too. He knew you'd taken the girl up into the woods, so he led you back there to try to trick you. You got suspicious of his motivation, and you drove up to Seeley Lake and forced Kell to take a boat trip. The Feds know the killer is a cop. They've been tracking you for months.'

'You're delusional. Henrik Mattich killed the girl in Lewis and Clarke.'

'Yeah, Frank, whatever. Tell your story to the judge and jury.' Sullivan breathes deeply, winching in pain. He coughs into his hand, red spittle on his palm. 'You know, Frank, I never liked you. You're a city type trying to make it good out here. All that false bonhomie like you were one of the boys, but you never were. You're a fucking outsider and always will be.'

'Just shut up, will you? I'm taking you to the nearest ER,' Locke says. There's a lot of blood wicking up through Sullivan's clothing, but the wound is nearer to the shoulder than the heart. 'I wouldn't want you dying before you discover the truth.'

'A good deed won't save you now.'

'I'm going to get the car,' Locke says. 'Don't move.'

He jogs around the building and back along the track to the turn-off. He gets in his vehicle, drives back to the shack and parks up. Only when he goes to find Sullivan, there's no sign of him aside from a large bloodstain on the boardwalk.

Locke bellows out Sullivan's name and circles the building. Checks inside. Nothing. He spends a few minutes surveying the woodland and listening for the noise of somebody moving. Not a sound apart from birdsong echoing in the trees.

This is trouble, he thinks. If Sullivan can get to where he can summon help, he'll spin the same story, and it'll be a case of who to believe. Sullivan's got a lot of mates, and then there's the small matter of Jim Swanson and the Bureau.

Locke gets back in his car. He takes one last look at the shack and drives off. He feels a bit guilty about leaving Sullivan, but if the man's fit enough to escape, then he's likely fit enough to survive until either he gets help or help turns up.

When he's back on the I-90, Locke makes three calls. The first is to the chief at DCI HQ. He explains what's just happened. She's none the wiser than Locke and believed Sullivan was at Billings doing legwork on the crack house job. The second call is to Karen Kell, but it goes through to voicemail, so he leaves a detailed message.

The third call is to Jim Swanson... There's no answer.

# Chapter 36

Heat. Like an oven. Sasaki lies still and breathes in a smell of vomit and urine, repulsed when he realises both odours emanate from him. He blinks in the dark and turns his head until a pinprick of bright light burns into his brain, hurting so much that he is forced to scrunch his eyes closed again. His head throbs, and when he moves a hand to the top of his neck, he finds a warm, sticky mess and a bruise the size of a golf ball.

Earlier, there was nothing followed by floating and rocking. A thudding noise over and over. Chop, chop, chop, chop. Deafening. The smell of a hot engine and aviation fuel. Choking dust.

*Who said anything about driving?*

Nothing more until the heat brought him round.

Tentatively, he opens his eyes again, letting just a fraction of the brightness in. Then, a little more and a little more until his vision adjusts. He's surrounded by darkness, but a shaft of brilliance beams down from above. He shifts his position so the light no longer falls on his face. Now he can see he's in a small space, and the brightness is sunlight spilling in through a hole in the roof.

He pushes himself up from the dirt floor. He puts a hand out and feels a rough wall of concrete blocks. In the gloom, he can make out three other walls, creating a small room that is not much bigger than a dunny. There's a door in one wall made from planks of wood roughly stitched together.

Now he's upright and away from the floor, the heat is overpowering, and a lack of fresh air has him gulping until he manages to quell the panic. He breathes slowly in and out several times, feeling calmer. He waits a moment longer, then stands and approaches the door. He pushes it, feeling resistance from top and bottom as if the door is double-bolted.

Steady, he thinks. He has to try to conquer the terror and the sense of claustrophobia, the feeling that this might be his last resting place.

He bends and lines up his right eye with a knot hole in the door. Blinks again against the harsh light. He's looking out across a dry, desert steppe. There are low hills in the distance several miles away, but closer, the terrain is a wasteland of loose shale and sand and dust. Sasaki pretty much knows everywhere near Darwin, and the landscape doesn't look familiar. He'd arrived at Anderson's place mid-morning, and the sun's angle suggests it is now some-time after noon. If his senses aren't playing tricks, Anderson and Pearce have taken him on a helicopter ride, meaning this could be anywhere within a few hundred miles of Darwin. Wherever he is, it's in the middle of no-where. There isn't a building or a vehicle or any sign of civilisation to be seen.

He pulls back from the door, a dawning realisation the situation is deadly serious. At its most basic, the heat in the little room is building all the time. In an hour or so, his core temperature will be at dangerous levels. Never mind that he's desperate for a drink of water; he'll be dead from organ failure long before he dies of thirst.

He rattles the door again, but the bolts are secure. He steps back and peers up at the roof. It's corrugated iron, and the hole with the sun piercing through is the only sign of any opening. He shields his eyes and looks closer, disappointed to see no sign of rust or damage round the hole. Anyway, even if there was, the roof is several feet above his outstretched hand.

He moves back to the floor and lies down. There's less heat on the bare earth, but everything is relative. Less is not cool enough, but it might buy him more thinking time.

Not that thinking is going to help much.

He closes his eyes and his mind races in circles. The girl at Tortilla Flats. The skid marks from the helicopter that dumped her there. The phone carried away by critters and later found by Malroony. The voice message extracted by Lamb. Ken Royston, Derek Pearce, and Kevin Anderson and the stupid, idiotic, solo mission that has ultimately led to him ending up in this literal shithole.

A blur of moisture forms before his eyes, and his father's face hovers over him. Endo Sasaki looks disappointed and resigned, as if he'd expected this all along.

'I'm sorry,' Sasaki says aloud. 'For failing to live up to your standards at the end.'

He imagines the newspaper reports, the tasty alliterative possibilities adding to the insult: Darwin Detective Dies in a Dunny in the Dunes. What a way to dishonour the Sasaki name. The only blessing is that his father, cocooned in blissful ignorance, is unlikely ever to read the headlines.

He wallows for a moment, feeling only despair and hopelessness, but then a basic survival instinct kicks in. He can either lie on the floor and slip into unconsciousness or try to get out of here and reclaim a modicum of honour.

Sasaki pushes himself upright once more. He stands and slips his hands into the pockets of his trousers on the off chance that he has something that might help him escape. No. They haven't been kind or stupid enough to leave him with a phone, gun, or useful multitool. He moves a hand up and pats the breast pocket on his shirt. Something there. He slips his fingers inside and extracts a rubber band. In the heat, it has softened, and there's a sticky residue on his fingers.

Great. An elastic band. He could, he supposes, chew it to stimulate saliva, but as an aid to escaping, he can't see how it could help.

The despair rises again, but he gets to his feet before the mood can overwhelm him. He moves to the door and carries out a more thorough inspection. The hinge side is tight against the blockwork, and the hinges are on the outside, so there's no possibility of being able to undo the screws, even if he had a tool to do so. On the opening side, there's a gap, and he can see the silver steel of the bolts top and bottom, but the space is not even large enough to squeeze his fingers into.

He sighs. He's never been much of a practical person, another attribute his father failed to pass on. When he'd lived with Anna, she'd been the one to put up shelves and flyscreens and fix blocked drains or leaking pipes; he was always more analytical. Perhaps yet another reason why they split up.

Sasaki reaches into his shirt pocket and retrieves the rubber band. He's about to pop it into his mouth and chew, but it slips from his fingers and falls to the floor. He bends to pick it up, but as he does so, he finds it has landed next to a thin twig.

*More analytical...*

He reaches over and rattles the door. The bolts are loose but shot across and secured. He snaps the stick in half and then ties the rubber band round one end. He bends to the bottom bolt and feeds the stick through, allowing the band to drop to the other side of the bolt. Then, he uses the second half of the stick to snag the band back. Now, he can hold both ends of the rubber band and tension it against the bolt, rotating it ninety degrees. With a little sideways movement, he can move the bolt a couple of millimetres. He repeats the procedure. And again. And again. Bit by bit, the bolt moves to the left until it comes free, and he can push the bottom of the door outwards. The top bolt is still in place, so he repeats the technique. In ten minutes, it too comes free, and the door swings open.

Sasaki staggers out into the searing heat. He takes a moment to orient himself and then moves round to shelter in the thin slither of shade that paints the sand dark to the right of the little building. With his back to the wall, he looks out across a desolate landscape of barren rock and sand. There's the occasional shrub, but not a tree in sight. Far in the distance, to what must be the south, an escarpment rises from the pan-flat terrain. Close to, about fifty paces off, there's a dilapidated prefab bungalow. One wall has folded in, and the roof has long since blown off.

He takes a breath or two. Right now, it doesn't look as if he's in any danger. There's no sign of Anderson or Pearce or the helicopter. They've left him here unguarded. And why not? There's nowhere to run to. Sasaki's been involved in his fair share of search and rescue operations for people who broke down in their cars and then walked off and got lost. The golden rule is to stay with your vehicle — or, in this case, *stay with your dunny* — do anything else, and it's as good as signing your death warrant.

He can see a track of sorts, curling into the sparse vegetation, but the fact he's been left alone suggests there's nowhere close to walk to. Still, what are his options? Unlike someone in a broken-down car, nobody knows he's here. He can wait until Anderson and Pearce return, head off into the wilderness, or follow the only route out of here and hope to duck off and hide if anyone should come along.

Option one doesn't sound good, and he can't see two ending well. Which, by the process of elimination, leaves option three.

Despite his better judgement, Sasaki moves out from behind the block building and begins to trudge along the track.

~ ~ ~

Chase is back at the hospital, where she finds Grainger has been moved from the HDU to a side room with a single bed. A bored PC sits on a chair outside the room and tells Chase that Grainger is much better.

'Unfortunately,' he adds. 'But, given the right circumstances, that could change.'

'Don't get any ideas,' Chase says and enters the room.

Grainger is propped up on the bed. His wrists are wrapped in bandages, and a drip stands to the side, the tube snaking down to one arm. As Chase closes the door, Grainger stirs.

'You again,' he says.

'We found the box, Alan. Your story checks out.'

'I told you.'

'But just because what you told me was true, that doesn't excuse what you did.'

'I had no choice. I could do as instructed or face a retrial here and extradition to the US. It was the very definition of between a rock and a hard place.'

'Perhaps you should have thought of that before you raped those men in New York.'

Grainger looks away. Not ashamed, Chase thinks, more disinterested in what she has to say.

'I want to know more about the instructions you were given, the message you left on the phone, why you cut Alison open, why you chose her in the first place, why you killed Lizzie.'

350

Grainger lowers his head. Chase can see that this is something he doesn't want to relive.

'Why Alison?'

'She was a sex worker,' Grainger says. 'There were specific instructions that the victim had to be a prostitute. I was to find her myself and then kill her. There had to be three slashes across her chest, and I had to mutilate her genitals and remove her arm, place the body on the island and the arm on the building nearby. I was given precise coordinates for where to go. I had to buy a high-end GPS unit because my mobile wasn't accurate enough.'

'And the phone and the message?'

'Christ.' Grainger swallows, his eyes swimming with tears. 'Do I have to go on?'

The emotion comes suddenly, and Chase doesn't buy it. If Grainger has any regrets, it's for himself and his predicament rather than for his victims.

'I need to know everything. You either tell me or, at some point, you'll be interrogated by other officers. Your choice.'

Grainger nods and then reaches over to the bedside cabinet, where there's a glass of water. He takes a sip.

'I had to get a phone and insert it inside the girl. God knows why.'

'You were told to cut her open?'

'Just to place it inside her. I interpreted that to mean surgically.'

'You enjoyed inflicting the pain, didn't you?'

'I merely carried out the instructions I was given.'

'And the message?'

'I was sent a sound file. I was instructed to call the phone and play the sound file, either to whoever answered or to voicemail if nobody did.'

351

'That explains the bearded reedling. The birdsong was captured when you called.'

'What?'

'Doesn't matter. Why Alison and Lizzie?'

'I knew them vaguely. I'd seen them at some fetish event, and they'd handed me one of their cards. They were dressed up to the nines in latex, a whip each, and boots with five-inch heels. Of course, I wasn't interested in women, but when I had to find a sex worker, I remembered them and had the card handy. I wasn't going to go kerb crawling.'

'Unlucky for them.'

Grainger doesn't respond.

'And Lizzie? Why did you have to kill her?'

There's a shrug from Grainger. 'They came as a pair. I booked an outcall at my place, and when they arrived, I spiked their drinks. As soon as they were biddable, I got them into my 4x4 and took them to the water tank.'

'But Lizzie, the violence? Was that necessary?'

'She managed to escape. I chased her across the fields, and when I caught up with her, she attacked me. I had to defend myself. What else was I supposed to do?'

Chase has to check her reaction to the matter-of-fact way Grainger is talking. He is a true sociopath who cares about nobody but himself and has zero empathy for his victims. And yet, if his story is true, there's nothing more profound to interpret about his character. Grainger had no motive other than to escape from the clutches of his blackmailer.

'Who is he, the man who made you do all this?'

Grainger shakes his head. 'I don't know.'

'Don't know or aren't telling?'

'He sent me emails, and at first I thought they were spam — some kind of phishing scam. I marked the sender to go straight to the junk folder. But then I received a regular letter by post telling me to check my email or else there'd be trouble. So I did, and that's when I discovered several emails with various pieces of evidence attached. I replied and asked what the sender wanted, assuming there'd be some kind of extortion demand. But that wasn't what he wanted at all.'

'You still have the emails?'

'I deleted everything.' Grainger stares at Chase. 'I guess your tech experts might be able to retrieve them.'

Possible, Chase thinks, but she doubts there will be any information they can use to trace the sender; he's been way too careful for that.

'Could the blackmailer be somebody you met when you visited the US?'

'That's what I assume. I figure it must be somebody in NYPD because whoever it is has access to police records. But what their underlying motive is, I have no idea. I just went along with their demands. I had no choice.'

'There's always a choice, Mr Grainger. You made yours years ago.' Chase turns to go but then remembers one last thing. Trivial, really. 'What happened to Max?'

'Max?'

'Alison's dog. You kept him in your spare room.'

'He... it...' Grainger shakes his head. 'You don't want to know.'

Chase presses for more information, but Grainger is done, and so too is she. She leaves the room and wanders the corridors, searching for the hospital exit. Emerges into the fresh air and fires off a message to Frank Locke. She, like Grainger, is no clearer on the motive behind the killing of Alison and Lizzie, but now she is convinced they were targeted randomly. Sickening though the killings were, there was nothing personal about them. If the pair hadn't encountered Grainger at some swish London fetish

353

party, they'd both still be alive. Providence, Chase thinks, is so very, very fickle. And totally and utterly unfair.

# Chapter 37

It's six hours back to Missoula and an hour to Jim Swanson's place in Seattle. It's a tough decision, but it is made easier when Locke takes an incoming call from Karen Kell.

'I got your message,' she says. 'What did you find?'

'Not what I was expecting,' Locke says.

Locke gives her the lowdown: Mattich's place, the New Mexico evidence, Leo Sullivan, Frank Locke the serial killer, Jim Swanson. Plus all the confusing information about the cases in Australia and the UK.

'Is Sullivan dead?' Karen says.

'I doubt it. And that's an issue because he'll be mouthing off about me being the killer. Swanson told him I'm ninety per cent likely to be responsible.'

'I'll call you back in a few minutes.'

And she's gone, leaving Locke staring at the road ahead until his phone blips out ten minutes later.

'You're no longer a suspect,' Karen says. 'And I'm cleared to investigate ex-agent Swanson.'

'*Investigate*? For what?'

'Breach of trust, misuse of Federal software and data, failure to secure a crime scene, deliberate provision of information likely to result in a wrongful conviction.' Karen smiles. 'Amongst other things.'

'The wrongful conviction, that's me, right?'

'Well...' There's a laugh. Playful. 'Assuming you didn't kill Robert or the girl in the woods, yes.'

'I'm on my way to Swanson's place,' Locke says. 'I was hoping to get an explanation from him about the errors in the database. You want me to hold fire?'

'I want you to pull over and wait for me. I'm only a couple of hours behind you.'

'You're on your way to Seattle?'

'While you were out in the woods looking for the arm, I was doing research into the X-Mex Slayer and the missing evidence that should have been in the GSCDB. I have a number of questions for Jim Swanson. Unfortunately, since he hasn't returned my calls, I need to pay him a visit.'

'But it's more than that now, right?'

'We'll see, but I have the authority to bring Swanson in for questioning if I see fit.'

Right, Locke thinks. And I have the authority to punch his fucking lights out for nearly getting me killed and causing me to shoot good ol' Leo Sullivan.

Locke pulls over at a turnout, and it's not long before Karen rolls up behind his vehicle in her Jeep. They leave Karen's truck and take Locke's car, and within an hour, they're approaching Swanson's place in Woodinville, a quiet area north of Redmond.

'Swanson worked for Microsoft before he joined the Bureau, right?' Karen says. 'Which explains why he owns a nice house in a peaceful neighbourhood near the campus.'

'I believe so.' Locke concentrates on finding the turning. 'He worked for them from when he graduated to his late twenties. He made so much from share options that he could afford to retire, but instead, he put his talents to work with you lot.'

'Yes. He oversaw an upgrade of FBI systems and dragged us kicking and screaming into the twenty-first century. Then, he developed analysis software to track murder victims, and that turned into the Global Serial Crimes Database. Another smile from Karen. 'Which, for a brief period, you were in with a ninety per cent probability you killed the girl in the forest.'

'My father told me never to trust cats, women or computers. He was obviously right.'

Karen doesn't answer because they're now winding into the little development where Swanson lives. Big houses on either side of the road, tall pine trees surrounding the area. Four and five bedrooms, a couple of cars on each driveway.

'And my Mom told me to follow my heart,' Locke continues. 'She was wrong. Software development would have paid better.'

'Have you been here before?'

'Yes, a couple of times. Long before his accident.'

'I checked the circumstances out. He was hit by a stray bullet in a shootout.'

'An unlucky ricochet, I heard.'

'Sure, but it was just a flesh wound in his upper thigh. The real damage came when he fell over and hit his head on a nearby wall. In all the commotion, he didn't receive any treatment for a good hour.'

'Right. Janet — his wife — left him a few months later. I wasn't close enough to ask him why, but I suspect things weren't good for a while, and the accident was just an excuse for the split.'

Locke pulls up in front of a property halfway down the road. A porch runs the width of the house, a double garage to the right, front door in the centre, and a large window to the left. There's no car on the driveway.

'Swanson isn't home,' Locke says.

'How do you know?' Karen asks.

'Jim does woodwork, or at least used to. It's a passion we share, and his garage is a workshop crammed with tools. There's a router table, drill stand, table saw, finisher, and more. No room for cars.'

'You OK?' Karen says.

'Sure. Let's do it.'

357

Karen reaches into her knapsack, magics out an FBI cap and puts it on her head. Slips a hand beneath her jacket and pulls out her weapon. Checks it.

'Go to each of the neighbours and let them know we're going to break in,' she tells Locke. 'I'll check round the side and back of the house.'

One neighbour next door is out, but the one to the right and the two on the opposite side of the street are in. Locke tells them calmly there's nothing to be worried about. He shows them ID, explains that he's here with a Federal agent, and asks them to remain inside. There's nonchalance from two neighbours, but an earnest guy in the house to the right insists on whipping out his phone and filming Locke. Rather than be confrontational, Locke holds his hands out and then walks away.

'All done?' Karen says as he joins her at the front door. Locke nods and Karen pushes at the door. 'The good news is we don't have to break in.'

The door swings wide, revealing an open plan area beyond. A kitchen sits to one side, a dining area is straight on, and a living area has a fireplace to the right.

'The unlocked door suggests he left in a hurry.' Locke peers in. The spotlights in the kitchen are on, as are the lights in the living room. 'And what a mess.'

Mess is an understatement; the floor is covered with fast food packaging, empty beer cans, soda bottles, and discarded newspapers.

'That isn't the Jim Swanson I know,' Locke says.

'Well, maybe you don't know the real Jim Swanson.'

'That's possible. I never would have figured he'd persuade Leo Sullivan to try to take me down.'

Karen takes a glance at Locke and then steps through the front door. Locke follows, and they begin to search, Karen upstairs, Locke down.

The ground floor doesn't reveal much about Swanson other than that he's been living a bachelor's lifestyle. The freezer is full of ready-to-eat meals, the fridge home to some dodgy-smelling leftovers and half a dozen beers. In the living area, the mess is slovenly and out of character but hardly indicative of anything else.

He moves over to a sideboard and rifles through several drawers full of meaningless paperwork, and then gets down on his hands and knees and starts to work through the lower reaches of a large bookcase. He stops when Karen hollers from upstairs.

'Come and look at this,' she says. 'It's pure gold dust.'

Locke pushes himself up and heads for the stairs. Takes them two at a time and jogs along the landing to another set of stairs that lead to an attic. He climbs the twisting staircase and finds a room with sloping ceilings and a window with a view over the nearby countryside. Karen is sitting in a fancy computer chair, staring at a map on one wall.

'Thread and map pins in there.' She points down at a wastepaper bin beneath the map. 'And if you look closely, you can see where the pins were stuck into the map linking the thread across the globe.'

Locke steps over and peers at the map. It's a giant-sized map of the world a couple of strides wide by one high. 'Give me a clue where to start.'

'I shouldn't need to, detective.'

Locke moves closer and cocks his head to the US-Canadian border. There's a pinprick mark just below the west-to-east black line. 'Lewis and Clarke.'

'Yup. And?'

Locke swings to the east, moving his finger across the Atlantic until he finds the odd shape of the British Isles where there's another pinprick. 'London.'

'And you can probably guess where the third pin was.'

'Yes.' Locke's finger traces a line across Europe and into Asia, alighting on the north coast of Australia. 'Darwin.'

'What do you think?'

'It's possible Swanson was tracking the killer, joining up the locations like we did. Remember, he has more than a passing interest in serial crimes.'

'You don't believe that?'

Locke looks at the map and then bends to the waste bin. He takes out the three map pins and the thread and links Lewis and Clarke to London to Darwin. Stands back and stares at the lopsided triangle. Swanson could have obtained the information from the FBI database or perhaps directly from Montana DCI. Still, the location data from the UK and Australia would have only been entered a day ago, if at all, and the map looks like it's been a permanent feature for a while.

'I'm not sure,' he says finally.

'What do you know about Swanson's backstory?'

'All the stuff we've already gone over. He joined the FBI after a career at Microsoft. He was head of the unit investigating serial murder, and he created the GSCDB. He's widely regarded as having revolutionised crime data collection, collation and analysis.'

'A glorious career, cut short by an unfortunate accident. A marriage breakdown, depression, alcoholism, possible drug use.'

'Depression? How do you know?'

'The Bureau paid for therapy. The alcoholism and drug use came up after routine testing. It's part of why Swanson had to leave, albeit he was allowed to continue in a consultancy role. His knowledge was too valuable to lose completely.'

'Are you saying he's been a suspect all along?'

'No, but before we started the investigation into the X-Mex Slayer, Robert and I made sure there were flags on our personnel records so we'd know if anyone tried to look at them. Swanson did.'

'Yes, because I asked him about Robert.'

'Sure, but to be safe, our mission was a verbal agreement between the deputy director and ourselves; nothing was on the record about our investigation. However, Swanson downloaded a high-quality image of Robert and his cell number.'

'That doesn't prove anything. He could have been meaning to pass the image onto me.'

'You'd just interviewed Robert. Why would you need to know what he looked like?' Karen pauses, and when Locke doesn't answer, she continues. 'Plus, the day before Robert was killed, a cell trace request on his phone was passed to the techies at FBI HQ.'

'It's not conclusive.' Locke gives a half shake of his head, but he's starting to wonder why he's bothering to defend Swanson. After all, the FBI man had sent Sullivan after him. Still, there are other factors to consider. 'There's Mattich. With the evidence I found at his place, he's the main suspect for the women murdered in New Mexico. It makes sense he would come after you and Robert if he knew you were on his trail.'

'But how would he know that we were? Mattich was a loner. He wasn't computer literate, his place was off-grid, he had no contact with anyone.'

'Are you saying Swanson blackmailed him?' Locke shakes his head. 'Also, even if Mattich killed the girl here in Montana and the women in New Mexico, he's not responsible for the murders in London or Darwin.'

'That's true.' Karen turns to the desk and points at the photo of Swanson with his wife. 'But the potted life story

361

of Swanson you gave me is missing one fundamental fact which could have a huge bearing on the case and who is ultimately responsible for this mess.'

'Go on.'

'According to his birth certificate, Jim Swanson was born in Australia in the Northern Territory in the city of Darwin.'

~ ~ ~

The heat is unrelenting, the sun merciless, and the only respite is the occasional patch of shade cast by a scraggy tree, a low shrub or an isolated boulder. After two hours of walking, Sasaki wonders if he's made the right choice. He moves from the track and stumbles across to a large hunk of rock, where he hunches beneath an overhang, grateful to be out of the sun. He sits with his back to the rock and wonders about waiting here until the evening. It would be cooler walking at night, and he'd be able to see the lights of an approaching vehicle or a distant farmstead; the first could spell trouble, the second salvation. On the other hand, the track is indistinct, just a rough trail meandering through a flat wasteland. He could easily wander off course and become lost.

After a five-minute rest, he staggers up and resumes his trek. His eyes focus on the track, but his mind runs over the events of the past few days. He tries to make sense of what's happened. Anderson in league with Pearce, some sort of friendship or bond forged decades ago persuading Anderson to kill Kirsty Downland and rig it so it looked like the work of the BUK. Only...

Sasaki wipes sweat from his brow.

... only that doesn't fit with the killing in the US. No way has Anderson hopped on a plane, flown to Montana, killed the girl in the Lewis and Clarke National Forest, and flitted back to Darwin without anyone noticing. Sasaki can understand Anderson copying the BUK, knowing that at some point, the police would need to visit Derek Pearce. But it's a stretch to imagine a visit leading to Pearce being given a chance to escape. If he remembers correctly, it was Malroony who suggested the trip and Sasaki who brought it about. No, Pearce's escape was serendipitous, Anderson placing the dummy body and hiding the gun only after the trip had been arranged. Unless…

More sweat. Dripping down his forehead and stinging his eyes.

… unless. Malroony? Sasaki veers to one side of the track physically knocked for six. Malroony suggested the aircraft trip, and Pearce immediately jumped to accept. Out at the Alligator River, Malroony let Sasaki climb the rock first and threw away her weapon all too easily. Her distaste of Pearce was all an act. But…

Now he's swaying back and forth, blinking away the moisture.

… but. Lamb? Surely not? Sasaki trips and falls to his knees. Gets up and staggers forward. The CSI has all the tools to obfuscate whatever is going on. Lamb is one of the old guys, like Anderson and Cooper. For all his friendliness, he's probably making racist jokes behind Sasaki's back. And who knows what he got up to back in the day?

Sasaki trips again, and this time, he's too weak to push himself up. He rolls over, lies on his back, and stares at the glaring sun. He closes his eyes against the light and laughs to himself. At least he escaped from the dunny. At least he tried.

A gust of wind brings him to his senses. Air washes down on him and provides a welcome coolness. And then there's a thud, thud, thud, thud, and Sasaki realises that Anderson and Pearce have returned to finish the job. He rolls on his side and scrabbles in the dirt until he finds a large stone. He won't go quietly this time. He'll show them what fighting means.

The helicopter is landing twenty paces away. It's the black one that snatched Pearce from the Alligator River. Dust swirls up from the ground in a cloud, and the helicopter disappears. Sasaki stands. There's no point running, but he swears the first person who emerges from the duststorm will get a rock smashed into their face.

The chop, chop of the helicopter continues, and the blizzard of sand shows no sign of abating. Then, two shadows appear at the border between calm and turbulence. Sasaki grips the stone and gets ready to strike. Pearce or Anderson? He can't make up his mind; both deserve extreme violence, and both deserve to die.

'Takeo?'

The figure on the right raises an arm and waves. It's Pearce, trying it on. Buddy, buddy. All friendly. But Sasaki isn't going to fall for the ruse. He raises the rock and lunges forward, intent on violence.

Pearce steps to the side, and Sasaki trips and falls, enveloped by the dust. He waits for the inevitable. The blow to the head. A savage kick in the ribs. The bang from Anderson's shotgun.

But there's nothing. Only the chop, chop sound slowing. The whine of the engine diminishing.

'It's me, Takeo. Linda.'

Sasaki rolls on his side. The dust from the helicopter drifts away on the breeze, and Linda Malroony stands a few metres away. Vicky Keelan, the owner of *Copter Catches*, is alongside her.

'Linda?' Sasaki squints and blinks just to make sure he's not delirious. 'Is that you?'

'Yes, sir.' Malroony reaches down to give him a hand up. 'Good to see you.'

'You too.' Sasaki takes Malroony's hand and stands. 'You're a sight for sore eyes.'

'I'll bet.' Malroony helps Sasaki over to the helicopter. 'What's going on, boss?'

'It's Kevin Anderson. He and Pearce are in cahoots together. Someone else, too. Someone from the US.'

'That figures, what with the information Detective Locke gave us.'

'I went to Anderson's place and Pearce was there. The two of them attacked me and knocked me unconscious. I woke locked in a building a few kilometres from here.' Sasaki climbs up into the helicopter and buckles himself in. 'How did you find me?'

'Down to Kieran Lamb, initially. He guessed you'd gone to Anderson's place, and when we drove out there, we found your car hidden round the back. Anderson wasn't home, but there were signs a helicopter had landed. Debris everywhere and the same skid marks we found at Tortilla Flats. Our next stop was Sandford Strip. Vicky told us you'd visited in the morning and confirmed that Anderson's brother, Pete, had flown out in one of the other helicopters later on and hadn't returned. We put two and two together, and luckily, Vicky was able to track the aircraft out to here.'

'Thanks,' Sasaki says to Vicky. 'Do you know where the helicopter is now?'

'No.' Vicky shakes her head. 'They've turned the tracker off.'

'Why didn't they think to do that before?'

Vicky shrugs, but Malroony chips in. 'Kevin Anderson isn't the sharpest tool in the box. I doubt he realised the helicopter was being tracked.

'But somebody did.' Sasaki leans back against the headrest, suddenly weighed down with tiredness. 'And that

365

person, whoever it is, is the key to all this. They set this up. They sprang Pearce from prison with the trick out at the Alligator River. And they're somehow linked with what happened when the BUK was active.'

Vicky Keelan is in the pilot's seat now and she restarts the engine. There's a whine and a roar and more dust. Malroony hands Sasaki a headset, and he puts it on, his mind elsewhere. He stares out as the ground falls away and the helicopter moves off.

'We'll work it out.' Malroony's voice comes through the headphones, all fuzzy and tinny. 'We just need a little help, right?'

'You mean from Detective Locke and his colleagues?'

'No, sir. I mean from your father.'

# Chapter 38

Vicky Keelan flies straight to the Royal Darwin Hospital, where Sasaki is checked over. Malroony puts him in a taxi, and he goes home and pops the painkillers he's been given. He takes a shower, tries to eat something, and crashes out. The following day, he wakes to a pounding on his front door. It's Malroony, armed with a box of pastries and two cups of fresh takeaway coffee.

'Up and at 'em, sir,' she says, breezing in. 'Work to do.'

The morning after the day before, Sasaki is aching all over, his body tie-dyed black and blue with bruises. Pearce and Anderson really went to work on him. Arms, legs, back. Pearce is a psychopath, so the behaviour was understandable, but something else was driving Anderson, a hatred Sasaki had first seen in his eyes decades ago.

Easing himself down onto the sofa, Sasaki reaches for a Danish. Relishes the sugar rush as he eats it. Sips the coffee and waits for the caffeine hit.

'You OK?' Malroony says.

'Thanks to all this, I will be.' Sasaki indicates the box of pastries. 'But it will be a while before I'm tanning myself on Mindil beach.'

Malroony laughs; Sasaki has snow-white skin that doesn't take sun well, and he spends most of the summer covering up rather than stripping off.

While Sasaki wolfs down three pastries, Malroony fills him in on what's been happening. There's an extensive search for Derek Pearce and Kevin Anderson, but Pete, Kevin's brother, has turned himself in.

'And what's he saying?' Sasaki asks between mouthfuls of Danish.

'That blood is thicker than water,' Malroony says. 'He claims his brother came to him desperate one day a couple of weeks ago. Kevin asked to be flown out to Tortilla Flats. Pete landed at Kevin's place, picked up Kevin and something long and heavy wrapped in layers of plastic, and flew him there. Kevin unloaded the bundle, and Pete claimed he didn't watch what happened, not wanting to know what was going on.

'I don't believe that.'

'No, neither do I. Anyway, as soon as the news of the murder broke, he'd have known what was in the parcel.'

'And what happened with Derek Pearce's escape?'

'Pete was up to his neck by then, so when Kevin said they had to fly to the East Alligator River, he had little choice. They headed out there, dropped off the mannequin and landed at a prearranged spot. Once Pearce had escaped from us, he rendezvoused with them, and they returned to the strip at Sandford. Then Pearce hid at Kevin's house, where you had the misfortune to bump into him.' Malroony pauses. 'But, even with all that info, we're no clearer on why Kevin Anderson killed the woman.'

'When I was at Anderson's place, I heard him and Pearce talking. Anderson said something about being forced to kill the woman, so it sounds like he was blackmailed. I guess there's something in Anderson's past, perhaps to do with his friendship with Pearce, that he didn't want to come out.'

'From around the time of the BUK?'

'Could be. Perhaps Anderson knew it was Pearce back then but didn't say anything.'

'Understood, but why recreate Pearce's crime?'

'I don't know. If we hadn't discovered the other killings in the US and the UK, we might have thought it was a ruse to get us to take Pearce on the plane ride.' Sasaki shakes his head. 'But the other murders must be connected to the mystery accomplice I heard Pearce and Anderson mention. Whoever that is has the money and power to pull strings. Pearce was talking about a new life in South America for both of them.'

'Unless it's some figment of his distorted imagination.'

Silence as Sasaki polishes off another pastry and Malroony finishes her coffee.

'Sir, I was...' Malroony pauses, hesitant.

'You were what?'

'We still don't know who cut the arms off the girls all those years ago. Pearce claims it wasn't him, so unless he had some bizarre reason to snitch on himself, we're missing something.'

'I know where you're going with this,' Sasaki says. 'But I don't—'

'It's the only way, sir. You must stop looking at the massive chip on your shoulder and face forward instead. You're letting your personal issues get in the way of the investigation. It's something your father would never have done. If the situation were reversed, he'd have spoken to you long ago.'

As close to Malroony as Sasaki is, she shouldn't talk to him like this. For a brief moment, Sasaki closes his eyes, intending to give her a second before he reprimands her. But then he's back in the dunny in the darkness, surrounded by heat and facing certain death. His father's face looming over him. Sasaki apologising. Senior nodding acceptance.

'I'm sorry, sir.' Malroony's voice intrudes. 'It had to be said.'

'No, Linda.' Sasaki opens his eyes. 'You're right and I'm wrong.'

'So we go and see him?'

'Yes,' Sasaki says.

~ ~ ~

Sasaki and Malroony are ushered inside by a smiling nurse. Sasaki is always struck by how happy the workers at the rest home are. He, for one, wouldn't be smiling if his daily routine was dealing with incontinence and dementia.

Endo Sasaki sits in a chair by a big bay window. There's a view of the nearby lake, and today, whitecaps sparkle in the sunlight as a strong breeze ruffles the surface. Sasaki reckons it must be mid-twenties in the room, but his father wears a thick cardigan and has a fleece blanket over his legs, the tin of old photos in his lap. He doesn't look round when Sasaki and Malroony approach and take a couple of chairs. A greeting from Sasaki produces something between a grunt and an acknowledgement, but Malroony's *hello* is met with a smile and a flicker of recognition.

Sasaki makes small talk for a few minutes as a nurse brings tea and biscuits. He asks about his father's health, mentions his move to a new apartment, and brings up some meaningless news about Darwin. Endo doesn't appear to be listening. He munches on a biscuit, raises the teacup to his lips with a shaking hand, and stares glassy-eyed.

'Dad,' Sasaki says. 'I wanted to ask you about the BUK. The Black Ute Killer. Do you remember the case?'

Endo puts the teacup down and looks out across the lake.

'We've got a similar murder, and I believe the crime is linked to the BUK. We've asked Derek Pearce, but he's not cooperating.' Sasaki doesn't mention Pearce's escape and has no idea if his father has read about it or seen the TV news. 'Pearce did tell us he didn't remove the victims'

370

arms and arrange them, and I believe him. After all, it made no sense for him to give you clues that would lead you to him, right?'

A gull, swooping low across the sky, appears to hold more interest to Endo than anything Sasaki is saying.

'We have three new victims with three arms removed. We know Kevin Anderson is involved somehow, but he wasn't the person who cut the arms off and led you to Pearce, was he?'

The gull climbs out of sight, and Endo reaches for another biscuit.

'It's no good,' Sasaki whispers to Malroony. 'He doesn't understand a word I'm saying.'

'Mr Sasaki?' Malroony says. 'Do you think you could help us?'

Tomoko?' Endo turns his head to Malroony. Smiles. 'Is that you?'

Tomoko is Sasaki's sister. She lives in Sydney and doesn't get home much. Looks absolutely nothing like Linda Malroony.

Sasaki gives Malroony a little nod. Mouths *yes*.

'Uh huh.' Malroony gives Sasaki a scowl as if she disapproves of deceiving the old man. But after a short pause, she continues. 'I'd love to know more about the BUK. About how you caught him. The pointing arms. Your theories and everything.'

'Sit closer, child, and I'll tell you,' Endo says. He taps the tin of photos as if knocking on a door. 'But first, I'd like another cup of tea.'

~ ~ ~

Endo Sasaki is nestled behind a police car drawn across the road of the quiet Darwin suburb. Neat fences and tidy lawns about the street. There are cars parked in the driveways, some still glistening with water and suds; it's a

Saturday morning, and until a few minutes ago, the neighbourhood was bustling with dads washing their prized possessions, kids playing in the gardens, footballs being kicked about, scooters and bicycles zooming up and down the pavements, people walking their dogs, neighbours stopping for a chinwag and a gossip.

Endo knows what most of the neighbours were talking about: the failure of the Darwin police to catch the BUK — the Black Ute Killer. The killer has been terrorising the area around Darwin, and three women are dead. Many more are affected, some not daring to leave their homes, some keeping their teenage-aged daughters inside, some making their opinions known on the local radio phone-ins.

*Everyone knows you can't trust the police to do anything these days.*

*They should stop hassling folk for minor offences and concentrate on catching the killer.*

*There's a bad culture in the Darwin force. They don't care about women being scared. If anything, they're part of the problem, not part of the solution.*

The statements infuriate Endo, but not because they're incorrect. He's angry because the sentiment is spot on. There are too many police officers who are racist and sexist. Too many taking backhanders or looking the other way. Too many who are lazy, inefficient and downright incompetent.

Endo knows he isn't one of them. He's a man of honour and industriousness and is proud to be a policeman in his adopted country, even if he isn't so proud of many of his fellow officers.

Still, at least he can be pleased with what the force has achieved today. Hiding in the low single-storey building on the opposite side of the road is the BUK. Endo knows this because, late last night, he finally worked out the puzzle with the severed arms. With a modicum of maths, he calculated a bearing and distance from the first victim's arm, which led him here, where parked on the driveway is a black ute belonging to one Derek Pearce. There are dozens of black pickups in the Darwin area, and all have been traced, and the alibis of their owners taken. But only one black ute sits at the precise point Endo's ratio leads to.

He should have solved the riddle before, but only with the third victim did he see the ratio repeated and thought to extrapolate from the first victim. If he'd been cleverer, he might have saved a life. Now, if the SWAT team assembling around him is anything to go by, there will be more bloodshed. Most people, especially his police colleagues, are intent on vengeance, and Derek Pearce gunned down while resisting arrest will not only be great front-page news but will be welcomed by nearly all and sundry.

Not Endo, though.

He despises Pearce for what he's done, but the law must be applied, Pearce tried and, if found guilty, incarcerated for a very long time.

The officer in charge of the SWAT team is giving his final orders. Pearce is to be taken alive if possible, but no chances should be taken. Any resistance and shooting to kill is the only response. There are murmurs of agreement and a couple of smiles. The orders are as good as a death sentence for Pearce, but Endo knows he can't protest because, as the officer is reminding his men, lives are at stake.

*Lives at stake…*

Inside the bungalow, along with Pearce, are his mother and younger brother. It's a potential hostage situation, and given Pearce's propensity to kill, no risks can be taken.

Better to try to talk him out then, Endo thinks, but he knows this option has already been taken off the table by an officer higher up the chain of command.

One by one, the officers move along a hedge, crouching low and keeping hidden. There are marksmen farther back, one using a ladder to climb onto a neighbouring property's roof. Pearce doesn't stand a chance unless he surrenders.

The lead officer takes a megaphone and barks out the obligatory *Come out with your hands held high*, but no one believes Pearce will comply. They expect a shooting gallery with Pearce caught in the crossfire, his body riddled with bullets, justice served.

Until the front door opens, and Pearce steps out, hands on his head, walking slowly.

'DOWN! GET DOWN ON THE GROUND!'

And Pearce lowers himself to the ground.

Officers rush forward, Pearce is cuffed and searched, and several kicks go in hard. As he's dragged to his feet, there's more than one punch, and when he's led away to a waiting vehicle, there's a definite sense of disappointment from the officers around Endo. He should go with Pearce, but something makes him decide to take a look at the house first.

There are already officers inside, and a team of CSIs are beginning to search for anything that could link Pearce to the crimes. Pearce's mother is in the central living area, distraught. But she's not arguing, not shouting, and appears to accept her son is guilty. Endo finds Pearce's brother in a small bedroom off the living area. He enters and closes the door behind him. It's neat and tidy, and there are maps on the wall and school books on a desk alongside a calculator. A boy a few years older than Endo's own son sits on the bed, his arms folded, a book beside him.

'You're Jimmy, right?' Endo asks.

The boy nods.

'What are you reading?' Endo asks.

'The Adventures of Huckleberry Finn,' Jimmy says.

'Is it any good?'

'Yes.'

'What is it about?'

'A journey.'

Endo moves across to the desk, where there's a blotter pad with ink markings and pencil scribblings. Crossings out. Numbers divided into each other. Above the desk, there's a map of the area around Darwin. Endo reaches out and moves his forefinger across the surface. Sees and feels the three pinpricks.

'He took you with him, right? As an alibi. Do you know what that means?'

'Yes.'

'And you went back afterwards?'

This time, there's no answer.

'It would have been simpler to have just told somebody. Your teacher or your mother, perhaps?'

Now, a shake of the head.

'I understand,' Endo says. 'You didn't want to be a sneak, especially not when it was Derek.'

'No. My mother would never forgive me if she found out.'

Jimmy eases off the bed, and for a second, Endo thinks he's going to make a run for the door or leap through the open window, but instead, he goes over to a wardrobe and opens it. Pulls out a grubby white towel, something wrapped inside. He walks across and hands it to Endo.

375

Endo unwinds the material and finds a serrated kitchen knife. Blood on the face of the blade. Little pieces of flesh caught on the serrations.

'You know I have a son almost the same age as you. He's clever, too. He's got a bright future if he works hard and stays out of trouble.'

'You won't tell?'

Endo rolls the towel back around the knife and slips the slim bundle under his jacket. He gives Jimmy an affectionate ruffle on the head and goes to the door. He reaches for the handle and thinks about rules and regulations. Thinks about abiding by an inner moral code. Thinks about doing what is right. How the three ideals twist together, at times conflating, at times conflicting.

Endo opens the door and steps out, turning back to the boy as he leaves.

'No,' he says. 'I won't tell.'

# Chapter 39

Locke is in the air somewhere over Australia. It's his third flight of the day — although *day* is a very loose description of the past twenty-four hours — and he's about ready to sign up to never getting on an aeroplane ever again.

His journey started with a short hop from Seattle to Vancouver. Then, there was a couple of hours of wait before the long fourteen-hour haul to Brisbane. Another two-hour stopover and a three-and-a-half-hour flight to Darwin. Hard to believe, but a whole day after departure from the US, there are still another sixty minutes before touchdown.

He eases his seatback forward, determined to be alert when he steps off the plane. Detective Senior Sergeant Takeo Sasaki will be there to meet him, and Locke wants to give a good impression. Emerging bleary-eyed and stumbling through arrivals won't cut it. He wonders if the trip is a good idea, but he's here by invitation.

*You know Jim Swanson. You can pick him out of a crowd. You might even be able to reason with him if it comes to that. We need you here on the ground.*

On the ground. On Australian soil. Because according to Customs and Border Protection, two days ago, Jim Swanson left the US from LAX and took a direct flight to Sydney. From there, the trail is cold, but as Sasaki told Locke on a call, it doesn't take a great detective to work out he's coming to Darwin. Perhaps not, Locke thinks, but for just what reason Swanson is returning 'home' is anyone's guess.

The aircraft lands ten minutes ahead of schedule, and when Locke steps out into the modest terminal, Takeo Sasaki is there to greet him.

'Welcome to Australia!' Sasaki says, hand outstretched, beaming smile. 'Despite the circumstances, we are very pleased to meet you.'

*We* being Sasaki and Detective Sergeant Linda Malroony. Sasaki is medium height, dark hair, formal. Malroony is half aboriginal, friendly as she insists on taking Locke's bag.

'Thank you,' Locke says. 'Tired, but glad to be here.'

There follows a whirlwind of information, the gist of which is that Locke is booked into a downtown hotel. They'll take him there to freshen up, meet him for dinner, and get straight to business.

'Sure,' Locke says, wishing instead he could get his head down but realising when you're hunting a demented killer, there's no time for a nap. 'Sounds good.'

The hotel is mid-range but comfortable, and after a shower, a shave, and an all-too-brief lie on the bed, Locke sets out to make the acquaintance of his new partners.

Over dinner, there's little time for chit-chat. Locke tells them what he knows of Jim Swanson, about the FBI man's career and his responsibility for setting up the Global Serial Crimes Database.

'He obfuscated information to do with the arrest of the Brit, Alan Grainger, in New York to ensure it wouldn't be passed to the UK authorities,' Locke explains. 'Then he used the details in the database to blackmail Grainger into committing murder in London.'

He goes on to tell the story of Henrik Mattich and the X-Mex Slayer. How data from New Mexico was altered to prevent it from being linked to Mattich's case in Seattle. How it looks as if Swanson forced Mattich to kill for him on the threat of the link being released.

'But here in Darwin,' Locke says, looking from Sasaki to Malroony and giving a shrug of his shoulders, 'I don't know how Swanson relates to your murder or why he's come back to where he was born.'

Sasaki and Malroony share a glance and a smile.

'Well, until yesterday, neither did we,' Sasaki says. 'But we do now.'

~ ~ ~

Back in the hotel, Locke sleeps for eight hours. Wakes and rises reluctantly when his phone alarm goes off. Washes, shaves, dresses, has breakfast.

Last night, the Australian detectives filled him in on Jim Swanson's childhood history. Without knowledge of subsequent events, the story can only elicit compassion. The young Jimmy watches his brother Derek kill three women. He understands the evil but isn't able to do anything about it until he comes up with a method of snitching on his brother without revealing himself. After Derek's arrest, he and his mother emigrate to the US to start a new life.

This was where Locke had taken over the story, telling Sasaki and Malroony the information discovered by Karen Holdsworth: the new life that turned sour so quickly. Swanson's mother down on her luck and forced to sell her body to support herself and her son, the tragedy of her murder and the effect that must have had on the young boy so soon after the events in Darwin. The strength to carry on and make something of his life. The accident and the head injury decades later that somehow triggered the desire to recreate the murders his brother carried out.

Which is the point when any sympathy Locke may have had for Swanson vanished into the warm Australian air.

After breakfast, Locke heads to a downtown car hire place and rents a vehicle. Sasaki and Malroony are chasing a tipoff that may or may not lead to Derek Pearce and Locke hasn't been invited. Even though he's disappointed, he understands why. He has no jurisdiction here, can't carry a firearm, and would only be in the way. It's frustrating, but he'd have applied the same policy if the situation had been reversed. Still, they've given him the location of Kevin Anderson's house. The place has already been thoroughly searched, but Darwin's chief CSI has offered to show him round and explain all the evidence to do with the case. The only problem is Locke has to meet him there. Hence the car.

He opts for a small Hyundai; Anderson's place isn't far, but Locke isn't confident about handling a stick shift while driving on the wrong side of the road. Throw in some jetlag, and it's a recipe for disaster.

The journey should take him around half an hour, Anderson's place being twenty miles from Darwin. He takes it slow, marvelling at the flat, brown and dry countryside. So different from the lush greenery and the soaring peaks of Montana. What is also different is the dust storm he drives into a few miles short of his destination. Sand and dirt swirl at the windscreen, reducing visibility to a few car lengths. He slows, aware the trucks and road trains are ploughing on regardless. One passes him at speed, and the little Korean car is buffeted from side to side. Fuck this, he thinks and pulls off at a gas station where there's a shop and a bar.

He checks his phone. Realises he passed Anderson's place a mile or so back. Still, he's early. Just time for a glass of something cool to ease the dryness in his throat. But definitely non-alcoholic. Add a sandstorm and monster trucks to his earlier problems with the car, and the last thing he needs is to feel a little tipsy.

Inside, the bar-come-coffee shop is cool and dark and almost empty. Something that sounds like Australian C&W echoes from a hidden speaker, and behind the bar, a redneck with the obligatory lumberjack shirt is polishing glasses. He raises his eyebrows at Locke's request for a non-alcoholic juice and pops the top off a bottle of J2O. Pulls out a glass but doesn't bother to pour the drink. Locke pays and ambles over to a booth with high-backed benches and a menu card on the table. Wonders about eating.

'Frank.'

A well-set man slips into the seat opposite, and Locke looks up into the wild eyes of Jim Swanson.

'Jim,' he says, his hand moving towards his non-existent weapon.

'You're not armed,' Swanson says. 'Not here.'

'No need to be,' Locke says. He fashions a smile. 'Not here.'

'Well, that's a loss because I am.' Swanson nods at the tabletop.

Locke cocks his head and takes a glance down. Swanson's holding a pump-action shotgun under the table, the gun partially wrapped in a fleece jacket.

'Easy, Jim,' Locke says. 'You're right, I'm not armed and no threat. Plus, we don't want any trouble, do we?'

He moves his head a little. A couple with three children have come into the café area. There's a kiddies' playpen with ride-ons and a low table with paper and crayons. The toddlers run across and make busy.

'I never wanted any trouble, Frank. That's the whole point. The trouble was made for me every step of the way. I never had a chance.'

'Really?' Locke tries not to sound too sceptical. 'You cashed big with Microsoft and then won plaudits for your work with the FBI. You had a chance, and — all respect to you — you took it. There are a lot of places worse to be than in your shoes.'

'Not in my shoes, Frank, up here.' Swanson taps his forehead. 'You don't understand what's going on.'

'No, I don't. I don't understand why those women had to die.'

'They were whores like my mother was. Whores like my brother killed. No whores, no trouble.'

'Sounds to me like you're blaming others for your problems.'

'I got smacked on the head, right? Something went wrong inside, and everything got jumbled up, but without what happened, I'd have come out fine. Before I was injured, I had almost no memory of my childhood. I don't even remember living here in Australia, just being with my mother in the US, her whoring, me watching. The concussion triggered something, and I began to remember. There were bodies of women, their arms cut off, but it made no sense.'

Locke has it then. 'You looked the murders up in the GSCDB.'

'Every serial crime is in there, even historical ones going back years, decades. Once I knew what I was looking for, it was easy. I saw who went down for the crime and a mugshot. Derek Pearce resembled me, and the name sounded familiar. I knew my mother had come from Australia decades ago. Here was the proof I needed.'

'And the justification?'

'I don't have to justify anything to you.'

'To yourself then.'

'I'm better than Derek, understand? And I'm better than my twelve-year-old self. I never should have shopped him to the cops. I replayed the crimes but made them bigger. I made sure the clues led nowhere but in a circle back to where it started.'

'And that's it?'

'I never killed any women.'

'You got people to kill on your behalf. Plus, you killed Robert Kell and tried to get me shot.'

'You gave Robert Kell away. If you hadn't interfered, he'd still be alive.'

'Interfering is what we do, right? You and me. Law enforcement. It's self-explanatory.'

Locke half glances at the kids in the play area. Three truckers have come in and are at the bar. A couple of women sit at a table sipping coffee. Mid-morning and the place is filling up. There are a lot of potential targets, and Locke is fearful of what might go down if Swanson completely flips.

'Shall we go outside?' Locke says. 'More private, right?'

'You needn't worry, Frank, I'm not going to hurt innocent people.' Swanson follows Locke's gaze. 'But leaving is a good idea. I have things to do. We'll take your car.'

Wrong-footed, Locke thinks.

'Where?' he says.

'Kevin Anderson's place is just up the road.' Swanson stands, the shotgun wrapped entirely in the fleece. 'Nobody's going to turn up there, are they?'

Outside, the storm is worse. Dust and debris and grit tumble through the air. In the lot, Locke aims the Hyundai at what he suspects is the main road and heads back towards Darwin. The house is only a few minutes away, and Swanson tells Locke when to turn in.

'Where are Derek Pearce and Kevin Anderson?' Locke asks as they get out and walk to the front door. 'Did you kill them too?'

'Enough with the chitchat.' Swanson lets the fleece slide off the gun and jabs Locke in the back with the barrel. 'Get inside and then we'll see where we're at.'

The wind catches the fleece, and Locke watches as it spirals into the dust. He steps onto the veranda and pulls at the flyscreen.

The house is dark, and when Swanson flicks a light switch on the wall, there's nothing.

'The state of this meant the CSIs probably turned the electricity off when they did the search,' Locke says. 'Safety codes or something.'

Anderson's place is a mess outside and in. The tin roof rattles in the wind, and there's a howl as air rushes through gaps in the window frames. Underfoot, the floorboards creak, and there's a smell of dry rot.

Swanson nods. 'Kevin's a pig.'

Locke isn't sure if he's referring to Anderson's job or lifestyle, but the latter is a world away from Swanson's plush house in Redmond. What exactly has brought Swanson here? Is it down to the bang on the head, or is there something else?

'All this effort and misery, Jim,' Locke says. 'And for what? To get one over on your brother? To recreate something from the past in a futile effort to influence the future? You had a wife, a comfortable life, a good job, recognition. To throw it all away and—'

'A *comfortable life*?' There's a sneer from Swanson. 'You have no *fucking* idea.'

'You had a tough childhood, and lately, the accident caused you problems, mental health issues, I understand. But has doing all this helped?'

'It will when it's done.'

'But the effort, I can see that's been tiring for you. All the planning, the research. I guess you got the information from the database. Still, you must have spent hours selecting the right men to blackmail, right?'

384

'There are more in there than you can imagine. Dozens who should be inside but are free to walk the streets. We think we have an effective justice system, but there are holes people can slip through.'

'Sure, Mattich, Grainger... but what about Kevin Anderson? What did you have on him?'

'Anderson knew the BUK was Derek, knew it from the first murder.'

'How come?'

'Derek's car broke down near the site of the first murder. Kevin borrowed a ute and towed the car back to our house.' Swanson stops. Pain. Worry. Concern. He shakes his head and moves on. 'I know because I was there in the car. When the body was discovered a few days later, Kevin realised Derek was the killer, but he said nothing. I used that to blackmail him.'

'Jim...' Locke tries to sound empathetic. 'I—'

'Enough.' Swanson thrusts the gun towards an old sofa. 'Sit. We're getting close. Now we just have to wait.'

'Wait for what?'

'I need to make a call, but not quite yet.' Swanson glances at his watch. 'Once I've done that, it's nearly over. Just one final job to do, and then I'll be at peace. We'll all be at peace.'

Swanson's words sound ominous, and Locke wonders if he should have made a move earlier. Then again, the odds weren't great. Poor old Leo Sullivan, the fall guy at poker nights, went up against Locke, and that was pretty much a flip since they were both armed. This is entirely different. It's like Swanson is holding Aces full of Kings and Locke nothing but a busted flush draw. Still, in poker, there's a way to win even when you don't have the best hand. Locke wonders if it's time to run the biggest bluff of his life.

385

'This stops here, Jim,' Locke says, refusing to sit. 'There's no way out for you. This whole thing has been a setup up, and even as we speak, cops are surrounding the house. In five minutes, they'll come in shooting.'

'I don't believe you.'

'They knew you'd target me, so I had a tail all the way from Darwin. You didn't spot them because of the sandstorm. The best thing would be for you to put the gun down, and we'll walk out together. With your mental condition, you'll be treated compassionately.'

Swanson half lowers the gun. His shoulders sag and he exhales a long breath. He blinks, his eyelids are heavy, he sways on his feet and shakes his head. He's conflicted, Locke can see that. He just wants it to end, and all Locke has to do is help him.

'Give me the gun, Jim.' Locke slowly extends his arm, palm up. Reaches, reaches, reaches. 'Easy now.'

I...' Swanson's eyes are watery. The jetlag, the stress, the heat, the thought of the cops surrounding the house: it's all playing a part in weakening his resolve. 'Do you understand why I had to do it? The nightmares, they were too much. I simply couldn't cope, Frank. I had no one to turn to.'

'I understand,' Locke says, easing his hand towards the gun. 'You suffered terribly when you were a kid. I'm here for you now.'

Vehicle noise through the open window. Tires slipping on dirt.

'SIT DOWN!' Swanson is jerked into the present. He rams the barrel of the shotgun forward, catching Locke hard in the chest. Locke stumbles and trips back onto the sofa. Swanson suddenly lowers his voice and whispers. 'Not a sound.'

A clunk from a car door. A voice hollering.

'Mr Locke?' The shuffle of feet. 'Frank Locke?'

The flyscreen flutters open with a creak, and someone comes into the hallway.

'It's Kieran Lamb, Mr Locke. The chief CSI.'

And there's a thin figure in the doorway, and Swanson swings the gun. Locke tries to get up, but Swanson is too fast, and there's a deafening retort. Lamb is hit in the chest, and he staggers backwards and collapses in the hall.

Locke is on his feet now as Swanson steps away and covers him as he pumps the gun and reloads.

'No, Frank,' Swanson says. 'Don't be stupid. My argument isn't with you.'

'That's what you're here for?' Locke stares at the doorway and at Kieran Lamb lying slumped against the frame, eyes open and unblinking. 'Retribution?'

'Isn't that what you wanted with Henrik Mattich? What the law round here wanted with Derek? What so-called good folk will want with me when this is over?'

'Retribution, vengeance, call it whatever you want, it doesn't do any good,' Locke says. 'I don't feel any different now that Mattich is dead.'

'Bullshit! You're a lying fucker. The world looked a whole lot brighter on the morning after you shot him, right?'

'OK, yes, but Mattich was guilty.'

'As are all those involved with this case. Simply recreating the crime hasn't been enough. I need to wipe the slate clean.' Only now does Swanson cast a glance across to the dead CSI. 'He's collateral damage, perhaps, but maybe he's one of the guilty ones. Now hand me the keys to the car.' Swanson puts out his left hand and raises the shotgun. His finger curls round the trigger, tightening. 'I don't want to kill you, Frank, but if you get in my way, I will.'

For a moment, Locke considers rushing Swanson, but it would be suicide. He reaches into his pocket and draws out the car keys. Hands them over.

# *Chapter 40*

Derek Pearce and Kevin Anderson seem to have disappeared from the face of the earth. That's not surprising, Sasaki thinks, not here in the Northern Territory. A million and a half square kilometres, the vast majority of it wilderness. Looking for Pearce and Anderson is almost pointless. Still, AC Cooper has pulled in a few favours, and various army units are being readied for a state-wide search.

The media, as Cooper suspected, have gone big on the story. They've detailed Derek Pearce's crimes from thirty-three years ago, linked them with the current case, and have done everything they can to scare ordinary people witless. The chances of actually coming across Pearce hiding in your garden shed are remote, but from the way the press is telling the story, it's an odds-on bet.

'They love a manhunt, the press do,' Cooper says. 'And that suits me. People tend to look to the police in times of trouble, and our popularity increases. So all we need to do is catch Pearce and we'll be quids in.'

To which end, there is extra security at international airports. Both in and out. But so far, there's no sign of Pearce, Anderson or Jim Swanson.

'Let's hope Frank Locke hasn't made a wasted journey,' Malroony says as they head south towards Tortilla Flats, chasing a lead called in by Bryce Mitchell. 'It's a long way to come on a hunch.'

Sasaki nods. Except it's more than a hunch. Jim Swanson, little brother to Derek Pearce, is here on some sort of personal mission. To put right what happened over three decades ago. To apologise to Pearce. To rescue him and restore family ties. Whatever the reason, if they find

Pearce, they find Swanson and vice versa. So Mitchell's lead — an anonymous call from someone who claims to have seen a man matching Derek Pearce's description hanging around at Tortilla Flats — is very welcome. And yet Pearce returning to the scene doesn't make a whole lot of sense to Sasaki since Pearce knows it was Kevin Anderson who killed the girl. Why would he want to go back to the flats?

Light filters through a thick haze as they drive south away from Darwin, dust swirling in a strong breeze. There's a storm forecast, hot dry air at the moment, but thunder and rain later. When they reach the turn-off for Tortilla Flats, the visibility is down to about two hundred metres.

'We'll have a hell of a job finding Pearce in this,' Malroony says.

'Yes,' Sasaki says. 'But on the other hand, he won't see us coming.'

They cruise down the flat gravel road and turn off onto the rutted track that leads to the crime scene. There's nothing here now to mark the girl's last resting place aside from the barbed wire coils. Visibility has worsened, and Sasaki can feel a hot static in the air when they get out of the car. Sand and dust sting his face and clog his eyes. He wraps his arm round his face and buries his nose in his elbow. Shouts into his clothing.

'This is hopeless,' he says as they struggle across the field to where the body was. 'We're never going to find the exact spot.'

Malroony doesn't answer, but she kneels and gestures at Sasaki. He moves over, peers down, and sees she's found the little lotus flower he left.

'It's still here,' she says, looking up at Sasaki. 'Good fortune, no?'

Sasaki isn't so sure. A flat feeling of disappointment has replaced the heightened sentiment he felt a week ago.

'There's nothing here,' he says. 'If Pearce visited, then there's no sign.'

He's frustrated, but then he doesn't really know what he expected to find. It was too much to hope that Pearce, Anderson and Swanson would be here with their hands up, ready to go quietly.

'Hang on, sir, there *is* something.' Malroony is holding the soapstone lotus flower. She transfers it from one hand to the other and looks at her now empty hand. There's a mark. Red-brown. She tilts the flower to reveal its base, where there's another smear of dark crimson. 'Blood.'

Sasaki kneels beside her, and she holds out the flower for him to look at. Now he can see the crimson is a smudge of fingerprint. Whoever picked up the soapstone had blood on their hands.

Malroony puts the flower in a pocket, and they scout around the area. Within a minute, Sasaki discovers a drop of blood a few metres away. And then another, double the distance.

'They were bleeding,' he says. He points into the sandstorm. 'That way.'

It's not easy following the blood trail with the dust swirling around, but Sasaki is pretty sure it leads in the same direction as where the arm was found. They move farther into the field, holding their hands up to block the sand from their eyes. And then, at what Sasaki guesses is the exact point where the severed arm lay, they find Pearce and Anderson.

'Fuck!' Malroony says.

The sight is horrific. Pearce lies on his back, his chest sliced open, organs and viscera visible, and only now beginning to gather sand and dust. Anderson is to one side, half his face blown away by a shotgun blast. The remaining part of his face is frozen in time, lips curled in a wry smile as if, in the last moments, Anderson heard something funny or unbelievable.

Sasaki reaches out and touches Pearce on the neck. Warmth.

'He's not been dead long,' Sasaki says. 'An hour or so at the most.'

And then there's a sound from the body that makes Sasaki jump. Not a human noise — Pearce is dead, that's for sure — but an electronic one.

The trill of a mobile phone.

~ ~ ~

Sasaki stands rooted to the ground. It's like the sand swirling around him has become a temporal vortex sucking time from the air and leaving him frozen between the ticking of the seconds. For a moment, there's nothing but the chaos of the storm. Then he sees his father's face made real in the tiny grains of dust clouding in front of him.

*I got my man all those years ago, Takeo, but now you are letting him slip away.*

There's no anger in his father's voice, more a tone of resignation as if he never expected anything other than this result.

'Bloody hell,' Malroony says, snapping him back to reality. She's kneeling on the ground, her right hand scrabbling inside Pearce's abdomen, her forearm up to the elbow in the loops of intestine, as she searches for the phone. 'Got it!'

She rocks back away from the body, a flat slice of iPhone in her hand, and then holds the device out for Sasaki.

He takes the phone. Smears away blood and pieces of viscera. Swipes to answer.

'Hello?' he says.

~ ~ ~

'You're too late,' the Architect says, one hand clutching the wheel, the other the phone. 'Good effort but in the end, a monumental fail. Your father was cleverer. Much cleverer. But his intelligence, paradoxically, led to all this death and pointless suffering. Back then, even as a child, I knew that things are linked together, but I never realised how disparate events can cascade down the years and affect the future. I tried to undo what had been done by replicating the past, but you can never go back. I get that now. That's why Derek had to die. I thought we could be brothers, just like before, but Derek killed without rationale. He was crazy. Still is. And ultimately, he is to blame for where we are now. Him and one other.'

The Architect pauses for a moment and takes a breath. The detective is speaking, but the Architect isn't listening. Something about Swanson stopping and handing himself in. Giving himself up. Getting the help he needs. The detective is wasting his breath just like Frank Locke wasted his. Nothing anyone can say will make a difference now.

'Shut up.' The Architect focuses on driving for a moment. Pulls up behind a slow-moving truck. Visibility is appalling and there is no way he can overtake. Better to hunker down and follow the truck at a snail's pace into Darwin. 'It's over. Don't you get it?'

'There's still time. Just stop the killing, please—'

'But I will stop the killing very soon. Derek is gone, so there's only one other person to deal with. When he's dead, the nightmare will be over, and I will finally be able to sleep easily. Goodbye, Takeo, goodbye.'

The Architect hangs up and concentrates on the road ahead, the sand swirling as bad as ever. Dust and turmoil and mayhem. The storm is a metaphor for how he's

393

*been feeling, but soon, the weather will change and calm will return. He glances down at the shotgun lying on the passenger seat. One more shot, he thinks, just one more shot. Then, peace and silence.*

*Not long now…*

~ ~ ~

Malroony is driving like crazy, pushing the car on through the sandstorm. Sasaki clings to the side of his seat, eyes straining to see through the murk, but there's little but a swirl of dust and debris. How his partner can even navigate, let alone drive, is a mystery. He turns to her momentarily as she leans forward, her face close to the windscreen, the speedo edging up. Sixty, seventy, eighty. If they come up fast on a truck, they'll rear-end it before she can brake. Game over. He should tell her to slow down, but if he does, then his father is done.

*There's only one other person to deal with…*

Swanson didn't mention Endo Sasaki by name, but who else can he be referring to? Derek Pearce is dead, Kevin Anderson, too. Sasaki's father is the one person left alive who had a hand in what happened to Swanson. The problem is Endo is seventy-five, a care home resident, and has dementia. He doesn't have much chance against Swanson, nor do the nurses and other residents.

Sasaki tries his phone again, but there's still no signal. There should be reception along the main road, but the storm has likely knocked out one or more cell towers. Until they get to Darwin, there's nothing to do but cling on and pray.

'It'll be OK,' Malroony says. She doesn't alter her position or look across; she just reads his mind. 'We'll get there.'

394

Sasaki hopes she's right but knows she's wrong. Swanson won't have left anything to chance. He wouldn't have phoned if he'd thought the call might prewarn them.

Except...

Sasaki stares through the windscreen. The only hope is that Swanson has been caught in this, too. Then he might have miscalculated. And he can't have factored Malroony's heroic driving into the equation.

The tail end of a truck looms suddenly, and Malroony swerves to overtake, blasting past. They're approaching the outskirts of Darwin now, and there's still no signal on Sasaki's phone.

'We go right at Berrimah, correct?' Malroony says. 'And then what?'

'Left on to McMillans,' Sasaki says. 'That's the quickest way.'

Malroony brakes hard and wrenches the steering wheel. The car side skids before she compensates, and they shoot forwards. Sasaki glares at his phone, and as if by some force of his own will, a lone signal bar appears. He hits a contact, and by another minor miracle, he's straight through to the duty officer at the station. He blurts out instructions and hangs up.

'All good?' Malroony says.

'All units alerted and a SWAT team's on the way,' Sasaki says. He notes a side street flash by. 'But we'll be there before them.'

He's right, and within three minutes, Malroony is making the final turn, swinging into the road where the care home is. She slows a fraction before pulling into the sweeping driveway that leads to the complex. Low buildings cluster round a central block, and light flares from windows through the gloom of the dust storm. Malroony steps hard on the foot brake, and Sasaki is thrown forward, his seatbelt wrenching at his shoulder. Then she yanks up the handbrake, sending the car into a sliding turn, the rear end lurching round. The vehicle stops sideways within a pace of the front steps and just nudges the rear bumper of a little Hyundai hire car parked out front.

Sasaki leaps from the car and up the steps, pushing in through the double doors. A nurse cowers behind the reception desk with a phone in her hand. There's a chunk missing from the wall next to her, torn and ragged edges, a smell of cordite in the air. The nurse points down the corridor.

He sprints away along a hallway dotted with doors until he gets to a cross passage. Left to his father's room and right to the communal area. Sasaki isn't sure where his father would be at this time of day, but then there's a shout from the left. He runs towards the shout, coming across an elderly woman lying sprawled on the floor, a gaping hole in her back. Further on, a terrified man with a walking frame nods to an open door a few steps away. Sasaki edges closer to the door and hears a raised voice. An American accent. Hears the voice say his father's name.

*Endo Sasaki...*

Which is when Sasaki realises he isn't armed. His weapon is in the car.

Then comes the shot, the retort echoing from the room like a thunderclap. Brave Sasaki is not, but he doesn't hesitate, doesn't think. He rushes to the door and leaps in.

To the right, slumped against the wall, is Jim Swanson. Blood gushing from a neck wound, a shotgun on the floor, Swanson twitching once, twice and then sliding down the wall, leaving a smear of blood on the flocked wallpaper. To the left, Endo Sasaki sits in his bed, a large pistol resting in his lap, the old tin of photos on top of the covers.

Sasaki steps into the room and moves across to Swanson. He bends, thinks about touching the neck and feeling for a pulse, sees the amount of blood, doesn't bother. Instead, he straightens and turns to his father.

Endo smiles at Sasaki.

'You're a little late, son,' he says.

# Epilogue

DI Jessica Chase is feeling a little out of the loop. It's all gone down down under. Party, party, party, but the SCU appear to have been left off the invite list.

'We could fly to Australia business class,' Stafford says. 'On a fact-finding mission designed to reinforce our international credentials and optimise interagency cross-border cooperation and data fluidity.'

'I don't know what the fuck that means,' Green says. 'But I doubt Boyle would even pay for a half-mile bus ride to Trafalgar Square to buy a celebratory ice cream.'

Chase, Green and Stafford are in the SCU, clustered round a table. Curry night has been abandoned in favour of pizza afternoon, three large Dominos boxes replacing the usual dozen or so foil trays.

The case has wrapped, but there are a lot of Is to dot and Ts to cross. Alan Grainger is almost certainly going to prison for the rest of his life for the murder of Alison and Lizzie, and the CPS will re-examine the Soho Sleeper material in light of the new evidence from the US. Green is all for making a midnight visit to the hospital where Grainger is staying, removing a few wires and tubes, and holding a pillow over his face. Watching the monitor flatline. Until Chase points out that it gets him off the hook. Better to imagine him living out his days in virtual solitary confinement.

Press coverage of the case has shone a favourable light on the SCU, with an investigative reporter highlighting the funding threat the unit has faced. When questioned, the Commissioner and the Mayor both say there is no threat; in fact, the unit is to receive additional resources to expand its remit.

Boyle is livid.

'All we have to do,' Green says, 'is catch the next one. And the next one after that. And the...'

'Shut it,' Chase and Stafford say in unison.

Talking of Boyle, Chase spies him wending and weaving, ducking and diving, heading their way.

'Defcon one,' she says. 'Ten seconds to impact.'

'Chase, Green and Stafford,' Boyle says. 'Three names you might expect to see on an estate agency board, not gracing the roster of a crack criminal investigation team.'

'Looks can be deceiving, sir,' Chase says. She half nods at a spread of newspapers on the far side of the table. Most of the headlines concern a Labour politician caught in flagrante with his Conservative opposite number, but nearly all the papers have a story about Jim Swanson and the SCU somewhere on their front pages. 'We *are* a crack investigation team.'

'Drivel,' Boyle says, taking a glance at the newspapers. He turns his attention to the pizza feast, and for a moment, Chase thinks he will either berate them for breaking office rules or pinch a slice for himself. Instead, he fixes Chase with a stare. 'Mark my words, there's going to be some changes round here.'

And then he's gone. Not wending and weaving or ducking and diving this time, but heading straight for the exit as if he can't wait to get away.

'Fucking wanker,' Green says.

~ ~ ~

Detective Frank Locke is back home. Sasaki had asked him to stay on for a week to help fill in the blanks, and he was happy to oblige. But when the week is over, Locke hops on a plane, then another, and then another. He lands at Sea-Tac, picks his car up from the long-term parking, and drives back to Montana.

He's promised Sasaki he'll return for a holiday sometime in the future. If he can persuade Elsie.

'Australia?' she says, with the characteristic wrinkle of her nose that implies mild disdain. 'Spiders and crocodiles and heat?'

They're sitting on the veranda, taking in the spring sunshine, taking in a couple of beers.

'You've got a point,' Locke says, breathing in the mountain air and looking across the valley to peaks still capped with snow. 'But perhaps one day.'

The case is as good as wrapped. There's the small matter of Locke shooting Leo Sullivan, but Locke's boss has said Sullivan was the one in the wrong: he should never have gone solo on hearsay evidence from Jim Swanson. Luckily, Sullivan survived, and he'll likely be pensioned off rather than pilloried as a bad apple.

When Locke's been home a couple of days, Karen Holdsworth visits to brief him on his appearance before an FBI panel investigating Swanson's actions.

'Nothing for you to worry about,' she says. 'Purely routine.'

They're out on the veranda. Same place as Locke and his wife. Two beers. Only Elsie is off somewhere doing something, and Locke realises he doesn't know what she's doing or when she'll be back. He glances across at Karen. Red hair, full lips, high cheekbones. Beautiful. Says, internally, *you idiot*, and promises himself he'll ask Elsie about her trip when she returns. Promises to try to reconnect. After all, Mattich is dead, and all that crap from Seattle can be buried too. Perhaps he and Elsie can take a vacation together, get away for a bit. Not Australia, too far. Maybe Europe. Revisit some of the places they went when they were younger.

'They want to know about Swanson?' Locke says.

'Yes. Your friendship, your impressions of him. Basically, there's a whole lot of ass-covering going on at the Bureau. Questions are being asked about how one man could have so much control of the system.'

'The GSCDB? Well, he designed it, I guess he found a way to get in and cover his tracks.'

'A backdoor, it's called. Swanson had a secret administrator's account, which allowed him to do pretty much anything without detection. I doubt he had anything sinister in mind when he built the database; quite the opposite. However, the head injury flipped his judgement.'

'You could say that.' Locke takes a pull from his beer bottle. 'The complexities of the human mind, hey? Now, there's an area that would reward further investigation.'

'The Bureau is already flagging offenders who are likely to move to a repeating pattern of criminality. The issue is what to do with the information. We can hardly lock people up because they *might* kill in the future.'

'Could be something in that, though.' Locke smiles. 'A lot of votes, at least.'

'It would be a case of Federal overreach.' Karen returns the smile. 'Can you imagine the backlash?'

'Yes, I can,' Locke says. 'On one side would be the libs moaning about who was getting imprisoned, on the other, the right-wingers crying about the State poking its nose in where it shouldn't. Piss off both groups, and I reckon you have policy about right.'

'Well, it's not going to happen on a widespread basis, but there is talk of looking closer at serial murder, about trying to identify those who are predisposed to it.'

'Makes sense.'

'And talking of serial murder, I've got a proposition for you.'

'Yeah?' Locke turns towards Karen.

'My boss would like you onboard. There's a vacancy in the Behavioural Analysis Unit for someone of your calibre.'

'Replacing Swanson?' Locke shakes his head. 'Sorry, computers aren't my thing.'

'Not filling Swanson's shoes, just the opposite. We're looking for someone to take the long view and do qualitative research on people like Swanson and Mattich.'

'Write papers on nutters?' Locke turns away. 'Sounds dull.'

'Not write papers, investigate. We've a number of cases, some active, some cold, that could do with further review by someone outside the Bureau. Fresh eyes, if you like. You could keep your rank and job here and be employed as a consultant as and when we need you.'

'I'd have thought the Bureau would have had its fill of consultants after Swanson?'

'Government and consultants go together like cream and apple pie.' Karen raises her beer bottle and makes to chink against Locke's. 'Are you in?'

'I'd have to come to Virginia?'

'On a regular basis, yes.'

Locke is tempted for about ten seconds, but then he thinks of Elsie, of the cool mountain air, of the twisty drive to work each morning, the coffee in The Daily Grind, the heady smell of pine up in the forests. He thinks about rebuilding his shop from the ground up, getting a whole set of new tools, creating some more artworks, some more furniture, about his neighbour Earl and how he's promised to help him on his own house.

'It's not going to fly,' he says.

'You don't have to give me an answer right away.' Karen snaps a card down on the table. 'Just promise me you'll think about it.'

Karen Kell — Karen *Holdsworth* — smiles.

'OK,' Locke says.

~ ~ ~

Detective Senior Sergeant Takeo Sasaki is visiting his father. The old man is in the day room watching TV. Some kiddy cartoon. A puppy running from tree to tree, chasing a squirrel that leaps effortlessly from branch to branch.

Sasaki sits next to his father, a little table between them. There's tea, biscuits, and a copy of a newspaper from a few days ago. The headline is all about Sasaki Senior taking on Swanson. There's a sidebar with a resume of Endo's career, and the main article details the events at the home. Towards the end, Takeo Sasaki gets a mention, but there's nothing about the complexities of the Swanson case, only a line for poor Kieran Lamb, plenty for bad cop Kevin Anderson and the Black Ute Killer — Derek Pearce.

Endo Sasaki isn't going to be charged with killing Swanson. When Sasaki brought the matter up with Cooper, the AC had dismissed the possibility.

'Charge Endo Sasaki?' he'd said. 'The Jap Cop? He saved lives back in the day and saved lives today. He's a bloody hero. Deserves a medal. *Another* medal.'

And Cooper would undoubtedly want to be the one to pin it on Endo's chest. Good publicity to counter the negative press around Anderson. The police are taking a lot of flack for not having wheeled out Anderson long before the events at Tortilla. Whether anything will change, Sasaki has his doubts.

While his father is in the clear, the care home will receive a reprimand for security and for the fact that Endo could keep the gun undetected in the tin box of photos in his bedside cabinet. Sasaki remembers his father clutching the tin box when he first moved there, refusing to let go of it. Endo can't have guessed that Swanson or anyone else would come looking for him, so there must have been another reason. Sasaki imagines his father, at some stage, intended to end his life; either he'd changed his mind or he'd gone past the point where he was able to make a rational decision.

Sasaki sits patiently and reads from the paper. When he finishes the articles, he begins to explain the Tortilla case from the start. He tells his father about everything from Ken Royston's lousy perimeter search to Jim Swanson and the way the ex-FBI man persuaded others to kill for him. He details the American cops and the British SCU. Frank Locke's brave attempt to save Kieran Lamb. His own role in the case.

When he's finished, the day room is nearly empty. The TV has been turned off, and two cleaners collect empty tea cups and plates full of biscuit crumbs. His father is looking out the window, his gaze somewhere over the lake where ripples dance in the late afternoon sun.

'I'm thinking of applying for promotion,' Sasaki says. 'Moving up a step. I've also had an offer from the Federal Police to move into one of their transnational special units. Anna thinks I should consider it.'

Anna.

His father probably doesn't even know Sasaki has split from Anna, but since she's been in touch again, suggesting they meet up, that's probably for the best. If Sasaki gets back with her, then his father will never have had a chance to get confused.

'What do you think of the promotion?' Sasaki says. 'Or about joining the AFP?'

His father continues to stare over the water, blinking at the intense light. Sasaki wonders if he's getting through, wonders if it's even worth him coming here any longer.

'Dad?'

'He'll never catch him,' Endo says, head shaking, a half smile on his lips as he looks up to the dead TV. 'The puppy will never catch the squirrel.'

'No,' Sasaki says. He lowers his voice to a whisper. Words just for his father. 'I love you, Dad.'

# About the Author

Mark Sennen was born in Surrey but spent his formative years in rural Shropshire, where he learnt to drive tractors and worm sheep. He has been a reluctant farmer, an average drummer, a failed PhD student and a pretty good programmer. He lives, with his wife and two children, beside a muddy creek in deepest South Devon where there hasn't been a murder in years.

Web: http://www.marksennen.com

Also by Mark Sennen

**The DI Charlotte Savage Series**
Touch
Bad Blood
Cut Dead
Tell Tale
Two Evils
The Boneyard
Puppet

**The Holm and da Silva Series**
The Sanction
Rogue Target

**Standalone**
The Sum of All Sins

.

Printed in Great Britain
by Amazon